CAVERN

OF

SPIRITS

Book Three
Stonehaven League

CARRIE SUMMERS

ISBN: 1724966405

First Edition: August 2018

Cover art : Jackson Tjota

10 9 8 7 6 5 4 3 2 1

more iron soon, that greatsword Bodenir ordered will need to be carved from stone."

"Wait, what?" Devon said. "I just saw a group of players coming to trade. That hardly seems like a poor economy."

"Yes," Greel said, speaking slowly as if she had just a couple brain cells. "And the only way we can *pay* them for goods is to send runners to the other shops to orchestrate complicated trades amongst our vendors until we've moved around enough goods to squeeze a coin or two out of our supply."

Devon pressed fingers to her temples. "I'm guessing this is what you were explaining earlier."

"It's *exactly* what I was explaining earlier," he said, voice sharp. "Bartering is fine and well amongst friends. But the starborn insist on using currency. Despite your generous donation to the village treasury, Your Gloriousness, we simply don't have liquidity."

"Don't the players use coins to buy things from us?"

"Yes, when they can afford to. But since they've decided it's their *divine purpose* to camp out in the jungle indefinitely, they aren't coming into new sources of currency either. Some have even shown the gall to suggest that our kind should be a bottomless source of funds." He shook his head and huffed. "As if we simply conjure gold and silver from thin air."

Devon sighed. Of course the players would think that. In every other game she'd played, NPC vendors always had the funds to buy loot from players. The situation inevitably led to inflation in the game economy regardless of which money sinks the developers put into the design. She'd always disliked that facet of gaming, but now that she had a glimpse of the alternative, inflation didn't sound so bad.

"And what's this about an iron shortage?"

Dorden grumbled. "'Twas flattering at first when so many players commissioned me finely smithed blades. A bit less pleasant when I checked the reserve of ingots yesterday."

Devon blew through loose lips. Bodenir, one of the dwarf fighters, had been waiting patiently for a weapon upgrade since the battle against the demons. "Is there really not enough for the tools and Bodenir's sword?"

"There is, but barely. And I've orders for chisels and axes and a skillet for Tom lined up behind. Of course, that doesn't even count for Garda's needs. The woman's at the forge even more than me, shaping armor plates and knocking the dents out of helms."

"So we need coin and we need iron. I hate to send the Stoneshoulder Clan's wagon and mule team to Eltera City on a trade mission."

Dorden's eyes bulged. "I'd rather give up me forge entirely and go look for that ironwood grove ye mentioned than visit that midden heap."

"Then does anyone have a suggestion?"

With a heavy sigh, Greel rolled his eyes yet again. "And now we come to the final portion of my report. The recommendations."

Devon pressed the back of her head against the tree, the bark's bite distracting her from the urge to groan in dismay.

"Go ahead," she said with a false smile.

"In *conclusion*," Greel said, "I recommend we form a party of qualified adventurers to escort our dwarven brethren who are skilled in the mining trade. This party shall skirt the southern edge of Ishildar then venture into the mountainous terrain directly bordering the ancient city to the east. Therein, they shall seek

Chapter Two

WHILE THE DWARVES cheered and toasted, reeling along the village paths with dazed grins and sloshing mugs, Devon retreated to the little clearing around the Shrine to Veia and sat down to go over her character and settlement information. Best to get the maintenance done *before* tasting any of the ale. And she definitely wanted to be done with character maintenance before the baby appeared.

She still wasn't sure what to expect of a dwarf infant. Would he really be the boy Heldi expected? Would he be born with a beard or something? She shrugged and pushed away the questions—she'd know their answers soon enough.

Focusing on the icon at the edge of her vision, she pulled open the settlement interface.

Settlement: Stonehaven
Size: Village

Tier 1 Buildings - 30/50 (25 upgraded):
3 x Standard Hut
2 x Canvas Shelter
21 x Simple Cabin (upgraded)
4 x Simple Shops (upgraded)

Tier 2 Buildings - 4/6 (1 upgraded):
1 x Medicine Woman's Cabin (upgraded)
1 x Crafting Workshop
1 x Basic Forge
1 x Kitchen

Tier 3 Buildings (2/3)
1 x Shrine to Veia
1 x Chicken Coop

After the refugees from the Fortress of Shadows had been incorporated into Stonehaven, housing had become a major priority. A few people were still sleeping in the giant fur tent made from the *Behemoth Sloth Hide*. It couldn't be very pleasant, so Devon had assigned Prester, the carpenter, to focus on building and upgrading cabins. He'd also improvised with his *One-room Shack - Flat Roof* plans yet again, adding a counter and shelves for the display of goods and creating a set of shops. The merchants who had joined the settlement slept in cots in those buildings for now.

Devon knew that Prester would much rather be working on a barracks—or any advanced project for that matter. But at least he had help now: one of Emmaree's refugees was also a carpenter.

As for stonework, Deld also had new help. He and the refugee stonemason were splitting their time between continued construction on the *Inner Keep* and fortifications work directed by Jarleck. For now, the keep's walls rose only to knee-height above the foundation. But that was okay. Castles weren't exactly built in a day.

Devon scrolled down to check out information on their defenses. Progress here was her highest priority, so much that she'd scarcely left the village over the past couple weeks. She might not be skilled in construction, but she'd been able to help dig.

Fortifications:
Status: Fort - Basic

Completed:
1 x Main Wall - Timber Palisade
1 x Wall-walk
1 x Merlons
1 x Main Gate - Iron-reinforced Timber
3 x Watchtower
1 x Wicket Gate

Required for upgrade to Fort - Advanced:
1 x Dry Moat
1 x Bridge
1 x Curtain Wall (Timber or Stone)
1 x Outer Gate
1 x Main Wall - Stone to Half Height

After rebuilding the main gates and repairing sections of the timber palisade, Jarleck had supervised construction on the wall-walk, a platform on the backside of the palisade which allowed defenders to peer over and shoot from anywhere along the wall. Higher sections of wall, the merlons, provided shielding for archers to duck behind.

With that in place, construction had begun on an outer curtain wall. Rather than build once in wood only to upgrade to stone later, Jarleck had suggested they take the time for stone construction now. The foundation and first course of blocks had been laid about fifteen feet from the main palisade. Much to Devon's dismay, Jarleck insisted on calling the empty space between the walls a "killing field." Any attackers who managed to breach the curtain wall would still need to cross the space under a hail of arrows and whatever else the defenders decided to drop on their heads. So even though the term might be correct, Devon wasn't a fan.

Outside the curtain wall, they'd been digging a moat. That was where Devon had been lending a hand, earning seven skill points in *Manual Labor* and seemingly endless sarcastic comments from the game about her puny muscles.

Even knowing how little she was adding to the process, she was still tempted to remain in Stonehaven until the upgrade to *Fort - Advanced* was complete. But she had a sneaking suspicion that she'd just find another excuse after that. It was hard to feel responsible for so many lives. At some point, though, she needed to move forward on her quest to restore Ishildar. Even if she didn't care about the power offered by the city, she *did* need to restore the Veian temple. The threat of demon incursions hadn't gone away just because they'd survived one assault.

Before closing out the settlement interface, she opened the population tab, which she'd recently reorganized into sections that made sense. First was the basic information.

Population:
Base Morale: 52%

Basic NPCs: 38
Advanced NPCs: 6

She cringed. Morale was falling. The villagers' basic needs were met, meaning they had food and shelter—even if that shelter was a giant sloth hide. But the integration of the refugees hadn't been perfect. Just like real world people, the citizens of Stonehaven wanted the chance to do work that matched their skills.

The advanced NPCs were generally happy, so she'd shuffled them off to their own section where their information wouldn't distract her. As for her basic NPCs, she'd organized them by category of profession.

<u>Resource gathering:</u>
Base Morale: 73%
3 x Lumberjack
2 x Quarry Worker
2 x Miner
2 x Hunter
1 x Fisherwoman

<u>Defense:</u>
Base Morale: 82%
5 x Fighter

These people were happy, except for the miners who would rather tunnel through solid granite than chip away at a single moss-agate vein. But it was in the other categories of professions that things started to go downhill.

Tradespeople:

Base Morale: 65%

2 x Leatherworker

1 x Tailor

1 x Jewelcrafter

1 x Weaver

1 x Blacksmith

1 x Armorsmith

2 x Cook

1 x Farmer (crops)

1 x Farmer (animals)

1 x Gem Cutter

Some of the tradespeople had a solid stream of work. Gerrald and his new leatherworking assistant had plenty of hides and requests. The cooks and farmers had a village to feed, and the blacksmiths had swords and armor to make. But without raw materials, the jewelcrafter and gem cutter had nothing to do but help dig the moat. Emmaree, the halfling tailor, was in a similar situation. Occasionally, she had a repair request from one of the players, but otherwise, she spent most of her time weeding the farm plots.

At least that situation would improve. In one corner of the farm, Bayle had planted a few cotton seeds that had arrived stuck to the plumage of Blackbeard the Parrot. The weaver already had a loom and makeshift spinning wheel set up in the crafting workshop, and the village could expect its first roughspun cloth soon after the first cotton harvest.

Devon grimaced as she moved on to the more dire categories.

Merchants:
Base Morale: 48%
1 x Clothier
1 x Armorer
1 x Weapons Merchant
1 x Grocer
1 x General Goods Vendor
1 x Luxury Goods Vendor

Between the problems with the economy, the general lack of goods, and the need to share four shops among six merchants, Stonehaven's vendors weren't happy.

Devon shook her head and moved onto the last category.

What am I supposed to do with these people?
Base Morale: 32%
1 x Shipwright
1 x Candlemaker
1 x Wheelwright
1 x Glassblower
1 x Poet

With a sigh of dismay, Devon shook her head. She'd tried inviting the poet to perform at an evening bonfire. He'd recited some long, non-rhyming piece about the delicacy of a particular flower blossom that had grown near his childhood home. To call it a flop would've been an understatement, particularly with a group of drunken dwarves in the audience. Unfortunately, when she'd gently suggested a new profession, she'd learned that the poor man had no other proficiencies.

As for the others, she might need to assign new jobs, but she'd been reluctant. Their trades weren't useful yet, but they might be as Stonehaven grew. For now, she'd asked Tom to cook up something special for the group in hopes of boosting the morale stat.

Devon took a deep breath and waved the settlement interface away. Despite the problems, things were going well when compared to the days leading up to the demon attack and the battle itself. She could afford to relax a little about Stonehaven's health.

As for her character, that was an issue.

Character: Devon (click to set a different character name)
Level: 16
Base Class: Sorcerer
Specialization: Unassigned
Unique Class: Deceiver
Health: 303/303
Mana: 476/476
Fatigue: 23%
Shadowed: 19%

She'd taken to checking her main character sheet every few hours, staring at the *Shadowed* stat. It seemed to tick down slowly, but every once in a while, it grew by a bunch. She couldn't figure it out, but she didn't like her inability to control it.

She'd tried grinding out another level, gaining attribute points and assigning a couple to *Endurance* to see if it would affect the

Shadowed percentage in the same way it did *Fatigue,* improving recovery in the stat. When that hadn't worked, she'd spent a point in *Strength*—her first. It had made her a better moat digger but hadn't done anything to change her resistance to *Shadowed* gain.

As for the abilities tab that showed a bunch of grayed-out demonic spells—written in a script she couldn't read, of course—she tried to forget it was there.

She'd messaged Emerson about the new info a couple of times, but the programmer hadn't responded, so she'd stopped nagging. She knew he was busy working on a fix for the unauthorized access to her implants. The sooner he patched the code, the sooner she could stop wearing the stupid tinfoil hat at night.

Anyway, the *Shadowed* thing was just another game mechanic. Would she message him to ask about spell combos? No. So it was kind of ridiculous to ask about a new mystery stat and ability page. For all she knew, it was some kind of reward for having defeated her inner demon. Maybe she should be trying to *leverage* the new abilities rather than cringing over her *Shadowed* percentage. Anyway, questions for another day.

Dragging her hands through her hair, she flicked away the character screen and stood.

She had a dwarven baby shower to attend.

Chapter Three

EMERSON HADN'T SHAVED. The scruff under his chin caught on the strap for his EM-shielding cap, causing his skin to get irritated and red. His eyes were red too, bloodshot after hours spent staring at his tablet display. He'd always thought the IT guys at E-Squared were kind of lazy and more into their beards than network security, but he was having a hell of a time trying to poke holes in the company firewall.

It didn't help that he was working in a suboptimal environment. The company had sent him a voucher for round-trip airfare anywhere in the world. Saskatchewan wasn't a usual destination, but he could be sure Penelope wouldn't be watching for an incoming connection from a town with a higher population of farming robots than people.

And he was *sure* Penelope was behind whatever plot had led management to decide he was having some sort of breakdown and couldn't be allowed near the code base. No doubt she also expected him to try to get around his network suspension by hacking through the firewall.

This was war, and unfortunately the woman had won the first battle. But Emerson was far from defeated. His assault on the other coder's defenses would be multipronged.

First, there was the ongoing attempt to defeat E-Squared's network security. Unfortunately, though he'd kept meticulous records of Veia's reports on network traffic between Penelope's assigned servers and the unconscious brains of sleeping players, he didn't have a snapshot of the offending code.

Emerson shook his head at the reminder of his error. He should have known better than to work off the corporate cloud instead of on a local machine. His overall strategy was to present management with a detailed report of Penelope's wrongdoings, but with the records of network traffic alone, he would have a hard time convincing Bradley "I don't speak programmer" Williams that the woman was doing anything wrong.

The code wouldn't do it either. But the comments she'd inserted between the lines of her C++ ought to do the job. He could see them as if they were burned into his retinas.

// Super-secret API call...ACTIVATE

// Processing power? We don't need no processing power. Let the players donate a little something to the cause.

// Hey Entwined? Ever heard of a symbols file? It's that place in an un-optimized library where your debug code gets shipped in a live build.

Recalling her flippant attitude made his nostrils twitch, a stupid tic that happened when he was angry. Emerson shook his head and prepped another supposed zero-day exploit he'd bought from some hacker on the darknet. It set his teeth on edge to have to resort to this kind of stuff. Emerson was a good guy, not some weaselly scum thriving on the misfortune of others. He'd even considered tweaking

Veia to do a little white-hat hacking for charity organizations, searching out vulnerabilities on the NGOs' networks.

But how did the saying go? Desperate measures for desperate times or something...

He launched the exploit and banged his fist on the hotel table when a popup appeared.

Nice try, sucker. Next time try using a vulnerability that wasn't patched in 2045.

Okay, so now he *really* found E-Squared's IT people annoying. It was way easier to make fun of their beard culture when he'd thought they were idiots.

Emerson shook his head, abandoning his intrusion attempts for now. Turning his tablet over so he wouldn't be tempted to futz, he pulled out a secondary display. He'd been careful to isolate the devices he used in his hacking attempts from those he used in normal communication.

He scanned through his messages, pausing for a minute on the questions Devon had sent a couple weeks ago. There was some kind of new stat on her character, which was mildly surprising, but he couldn't really do anything to investigate. Even if he did have access to the company database and server farm, the answers weren't just something he could pull out of Veia's neural net. Many times, he'd thought of responding and telling her that, but the response might raise a flag with E-Squared's network snoops—the company had a tight relationship with the developer of the current in-fashion messenger app due to the integration with Relic Online. Emerson wouldn't be surprised to learn that this "friendship" allowed E-

Squared the ability to spy on their employees' activity. Or maybe he was just paranoid.

Regardless, he was supposed to be on vacation. No work-related activity. Better to let E-Squared believe he had taken their suggestion seriously and shipped out for a Tahitian beach.

The rest of his messages were mostly marketing spam—the other negative of being kicked off the corporate network and its sophisticated filters. But at the very end of the list, a message caught his eye. He swallowed, his heart thudding as he read the subject line, a particular combination of characters he'd been hoping to see for days.

> From: @Worried_in_Atlanta
> To: @EmersonGeorge
> Re: Your FREE gift!!1
>
> Dear Sir,
> In response to your inquiry and the mysterious package we recently received, I am writing to let you know that we believe there may be untold benefit and wealth. However, we are only reserve this benefit for a limited time. Please respond with your address and information such that you may reclaim this incalculable sum.
>
> Sincerely,
> A Nigerian Prince

Emerson dropped his head into his hands, sighing in relief. Owen's girlfriend had not only received the EM-shielding cap, but she'd also read and followed the instructions carefully. Guessing that his network traffic might be watched, Emerson had insisted she message him in a way that looked as if it were a crappy auto-generated phishing attempt. From what he could gather from the email, she'd found a way to briefly shield Owen's implants with the cap. Something must have happened to lead her to believe the EM-shielding could help him, but her message also suggested she'd heeded his warning about not telling anyone. Emerson needed more information and cooperation to assure that Owen wouldn't be harmed by forcibly cutting his connection. Moreover, the doctors, Owen's family, and the army of E-Squared and Entwined lawyers would surely complicate the situation.

Emerson scratched his stubbly chin. Regardless of the difficulties ahead, this was a breakthrough, the first part of his counterattack that had succeeded. He needed to think about how best to leverage the results, but for now, he needed to reassure the girlfriend—and ideally, convince her to meet him.

Reopening the message window, he started typing a response.

Chapter Four

SPRAWLED IN RANDOM spots around the village, the dwarves—except Heldi, of course—were sleeping off what Dorden had called "round one." Devon shook her head as she stepped over the armorsmith, Garda. The dwarf woman snored. Loudly.

She passed Hezbek, who sat on the porch of her cabin looking intently at the closed door to the home Dorden and Heldi shared. As difficult as it was for Devon to contain her worry for Heldi and the baby, it must be much harder for the village medicine woman to stay away. But Dorden had been adamant. This was how it was done in their clan; the women brought forth their children alone. And worse—according to Dorden anyway—they weren't even allowed ale to pass the time.

"It's as if they're worried we'll forget they're twice the dwarves we are. Ha!" he'd said, lifting his mug. "Last time I tried to arm wrestle me wife, me wrist ached for a week. And it wasn't even her good arm."

This had brought another round of cheers and toasts. Devon wasn't sure how they could even see straight enough to connect on the toasts, though maybe that explained why they were now sleeping.

"She'll be fine," Devon said as she stepped closer to Hezbek's porch.

"Oh, I know it, child. But it's still in me to worry. The summoning of a child is a difficult task to face alone."

"Wait," Devon said. "Back up. Summoning?"

Hezbek raised an eyebrow. "Of course. That's what this is about, isn't it? Summoning their new child into the world."

Uhh...Devon chewed the corner of her lip, unsure what to say. "You mean she doesn't..."

"Doesn't what, child?"

Devon laid her hands over her gut, then pushed them away to mimic a swelling stomach. "She doesn't...grow a baby inside her belly?"

Hezbek grimaced. "What the...? Frankly, child, I'm not sure I like where this conversation is going. I'm guessing by your reaction that the summoning of an infant must be a different process in the starborn realm. And a somewhat gruesome one. The child doesn't claw its way out like a hatchling leaving an egg, does it?"

"You know...I think we should probably drop it. But yes, it's different." Devon glanced at Heldi's cabin. "So she's in there...channeling a spell or something?"

A sad look crossed Hezbek's face. "More or less. But the truth is, I can't tell you exactly what happens, as I was never blessed with a child. The summoning is something only an expecting mother can perform, and due to the great difficulty and exertion, she generally forgets the details."

Devon squeezed her temples. Sometimes, Relic Online was just too much.

Shaking her head, she glanced at the screen of leaves that shadowed Hezbek's stoop. Over the past few days, the jungle canopy had all but vanished from Stonehaven. Where giant trunks had once stretched impossibly high, most of the trees were now stout and broad, spreading low boughs over enticing patches of shade. Tall, fine-bladed grass filled the space between trees, brushing gently against the legs of villagers who wandered off the paths.

She hadn't been online to see any instances of the new type of tree replace the old—the game probably did that on purpose—but she had asked Hezbek about it. The woman had smiled fondly and muttered some mumbo-jumbo about magic and the changing face of Veia's creation.

Devon stepped out from beneath the shade of the tree and turned her face to the sky. A shift in temperatures was another nice change as the jungle receded. In the middle of the day, it still got a bit hot in direct sunlight, but the weeks of sweltering heat and humidity were over, at least inside Stonehaven's borders. Idly, Devon wondered how far the change extended, then shook her head in dismay upon realizing how long it'd been since she'd ventured away from the village. Not since the first days after the demon battle.

She glanced again at the dwarves' cabin. "This wait is killing me."

Wrinkles formed in the corners of Hezbek's eyes when she smiled. "You'd think you were the expectant father the way you're pacing around. Perhaps you should head out for a little exploration or hunting."

"Yeah, but if I leave, how will I know the baby's been born—or do you say summoned? I want to see him."

"We say *born*, of course. It's a special type of summoning spell called a birthing. Anyway, do you think he'll grow up in the time it takes you to slay a few monsters?"

Well, to tell the truth, Devon wasn't sure. This was a fantasy roleplaying game, not a childcare simulator. But yeah...even if she headed out for an hour or two, she probably wouldn't come back to see Dorden and Heldi's son fully grown and heavily bearded.

"Gerrald did tell me he had some fancy new piece of gear for me. Said I couldn't have it if I was just going to dirty it up digging the moat."

"Well there you go," Hezbek said. "Leave the worrying to me and take yourself on a little adventure. You shouldn't have any problem knowing when the guest of honor arrives."

"How?" Devon said, furrowing her brow.

A sly smile tugged at Hezbek's lips. "You'll know it when you see it."

Devon narrowed her eyes, imagining the woman casting fireballs into the sky like flares. "You aren't getting back into sorcery, are you? I thought that battle with the demon was an exception."

The woman looked at the sky as if innocent. "I never said I'd given it up. Only that I wouldn't use my skills for warfare or violence." A somber expression descended over her features. "Truth is, I never thought I'd cast some of those spells again. But when I saw that demon standing over you...I couldn't even imagine holding back. Goes to show how easy it is to lie to ourselves when it comes to people we care about."

Devon stepped closer and grasped the woman's wrinkled hand, cradling it between her own. "You helped save me and everyone in the village. And no one was harmed except Zaa's minions. I hope you don't regret what you did."

"I don't regret it, child. Not for a moment. But I have learned a bit of humility when it comes to the strengths of my convictions."

"Fair enough," Devon said, knowing better than to argue with the medicine woman. "In that case, I eagerly await your signal."

Hezbek raised an eyebrow. "I never said it would be *my* signal. That was your conclusion. But the conjuring of a new life isn't like summoning a *Glowing Orb*. It tends to be noticeable."

Right. With a smirk, Devon set off for the crafting workshop. Inside, Gerrald was instructing the newer leatherworker, one of the refugees from Emmaree's village, in his technique for stamping runes into pieces of leather. Devon was glad to see it. The two groups of villagers had been learning quite a bit from each other, granting a temporary bonus in skill gain.

"Not celebrating, Your Gloriousness?" Gerrald asked as she stepped into the building.

Devon tucked her arms close as she looked around. It'd gotten rather crowded inside with Emmaree bent over some clothing repair and the new weaver dribbling vegetable oil into the moving parts of her equipment. As soon as Stonehaven became a Hamlet, allowing Devon to expand the list of tier 3 buildings, she'd definitely have to look into specialty workshops for her crafters.

"I'm having a hard time with the wait for Heldi's...summoning," Devon said.

Gerrald nodded. "Not interested in joining the rounds of drinking?"

Devon cringed. "I'm not too eager to wake up face down in the brook again."

The leatherworker laughed. "Then since you're here, I'm guessing you're finally going to take a break from the moat to try out your new doublet?"

Devon's eyes widened. "Ooo, chest armor. I was worried you were going to try to stuff me into some closed-toed boots again."

Gerrald sighed and rolled his eyes. "I've given up on that little quest. I figure eventually you'll stub your toes one time too many and you'll come begging for something to replace those sandals."

"As if," Devon said with a smirk.

With a sigh, the leatherworker opened one of the chests and tugged out a fancy-looking leather jacket. He held it up for her approval, and Devon nodded, trying to keep a cheery expression even as dismay settled into her belly. The new armor piece was decorated in a similar manner to her *Bracers of Smoke*, edged with— unfortunately—more demon skin. If she squinted, the dark piping and hem decorations *could* look like they'd been made from dyed leather. Very thin leather, dyed very black. But as long as she kept telling herself that, it didn't feel *too much* like she was garbing herself in the skin of underworld beings.

"Well?"

"It's...surprising," Devon said, forcing a smile. It *was* well-crafted. But she really had hoped for something a little less macabre. The problem was that if she told him that, it would impact his morale and hurt his feelings. If only she hadn't dropped her *Demon Skin Scraps* into the crafting resources chest. It was an old habit of hers...hoarding everything she looted just in case she could use it or sell it at auction sometime.

Gerrald shook the garment, urging her to take it.

With a swallow, she accepted the jacket.

You have received: Leather Doublet of Darkness
Oh yes. You have to live with the cheesy name, too.

Despite this disturbing practice of wrapping yourself in the flesh of your enemies—some of whom were your alter-ego—this doublet is pretty snazzy. The dark accents really bring out your eyes.

+1 Cunning, +1 Charisma | 80 Armor | 50/50 Durability

Use: Casts *Night's Breath* on enemies within 3 meters. Your opponents feel watched by unseen eyes peering from dark and disturbing places. Greatly reduces targets' melee and spell accuracy.

Recharge time: 2 hours

She kept the smile tacked on her face. "It's very...powerful."

Gerrald nodded, touching his brow. "And look here, Your Gloriousness. I lined the collar with some of that skin you brought. Should be quite soft against your neck. And there are moonstones on the back. I put them over the shoulder blades to look like glinting eyes."

"I'm not sure what to say."

The man grinned. "The look on your face is more than enough thanks."

Was she that good at hiding her reaction, or did he mistake her discomfort for awe? Either way, the armor *was* an upgrade. The attribute bonuses weren't quite as good as her previous chest piece which added +3 *Constitution* and +1 *Bravery*, but it had 10 more armor, and the accuracy debuff could be clutch. Not to mention, both *Cunning* and *Charisma* increased her mana pool, the resource she needed most.

"I'm looking forward to testing it out," Devon said with what she hoped was a cheerful tone.

"If you like, I *could* start on a pair of upgraded trousers," Gerrald said. "Now that there are two of us working, we can keep up with repairs and meet other village needs much more easily."

Devon shook her head, possibly a little too quickly. "You've already outdone yourself. I'll need to practice moving with the added protection for at least a few days before I'm ready."

He looked faintly disappointed but seemed to accept her excuse without suspicion. "I'll look forward to your return then, Your Gloriousness."

Devon smiled and nodded. Hopefully in that time she could figure out an excuse to make off with the rest of the demon skin.

And this time, she'd burn it.

***

The thicket Devon used to change clothes was thinning, though not at the same rate as the jungle canopy. And unfortunately, with 37 Charisma after spending a couple points from her level 15 and level 16 attribute allocation plus the bonus from her new *Leather Doublet of Darkness*, there was no way she could get away with undressing anywhere remotely public. Sometimes she even caught the dwarves staring as she walked across the village. Ordinarily, they didn't even find scrawny human builds attractive.

Between her lack of a private changing room and the continued practice of storing her stuff in random chests throughout the village, she was beginning to think she needed a space of her own. The demon skin situation wasn't the only instance where she'd left something only to find it repurposed by a well-meaning NPC, and Hezbek often complained when Devon started rooting through the trunks in her cabin.

But she didn't want to take housing from those who actually needed it. Maybe once the carpenters had knocked together enough cabins she could move into the sloth-hide tent. So far, the game didn't count it against her limit of structures that could be built in the village.

Eventually, of course, she'd move into the keep. But that was a ways off. For now, she added the problem of a personal space to her long list of things to sort out.

Clad in the new chest armor, Devon stepped out of the brush and started for the main gate. She tried to ignore the silky-smooth feeling where the garment was lined with demon skin. The fact that it was actually kind of comfortable somehow made it worse.

"Mayor Devon?" a woman called as Devon neared the wicket gate.

One of the new villagers, a merchant if Devon remembered correctly, scurried from one of the shop buildings. She was slight of build with a scarf tied over her graying hair.

"Yes?" Devon asked.

Having captured Devon's attention, the woman now seemed to struggle with her words. She had a glum aura about her, no doubt caused by the low morale among the village vendors.

"I'm not sure we've ever been formally introduced," Devon said, hoping to draw her out.

The woman kept her eyes downcast. "No, Mayor, I don't believe so. Bess is my name."

"What is it that you sell, Bess?"

"General goods, Mayor. Ordinarily, that would be any of sorts of supplies an adventurer needs. Waterskins. Crafting supplies for field repairs. Reagents for the alchemists."

Devon cocked her head. "You said *ordinarily*. Does that mean you aren't selling such things at the moment? I know that we have problems with the supply of available coin right now, not to mention the shortage of shop buildings, but that should hopefully be addressed soon."

Bess clasped her hands in front of her belly. "I do have a few odds and ends, and you're right about the general difficulties we merchants are facing. But it's more a question of supply. The leatherworkers have been making me waterskins, and your medicine woman has kindly sold me a few potions so my shelves aren't so bare. Other things will have to come once we've grown enough to attract trade caravans...and once there are roads which can support wagons."

Devon smoothed an eyebrow. Roads? Trade caravans? She'd never realized how much went into establishing a settlement.

"All right..." she said, sensing that the woman was working around to her real request.

"But there is something you could help me with, Mayor. During our months in the swamp, I wasn't able to ply my true trade, so I worked on a skill that is common among merchants like me. I've become quite good at fletching arrows. Your fighters tell me they've been running low, and if I had a ready supply of feathers, I could create one batch for the village and another to sell to players."

"Certainly. Have you spoken with the hunters?"

"Well..." Bess said, scuffing her feet on the packed earth of the path. "Yes, but they tell me it's forbidden."

"Forbidden?" Devon said, pulling her head back in shock. "I don't understand."

"They say you won't allow hunting of parrots, and the other types of birds are too rare or too dangerous for our hunters' skill levels. I talked to the farmer working the chicken coop, but he said the birds won't molt for some time."

Right. The parrot thing again. Well, no matter the NPCs' complaints, she wasn't caving on that prohibition. "I suppose Blackbeard's plumage is out of the question."

"Even if that...*creature* didn't insist on telepathically calling me a brainless ape the moment I try to open a conversation, his feathers would need an arrow shaft the size of a small tree."

Devon blinked, envisioning constructing a massive ballista atop the wall and firing giant arrows fletched with scarlet-hued feathers. It actually sounded pretty awesome. For the moment, though, it seemed their ordinary ranged fighters needed mundane ammo.

"Well, I'm sure I can work out a solution." Maybe the parrots would just migrate away as the jungle retreated, opening the niche for some other types of birds. If not, she could always revisit the area where she'd encountered harpy eagles.

The woman brightened, the first glimmer of life Devon had noticed in her eyes. "Would you?"

> **Bess is offering you a quest:** Crossbow Crisis (repeatable)
> *Solve the arrow and crossbow bolt shortage by bringing Bess feathers. Whether you want to give up on your crusade to defend the parrots is up to you.*
> **Objective:** Bring Bess 20 flight feathers.
> **Reward:** 40 arrows or bolts for the village.

Reward: 1000 experience (it's not like you're heading out to slay a dragon)

Accept? Y/N

Well, it was something to do, anyway. A goal would help get Devon's mind off Heldi, and it would help the village at the same time. Devon accepted the quest and headed for the gate.

Chapter Five

DEVON SHOOK HER head again, still amazed at how much had changed. Though patches of steaming jungle still lingered, the area surrounding Stonehaven now reminded her of the pictures she'd seen of the African savanna. She half-expected to see a pride of lions lounging on a nearby rise, but if there was any wildlife nearby, the tall grass hid it.

It didn't, however, hide the pair of wide trails leading away from the area of raised earth where a bridge would eventually cross Stonehaven's moat. She stood at the trail juncture and looked back toward the main gate. As suggested by Jarleck, the openings in the curtain wall and the inner palisade were offset by a few hundred yards. It meant that even if attackers crashed through the first gate, they'd need to cover a long distance inside Jarleck's killing field to reach the main settlement entrance. It was a good design, she thought.

The wider trail headed south to the quarry, a relatively straight shot now that there was no need to keep Stonehaven's location secret. Or rather, there was no *way* to keep it secret with so many players nearby. The other track struck west through the grass and detoured around a tangle of stubborn jungle. It had to be the trail to the players' encampment. Devon looked at the path for a few seconds, considering. She was a little curious about their camp and conditions. Without intriguing quest lines or dungeons to explore, it seemed pretty boring to hang out and wait for a group of shithead players to arrive and attack Stonehaven. Not that Devon was complaining about the help. She just didn't understand what motivated them.

Moving off the trail by about twenty paces, she set out in roughly the same direction as the track. It couldn't hurt to see what they were up to as long as she didn't have to run into anyone and make small talk.

Unlike the village greens where the grass blades were soft and gentle, the tall stalks in the surrounding savanna seemed to find every gap in her armor, poking and itching. The experience was slightly more pleasant than cutting through dense jungle, but not by much. Not long after she started marching, she was already cursing and wondering whether she should go back to the trail after all. But she decided to stick with the plan, in hopes of getting a better sense of the land if nothing else.

The biggest surprise was the rolling terrain. When the landscape had been hidden by the overgrown forest, she hadn't noticed how much the ground rose and fell. Though not quite hilly, it formed rounded crests and dipped into shallow troughs. Here and there, outcroppings of weathered rock surfaced through the grass. Some were natural, and some the ruins of the long-dead Khevshir vassaldom, countless stone buildings fallen into decay.

It didn't take long for the gentle folds and scattered trees to hide Stonehaven from sight. Once she was alone, Devon paused and took a few breaths, enjoying the silence despite the scratching grass. The truth was, she enjoyed solo missions and hadn't had much opportunity to indulge in them lately.

The afternoon sun colored the landscape a pale yellow, and currents of air riffled the grass, causing her surroundings to wave and bend. Sometimes the breeze wafted from the north, carrying the hot breath of the jungle. Laden with steam and smelling of riotous greenery, the air was pulled from the ruins of Ishildar where vines and trees still cloaked the ancient city. Other puffs of air smelled like hay and warm earth and brought the buzzing of insects to her ears. Her sandals crunched through grass that wasn't dead but wasn't lush with moisture either.

Just as she started to wonder whether any wildlife had moved in behind the jungle's retreat, she yelped when she brushed aside a patch of grass with her *Wicked Bone Dagger* and revealed a long-snouted mammal with squinty eyes. She took a step back and used her *Combat Assessment.*

Anteater - Level 2

Listen. You could probably kill the poor thing with one hit. But you did want the ecosystem to weather the transition, right? We're talking resource management here.

"For your information, I was just curious what kind of creature it was," she said.

You never know with your kind...

Shaking her head, Devon let the grass spring back into place and sidestepped the snuffling animal. Out of the corner of her eye, she saw it amble off toward a dun-colored mound speckled with dark holes.

"Termites?" she muttered to herself.

You have gained a skill point: +1 Foraging
Not saying you should eat termite larvae. But isn't it nice to know you wouldn't starve if you got trapped out here?

"I think I'd rather dive under a rhino stampede."

Your preference is noted. Perhaps the death penalty is too soft for players under level 20...

Devon sighed. Why did the game have to be such a jerk?

Ahead, a stand of trees grew thicker, promising shade. Spotting the welcoming darkness, Devon hurried her pace. Demon skin might be silky smooth, but it attracted quite a lot of heat due to the dark color, and it was unfortunately even slimier than regular leather when wet.

When she ducked beneath the wide boughs of the first tree, the grove erupted in a loud chorus of squawking and flapping wings. Devon whipped out her dagger and darted behind a tree trunk, then peered out and dropped her arms to her side. In the center of the trees, a shallow pond reflected the leafy ceiling of the grove. In the water, a flock of flamingos strutted and flapped and looked generally annoyed by her intrusion.

She groaned. Even if she could bring herself to wade in and slash a few graceful necks, no one was ever going to respect a village whose trademark was fletching their arrows with pink feathers. She flopped to a seat beside a stately tree and leaned back against the smooth bark. Pulling out her *Everfull Waterskin*, she took a couple swigs of the lukewarm contents while watching the flamingos settle down and resume fishing for minnows.

"Got any bird friends who aren't kept as pets or used as plastic decorations in old peoples' yards?" she called. "I'm thinking maybe a flock of vultures or some kind of wild turkey."

A strange *gorble* brought the flamingos' heads up. Moments later, an ostrich strutted into the grove. The massive bird seemed to be laughing at her as it stretched out its long neck and blinked long-lashed eyes.

Devon shook her head.

"I could just log off, you know."

The logout button flared a bright, inviting green.

"Jerk..."

Devon stretched and stood. The truth was, she wasn't quite as freaked out at the prospect of ostrich hunting as she was of murdering flamingos or parrots. There had to be some nice steaks on a body that big, even if the feathers were too floppy and frou-frou for arrows. But she remembered something from back a couple years ago when she'd made a doomed attempt to improve her real-world cooking by watching a reality show where hopeless cooks were taught by robot chefs with the latest culinary AI. To improve ratings, the producers had made them work with at least one ridiculous or gross ingredient per episode.

Which was how she knew that ostrich egg omelets were a thing. Also, she'd learned that a frustrated neophyte chef who'd once hoped to play professional American football could do a lot of damage throwing one of the eggs at a robot chef's head.

"Hey, birdie," she said, popping open her rucksack and activating her inventory interface. If she could lure the thing back to

47

Stonehaven, it could be the start of their ostrich farm. The crafters might even be able to work shed feathers into interesting items, even if they weren't very useful as fletching.

She focused on the icon for a stack of lychee fruit she'd plucked from Stonehaven's orchard and felt the little fruit plop into her hand. Holding it out, she stood and smiled at the ostrich.

The bird cocked its head and blinked.

"It's yummy," Devon said, using her thumbnails to slice the fruit's hairy skin and expose the translucent white flesh. The ostrich took a step closer.

"There you go...this way."

Devon glanced over her shoulder as she backed out of the grove. Strutting, the ostrich picked its way forward, a sharp eye fixed on the fruit. Devon nodded, pleased with herself.

You have gained a skill point: +1 Animal Taming
Aren't you just the circus performer...

The sun fell warm and heavy on her shoulder and the side of her face as she stepped from the shade of the grove. Devon grimaced. It was going to be a long walk back while coaxing the bird, but maybe she'd get some good skill points out of it. It wasn't like she was super interested in becoming an expert animal tamer, but unusual talents often came in surprisingly useful.

Grass bent and broke beneath her sandals as she backed up a low hill. When she reached the crest, she glanced behind her to make sure she wasn't going to trip over a termite mound or something on the way down the other side.

Movement caught her eye, just a flicker atop another rise that lay maybe a hundred feet away. Jiggling the lychee fruit to keep the ostrich's attention, she squinted. Yes, there was *definitely* a shadow moving through the grass, and it was just now coming over the top of the hill. She couldn't make out any details, but whatever it was had considerable bulk. As it moved higher onto the rise, she spied a sleek back that reminded her of a lion and...at least two tails. She cringed.

Something smacked her hand. She yelped, whirled, and watched the round lump of fruit travel down the ostrich's long throat.

The hidden creature roared, bringing her whirling back to face it.

A spout of fire ripped across the hilltop opposite, blackening a trough in the grass.

Finally, it bleated.

When the monster leaped from the grass, Devon backpedaled. What the hell was that? As she'd thought, the beast's body was similar to a lion, but it didn't have two tails. It had three. It also had three heads. In the center, a lion snarled and bared its rather impressive teeth. On the left, some kind of dragon-looking thing sent smoke wafting from its nostrils as it craned a sinuous neck to try to see around the lion's mane. On the right, a goat stared off in the wrong direction and bleated again.

Devon took another couple steps backward as the monster dropped into a combat crouch and prowled down the opposite slope, through the dip, and up toward her.

The stupid ostrich started pecking at her rucksack in search of more fruit.

"Scat," Devon said, waving it off.

The ostrich cocked its head, then made that strange *gorble* sound again. It gave her weapon arm a solid stab of a surprisingly pointy beak, hitting a nerve. Her hand spasmed and tingled.

Flinging her inventory open, Devon grabbed a whole stack of lychee fruit and threw them back down the hill she'd just climbed. With high knees and another awkward squawk, the ostrich ran down the hill after them.

Taking a breath, Devon clenched and opened her fist to get the feeling back into her fingers before drawing her *Wicked Bone Dagger*. She conjured a *Glowing Orb* and held it high, but the glare of the sun hid any shadow cast by the crackling sphere. Worse, the waving grasses fractured her sun-cast shadow so badly that she couldn't gather enough awareness of it to get a valid target for her *Shadow Puppet* ability.

She clenched her teeth. Damn it. Sometimes it seemed like the changes to the game were deliberately trying to ruin her most effective strategies. Of course, there was some truth to that theory. Emerson had recruited her to help the AI build challenging and immersive content by responding to her creative play style. If she could stop trying to be clever, maybe things would get easier.

She snorted. Yeah right.

A roar shook the ground. Devon's breath caught, and she jumped back as the beast covered the final distance with a massive leap. Suddenly frantic, she groped again for a valid target for *Shadow Puppet*, but she came up empty.

Another spout of fire shot from the dragon's mouth, burning a stripe through the grass but missing Devon by a good five feet due to the bad angle. The dragon gave a reptilian shriek and tried to headbutt the lion out of the way. The big cat was having none of that, and the fur-tufted lion's tail whipped forward to smack the dragon on the back of its head.

The goat bleated at the distant horizon, purplish tongue vibrating.

Devon used *Combat Assessment.*

Chimera - Level 17
Though feared by many ancient cultures, this beast seems to have issues.

Yeah, the whole three heads and one body thing wasn't working out too well. She tried circling toward the goat head, figuring the worst the herbivore would be able to do was gnaw on her a bit. To the chimera's credit, it had enough coordination to recognize the tactic and pivoted until the lion's head faced her again. This seemed to enrage the dragon even more, and the reptile started snapping at the lion's mane, ripping free hunks of hair and spitting them out with little puffs of fire.

Okay, so maybe her inability to use *Shadow Puppet* wasn't a death sentence after all.

After another half-hearted blast from the dragon head, the warm scents of baked earth and ripe grass were replaced by the stench of burned mane.

Its eyes rolling in panic, the goat started *screaming* and trying to look for the source of the threat.

Devon grimaced as the beast—apparently under the control of the lion's head—lowered the front of its body and started wiggling its butt in preparation for a pounce. It almost seemed cruel to fight the screwed-up thing, but it *had* attacked first.

She cast *Freeze*, locking the monster in a case of ice. Darting to the side, she called down a *Flamestrike,* but the flames seemed to wash over the monster, melting the ice but doing no damage. The chimera pounced and landed where she'd been standing.

> *Normally, combat notifications are suppressed. But since you've been sitting around your village for a while, it seemed worthwhile to remind you that fire-breathing creatures typically resist fire damage. Too many injuries to the nose and throat otherwise.*

Devon rolled her eyes. Okay. Maybe that was fair. The problem was, her *Freeze* spell hardly did any damage, and her *Shadow Puppets* weren't working out here in the grass. Despite its problems with arguments amongst its heads, the chimera was one level higher than her. Devon's melee skills were pretty weak. She didn't think she could beat the monster in a straight up stabby battle.

Time for a new plan.

First things first, she froze the monster to gain a little time, then slapped a hand on her doublet and activated the armor piece's special ability. The hilltop darkened as the *Night's Breath* spell blanketed the area. Wrapped in a shell of ice, the chimera remained motionless, but the goat's eyes widened further. No doubt it would have more to say about the situation in a moment.

Next, Devon closed her eyes and formed a mental image of herself. She cast *Simulacrum* to create a vague representation of her figure near the dragon's head. The spell description claimed it wouldn't work very well for creatures of medium or high intelligence. Hopefully the unfortunate situation of sharing a body meant the heads would qualify as stupid.

Finally, she stepped in close to the monster's shoulder just behind the goat's head and stabbed through the ice. The casing immediately shattered, freeing the beast. But her dagger grazed the fur-covered flesh, raising a line of blood and knocking off just a sliver of the animal's health bar.

She jumped back as the dragon roared and sprayed a tremendous blast of fire through her illusion. The reptilian neck tugged hard at the chimera's torso, and the animal staggered.

Devon grinned.

The goat bleated.

Unfortunately, the lion quickly resumed control and turned back toward her. This time, it didn't wind up for the pounce. Before she could get off another *Freeze*, the beast was on her. A claw tore through the leather of her pants, opening skin and muscle beneath. Devon tumbled onto her back as the chimera's momentum carried it over her. A quick glance at her health bar showed that she'd lost 80 hitpoints. Over a quarter of her health.

"So much for the awesome accuracy debuff," she muttered.

> *As it happens, the monster was aiming for your belly. With both claws. Be glad you're still alive.*

Devon shook her head in disgust. Rolling and wincing, she jumped to her feet. Blood ran down her thigh while the cast bar for *Freeze* filled. A patch of ice erupted from the earth and grabbed the beast.

The ice immediately shattered.

53

Crap. Was that a resist? She backpedaled as the lion sprang again. As the beast flew through the air, another jet of flame blasted from the dragon's mouth. The thrust from the eruption pushed the chimera sideways, rotating the monster until Devon was staring into the long slits of the dragon's pupils.

She frantically tried to get another *Freeze* off, but a blast of fire hit her in the face, interrupting the cast. Devon fell backward, body smoking. Her health plummeted to 30%. Fumbling for her rucksack, she tried to get her inventory open to grab a health potion, but the backpack was crushed beneath her.

The dragon pulled back, mouth opening for another gush of flame. Just in time, the lion roared and sent the dragon's attack off target as the cat turned a snarl on Devon.

Desperate, she rolled backward and gained her feet. Gritting her teeth, she shoved mana into another *Freeze* attempt.

Her knees buckled with relief as ice enveloped the monster.

Half a breath later, the frozen prison shattered.

What in the ever-living hell? She'd never had problems with spell resists before, at least not on creatures near her level. Furious, she dragged open her combat window.

> *Your Bone Dagger Poison hits the Chimera for 23 damage.*
> *Freeze effect canceled due to damage taken.*
> *You wish your wounds would stop BLEATING so much. Haha!*

Ahh, shit. Devon shook her head. What had she been thinking? She *knew* the dagger had a chance to cast poison...that's why she'd gone for the scratch to the beast's shoulder, planning to whittle the monster down. But, idiotically, she'd forgotten that damage almost always broke effects that rooted monsters in place.

Fist clenched around her dagger's hilt, she backed away and dropped another *Simulacrum*, this time in front of the lion's head. The beast wasn't fooled a second time. It didn't even pause.

Bounding forward, the beast raked claws across her shoulder, knocking off another hefty slice of health and leaving her with less than a quarter remaining. Another attack or two and she was toast. Shaking her head, she threw down a *Freeze* anyway, but her focus was off. A slab of ice erupted just in front of the monster. Unable to stop its charge, the lion rammed the frozen barrier and rebounded, losing a bit of health.

> **Congratulations! You have learned a new ability:** Wall of Ice - Tier 1
>
> *You cast an impenetrable barrier of ice up to ten feet wide and seven feet tall. The wall is impassable until it has taken 350 hitpoints of base damage (scales with your Focus attribute). Once reduced to zero hitpoints, the wall shatters.*
>
> **Cost:** 40 mana
>
> **Duration:** 10 minutes or destroyed by damage
>
> *It's a cool spell as long as your enemies can't just walk around it...*

As Devon flicked the message away, the monster sprinted around the edge of the wall. Devon shook her head. She was so screwed.

She used *Combat Assessment* again, hoping for something more useful than an update to the chimera's mostly full health bar.

Forgetful much?

Chimera - Level 17
It seemed messed up, but this thing is pretty much kicking your ass.

Devon racked her brain for other ideas, but nothing came. Time to evac. She reached for one of her *Bracers of Smoke,* intending to cast the *Vanish* ability as the monster roared and charged.

A sharp pain from her shoulder knocked her hand away from the bracer.

Devon tried to yelp, but everything went black.

You take 46 pecking damage.
You have been slain by a Hungry Ostrich.

Respawning...

Chapter Six

WELL, THAT HAD royally sucked. Devon groaned as she stood from her "respawn of shame" cross-legged seat beside Veia's shrine. Her armor was seriously wrecked due to the death penalty, and she could still hear the echoes of that idiot goat's bleating. She didn't even have a single feather, much less the 20 needed to satisfy Bess's quest.

At least most of the dwarves were still passed out, and most of the rest of the town was finding excuses to walk past Heldi's house and look expectantly at the door.

No one noticed as Devon sauntered away from the shrine and made a beeline for her changing thicket. Now that she had a rucksack with decent inventory space, she carried a spare set of clothing around for situations like this. It saved her from annoying Hezbek by digging things out of a trunk.

She sighed. Maybe she should get Prester to build her a chest here in the thicket. If she hung a couple pieces of hide as curtains, it probably wouldn't count toward the settlement structure limits. For now, though, she quickly glanced through her equipment to see what needed repair.

The *Wicked Bone Dagger* had taken around 5 points of durability damage—she didn't keep precise track of that since it had started with 869 out of 1000 durability and it wasn't repairable anyway. Pulling it from its sheath, she set the weapon aside.

Her leather armor and sandals had been badly damaged, losing between a third and half of their durability points. Sighing, she stripped everything off and pulled on her spare clothes. Provided everything went well with Heldi and Dorden, she'd soon be leaving on a longer expedition. Starting with half-broken gear was a sure way to fail her objectives there.

Fortunately, the *Greenscale Pendant* didn't seem to take damage. Devon wore it at all times in hopes of getting the thing attuned—the necklace was up to 75% now. She had a theory that the area's dissipating jungle was related to her attunement percentage. Maybe by the time they returned from the mountains, she'd be at 100% with the pendant, and the jungle would be eradicated from the surroundings.

Of course, given how well she'd fared in a grasslands battle, maybe it would be better to go back to hacking through endless foliage.

Sighing, Devon bundled up her damaged gear and started for the crafting workshop.

Gerrald shook his head when she slipped through the door.

"Sorry," she said with a shrug. "Got in a little over my head. But I did get to use the doublet's special ability."

The man shook his head sadly. "Well, I make the gear to be used. I'm just sorry I won't be able to follow through on my plans for the trousers."

"Oh?" Devon asked, nearly cringing when she realized how hopeful that had sounded.

Gerrald didn't seem to notice her tone. "It takes materials to repair things, you see. I suspect it will consume all the demon skin we have remaining to fix up these bracers and doublet. Real sorry about that, Your Gloriousness."

Devon tried to keep a straight face. At least that was one bright side to her pathetic adventure.

She clapped him on the shoulder. "It's my own fault, my friend. But I'm sure there will be new components for you to incorporate in the future."

And she would be far more careful in supplying them.

Gerrald took a deep breath and seemed to recover from his disappointment. "Well, I'll get these repaired within the day. Now that the wee one is here, I hear you'll be heading out soon."

"Wait, what?"

"I thought you came back because you saw the beam of astral light signaling the final stages of the summoning. Figured the...damage to your gear was on account of extricating yourself from battle when it wasn't tactically advisable."

Devon pressed her lips together. She'd been sure he knew she'd died due to incompetence, but apparently he had too much faith in her. She must have missed this beam of light during the heat of her ill-fated combat.

"I...I did hurry back, that's for sure. Figured I'd play dumb about the summoning just in case the proud parents wanted to surprise me."

Fortunately, Gerrald was too gullible to ask any follow-up questions. She didn't want to lie outright, but it *was* pretty embarrassing to get killed within her first hour outside the camp.

The lines bracketing Gerrald's mouth deepened when he smiled. "To tell the truth, I think everyone in Stonehaven is about ready to jump out of their skins with impatience—except the dwarves who haven't woken up yet, I suppose. Dorden's in with Heldi, and they won't let anyone see the child because they say you should be first."

Well, crap. "I guess I better run then."

Dashing toward the dwarves' home, she felt the eyes of the village on her. Did they wonder how she'd snuck inside the walls without being noticed, or were they just waiting to see her reaction to the child? Unfortunately, when she made eye contact to try to figure out the answer, people looked away out of respect for their leader.

Hezbek had no such qualms. The medicine woman stood on the porch of the dwarves' cabin, arms crossed, foot tapping.

"Took you long enough," she said before narrowing her eyes. The woman chuckled. "Equipment in for repair, is it?"

Devon shook her head. "Don't ask."

She stepped up to the door, tapping lightly. Heavy footfalls shook the floor, and the door flew open, exposing a grin so wide Devon worried Dorden's jaw would lock.

The dwarf seized her by the arm, yanked her inside, and slammed the door.

Devon blinked as her eyes adjusted to the dimness. When her vision returned, she tiptoed forward.

Heldi sat in a straight-backed chair, her hair unbraided and falling in loose waves over a linen tunic. The dwarf woman looked down adoringly at the little package in her lap.

Devon hadn't known what to expect. She'd imagined the baby would basically be like a miniature version of the adult dwarves but without the beard. She wasn't sure what to compare the baby to, but he certainly wasn't what she'd expected.

Luminous over a tiny button nose, the child's green eyes were genuinely enormous. Like...anime-sized. He had an eensy-weensy mouth all pursed up in a sweet little pucker.

When she drew near, he focused on her and blinked, then made a tiny cooing noise.

The miniature dwarf was undoubtedly the cutest thing she had ever seen.

Devon tried to look up at Heldi, intent on congratulating her, but her eyes kept returning to the little face.

"I...hello boochie," she said. "Whatcha doing wittle cutie?"

Devon blinked. Where had that come from? She swallowed, unable to wipe the stupid grin off her face.

*A dwarf baby has afflicted you with **Adoration**. You seem unable to think straight or speak like an intelligent adult while within 3 meters of the caster.*

"Oh, for crying out loud," Hezbek's voice penetrated Devon's trance. "Someone drag her out of range. We'll never get to see the child if we wait for Devon to remove herself."

The baby blinked again, blowing a tiny spit bubble from his perfect little mouth. Devon tickled his tummy, and he giggled.

"Who's getting the baby's tummy?" Devon crooned. "*I'm* getting the baby's tummy."

Hezbek groaned. Loudly. Dimly, Devon noticed a glow spreading from the entrance to the cabin. A moment later, a chill wave struck and passed through her.

*Hezbek has cast **Inner Armor** on you, increasing your resistance to mind-altering spells.*

Devon blinked and swallowed. The baby cooed, and she smiled. But the impulse to raspberry the child's chubby cheek was now manageable. Mostly.

"He's..." She trailed off, once again struck by the deep emerald shine of the boy's eyes.

"Adorable. Yes, we know," Hezbek said. "And most of us are smart enough to train resistances before exposing ourselves."

The medicine woman sighed, and her stomping feet shook the floorboards. Moments later, her hand latched on Devon's shoulder.

"Come on, child. Better to take this in small doses until you've learned the tricks of it."

Devon shook her head. "But he's so..."

Heldi looked up and leaned around Devon and Hezbek to catch her husband's attention. "Come on, Dorden. You've had your fun. Help our poor starborn friend."

With a low chuckle, Dorden crossed the small room and stepped between Devon and his child. Suddenly confronted with his bulbous nose and scraggly beard, Devon recoiled as the *Adoration* effect was canceled. She couldn't help grimacing, which only caused Dorden to laugh harder.

"Let's get you out of here," the dwarf said, pushing her by the elbows as Hezbek tugged on Devon's shoulder. Stumbling, Devon shuffled back. Once in the safety of the doorway, she took a deep breath.

"Well, that was unexpected," she said. "I thought he would be..."

"Thought he'd be as handsome as his father?" Dorden said, puffing his chest. "Someday."

"What's his name?" she asked.

"Ahh. Now that's a good question. And it demands a long answer. What do you say we speak of it on tomorrow's trek? For now, I have plenty of eager clan members and villagers who want to see me boy."

Devon dragged her hand through her hair, avoiding glancing toward where Heldi sat with her child. When she'd first heard that the dwarf parents planned to leave the baby soon after his birth, she'd been concerned. Now the idea was alarming.

As if noticing her hesitation, Dorden caught Hezbek's eye. Some unspoken communication passed between them, and then Hezbek leaned close to her ear.

"I think we need to have a little talk about how things work with babies, starborn. Aside from the actual summoning."

Raising an eyebrow, Devon turned. "Seriously?"

The woman smirked. "Not that. I mean, *after* the baby is made. And I believe you owe me a story about your explorations today."

Devon sighed. "I suppose I do."

"Then let's get out of here and let these people have a chance."

Devon turned and immediately blushed to see what appeared to be every citizen of Stonehaven standing just a few paces away. Had they all heard Hezbek offer to explain about babies?

Shaking her head, Devon groaned. With luck, they'd forget all about it once they saw that disgustingly adorable creature inside the cabin.

***

Hezbek swung a little kettle over the flames in her hearth and sprinkled in some minty-smelling herbs. Pulling over a stool, she encouraged Devon to sit and then lowered her weight onto the cot.

"So," she said, "run into a little trouble out there? It can be difficult when conditions change away from those you've become accustomed to."

Devon sighed. "I ran into a monster with an annoying resistance to fire."

Hezbek hummed and nodded. "Yes, I can see how that could make things a little more difficult. At your level of experience, such encounters are rare. But you aren't helpless in any case."

"I don't know. I felt pretty damn helpless. I tried *Freeze*, but it doesn't do enough damage, and unfortunately my dagger has a poison effect which kept breaking the ice. My Deceiver abilities had issues in deep grass."

The medicine woman cocked her head. "And that's all you tried?"

Devon blinked. "Well, I used an ability from my new chest armor, but the problem is that even with reduced accuracy, the chimera still wrecked me."

"Ahh..." Hezbek nodded. "A fearsome beast. The melee attacks from the lion are powerful, and if you have the misfortune of letting the dragon hit you... Well, we know how poorly adventurers of your strength usually fare against such beasts. Fortunately, the dragon's fire is easy to avoid, and the goat is totally useless."

"But the bleating...it sounds like a herd of screaming toddlers."

Hezbek nodded again. "I suppose the ruckus could cause some otherwise hardy fighters to, as you say, wig out."

The medicine woman plucked a pair of earthenware mugs from the shelf and ladled out portions of tea. She handed one to Devon. "I'm surprised though..."

"About what?"

"I thought you would derive great pleasure from the *Conflagration* ability."

"Actually..." Devon grinned. "I never got a chance to tell you about the skeleton fountain. It was awesome."

Hezbek stirred the contents of the pot before hanging the ladle on a hook. "I look forward to the tale. But if you found the spell so *awesome*, why not use it against the chimera?"

Devon pressed her lips together. She didn't want to make Hezbek feel embarrassed for asking the question, but she wasn't sure how to answer. "Is there a way to get around the fire resistance with it?"

A look of understanding crept across the medicine woman's face. "I get it now. You are thinking of the spell's target, not the damage type."

Confused, Devon pulled up the ability description for *Conflagration*.

Spell: Conflagration - Tier 1

A bolt of lightning shoots from your hand and causes an existing fire to explode for between 3 and 50 base damage depending on the size and nature of the source fire. Final damage scales with your Intelligence.

Cost: 41 mana

Target: An existing source of fire.

"A bolt of lightning shoots from your hand..."

Hezbek smirked. "As I said, you aren't completely helpless. Though I do agree it would be a challenging battle given the need to combo the spell with a target fire."

Devon shook her head. "I wasn't thinking. I probably could have burned an area of the grass so that I could use my *Shadow Puppets* too."

The medicine woman patted her knee. "Fortunately, you learned. Now, tell me what questions you have about children in this realm. Dorden already explained that the babe belongs to the clan as well as the parents. Surely that reduces your concern for his welfare..."

Devon cupped her mug and inhale the steam. It smelled delicious. She blinked, ordering her words. "I guess I'll be blunt. Doesn't the baby need to eat?"

A slow smile spread across Hezbek's face. The woman leaned back and laughed. "Sometimes I forget how things work in starborn realms. Your infants are dependent on their mothers, aren't they? Feedings every Zaa-cursed hour or something. I can't imagine how your mothers do it." The woman shook her head. "Fortunately, this world is what I believe you call *mawrpig*. We are allowed some conveniences."

"A what?"

"Perhaps I am pronouncing it wrong. The spelling is quite strange. MMORPG?"

Devon nodded. Of course. Hezbek couldn't say it outright, but she was trying to explain that the game had different rules. "I see what you mean. So I take it Heldi doesn't need to be here for her child to eat."

"Quite so. But that doesn't mean she won't be caring for the babe. In fact, many adventuring parties quite enjoy having a new mother along for the magic she gains while her child is young. Of course, the spells have a much longer duration when cast on the infant, but they're still quite useful for groups."

Devon sipped her tea, eyebrows raised. "Such as?"

"Well, the most necessary is probably *Growth*. For children, it causes maturation from infant to toddler. But on full-grown adults, it has a regenerative effect."

"Are you saying Heldi's a healer right now?"

Hezbek nodded. "And quite proficient at it. The other major spell is I believe what you'd call a damage shield. When cast on the baby, it prevents all injuries until the end of adolescence. Anyone trying to wound the child suffers damage in response."

"I'm guessing it's not quite that powerful on grown-ups."

"No. But it might've helped you against your chimera nemesis."

Devon sighed. "Thanks for the reminder."

"Any time."

Devon fixed Hezbek with a suspicious stare. "Sometimes I think you enjoy watching me muddle through."

The woman laughed. "Or maybe I like watching someone with your talent solve problems in unexpected ways."

A loud squawk filtered through the walls of the cabin, followed by a few out-of-tune lines from a sea shanty.

"Sounds like Blackbeard is home," Devon said. "I suppose if we are leaving for the mountains tomorrow I should see to a few things." She'd been thinking about the parrot lately and had a new idea for his beak problems. Birds typically learned to speak by listening and repeating. And she happened to have a poet NPC with no audience. Not to mention, her real-world clock was edging toward midnight. Best to get a little sleep before the journey.

Hezbek inclined her head. "I wish you a journey full of adventure and camaraderie."

"I can't imagine we'll find any shortage of that."

Chapter Seven

MICROWAVE POPCORN WAS awesome. The stale smell of the bag she'd cooked for breakfast fourteen hours ago was not. Devon groaned as she climbed off the couch and shuffled to the window. As she cranked the handle to open the glass pane to admit some night air, the faint scent of evergreen bushes from the scrappy hedge below the balcony swirled into the room.

She stretched and rubbed her eyes, yawning.

The fridge was getting low again, which meant placing another order with the grocery delivery company. The guy who usually brought her items definitely seemed to think she was some kind of freaky recluse. At least, that was the impression she got from the side-eye glances and his not-so-covert attempts to peek through her window. But he picked out decent-quality produce and hadn't screwed up an order yet, probably because she tipped him even though she didn't make him carry the stuff all the way to her counter.

Anyway, for now she had a squeezy bottle of something called tikka masala sauce and a box of spaghetti noodles that were pretty hard to screw up cooking, as long as she remembered to stir them a couple times. Yawning again, she grabbed her lone pot from the cabinet. It had come with the apartment and had quite a few dents, but it seemed to boil water okay.

While the pasta cooked, Devon strolled out onto the balcony that accessed the second-story apartments and leaned her elbows on the railing. Across the sprawl of subdivisions and thoroughfares with their snakes of autocab traffic, the sandstone cliffs near Snow Canyon State Park rose to cut dark shadows from the starlit sky. She shivered in the chill autumn air, but the contrast from October, when the city had sweltered, was nice.

The terrace vibrated as someone stepped from the stairwell. The young man cast a furtive glance at her as he passed, and Devon fought the urge to pull her arms close. His quick look was probably just evidence of the ordinary curiosity that people had about their neighbors, but she couldn't help feeling judged. She knew her hair was a mess and that her rumpled clothes probably made it obvious that she'd spent the last twelve hours on the couch.

She wasn't always this self-conscious, but it didn't help that most of her current life was spent with 37 *Charisma* and a village that adored her while in the other parts—the bits that were supposed to be *real*—she was just an average woman living in a crappy apartment. She had a grand total of one friend outside Relic Online, and she hadn't exactly been doing a good job with that relationship lately. The last time she'd hung out with Tamara, she'd turned down an invitation to go camping in Arizona. It was probably too cold now with Thanksgiving on the way.

For that matter, even though her relationships with some of her old guildmates had improved, she hadn't exactly made an effort to keep in touch since Hailey and Chen had set off to explore undiscovered areas of the game world. She sighed.

Fifty feet or so down the terrace, the man stopped at his door and laid a finger on the sensor to unlock his apartment. Devon pushed off from the railing and shuffled inside. She wasn't usually so hard on herself. It was probably just tiredness talking.

But she *did* need to pay more attention to Tamara.

The water was boiling, so she shook out a portion of dry noodles from the pasta box, broke them in half, and dropped them in. The water frothed and overflowed the pot like usual, but quickly settled down.

Flicking her gaze to the Entwined dashboard at the edge of her vision, she set a ten-minute timer and grabbed a beer from the fridge.

Unsurprisingly, her message queue was empty. Emerson's contact card grabbed her attention, and she hovered over it for a second or two before shaking her head. Seriously, what was he going to tell her? Get back to the newbie zone and look for a tutorial about what to do when a demonic shadow infests your character sheet? She brushed past his card and focused on Tamara's.

The last message they'd exchanged was from three weeks ago.

Hey Dev. I'm heading out to Flagstaff. Be back in a week or so. Drop a line when you want to ride. (Or if you just want to grab dinner, I won't call you a wuss or anything.)

Devon selected the message window and started subvocalizing a message.

"Hey. Sorry to be such a flake lately. I got kinda caught up in..." She paused. Caught up in what? For the last couple weeks, she'd mostly been hanging around in Stonehaven, too nervous to leave, but not really accomplishing much. But Tamara didn't need to hear the details about her in-game activities, and she would probably just laugh at Devon for thinking she needed to apologize. The woman always seemed so confident and easy-going.

Devon deleted the message and started over.

"How was Flagstaff? Ride off any cliffs? I'm finally out of my 'I can't sleep' phase. If you're ready for a good laugh, I'm ready to make another attempt at that mountain biking stuff. Lemme know and I'll figure out my work schedule."

She focused on the 'send' button, then hesitated. What if Tamara didn't want to take time off from her real riding to teach a rank beginner? The other time they'd gone biking, the midday heat had been making it too hard for the other woman to get long rides in anyway. Not to mention, Devon had passed out halfway through the ride...

Sighing, Devon shook her head. Really, why was she feeling so insecure tonight? Before she could second-guess herself any more, she clicked send, then brushed the messaging app out to the very fringe of her awareness.

Another cool swallow of beer slid down her throat as the pasta timer went off. Wooden spoon in hand, Devon turned off the burner and peered into the cloudy water. A thick mass of noodles rested on the bottom of the pot.

She pressed the knuckle of her thumb between her eyebrows. Hadn't she just been thinking that pasta was easy as long as she remembered to stir it?

The water and noodle-log went into the sink in a cloud of steam. Devon started to refill the pot, then changed her mind. It might be the first time anyone had eaten microwave popcorn with tikka masala sauce, but maybe she'd get a point in *Improvisation* for trying.

Or if not that, *Bravery.*

Chapter Eight

HELDI WAS GLOWING, and it wasn't in the figurative sense like people said about new mothers in the real world. She was quite literally surrounded by a shimmering white halo. Devon tried not to stare, especially because no one else seemed to notice the changes. The dwarf woman stood with the rest of Stonehaven's fighters beneath a tree they'd taken to calling the Council Tree. Thick and gnarled at the base, it branched into an umbrella of greenery that stretched wide over a circle of ground cushioned by moss.

Pulling her eyes from Heldi, Devon crossed her arms and stepped onto a low stump. In the corner of her vision, the new dwarf baby was a white cocoon in woolen wraps. She knew better than to look directly at the child, but even now she could feel the urge to start babbling like an idiot. Before the meeting, Hezbek had explained about resistances in Relic Online. Though they were typically increased by buffs and gear, she *could* develop some natural tolerance against certain effects and damage types with deliberate and controlled exposure. Apparently, some dedicated adventurers practiced this tactic by subjecting themselves to burning, freezing, poison, and so on. Devon was tempted to test it out—no doubt every serious raider in the game would be sticking limbs into campfires once they caught wind of the opportunity. But for now, it seemed she could learn to keep her wits around the baby by taking it slow with him.

"All right," she said, addressing the gathering. "You're aware that I'll be leading a party into the mountains, I assume?"

The fighters, including Dorden's dwarves as well as Bayle and her fellow human fighter, Falwon, nodded. Jarleck's mouth twisted in worry as he glanced toward the fortifications. No doubt the man was wondering whether his efforts had provided a suitable defense, particularly when a number of the village's fighters would be leaving. Greel rolled his eyes as if annoyed she felt the need to reiterate the point of the meeting.

"Then you know we may be gone for quite a few days. We don't know what conditions we'll encounter or how long it will take to locate a site for mining."

"If you're asking if we're up to the task," Dorden said, "we can end the meeting right here. Just the thought of mountain air and deep caverns has me and me clan ready to chop through the gate to get out of here."

"Now wait," Jarleck said. "That's why we built the wicket door. You just have to pull the rope to lift the latch—"

Dorden cut him off with a loud guffaw. "Ye take me too seriously, me friend."

Devon smirked. "Anyway, I'd like to take four fighters to escort the miners. Because of the potential dangers, I'm inclined to bring advanced citizens who could be restored at the Shrine to Veia."

She paused at this point because the math presented a problem. Of the fighters, five were advanced NPCs, which meant she could make offerings at the Shrine to Veia to resurrect them—unlike the basic NPCs who were permanently lost if they died. But if she invited just four advanced NPCs to group up and head out, she'd have to leave one behind. It was an unfortunate situation, but she had a feeling the problem would solve itself if she held her tongue.

When Jarleck cleared his throat, she breathed a silent sigh of relief.

"I hope you'll forgive me," he said, "but until the curtain wall is finished, I don't feel right leaving the construction."

She nodded as if disappointed but approving of his sacrifice. "Of course your combat skills would be a big help to us in the wilderness, but I understand. And Stonehaven appreciates your hard work."

You have gained a skill point: +1 Leadership.

Devon turned to the rest of the group. "I hope those of you who can't be reborn at the shrine understand my concern for your safety. I nearly lost Bayle before she became an advanced citizen."

Though the other fighters stood with faintly slumped shoulders, especially the dwarves, they nodded. Devon swallowed. She'd never liked picking teams in elementary school, and she didn't enjoy selecting favorites now either. But she had to think of the greater good.

"And I'm afraid there is danger even here," she said. "Stonehaven could be attacked at any time. I need brave fighters to defend the walls."

In fact, it was difficult to stomach splitting her small force of fighters no matter who stayed behind. Now that the villagers' basic needs were taken care of, the lack of defenders was Stonehaven's greatest vulnerability.

"If I might make a suggestion, Mayor Devon," Jarleck said.

She raised her eyebrows, surprised he had more to say. "Of course. Anyone is welcome to speak up at any time."

"Well, you see, the starborn have been coming to me asking to help with construction. I've been putting them off because I know you have reservations about the starborn. But what if we were to give them specific tasks catered to our needs? I could put them to work on the moat and wall. That way, if Stonehaven were to come under attack, many of them would already be here and ready to defend."

Devon realized she was clenching her jaw, and she forced herself to relax. It sounded like Jarleck was talking about giving the players quests. The game would probably award experience for the tasks, gaining the village free labor while costing them nothing. If the players were willing to help, it seemed dumb to ignore the opportunity.

"Do you feel confident you could put them to work effectively?"

Jarleck crossed his arms and looked almost smug. "More than confident."

Devon took a deep breath. "Do it. Offer any tasks you think they can handle that won't take work or resources away from Stonehaven citizens."

"There's one more thing I'd need," Jarleck said, not quite meeting her eyes.

"Yes?"

"You will need to be there for the first assignment. Charters for villages such as this one won't allow the use of outside workers without the approval of the village leader."

Devon groaned inwardly. "Okay fine. I'll be there to nod and smile."

The fortifications master shuffled. "About that...I know you're the strong silent type, but you *could* greet them. Maybe make a little small talk."

She sighed. "Okay, so I'll nod, smile, and talk about the weather. Good enough for you?"

Around the circle of fighters, grins broke out.

"I told 'im ye'd come around to letting them 'elp us," Heldi said. "He just had to put it the right way to convince ye."

"Ironic isn't it," Dorden added. "Seeing as we are the ones who were supposed to hate starborn."

Devon shrugged. "Just don't let our good luck with these particular people steal your caution. There are still jerks out there."

"Understood," Jarleck said. "We won't forget."

Devon swallowed. She hoped she wasn't wrong to believe that.

***

The player, a paladin in armor so polished he must have shined it at least once a play session, looked askance at Devon as she stood behind Jarleck's shoulder. She smiled, kind of, and gestured toward the fortifications master.

"Jarleck has a quest for you, and I need to be here to approve it," she said. After an awkward pause, she added, "Thanks for helping."

The paladin gave a very role-playery bow. "I figured as much considering there's a quest popup in front of my face."

Devon contained her wince. Barely. Okay, so no more stating the obvious. Small talk. Smile and wave.

"Sorry. I don't really know how this works."

The player smirked. "I was just giving you shit. I didn't know your NPCs could give quests either."

Devon glanced at Jarleck to judge his reaction. She deliberately avoided calling the villagers NPCs in conversation, and she certainly didn't refer to them as *her* NPCs. It didn't seem right considering they didn't think of themselves as non-player characters controlled by a computer, nor as followers slaved to Devon's will. But if the player's word choice bothered Jarleck, he didn't show it.

"Wait, didn't you guys come asking for tasks?" Devon said.

"We asked to help with the construction because it would help Stonehaven's defense. Getting a quest reward out of it is just a bonus."

She raised an eyebrow. Really? They were helping build a village out of the goodness of their hearts? Where had Hailey found these people?

She wasn't sure what to say for a moment, so she glanced at the sky and started formulating a comment about the weather. Fortunately, Jarleck saved her by clearing his throat.

"We are nearly done with the southern half of the moat if you have any interest in helping there," he said.

The player's eyes went distant, likely as a new objective was added to the quest dialog. He nodded. Devon couldn't help staring and wondering what his motivation was. Then again, what was hers? She wasn't exactly grinding out the levels either. But she was the leader of Stonehaven and champion of Ishildar. Compared to digging a moat for a bit of XP, she was pretty much a power-leveler.

The player turned back to her. "I think this is where you have to approve."

As if on cue, a popup appeared in her vision.

Will you allow Jarleck to be a quest provider for Stonehaven?
Accept? Y/N

Devon selected yes then brushed the popup away. The player was still staring at her, a faint moon-eyed expression on his face, and she felt the color in her cheeks. It was probably her 37 *Charisma* at work again. Though she had to admit that the paladin wasn't hard on the eyes either. For someone whose armor was way too shiny, he had a faint roguishness about him. Of course, as soon as she realized she was even paying attention to that, Devon wanted to smack herself. She was spending way too much time in game if she was starting to consider other characters hot.

Hopefully Tamara would take her up on a dinner invitation soon. She needed to see some real-life human faces.

Blinking, she turned her head and pretended to be inspecting something about the village. Jarleck again cleared his throat and nodded.

"On behalf of the settlement, thank you for your offer of assistance. There are shovels beside the trench, and once you've tired yourself out there..." Jarleck paused and looked the man over. "Yes, I believe you have sufficient strength. The workers at the quarry have stacks of blocks ready to be carried back. For every five blocks transported, we would reward you."

The paladin finally tore his gaze from Devon and peered over the low foundation of the curtain wall to examine the trail leading to the quarry. "You know, one of the clerics invited a crafter friend to come hang out at our camp. She's been working on obscure skills to see what's available and is apparently some kind of wheelwright now. She made some of us handcarts."

Jarleck shook his head. "Our dwarven friends learned the hard way how wheels can become mired out here. The jungle might have retreated, but the soil is still soft."

Crossing his arms, the paladin nodded. "What if we were to help out with that? Even with the changing environment, there's plenty of wood we could use to build a plank path, or if you feel you could spare the scrap stone, we could construct a cobblestone trail."

At this, Jarleck seemed to realize the conversation had gone beyond his pay grade. He glanced at Devon expectantly.

It sounded like a good idea, actually. She was about to ask the player for his name so she could stop thinking of him as anonymous paladin when she realized she could just inspect him. With the NPCs, she'd taken to introducing herself like normal people did in real life. She honestly didn't even know if the introductions were necessary or if they could just pull her name from the digital ether, but they always seemed to appreciate the effort.

But the player would think she was really weird or a hard-core role player. She pulled up his inspection window.

Torald - Level 21
Base Class: Paladin
Specialization: Unassigned
Unique Class: Unassigned
Health: 676/676
Mana: 104/104
Fatigue: 13%

As she flicked the window away, her chest tightened. Did other players see the full details on her main character sheet? If so, did they see her *Shadowed* stat, too? The thought made her vaguely uncomfortable.

Both men were looking at her now, and she hardened her expression as she glanced toward the quarry trail.

After a moment, she nodded. "It's a good idea. Talk to Deld and the quarrymen, Jarleck. If there's waste stone, let's go straight to the cobblestone path. Otherwise, planks will be an improvement." She thought about suggesting that the players could improve the path between their camp and Stonehaven as well, but decided that could wait. Just allowing the newcomers to help out with Stonehaven's development was a big step for her.

Jarleck nodded and turned to Torald. "Come back tomorrow and I'll let you know what sort of construction we'd like on the path. For now, the help on the moat and carrying stone blocks are the only tasks I can offer."

To Devon, that sounded like a clear dismissal, but Torald continued to stand there. After a moment, he finally caught on and tugged a gleaming helm from a small pouch slung over his shoulder, a trick that made Devon do a double take and inspect the piece of gear.

Item: Manpurse of Holding
This delicate pouch is both fashionable and convenient. Tucks neatly under a guild tabard or other heraldry garments, but the chic styling also makes this manpurse ideal for accessorizing the modern warrior's daily wear.
Container: 10 Large Slots, 20 Medium Slots, 20 Small Slots

The paladin noticed the direction of Devon's gaze. "Don't even start," he said. "It's one of the highest priced items on the European auction house."

Devon fought to keep a straight face. "It does have a lot of slots..."

Torald's mouth made a hard line as he waited for the punchline.

"And I like the way it complements your battle regalia," she finished.

The man gave her a flat stare. "I have a rule. Never carry inventory overflow for anyone who mocks my manpurse. Watch yourself, Miss Enhanced Basic Rucksack."

Devon smirked. "Should make it easy to transport stone blocks back from the quarry, anyway."

"And for carrying the spoils of my fight against darkness," he said with a laugh.

Jarleck was shuffling as if ready for the conversation to be over. He kept glancing at the unfinished curtain wall. Devon patted him on the shoulder, then glanced back toward the wicket gate leading into Stonehaven.

"I should go finish getting supplies together for the trek," she said.

"Trek?" Torald asked.

She hesitated, abruptly unsure whether she wanted the players to know she'd be gone. "Just a little exploring," she said.

He nodded. "Well, if you ever want to group up with some of us, we tend to meet up at the camp. Usually on the hour or half-hour. I'm sure anyone would be keen to see what your Deceiver abilities are all about."

She blinked and swallowed. "Thanks," she said after a moment's hesitation. "I may take you up on it after this."

With a slight bow, the man shoved the helm onto his head and glanced at the moat. "Seems I have some ditches to dig."

"Enjoy," Devon said as she turned for the gate into the village.

Chapter Nine

THE MORNING SUN was cresting the cliff behind Stonehaven as the party formed up inside the gate. Dorden and Heldi leaned over their baby and crooned their goodbyes. The infant was tucked tight against Garda's massive bicep, his enormous green eyes open and staring. Occasionally, he smiled and gurgled.

Devon kept her distance.

After some deliberation, they'd decided to bring the mules along. Though patches of jungle still lingered in the hollows near Stonehaven, and there'd be more dense foliage as they skirted the southern edge of Ishildar, the spreading savanna meant the animals could travel much more easily. Devon had spent the nighttime hours collecting and packing supplies for the journey while the NPCs slept. Each of the beasts now wore saddlebags with space for fifty medium items, while large equipment like their canvas tents was tied over the mules' backs.

For now, the animals carried rations for the group for ten days, plus assorted spare armor, repair kits, tools, and potions. There were eight people total on the expedition, five fighters plus the pair of miners and Hazel, the village scout. It was a lot of equipment to take into the wilderness.

Devon scratched one of the mules under the forelock. The animal twitched his long ears appreciatively, flaring his nostrils as he sniffed her forearm.

"Are you going to let me try to ride you if we have downtime?" she asked.

The mule snorted and looked away.

"I'll take that as a no."

"All right, me wee lad," Dorden said, laying a thumb on his son's forehead. "Don't cause too much trouble."

Heldi smiled at the baby, and a stream of light passed from her hand into the child.

"You waited until now to buff 'im?" Dorden asked, faint alarm on his face.

Heldi rolled her eyes and patted her husband's back. "Fool man. No. I buffed 'im the minute he started squalling. But never hurts to refresh the timers."

"Even when the effects last for years?"

"Even so."

Smirking, Devon sent group invites to the dwarf couple, Greel, Bayle, and the three noncombatants. As the party joined up, a glimmer stole into Dorden's eyes. He turned to the northeast and shaded his eyes. From their current position, Stonehaven's cliff blocked the view of the mountains to the east and north of Ishildar's ruins. But it was obvious the dwarf was already imagining himself in the high crags. Or just as likely, in some dark cavern that tunneled beneath those crags.

"Everyone ready?" she asked.

As the party members nodded, a commotion rose from within the cluster of cabins where the dwarves made their home. One of the fighters who was staying behind, Bodenir, came running on short legs with a cask of ale over each shoulder.

"Ye didn't mean to forget these, did ye, Dorden?" he called.

Dorden turned a horrified glance on Devon. "Don't tell me ye were going to have us leave without the ale? Some quartermaster ye are..."

"I...I guess I didn't think of it."

The man shook his head. He couldn't have looked more shocked if another demon rift had opened in the village floor. "Lass, ye realize if we'd reached camp to find the ale missing, we'd have had to march back through the night."

She cocked her head and raised a skeptical eyebrow. "Really?"

The man's nose twitched. "Well, maybe not. But how under Veia's stony gaze are we supposed to celebrate the discovery of a mine without a frothy mug or two?"

She sighed. "Okay. It's a fair point."

As she tugged open the saddlebags to make room for the casks, Greel started pacing. "And meanwhile, the sun continues its climb toward its zenith."

"Feel free to head out with Hazel and scout ahead, if you can keep up," she said.

The lawyer gave a beleaguered sigh. "Just reminding you to keep watch on the time, *Your Gloriousness.*"

"Are you sure you want to come on this venture? Maybe Jarleck could leave instructions on completing the fortifications."

The man snorted and rolled his eyes.

"Anyway," she said, "I do believe we're ready to set out."

"Not without agreeing on a marching song," Dorden said.

"Oh no," Heldi muttered, dropping her head.

Devon laughed. "Maybe once we're clear of the village. Don't want to wake those who are still sleeping."

"Or give them nightmares if they sleep through it," the dwarf woman added.

**

The party set off to the north and east, cutting a trail through the gently waving grasses. Hazel roved ahead, not quite as invisible as she'd been in the jungle, but still remarkably hard to make out. The grass came to the small woman's ribs, and she often moved in a crouch. The others walked single file, taking turns in the lead. Though the march was nothing like what Devon had experienced while trudging through in-game snow while playing other games, the effort of pushing aside the tall grass caused the lead party member's fatigue to rise faster than the rest of the group's.

As Devon walked, she kept her eyes on the ground in search of animal signs. Not only did she hope that more wild game would fill in behind the retreating jungle, she kind of liked the idea of the ostrich egg farm. Or maybe she just wanted revenge after being pecked to death.

The sun climbed toward its midday apex, and sweat started to trickle from her hairline. Devon pulled out her *Everfull Waterskin* and squirted some over her head. Unlike trekking through the humidity of the jungle, where being wet just meant being more uncomfortable, the dry air of the savanna cooled her as the water evaporated. She sighed in contentment, enjoying the march.

Dorden started to sing. The little ditty was okay, at first, a good rhythm for walking. The words were something about pickaxes and busting stone, not really her thing, but that didn't matter. Unfortunately, after the first minute, it quickly became clear that every line had the same repetitive tune. The damn thing made "ninety-nine bottles of beer on the wall" sound complicated and varied.

Devon groaned and fell back from the group. She wanted to test out some spell combos anyway.

Focusing on a section of grass, she cast a *Wall of Fire* in a stripe beside the trail made by the party's passage. The grass blackened and turned to ash that swirled up on the light breeze—fortunately, without spreading beyond the area covered by her spell. Once charred soil showed at the base of the flames, she dispelled the effect and stepped into the cleared area.

Her shadow was a tiny pool beneath her, almost invisible between the darkness of the earth and the sun's position directly overhead. Focusing on the small patch of shade, Devon cast *Shadow Puppet*. Thankfully, the spell took this time, and her minion rose from the ground. With a nod, she dismissed the effect.

So...she wasn't completely helpless in the grass, but having to burn a hole in the vegetation was a clunky way to get access to her ability, and needing to occupy a narrow strip of burned terrain limited her tactics.

She glanced up. The group was starting to get pretty far away, so she started walking as she chewed her lip and thought.

Cocking her head to the side, she put mana into a *Wall of Ice*. The translucent slab appeared across the trail in front of her, and she stepped up to it. Pressing her palm against the frigid surface, she pushed. Unsurprisingly, the mass didn't budge. But it did feel nice to stand beside. She pressed her cheek against the chill substance before banishing it—realizing too late that she ought to have backed off. Ice-cold water sloshed over the trail, submerging her sandals. She yelped, causing her party members to whirl in panic, then waved apologetically as she pranced out of the wide puddle.

"Sorry," she called, "just trying some things out."

Despite the distance, she could hear Greel's huff of disgust.

As she squelched forward, water dripping from her trousers and *squooging* between her feet and the soles of her sandals, she pondered. Targeting an area of the grass—off the trail this time—she tried casting another *Wall of Ice*. Only this time, she imagined it materializing horizontally rather than vertically so she could stamp out a flat square of grass.

*Cast failed. Did you think the spell was called **Floor of Ice?***

She sighed and shook her head. The game didn't have to be such a jerk about it.

As she started forward, intent on catching the group, something stabbed her shoulder. Whipping out her dagger, she whirled. The ostrich cocked its head at her and blinked.

***

"So tell me again why we're bringing this bird along?" Greel asked as he glared at the ostrich and laid down his bedroll. The sky was clear and the savanna warm, so they'd decided to sleep in the open rather than pitching the tents. Even if a bit of weather did come in later on, they'd selected the mossy ground inside a grove of wide umbrella trees as a camp. The arching boughs would keep off much of the rain.

"I thought you'd enjoy its company, given your fondness for chickens," Devon said.

"Whether I enjoy it or not—and I'm not—don't you think it makes us rather conspicuous?"

"To whom? It's not like we're marching through the central bazaar in some massive city."

"I don't know...to the bird's natural predators perhaps?"

Devon rolled her eyes. "Are you telling me you're afraid we'll be attacked by lions or something?" As she spoke the words, the memory of her unfortunate encounter with the chimera flashed to life. She brushed it aside.

He shrugged. "You must agree that it seems odd to trek into the mountains with an ostrich following."

Okay, maybe he had a point. And Devon might be a little overly defensive about the bird, especially since she couldn't seem to get rid of it, and instead had to relive the ill-fated chimera battle every time the thing pecked her shoulder. Whatever her single skill point in *Animal Taming* gained her, it certainly didn't seem to convey the ability to shoo her "tame" ostrich away.

As if to punctuate her thought, the ostrich sidled over and fussed at the flap of her rucksack with its oversized and surprisingly pointy beak.

"It *is* strange, Your Gloriousness," Hazel said. "What reason might the bird have for its fascination with you?"

Devon hadn't yet explained the situation, mostly because that might lead into a discussion of her embarrassing encounter with the chimera. But it wasn't very fair to keep pretending the large bird's behavior was normal. With a sigh, she explained her plan to lure the ostrich back to Stonehaven as their inaugural member of the ostrich egg farm. At least, she assumed this was *the* ostrich, and not just *an* ostrich. If the entire species had developed a fascination with her rucksack following the offering of lychee fruit to a single individual, she might have to quit the game in protest.

"So why weren't you able to bring the bird back to Stonehaven?" Dorden asked, his voice carrying a faint note of suspicion.

She sighed. As long as she was simply omitting details, she didn't mind keeping the story from her followers. But she couldn't outright lie to friends.

"Unfortunately, I was surprised by a chimera. It didn't go very well."

"See!" Bayle said, turning to the others. "I told you she wasn't bothered by it."

"Huh?" Devon asked.

"Some of the dwarves thought they saw you sneaking away from the shrine. We know that's where you're reborn if you die."

Devon blinked. "The dwarves were passed out..."

"Resting," Dorden said. "The best way to prepare for another round of celebration is to lie perfectly still until the world stops spinning."

With a sigh, she laid a hand on the ostrich's fluffy back. "Yes, when I say it didn't go well, I mean, I lost the battle. Rather spectacularly. Anyway, it seems this ostrich thinks I'm a lychee fruit dispenser."

Hazel had already spread her bedroll near one of the tree trunks. She walked over and inspected the ostrich, catching its eye and prompting the bird to stretch its neck toward her.

"I've heard that some adventurers fight with an animal companion. Have you considered it?"

Devon's lip twitched as she shook her head. No way. In Avatharn Online, she'd leveled a Wildsense Ranger to 250. The class hadn't been totally about fighting with pets, but she'd been able to charm and calm wildlife. Going back to something like that would be like clinging to the past or something. But even if she *were* interested in becoming a pet class, she definitely wouldn't choose an ostrich as her fighting companion.

"I don't think it's my natural talent," she said, hoping to be politic.

Hazel smiled as the ostrich blinked. "I don't know. It certainly seems to like you."

"The bruise on my shoulder disagrees," Devon said. "Hopefully it will wander off if no one feeds it."

She took a moment to meet the eyes of everyone in the group.

"Ah well," Heldi said. "I was thinking it would make a lovely steed for our boy."

"You're serious?" Devon asked.

The woman shrugged. "Seeing as there's a shortage of bighorn rams or hardy mountain ponies, I figure we'll have to improvise."

Shaking her head and turning from the bird, Devon paced a circle around the grove. Though the NPCs needed to sleep, she had another few hours before she needed to log off. She *could* spend that time grinding out a little experience or raising some skills or just keeping watch. But she had been scolding herself for spending too much time in game. Her followers could handle themselves for a little while.

When she returned to the group, the ostrich had bedded down amidst the reclining party members. She rolled her eyes.

"I'm going to vanish for a short while, but I'll return before we're ready to set out in the morning." Saying it, she felt strangely like Gandalf abandoning the hobbits at the edge of Mirkwood. Clearly, she'd started to develop quite a high opinion of herself.

The others nodded and kept about their tasks, unbothered by her starborn ways. With a shrug, Devon sat down, glared at the ostrich, and logged out.

Chapter Ten

DEVON'S PONYTAIL SWISHED over the collar of her light jacket as she stepped onto the balcony outside her apartment. With her purse slung securely across her chest rather than dangling off a shoulder, it was harder to fiddle with the strap, her habit when unsure what to do, but when going downtown it was a better defense against purse snatchers.

She took a breath of the chill evening air. It was around six-thirty and fully dark outside, typical for November's short days. The city of St. George spread to the south and west, lights glittering beneath the desert sky.

She'd showered, brushed her hair, and gotten dressed in something besides yoga pants with the intent of getting out of the apartment for a while. Back when she'd needed to head to a VR parlor to log in, the trip downtown had been a daily pilgrimage. Now, she wasn't sure she could remember when she'd last visited the city center. Maybe when she'd met Tamara for tacos.

Devon shook her head. That was way too long to go without contact with civilization.

Of course, since Tamara hadn't yet responded to her message about getting together, she wasn't exactly sure what she was going to do with an evening in town. The central area of St. George had plenty of fast food joints and food carts where she could eat alone without attracting pitying stares. Beyond that, maybe she'd just walk around a little bit.

Flattened chewing gum and grease stains darkened the concrete stairs that led to ground level. At the exit to the stairwell, she laid a palm on the autocab hailing pad.

"Your vehicle will arrive in three minutes," a friendly voice said from the speaker above the pad.

Yawning, Devon leaned against the wall to wait. Somewhere in the weeds across the asphalt pull-through that fronted the apartment complex, a cricket chirped. The low hum of tires on the thoroughfare a few hundred yards away flowed through the night air. In one of the apartments behind her, a couple yelled at each other.

The cab turned onto the pull-through and glided to a stop, the door sliding open.

"Please confirm credit," the car's AI said as she slipped into the seat.

Devon held her wrist over the scanner and was rewarded with a chime.

"Thank you. What is your destination?"

She shrugged. "The center roundabout, I guess."

"Thank you. Please fasten your seat restraints, and we will arrive shortly."

Ten minutes later, the cab pulled to the curb, depositing Devon on a sidewalk guarded by palm trees and a few artfully placed volcanic boulders. As she stepped back from the street, a young couple ducked into her abandoned vehicle and were whisked away. Devon swallowed and straightened her shoulders, walking through a scattering of people awaiting rides. Most looked to be office workers and retail employees on their way home from their jobs, but a few families stood at the curb, likely having eaten an early dinner out.

Strings of white LED bulbs that Devon couldn't help thinking of as Christmas lights spiraled up the trees. Where a pedestrian pathway left the central roundabout, the lights draped over the sidewalk to form a glowing tunnel. Downtown, three main walking malls extended from the roundabout like spokes, the commercial areas having been carved out from the former grid of streets when the autocar boom had changed the way people in the city got around. On the malls, electric carts moved along the lengths of the bricked streets, granting free rides to shoppers and diners who didn't want to walk.

Devon decided she needed the exercise and ignored a cart that stopped questioningly beside her. Tucking her purse against her hip, she started along the row of storefronts and restaurants, waiting for something to grab her interest. Around her, people moved in twos and threes, with just a handful of solo shoppers. Judging by the size and number of their bags, the people out alone were probably trying to get some early Christmas shopping in.

She stopped in front of a hole-in-the-wall Thai place and read the menu. It didn't look bad, but as she headed for the door, a trio of laughing college-age girls pushed in ahead of her. The door opened to show a room of nearly full tables.

Devon moved on.

She noticed the crowd of people spilling onto the mall from a storefront and started to make a wide arc around the group until she noticed the sign over the shop's door. It was another Pod People location, the chain of VR parlors where she'd spent so much time over the last years, but she'd rarely gamed at this particular arcade because there'd been another parlor nearer to a stop for the free bus line. Her footsteps slowed as she tried to figure out what was going on. After Avatharn Online had shut down, everyone had assumed the VR pod industry would suffer and possibly collapse unless another game quickly filled the void. Relic Online could have, but the partnership with Entwined and their implants meant even worse news for the VR capsule industry.

Which led to the question: what the heck could attract a crowd like this to a dying store franchise?

Devon took a step back as a holo began to materialize in the door alcove. The crowd retreated as well, not wanting to disrupt the projection. As the onlookers shifted, Devon got on tiptoes for a better look at the holo.

Her own face looked back.

Well, not her real-world face. Her character. That didn't matter. It was still her. Though there weren't mirrors in the game, at least not in Stonehaven, she had seen her character through Hailey's eyes. And if that weren't enough proof, the gear was. Devon's *Wicked Bone Dagger* was sheathed at the holo's hip, and the *Leather Doublet of Darkness* wrapped her perfectly proportioned torso. Stupid fricking 37 *Charisma*.

The bricks of the walkway seemed to fall away from her feet as she struggled to keep her composure. This was out of control. When did she agree to allow E-Squared to use her as a spokeswoman? Never.

The urge to sprint forward and swing her purse to knock out the projecting hardware was nearly overwhelming. In a loose semicircle around her character, gamers gawked and spoke excitedly. Suddenly weak-kneed, Devon rushed to a bench so she wouldn't collapse.

She closed her eyes, trying to get a grip. There was an operative phrase here. People were looking at *her character.* An avatar generated by a computer system. By *E-Squared's* computer system. They had every right to use pictures and holos of in-game characters since it was their content. And anyway, the gamers weren't staring— and in some cases, ogling—*her.* She, Devon Walker, was the woman sitting on a bench and starting to shiver because it was night time in November.

Unfortunately, trying to logic her way through this wasn't helping.

Her character began to speak.

"Hi everybody," she said, flashing a heart-stopping smile. "I take it you're here to try out a little Relic Online."

Gamers grinned and cheered as Devon's avatar held up a hand and summoned a *Glowing Orb.* Devon felt sick.

She pulled open her messaging app and started subvocalizing to Emerson.

"I thought you said I didn't have to stream or have a big public presence. So why are you guys using my character as a booth babe?"

Gritting her teeth, she highlighted the text and reread it. The shock was starting to wear off. She really didn't have a reason to be so mad. She *was* a salaried player after all. And it wasn't like they'd made her get up there and look hot for the crowd. The fact that her identity was so tied up with her character probably meant she needed to do more things like this, getting out and inhabiting her own skin for a while. It had been bad enough when Avatharn shut down—like part of her soul had been ripped out. If she wasn't careful, she'd fall so out of touch with reality that she wouldn't be able to handle if the same thing happening to Relic Online. Not a good situation.

Of course, it would have been nice to have been asked about this. Or even warned so she didn't stumble upon herself while out to get dinner. But she didn't need to send an enraged complaint to her contact at the company. Given Emerson's silence lately, he was probably so heads-down on the fix to the unauthorized implant access that she'd only be an unwelcome distraction.

With a deep breath, she deleted the text and turned sideways on the bench to watch herself—her *character*—interact with the crowd.

"Now I hope you'll understand that the experience inside the capsules is nothing like you'll feel with Entwined implants. Imagine. You could *be me*. Feel everything I feel as I adventure through the jungle. The damp air on my face. The hiss of the snakes. The VR capsules will tell you that's happening. With the Entwined hardware, you will *live* it."

Devon shook her head. The Pod People corporation had to be really desperate to allow an E-Squared holo-babe to stand in front of the store and diss their technology. Maybe they were just trying to get a cash infusion to pay off debts or something. Anyway, she hadn't realized that Relic Online even *allowed* play through traditional VR capsules.

"Of course, only some of you will be lucky enough to experience this today. During this promotional period, we will give one hundred gamers per location a chance to try out the game. Afterward, these lucky winners will be given coupons for 50% off on the installation of Entwined hardware. Most of you have only heard about the game by reading forums and watching livestreams or even plugging into sense streams. That's why we've instituted this trial program in cities across the US. By the time it's over, each of you will have a friend who has logged in even if you haven't been online yourself. We realize the hardware is expensive, and while we can't offer the coupons to everyone, we want you to know what you would get."

Devon sighed. What would these people think if she walked up and explained that the holo standing before them was her character? They probably wouldn't believe her. They *might* believe she had a RO account after seeing her implants. Just for that, she'd be an instant celebrity among this crowd.

She actually considered it for a moment. Hadn't she come down here thinking she needed more social contact? But then she huffed and shook her head. Not like this. She wanted real friends like she had in the game. Not fans who clung to her because she'd had the good fortune to be offered a job with E-Squared.

It was getting a little late anyway. Her party would be waking up soon. Standing, she spied a food cart selling pitas and gyros. She could eat on the way back home, leaving the smell of Greek food in the autocab for the next passenger.

Chapter Eleven

EMERSON SLIPPED A hand under his EM-shielding cap and moved some hair that was tickling his ear. Around him, the Cincinnati hyperloop station hummed with activity. Travelers moved back and forth between platforms on Emerson's level and hurried to escalators leading to other sets of destinations. As they passed, the adults gave his so-called tinfoil hat quick glances before averting their eyes. Children stared openly.

Neither behavior particularly bothered Emerson. He'd been on the receiving end of social skepticism since middle school. Turned out, his obsession with the intricacies of math proofs and code algorithms made it difficult for others to know how to relate to him. Occasionally, though, he had considered that a less conspicuous shielding device might be nice, especially if he didn't want Penelope tracking him down.

He glanced at the clock in the corner of his tablet's screen. His hyperloop capsule to Atlanta wouldn't leave for another hour. Unfortunately, there hadn't been a direct tunnel from Calgary, the nearest h-loop port to his Saskatchewan hideout, to Atlanta where he'd arranged a meeting with Owen's girlfriend. The layover in Cincinnati was inconvenient, but he supposed it was a good chance to review his strategy.

Swiping through screens on his tablet, he pulled up the obscure messaging app he'd agreed on using to communicate with Miriam, the engineer at Entwined who was helping him find and fix the vulnerabilities in the implants' software layer.

She'd messaged while he had been in transit from Calgary.

I've got something. Urgent. Can we video chat?

Emerson selected the field for entering his response and started subvocalizing. "Sorry. Was data-shielded during hyperloop transit." He paused and looked around at the stream of travelers. "Probably better to stick to text or voice...too public."

Voice then.

As Emerson pulled his earbuds from a pouch on his traveling carryall, he thought back to how convenient his cochlear implants had been. Sure, the Entwined hardware was supposed to make everything better and more seamless, but now that he was forced to keep it shielded to avoid intrusion from Penelope's AI, he'd been tossed back to the technological Stone Age.

"Okay," he said in a low voice once his earbuds were in. "What have you got?"

"Good news first," she said. "I'm making solid progress on the patch. I'm guessing I'm two weeks for completion on my end, but who knows how long it will take for me to convince management to push an update to live customers. And...I'm not sure it will be that simple."

Emerson ignored the inner voice that wondered how the removal of a debug library from the implants' software could take two weeks. Maybe their code had some strange dependency issues that he didn't quite get. Her last statement was what really grabbed his interest.

"What do you mean, not simple?" he asked.

She hesitated before responding. "Well, as you know, I've been running some tests in our neuro-lab, particularly ones that stimulate the unconscious mind. I was able to verify that the pain response was due to overexposure to the added sensory input."

"And?" Emerson said. "That should be good news, right? With proof, we'll have more leverage."

"True, but the problem comes when I take my test subjects back off the trial. I've seen some troubling responses."

Emerson sat straighter, nervously shifting the EM-shielding cap that covered his skull. "Troubling how?"

"It seems the abrupt cessation of regular stimulation leaves the subjects' minds in a variety of states. In some ways, the results are similar to withdrawals from an addictive substance, but they're also very different. Some people are left with a sort of residue of the experience...endlessly cycling memories that seem to cling to their subconscious—they show up in recurring dreams more than anything. Other subjects have a bit of shock from the sudden loss of stimulation, which seems to lead to mild mental paralysis. Most commonly, we've seen a strange bleed-over where the unconscious mind keeps trying to synthesize the sorts of experiences it was fed, and this process seems to leak into conscious awareness."

Emerson fought the urge to rip off his cap. "That doesn't sound good. What about the player I was able to shield? Is she in danger?" He didn't mention his own use of the shielding device due to sudden paranoia that she might start to doubt his judgment or mental competence.

"The moment I saw the results, I talked to a couple of our neuroscientists and psychologists. For my test subjects, the responses are fairly subtle. I put a couple of them back on the stimulation in the short term, and we are trying to wean them off slowly. In the case of Relic Online players, though, if they seem stable, I'd suggest leaving them shielded. They likely have the mental strength to fight through and recover alone. I think we should be careful with shielding new subjects until we have better answers, though. The psychologists suggest some sort of guided exit from their unconscious experience. Something to help their minds to recognize what's happening as the stimulation is phased out."

Emerson pressed a fist against his forehead, the insulation of his cap crinkling. "Management needs to know this is happening. Penelope has undermined my credibility, but maybe I need to do something drastic to get their attention."

"I think we may be safer to just hold tight for a few days. I can crunch to get the patch ready. I'm afraid to bring it forward when we have no solution because I don't want them to get into cover-your-ass mode."

Emerson nodded. He was—unfortunately—well aware of that danger. He took a deep breath, thoughts straying to Devon's messages. Was this "shadowed" thing due to her sudden disconnection from Zaa's stimulus? Maybe, maybe not. Either way, he should check in with her.

"Thanks, Miriam. Keep me updated, okay?"

"Will do."

Her icon went gray as she disconnected.

Chapter Twelve

BACK IN THE game, predawn light flooded the grasslands, but gloom still lingered beneath the wide canopy of the umbrella trees. Devon quietly climbed to her feet and tiptoed through the spongy moss, avoiding the sleeping forms of her companions. She stepped into the gently waving grasses and stretched, rubbing her eyes. Motion from one side caught her attention and nearly pulled a yelp from her throat. She fumbled for her dagger and pressed mana into casting a *Glowing Orb* before she recognized Hazel slipping through the grass.

Devon canceled the cast and started toward the scout. The woman waved as she approached.

"What are you doing up so early?" Devon asked.

Hazel chewed her lip, looking uncharacteristically bashful. "You weren't supposed to know, Your Gloriousness."

"Know what?"

"Hezbek said you didn't need to be bothered. She said that the two of us would work it out."

Devon kept her face even, hiding her faint annoyance at the woman's dithering.

"But you're going to tell me, right?" she asked in a deliberately patient voice.

The little scout shrugged. "You are the leader. I suppose I can't keep it from you. The problem is, as the jungle has moved off, Hezbek is struggling to keep producing."

Devon's eyebrows drew together while she tried to understand what Hazel meant. Finally, comprehension sank in. Of course. *Jungle Healing Potion – Mid. Potion of Jaguar's Speed.* They were all jungle-based. Hezbek had trained herself as a medicine woman by experimenting to make potions from ingredients found in her environment. The changing ecosystem didn't just affect the hunters. It affected foraging efforts for both medicinal and food ingredients.

"So you're collecting components for her?"

Hazel nodded. "She was very adamant that I didn't delay the expedition. She said you know best about what's good for Stonehaven, and that you wanted to hurry to the mountains."

"But if I'd known, I'd certainly have agreed we need to find ingredients so she can learn new recipes. We avoid using the potions except in dire situations, but that's only because they taste so foul. They're still an important part of our village's success."

The woman pressed her lips together. "I don't want to argue either way, Your Gloriousness. Only conveying what she said."

Devon nodded and touched the woman's elbow to put her at ease. "You're right. It's between Hezbek and me. I'll speak to her and make sure she knows that her work is important to us. I guess she was right about priorities—to a degree, anyway. We have a long hike and a lot of work ahead of us in the mountains."

Hazel glanced toward the stony ridge in the east. The peaks were closer now, the foothills reachable before evening if they kept a good pace. Still, the journey was much longer than any they'd made before.

"Have you found anything yet?"

Hazel smiled. "A few promising components."

"Keep at it. You cover much more ground than the rest of us while scouting ahead. Keep your sweeps a little shorter, and you'll have time to forage without delaying our march. Maybe you and I could work together on the gathering."

Though her efforts had languished recently, Devon had been trying to learn to recognize the jungle herbs that Hezbek needed. It would be nice to continue that practice. Maybe she'd even pick up some *Herbalism* skill.

Hazel brightened a bit. "I'd greatly appreciate the help. I'm sorry I kept the truth from you, Your Gloriousness."

> **Hazel is offering you a quest:** Pharmacopeia Failings (repeatable)
>
> *Hezbek is struggling to keep up her potion production and needs help collecting new components. It will take some trial and error but providing her with a range of ingredients would help tremendously.*
>
> **Objective:** Gather 5 x different types of roots, fungi, bark, and so forth.
>
> **Reward:** The village potion supply will continue to be replenished, possibly with less foul-tasting concoctions. Reward: 10% chance of rare potion discovery per ingredient delivered.
>
> **Accept?** Y/N

By the way, don't try to test any components on yourself. That's how people end up seeing Elvis.

"I'd be glad to help," Devon said as she accepted the quest.

She cocked her head and glanced beneath the shade of the trees. "What happened to the ostrich?" Was it too much to hope that the bird had given up?

Hazel twisted the toe of her boot into the ground. "About that..."

***

Devon looked from the pile of assorted loot to the ostrich, which now sat at the very edge of the grove looking glum. As she stared, trying to figure out what had happened, a shift in the morning breeze brought the smell of *Jungle Healing Potion* from the bird's plumage to her nose. Plumage which now looked rather ragged, having lost at least half of the froofy tail feathers.

Shaking her head, she crouched and sorted through the loot.

You have received: 2 x Lion Pelt – Poor
Someone clearly tenderized these while their former owner was still alive.

Devon shot a look to Dorden, who shrugged. "Sometimes Agavir the Pummeler has a mind of 'is own," the dwarf said with a shrug as he patted his warhammer.

You have received: 200 x Tiny Scintillating Dragon Scales
These would be cool if they were useful for anything. Well, they could be stitched into some very glitzy garments.

Bright green and flashing, the dragon scales shifted like sequins in her palm. Regardless of the item description, she wasn't ready to believe that dragon scales would be totally useless. She dumped them into a tiny slot in her inventory.

Quest updated: Pharmacopeia Failings
Objective: Gather 5 x new ingredient types for Hezbek. (1/5 found)

Ha. Not so worthless after all.

The remaining loot was 2 x *Head Cheese – Goat*. She left the gelatinous mass with chunks of meat and fat alone.

Standing, she dusted off her hand and faced the party. "Chimeras, I take it?"

Dorden grunted and nodded. "Our scout here"—he nodded at Hazel—"figured out the situation. It seems ostriches are the chimeras' natural prey."

Devon rolled her eyes. Oh brother. At least the smell wafting from the bird made sense now.

"So you soaked the ostrich's feathers in *Jungle Healing Potion* to disguise the scent."

"And it seemed to work. Hazel spotted more sets of big cat tracks that came close overnight, then veered away. But the situation still brings up the question as to what we should do now." Dorden cast a pointed glance at the large bird, which gave a little, pitiful *gorble*.

"Yeah," Devon said, chewing her lip. While she'd like to hope the bird would quit following them, she wasn't optimistic. And anyway, she wasn't sure she could let it wander off to be slaughtered by chimeras. Not that she wanted to make it into a pet, but the fact that it had trusted her, and had come to her for food and—probably—protection made her feel responsible.

Of course, what if the end were quick and merciful? She stared at the bird, trying to imagine turning it into ostrich stew, but couldn't bring herself to give that more than passing consideration.

Maybe she should just use the excuse to continue her plan of founding an ostrich egg farm. Could they deal with a giant smelly bird following them into the mountains and back to Stonehaven? Surely the bird's natural predator wouldn't break down the gates of the village just for a taste of its favorite meal.

She sighed. "With Heldi able to heal, we can probably spare enough potions to keep the scent covered."

"Are you really thinking of adding an ostrich to our party?" Greel asked.

Devon cast him a flat stare. "Do I need to remind everyone here that you spend an hour a day in the chicken coop talking baby talk?"

The lawyer glared. "That's different. They are domestic livestock, and they need encouragement and praise for continuing to lay eggs."

She raised an eyebrow. "I might be starborn, but I'm pretty sure that chickens are the same in all realms. Give them a nice coop and generous feed and you earn yourself an omelet."

Greel glowered but said nothing.

"You realize traveling with the bird offers no advantages," Heldi said gently.

"Yeah, I know. I get it." Not only did the ostrich add nothing to the group but a bad smell and the chance of more chimeras seeing—or rather smelling—through the disguise, the bird was an NPC. Just a random part of the local wildlife who had started following her around.

This was a game. She wasn't supposed to care about a non-humanoid zoo animal that had decided to stalk her. But she did. Just like she cared for these NPCs despite their digital origins. Devon had long ago let go of the illusion that the NPCs in Relic Online had no self-awareness. They were just as alive as she was.

"It's inconvenient, but I just don't see another solution that isn't needlessly cruel. It was my fault for luring it from the grove with that lychee fruit. So I'll take responsibility. The rest of you won't be stuck caring for it."

"It's not the bird's care that's the problem," Greel said, sniffing and wrinkling his nose.

Devon sighed. "Yes, fine. The bird and I will stay downwind."

"Then it's settled," Dorden said.

Dorden has sent a party invite to Bedraggled Ostrich.

Devon's eyes widened. She wasn't surprised that the group leadership had transferred to the dwarf when she'd logged out. But she'd had no idea that he could invite a simple animal to the group. Regardless, it worked. Whether due to some impulse in the ostrich's walnut-sized brain or due to the game auto-accepting, an entry for the bird appeared in her group interface.

Dorden chuckled, apparently noticing the surprise on her face. "I was going to mention this," he said, adding invites for the pair of pack mules. "It's a good way to keep track of everyone traveling with us, not just those of us who can think and speak."

The situation made her wonder what the NPCs saw for a group interface. Did they have health bars and other status information somehow layered over their vision? Or was it some other sort of digital awareness? She shrugged, deciding not to ask. There was no point in highlighting the differences between her and her friends.

With a nod, she glanced back to the smoldering coals in the fire ring. "Shall we get breakfast going and prepare to march, then?"

"Indeed, lass," Dorden said. "I want to taste the mountain air before sundown."

Chapter Thirteen

AS THE PARTY neared Ishildar's ruins, patches of jungle once again began to intrude into the landscape. Tangles of vines and the springy underbrush replaced the swooshing of grass against Devon's thighs. She'd hoped to pass close to the city, having not ventured inside its limits since her ill-fated encounter with the Stone Guardian on her first day in Relic Online. But the increasingly slow going made the prospect less and less appealing.

She was about to suggest veering back toward the savanna when she crossed some invisible threshold and felt a sudden and incredible longing. The sensation was both warm and cold and spread from her chest where the *Greenscale Pendant* pressed against her breastbone.

Devon pressed a hand over the relic and felt it singing beneath her palm. Despite the intervening jungle, she almost felt the ruined city hum in response. Glancing at the item inspection window, she saw that the pendant was now 90% attuned.

Somehow, as she stood listening to the vibrations and feeling the pull they exerted, she felt the power and wonder that Ishildar promised. Restoring and ruling the city was her destiny, and for the first time, she believed this down in the core of her being, not because a quest dialog told her that was the case.

She shook her head, overwhelmed and trying to free herself from the spell. Sure, the Entwined implants created an immersive experience. But she hadn't known they could do so much to her emotions. Or maybe the emotions had nothing to do with the implants' influence on her mind. Maybe her feelings were genuine, spawned only from the physical sensation connected to the pendant.

Of course, thinking of the dark emotions that occasionally came over her, vestiges of the time her subconscious mind had spent controlling the demon Ezraxis, she suspected the game had more control over her feelings than she liked to acknowledge. The idea sent a chill through her and brought her footsteps to a halt. Better to find some answers about the hardware's capability before she willfully subjected herself to possible emotional influences.

She cupped her hands around her mouth and called to her friends, who were marching around fifty paces ahead to avoid the ostrich's stench.

"Let's scrap the idea of checking out the city. Like Dorden said, we want to be in the mountains by sundown."

Every dwarf in the party gave a little cheer as they whirled and started cutting a course back toward the thinning edge of the jungle.

Skirting the tangled growth set the party on a less direct route, but it was still much faster. By early evening, the group reached the first gentle rise of the foothills. The faintest of trails, likely the result of traffic by wildlife, curved up through a shallow valley where a stream trickled from the higher peaks. This time, Devon took the lead, leaving the others to choose how close they marched to the ostrich.

As they climbed, the grass became short and tufted, exposing stony earth dotted with low-growing wildflowers in between patches. The air grew fresher and carried the sweet smell of mountain lichens and the nectar of the blossoms.

At the top of the first set of hills, Devon stopped short at the sight of a circle of standing stones, which were thrusting up from the meadow and decorated with age-muted runes and carvings. In the center of the circle, a large monolith of gray granite towered at least twenty feet high.

You have discovered: Argenthal Vassaldom.
You receive 6500 experience.

Quest Complete: Discover the Argenthal Vassaldom.
You receive 25000 experience.

Devon waited, staring at her interface. When she'd discovered the Khevshir and Grukluk vassaldoms, she'd received quest updates asking her to search the new areas for relics. After waiting for a few seconds, she sighed and focused on her surroundings. Maybe the game had decided she didn't need quite so much hand-holding. Hopefully, the lack of an update didn't mean the next relic was elsewhere.

Forgetting she had a reeking companion, Devon turned and backtracked to meet Greel as he crested the hill. "Can you read those runes?" she asked, gesturing toward the stones.

The lawyer glared and pulled his undershirt up over his nose and mouth. "I don't know."

"You don't know?"

"It's not like the interpretation of ancient and forgotten languages is an instant thing."

"I didn't ask for an answer right now. I just wanted to know if you *could*."

Greel rolled his eyes. "Give me some time, and perhaps I'll have an answer. But I make no guarantees."

Devon ignored his annoyed tone. "And here I thought you would be excited about the chance to prove your abundant education and intelligence."

The man did a terrible job of hiding his sudden excitement at the realization that she was right. She smirked as he hurried off and began examining the stones.

She turned to Dorden and Heldi. "Is the air here fresh enough for an evening's camp?" she asked with a smile.

Dorden cast a skeptical glance at the ostrich.

"I mean, present company excepted," Devon added.

The dwarf grinned. "Indeed it is, lass. Never thought I'd taste such sweetness again after we had to abandon our home."

Heldi, the quieter of the pair, simply nodded and smiled. But Devon could see the joy in her eyes.

"Then you agree we should stop for the night?" she asked.

"Stop, breathe, and watch the stars come out. Can't think of anything better, unless me son were here to share it," Dorden said.

With a smile, Devon gestured the party forward then moved off with the ostrich. She watched as the group quickly set to establishing a camp near the standing stones.

After a minute or two, she yawned. It was time for her to sleep as well. As the bedrolls unfurled on the meadow grass, she lowered to a cross-legged seat and logged out.

***

Devon was feeling out of sorts when she logged back in after a night's sleep. Tamara still hadn't responded to her message, and Devon wasn't sure whether to send another to apologize for being out of touch or whether to do nothing to avoid annoying her friend.

Or maybe she needed to accept that the other woman's silence might mean something else.

Even though rationally, she had no reason to think Tamara was done with the friendship, Devon's thoughts kept running that way. She blamed herself for being flaky in her communication, for turning down the chance to go camping, and especially for her half-hearted response to the invitation to learn mountain biking.

Maybe over the next few days she should go down to the bike shop where Tamara worked. Show a little effort in keeping up the friendship. If she could work up the courage...

Regardless, loading into Relic Online felt like the relief of getting out of a bad relationship, only the relationship was her real life. She shook her head as she stood, evening breezes carrying the sounds of buzzing bees and rustling grass. This kind of self-pity really wasn't her style, and she couldn't figure out why it had been happening so much. Maybe the emotions were related to the experiences injected into her mind by Zaa. In fact, the more she considered that, the more it seemed her bad moods had started after the battle with Ezraxis.

Of course, if that were really the problem, what was she supposed to do to fix it? Go to a psychologist and explain that there was a demon—or at least the ghost of a demon—working on her subconscious? That it had been planted there by an AI whose coder had taken advantage of some undocumented code in her implants? Even if she convinced a shrink to believe her, what would they say? That the path to peace lay in banishing her inner demons?

121

Devon snorted and shook her head.

Professional help would probably be anything but helpful. But if this new theory was valid, she could probably use the knowledge to improve her situation. Recognizing that she felt off due to a certain circumstance could probably help her find a way to beat it. Maybe.

Thinking about the demon issue prompted her to pop open her character sheet to check the *Shadowed* stat. Sometime around her ill-fated encounter with the chimera, it had shot up to 32%. She couldn't be sure when it had happened because she'd been too focused on the combat and then on Heldi's baby. Regardless, she was glad to see that it had been slowly ticking down again and was back to 23%.

She shrugged. Maybe the uncertainty about this stat she didn't understand and couldn't control was contributing to her bad mood. Brushing her character sheet aside, she turned her attention to the camp.

Though she'd been offline for just eight hours, the time compression meant that nearly a full day had passed in game. If she were in the NPCs' shoes, forced to wait around while someone vanished for twenty-four hours at a time, she'd definitely be annoyed. But the situation didn't seem to bother her party members, probably because that was just the way things worked in Relic Online. Starborn came and went in strange ways with odd timing, and natives of the realm just accepted it.

In the time she'd been away, her followers had set a nice camp and, judging by the contents of baskets near the circle of tents, had hunted and foraged to bolster their supplies. A few chunks of stone had even been piled at the edge of the camp, no doubt collected by the miners intending to inspect the rocks for potential ore-bearing qualities. She cringed when she saw the makeshift pen the group built for the ostrich a good two hundred yards away from the main camp. Devon probably should've done that herself. She hadn't been thinking.

As she walked into camp, Bayle looked up from her seat near the fire.

The woman jumped to her feet, stark relief on her face. "Thank Veia you're back."

Devon's heart slammed against her ribs. "What? What's wrong?"

The archer raised a hand in apology. "Sorry, Mayor Devon. I didn't mean to scare you. It's just that we've had strange things happen, and we don't know what to make of it. We need your help."

"What sort of strange things?"

Bayle chewed her lip, then stooped and flipped a sweet potato that was roasting in the coals. "Noises, for starters. Odd lights. The rest is actually difficult to describe. It's a feeling as much as anything. Dorden and Heldi set off to investigate, but I'm sure they'd appreciate your help if you could track them down."

Bayle is offering you a quest: Gather information on the bizarre happenings.
Dorden and Heldi have left camp following strange noises. Track them down, make sure they're okay, and move on from there.
Reward: Your friends need you. That should be reward enough.
Reward: But you can have 5000 experience for finding them.

Devon scanned the surroundings, perplexed about which way to head. The hilltop crowned by the standing stones was flat and spacious, offering plenty of room for the camp. Behind her, the faint trail they'd ascended flowed down through undulating terrain to the savanna below. Ahead, the terrain dropped off only slightly before rising through thin pine forest toward steep and craggy ridges.

"Do you know which direction they went?"

Bayle shook her head. "I volunteered to take over the cooking. Figure living with Tom ought to rub off a little, right?"

Devon was already starting toward the edge of the forest. She paused and looked over her shoulder. "Where's Hazel? I could use her help tracking."

Bayle shook her head. "Haven't seen her for a while. She said something about heading out to map the area, back around dark."

Devon sighed. Well, but it would be a chance to improve her tracking skill. She headed toward the scraggly forest, figuring that Dorden and Heldi wouldn't search terrain the party had ascended together. As she crisscrossed the meadow, looking for trampled grass, she passed the pair of dwarven miners. They sat with their pickaxes and another pile of rubble and were pecking at the stone chunks with rapt attention. They nodded at her, but that was the extent of their break from their work. If not for her concern for the other dwarves, Devon might have found their single-mindedness amusing.

As she neared the first of the scruffy pines, Greel came hurrying up from behind.

"I thought your request for the deciphering of the runes was important to you," he said, sounding even more petulant than usual. "Apparently not."

She turned and took a deep breath. "What did you discover, Greel? I'm fascinated to hear."

Oblivious to the sarcasm in her voice, the lawyer looked positively smug. "Well I've only begun on the first of the stones, but I can tell you this. The runes were carved by an ancient race known as the felsen. They were—"

"I know who the felsen were," Devon said, cutting him off.

He looked briefly affronted but continued. "Well, as I said, I've only been able to decipher a modest amount of the script, though I'm confident I will uncover more if given the opportunity."

"And you discovered...?" she prompted.

"It seems the stones were placed around the central monolith as part of a ritual. There is, shall we say, power in the placement and runes. I believe the best term would be a curse."

"Wait, so we're camping in a cursed area?"

"You might have noticed we located the tents outside the circle. But yes, I believe there may be some fel magic associated with the region in its entirety."

"Wait. You knew this, but you let Dorden and Heldi set off alone?" she said, glaring.

The lawyer shrugged, showing his palms. "Only just now was I able to translate the rune for *curse*. Until then, I only knew there was power represented in the configuration. Seeing as the stone in the center has its own magic, I wasn't terribly surprised."

"And what magic does the stone in the center have?"

He looked at her as if she were a complete idiot. "I cut you a lot of slack due to your starborn origins, but I thought *everyone* knew what those are."

"It really is sad for you," Devon said after a deep breath.

He cast her a confused glance. "What is?"

"To have such a complete moron as a leader."

For once, he seemed to catch the hint from her tone. "Okay fine. I understand your experience has been somewhat different than that of most starborn immigrants. So I'll explain. The tall stone in the center of the circle is a bindstone. You can use it to—"

She raised a hand to stop them. "I get it. I can set my respawn point to the stone."

"Then I guess you're only partly a moron," he said with a smirk.

"Gee, thanks," she said. "Well if there's nothing else, this fumbling doofus better go try to find our missing party members."

The man actually huffed in amusement. "Good luck dimwit," he said, lips twitching at his joke.

Chapter Fourteen

You have gained a skill point: +1 Tracking.

When the skill gain notification popped up, the signs of Dorden and Heldi's passage got easier to see. Almost as if she'd just looked a little more carefully, the areas where their footsteps had disturbed the layer of pine needles had taken on more contrast, the little mounds of needles standing higher from the surrounding soil. Clear outlines of footprints appeared in some places. The tracks caught the waning light in a way that seemed almost natural, yet the game's efforts to enhance the prints were obvious. It was a good compromise between drawing some sort of glowing trail to indicate her increased skill, a technique that would ruin the immersion, and absolute realism. To keep things realistic, Devon would have to actually learn how to track. At that point, maybe she'd get recruited by the FBI or something.

As she continued uphill, pine needles crunching and twigs cracking beneath her feet, her worry and discomfort grew. Maybe it was some holdover from childhood ghost stories, but the fading light and the eerie calm made her hyperaware of the racket she made. Disturbing noises...was that what Bayle had said? And what was this about a strange feeling? For a moment, she almost wished she'd asked Greel to accompany her.

That moment passed quickly.

Regardless, the presence of enemies seemed likely. Even if this curse had no truth behind it, they'd entered a new biome. Given how games usually worked, the area was probably higher level than the jungle-turned-savanna. Devon slowed her footsteps and tried to focus her awareness more deeply on her surroundings to make sure she wasn't surprised. A trip back to her spawn point two days' walk from here would really, really suck.

Speaking of, she wondered if she should bind at that monolith inside the standing stones. It would spare her the worry of resurrecting so far away. But given the curse, she wasn't sure that was such a good idea. The magic might do something wonky like send her halfway across the world to reconstitute her as a male half-orc barbarian.

Besides, if the rest of her party got wiped out, everyone else would need to be resurrected at the Shrine to Veia. As far as she knew, she had to be the one to operate the shine and ask for the boon. Some lot of good it would do for her to respawn all alone at the edge of the mountains.

She sighed. As a level 20 Sorcerer, Hezbek had a teleport spell, so theoretically, Devon would get that sometime within the next few levels. Of course, she wouldn't put it past the game to have different rules for spell progression between NPCs and players. So maybe not.

She hadn't realized how far she had let her thoughts drift despite her desire to stay focused, until she heard a bellow from up the hill.

Adrenaline surged through her body. That had sounded like Dorden, and he hadn't sounded happy. Yanking out her dagger and pouring mana into her first *Glowing Orb*, she started sprinting uphill.

When she got close enough, Dorden and Heldi's health bars appeared in her group interface. Still full. Thank God...or Veia...whatever.

"Hold tight," she shouted when she glimpsed the shadowy pair. With the falling night, her darkvision flickered on and off in the most annoying way. Kind of like a crappy light sensor. But she could easily make out the dwarves standing back to back, warhammer and crossbow raised.

Devon saw no hint of an enemy.

With a last burst of energy, she plowed into the sloping clearing where the dwarves stood. She searched the perimeter. Still no sign of the attackers.

When she realized the surrounding trees made a perfect circle around the open area, another chill traveled her spine.

"Guys? What's happening?" she asked as she backed into the center of the clearing. The dwarves shifted to add her to their formation, the group now forming a triangle.

"Wait for it," Heldi said. "They retreated when you shouted."

"What retreat—oh."

Eerie greenish light bloomed between the surrounding tree trunks, shifting through amorphous shapes. Low moans drifted through the night.

"Well, that's creepy," Devon said as she threw the *Glowing Orb* she'd summoned and stuck it to a tree.

Focusing on a patch of the green glow, she used *Combat Assessment*.

Ghost light is not a combatant.

Ghost light? Ugh. Yeah. Super creepy. Devon really didn't like ghosts. But if it wasn't a combatant, why did the dwarves' health bars have the little gold frame that indicated they were in combat?

"I don't...what am I missing, guys?"

"There!" Heldi said. The snick of her crossbow followed her words.

Dorden's shoulder nudged Devon in the back as he sidestepped to rotate the triangle and face whatever Heldi had seen. He growled, low in his throat. Devon squinted and searched the trees. Still nothing.

"Did you hit?" Dorden asked.

"I don't think so," his wife replied.

"Zaa's stinking caverns. The bastards."

Devon blinked furiously as if it could help her understand what was going on. Her heart stuttered when a high-pitched giggle pierced the air. A flicker of motion caught her eye and she whipped her head in time to see a shadow form with greenish-yellow eyes and contorted features. A limb whipped forward, and a thrown rock clanked off Dorden's armor. The figure vanished.

"What are they?" she asked.

Before the dwarves could answer, another flash of movement grabbed her attention. Devon fired off a *Combat Assessment.*

Felsen Poltergeist - Level 17

She threw mana into a *Freeze* spell, but by the time the cast timer finished, the target had vanished. Not just stepped behind a tree, ruining her line of sight and canceling the spell. The poltergeist was totally gone.

Another giggle. A handful of pebbles sprayed into the clearing, pattering harmlessly on the ground to her feet.

"Did this start when you reached the circle?" Devon asked. Maybe this wasn't the best place to hang out...

"Earlier," Dorden said. "They fell on us farther uphill. Started raining light blows...nothing me bride couldn't heal. But when I tried to strike back, me warhammer passed straight through them. We started fleeing for camp, but when we reached the circle, they couldn't follow. Seems they can't enter."

Devon chewed her lip, thinking. It sounded like some sort of protective ring encircled the clearing. She scanned the edge but spotted nothing.

Another shrill laugh shot through the night. Moments later, wood crackled and a tree limb fell from one of the tall pines. It crashed down, missing the group, but prompting a yelp from Heldi.

"I got a *Combat Assessment*," Devon said. "They're poltergeists. What do we know about them?"

As if on cue, another light joined the scene. Bob radiated a white glow as the wisp swirled down from a treetop. "Perhaps you would like to ask your guide wisp for information. I *am* rather knowledgeable..."

Devon groaned. "Yes. Dear guide, can you please enlighten me about our current enemy?"

Bob shimmered self-importantly. "I'd be glad to. Granted, I don't know any specifics about *felsen* poltergeists."

Devon dodged a hurled pine cone. "Just..." She paused and took a deep breath. "Tell me what you know, Bob."

"Well, for starters, poltergeists are rather difficult to damage by physical or magical means."

"I kinda got that when Dorden said his warhammer passed straight through them."

The wisp booped her nose. "If she wants the elite info, she will kindly shut up."

Devon rolled her eyes and clamped her lips in a hard line.

"A poltergeist's resistance to damage is due to rapid phasing from the physical plane. If you can capture them and hold them to our physicality, you can pound the daylights out of them. But beware. Poltergeists generally don't attack to kill, but rather to annoy. Unfortunately, they have a fearsome reputation for growing very angry when provoked, and their power and damage increases tenfold."

"So you're saying if we leave them alone and ignore their annoying attacks, they won't try to kill us?"

Bob swayed from side to side as if considering. "Well, yes and no. When a poltergeist attaches to a target or set of targets, it rarely loses interest. Even if they don't intend to cause severe damage, it does stack up. And anyway, I hardly think any of you wish to spend the rest of your lives being pounded on, even if those hits are minor. Living in a state of perpetual combat might be rather challenging."

"So we should fight them."

Bob swelled and then shrank, its version of a shrug.

"You want me to make all your decisions now?"

Devon rolled her eyes and dodged another pine cone. She backed closer to the dwarves and called over her shoulder. "You ready for a real fight, friends?" As she cast another *Glowing Orb*, Bob seemed to shiver in appreciation. The wisp booped her nose and flew off.

"Agavir the Pummeler wants nothing more than to smash a few geists," Dorden said. "I'm at your command, Mayor."

"Okay then. Here we go!"

***

Ten minutes later, Devon had to accept that the tactic wasn't working. It had seemed awesome to chill inside the circle where the poltergeists couldn't come, damaging the phantoms while remaining untouchable. Unfortunately, they weren't making any headway on the whole "damage" portion of the plan. *Freezing* the spirits to lock them to the physical plane should have worked—in theory. But by the time Devon noticed the flicker of motion and the glowing green eyes, then dropped mana into a *Freeze* attempt, the newly appeared phantoms had already hurled rocks or made some giggling raspberry noise and vanished.

"I'm open to ideas here," she said after another fizzle when her target disappeared.

"I tell ye, I got no blessed clue on what we are supposed to do with a yellow-bellied enemy that won't stick around and fight," Dorden said. "Cowardly Zaa-spawn."

"Can ye start casting and hope one appears?" Heldi asked.

Devon shook her head, then realized the dwarves were facing away from her and answered aloud. "The spell needs a target. I can cast it on the ground, but I can't change the target if they appear before the spell fires. I'd have to cast and hope they were dumb enough to walk into it."

Though that did give her another idea. After letting her mana refill a bit—it was slow due to the combat state, but still ticking upward—she cast *Wall of Ice* along one edge of the clearing. The slab of frozen water appeared, locking trees and branches in its grass. But no poltergeist. Another giggle cut through the night.

They needed a way to make the phantoms hold still long enough that they could be frozen. Though thinking about it, Devon wondered if it would do any good. The moment Dorden whacked one with his warhammer, the *Freeze* effect would break, and the phantom would be free to change phase again. Only now, it would be enraged and capable of ten times the damage.

"Tell me about your damage shield, Heldi," Devon said.

"Ye mean *Impervious*? Me shielding buff for the wee one?" the dwarf asked.

"Yeah, that one."

"It's a mite different for adults than for babes. On us, it blocks just some of the damage from getting through, and in retaliation, hits the enemy with a fearsome counterattack."

"Does that counterattack do magical damage?" Devon asked.

Heldi was silent for a moment as if thinking. "I reckon so," she said. "Can't say for sure, but my inner knowledge tells me that it 'hits back like an enraged mother bear.'"

Devon chewed her lip. So probably magical, but she couldn't be certain. Not that it mattered much...it just seemed more likely that magical damage could chase the phantom to its...wherever it went when phasing away. But even if the damage counted as a physical attack, the instant retaliation would probably allow it to hit before the poltergeists disappeared.

Of course, she doubted the damage shield would fire in retaliation for the person it protected from being hit by a flying pine cone. They'd have to leave the circle—or maybe, send just Dorden out of the safe zone to lure attacks. And that strategy assumed they could kill the poltergeist with just the mother-bear damage. Seemed a sketchy assumption.

Could they somehow try to combine Heldi's damage shield with Devon's abilities? Devon's only instant-cast spell was *Shadow Puppet*, which wasn't very helpful unless the poltergeist appeared right on top of her shadow. Unless...

Devon edged toward the perimeter of the clearing, stopping when she entered the pool of light from a *Glowing Orb*. Focusing on her shadow, she pulled a puppet from the ground. She hesitated for a second, considering raising another from the green glow of the ghost light, but caution overrode her curiosity. Maybe once they figured out how to deal with the poltergeists.

"Can you target this with your shield, Heldi?" she asked.

The dwarf woman turned, cocked her head, and then smiled in satisfaction as she raised a hand and sent a stream of shimmering light over the shadow.

Devon nodded. Nice.

As she stepped back to join the dwarves, she sent her puppet into the forest. Shoulders tense, she waited. Another shrieking laugh burst from the darkness. The ghost light flared, bathing the clearing in sickly green.

The poltergeists ignored her shadow.

She sighed. Crud. Yes, she'd discovered a cool new combo to use with Heldi. But unless she could bait the poltergeists, the trick was utterly useless here. Figuring it wouldn't hurt to try, Devon cast *Ventriloquist.*

"Hey, stupid," she said, projecting her voice from her *Shadow Puppet.* "This is getting pretty boring, don't you think?"

A phantom flickered into being beside her puppet. Devon held her breath. She groaned when, with a giggle, the poltergeist threw a stone into the circle and vanished. The crown of the nearby tree bent and then broke. It came crashing down into the clearing.

With a frustrated sigh, Devon shook her head. She had one last idea.

"Okay. New plan. Heldi, we'll need you to focus on healing. Don't leave the circle."

"I'm not sure I like the sound of that."

Devon shook her head. "To be honest, me neither."

"I hate to ask this, but what if ye...I mean, what if I can't heal ye quickly enough?"

"If we die, do your best to warn the others and get to safety I guess."

The dwarf woman gave a grim nod.

"Would you please put a shield on me?" Devon asked. She glanced at Dorden, then decided it would just confuse the plan to have him drawing aggro as well.

"Incoming," Heldi said as her hands began to glow.

Shimmering energy soon surrounded Devon and sank into her flesh. Immediately, Devon felt as safe as a little baby swaddled and laid gently in her crib. She shook her head as she fought the impulse to suck her thumb.

"Seriously, game?"

There has to be a downside to having your ranged fighter miraculously develop cleric powers, right?

Sighing, she rolled her eyes. To reassure herself about this plan—for all the good that would do—she pulled up the description for *Freeze*. It didn't say anything about potentially invalid targets, so she tried targeting herself, interrupting the cast when it seemed to work. That was good news, even if she'd still have to hope for good timing. As the last step in her preparations, she cast *Wall of Fire* and then raised a fire-based *Shadow Puppet*, leaving it stationed near the edge of the clearing.

"Okay. Let's munch some poltergeist," she said. After glancing at Dorden to assure he was ready, she jogged from the circle and stopped a few paces into the woods. Almost immediately, a shadow limb came out of nowhere and slapped her face. The flicker of motion was gone almost as fast as it appeared, but Devon both felt and heard the whip-crack as her damage shield struck a retaliatory blow.

The moment seemed to drag on until abruptly, a roar shook the forest. The surrounding ghost light flared and shifted to an angry scarlet. Just a few feet away, a tree tore free of the earth, its roots exposed and dribbling soil. The unseen hands that wielded the trunk swung it in a wide arc, and Devon ducked just in time. Gritting her teeth, she started casting *Freeze* on herself.

The spell landed, ice engulfing her and sending a chill deep into her bones. Devon fought the urge to panic. Rotating her eyeballs, the only part of her body that could move, she spied a contorted face with glowing red eyes. Locked in ice, the poltergeist radiated rage so strongly she was surprised it didn't melt them free.

137

"Gotcha," she tried to mutter, only to be severely thwarted. The good news about her *Freeze* spell was that she apparently didn't need oxygen while affected. The bad news was that she couldn't talk.

Focusing inward, she reached for her awareness of her fire-based *Shadow Puppet*. There, a flickering presence just a few feet to her left. Focusing on it, Devon cast *Shadow Step*.

A heartbeat later, she gasped in relief at the sudden release from the chill prison. She was back inside the protective circle, looking out at the ice-encased poltergeist. As Heldi's heal landed, repairing the small hitpoint loss from the *Freeze* spell, Devon whipped her head around in search of Dorden. The dwarf was standing just inches from the edge of the trees, warhammer raised.

"All right," Devon said. "Step close to the frozen one but ignore blows from any adds."

He nodded and jogged to the side of the trapped poltergeist. After a moment, his brow knit.

"No more attacks? Was there really just one of them? All that bothering from just one of the little pukes?"

Devon shrugged. "I guess so."

The information seemed to anger Dorden further, and he raised his weapon to strike.

"Wait! We'll hit it together."

She started casting *Flamestrike – Tier 2*. An instant before the spell fired, she shouted, "Now!"

A column of fire geysered over the frozen phantom as Dorden leveled a massive swipe with his warhammer. Devon caught a split-second glimpse of the poltergeist's health bar, enough to see it drop by maybe 20%. She cringed when a phantom struck with a shadowy limb, punching Dorden in the gut and sending him flying with a huge chunk of health missing.

"Ouch," Heldi muttered, throwing herself into another heal.

With a bellow of fear or anger—Devon wasn't quite sure which—Dorden hightailed it back into the circle. The moment Heldi's heal landed, she started casting another. Devon searched the forest for signs of the poltergeist but saw nothing.

A loud crack shook the ground as another tree was snapped off at the base. Devon had just a second or two to feel relieved that they were all within the circle before the tree came hurtling at them at an insane velocity. On instinct, she threw up a *Wall of Ice*, the spell barely landing before the tree smashed against the frozen slab. The ice shattered as the wood splintered.

"Duh..." Devon muttered, remembering the pine cone assault. Just because the poltergeist couldn't enter didn't mean its projectiles were banned.

They needed to get on with this.

"Ready for round two?" she asked, swallowing. "Same plan."

The dwarves nodded, looking only a little nervous. With a deep breath, Devon ran from the circle.

The party repeated the process four times. On the last, Devon's health dropped to below 15%, and she thought she was a goner. But Heldi's chain-heals saved her, just barely.

Finally, with an ear-splitting wail, the poltergeist faded the physical realm and died.

> *You gain 2300 experience.*
> **You have gained a new attribute point:** +1 Cunning.
> **You have gained a new skill point:** +1 Improvisation.

Congratulations! You have reached level 17!

The forest chimed and then fell quiet as a tomb.

After a moment, Devon took a breath and hugged Heldi around the shoulders. "Nice heals. That was...unpleasant."

Dorden grunted in agreement. "I'd rather face twenty opponents than one cowardly geist who won't stay put."

"Thanks for coming to the rescue," Heldi said, turning a smile on Devon.

> **Quest Complete:** Gather information on the bizarre happenings.
> *You gain 5000 experience.*

Well, now you know.

Devon shook her head. She might have learned about the problem, but she didn't like what she'd discovered. If fighting just one of the poltergeists was this bad, what would happen if they encountered more? They certainly couldn't establish a mine out here with those things roaming around.

"I don't even know if we can stay in the mountains until morning," she muttered.

Crouching, she scooped the single piece of loot from the ground.

You have received: Ruby-crusted Chalice.

Among other hobbies, poltergeists are rather fond of thieving. Who knows where they found this. Lucky for you though. Finders keepers.

Use: Drinking from this chalice grants +1 Bravery. Drinking alcohol from this chalice grants +2 Bravery, -2 Intelligence.

Duration: 30 minutes

Recharge time: 2 hours

Well that was kind of cool, at least. As Devon sighed and stood, Bob reappeared, this time drifting in from a thicker stand of trees to her right.

The wisp booped her nose. "You know, there's one thing I forgot until your comment about leaving the mountains made me think of it. Though the poltergeists are a pain, you can avoid them in the short term by remaining indoors with a steady light source any time after dusk."

"Does a tent count as indoors?" she asked.

Bob shrugged. "Your guess is as good as mine. But I will say that a true Champion of Ishildar wouldn't just turn back at the first sign of a haunting."

"Sure, but it would be pointless to establish mines out here with this going on. I should at least send the miners back to safety."

"You could, or you could take control of your destiny..."

"I assume you have a suggestion."

Bob is offering you a quest: Get rid of the curse, dummy.
Greel probably has more information by now. Shouldn't you at least investigate a little before throwing in the towel?
Objective: Clear the felsen curse.

Reward: 30000 experience
Accept? Y/N

Devon sighed. "Okay fine." She clicked yes and turned to the dwarves. "Ready to head back to the tents?"

"Please," the couple said together.

Chapter Fifteen

SEEING AS DEVON did her sleeping out of game, they hadn't brought a tent or bedroll along for her. Fortunately, Bayle and Hazel were agreeable about having Devon squeeze in.

Of course, with everyone else asleep, and nothing to do but listen to the faint laughter of the poltergeists roaming the forest, it got boring real quick. For a while, Devon practiced casting her *Simulacrum* spell, figuring the illusion wouldn't wake up her tentmates, but her tier 1 mastery leveled off at 70%. As with most skills and abilities, she probably needed an enemy nearby to keep improving. Or at the very least, a new situation.

Sighing, she rubbed her face. It had been a couple hours since she'd logged in, but it was still only around 10 AM in the real world. Unless she wanted to face a poltergeist alone, she was either stuck in the tent waiting for dawn to arrive after another six in-game hours, or she might as well log and kill a couple of hours of real-world time to take advantage of the time compression.

She *had* been meaning to head over to the shop where Tamara worked. Now would be as good a time as any for that.

Glancing again at her slumbering companions, Devon sighed and logged out.

***

The door to the bike shop clapped shut with a jingle of bells, sealing Devon in with the smell of rubber and grease. A man looked up from behind the counter, and she fought the urge to sidestep behind a rack of brightly colored clothing. Everything looked to be sized and cut for superhumans like Tamara, the garments tiny and stretchy in a way that promised to show every flaw. She reached for her ponytail to fiddle, then dropped her hand to the side. There was no need to be such a wussy.

With a deep breath, she walked up to the counter and flashed the attendant a smile. After knowing Tamara, she shouldn't have been surprised to see that both he and the pair of young guys working in the back room were deeply tanned and sculpted like they'd stepped out of some holo advertisement for cologne or menswear.

Her flash of insecurity passed when she forced herself to remember that her mood changes lately were likely a result of Zaa mucking with her brain. Meeting the attendant's eyes, she leaned to the side as if to look deeper into the shop in search of her friend. "Hey, is Tamara around?"

The man blinked and a flash of...something crossed his face. His brows drew together. "She's not here right now. Been out for a couple weeks."

A couple weeks? That was weird. "Really? What's she been up to?"

The man hesitated for a few long seconds before speaking. "How do you guys know each other?"

Unease crept into Devon's belly. "I'm just a friend. We used to work together at Fort Kolob, and I haven't heard from her for a while. Thought I would just stop in rather than sending more messages."

144

The man's face grew grim, and all of a sudden, Devon felt as if the walls were pressing in. Bike parts gleamed, all teeth and hard angles. The air was abruptly stuffy, and she felt short of breath. Somewhere in the back of her mind, fear stirred, accompanied by a flicker of demon's rage.

"I don't know if I'm allowed to share this," the man said, "but Tamara is in the hospital. ICU."

Shit. Devon closed her eyes, struggling against a sudden flash of anger and guilt. If she'd been a better friend, she would've known. She would've realized that Tamara's silence after the Flagstaff trip meant trouble, but she'd been too wrapped up in Relic Online and her own insecurities.

"Is she allowed guests?" Devon asked.

The man's nostrils flared. "I've been trying to see her since the crash. Her control-freak mom told the hospital not to let us in. Says it would be too much stress. I think she just blames us for what happened."

Devon swallowed, finally mastering her swelling rage...mostly, anyway. She still felt like a shitty friend.

"Tamara's an adult, right? Doesn't she have the final say in who gets in to see her?"

The guy looked down at the counter, face full of regret. "I guess they have her too sedated or something. Next of kin is making her decisions for the time being."

Devon's chest was so tight it hurt to breathe. "How did it happen?"

The guy shook his head. "It was stupid. We were trying some big drops and she—"

"Drops?"

145

"Like jumps. Riding off ledges with good landings."

Devon swallowed. She'd been joking when she'd accused Tamara of wanting to teach her to ride off cliffs on a bike. "How high?"

The guy pulled some kind of component from beneath the counter and started fiddling with it. The thing clicked as he moved a lever back and forth. "Only about seven feet. It should have been safe, but her front wheel landed crooked and she went over the bars. Came down on her chest on a chunk of sandstone, which is about the only good news. She had something called a tension pneumothorax—air leaking into her chest cavity from a punctured lung—and by the time we got her into the helicopter, her lung capacity was down to like thirty percent."

"That's good news?"

"Better than a fractured skull," he said with a shrug. "Anyway, there were multiple lung injuries from splintered ribs and something with her spleen." He turned regretful eyes on her. "I shouldn't have encouraged her to try, but she's pretty gonzo, you know. Didn't want to be the condescending jerk that tells a woman rider to take it easy."

"I doubt Tamara would have listened anyway."

He looked a bit reassured by her words, but the guilt still shadowed his eyes. "Anyway, maybe the mom will let you in. If she does, tell Tamara we're all pulling for her to make a quick recovery."

"You haven't even been able to send cards or anything?"

The guy shrugged. "Sent them. Even sent flowers, though that might piss her off. We just don't know if the mom's letting the gifts through."

"You said a quick recovery...she *will* heal up eventually, right?"

His Adam's apple bobbed. "If you're asking if there's a chance she could die, no, I don't think so. I'm just hoping her lungs work right after this." He shrugged again. "I'm not a doctor, but bone fragments in your lungs doesn't sound good, right?"

Devon took a shaky breath. "No, it doesn't sound good."

Another customer entered the shop, and the attendant acknowledged her with a nod. Devon took the opportunity to take a step back from the counter.

"St. George General? Or Dixie Regional Medical Center?"

"General. If you hear anything, mind giving us a ring?"

"No problem," Devon said as she headed for the door.

***

After placing her hand on the autocab hailing pad, Devon pressed her lips together. She needed a cab, but where to? Her group would be awake in less than an hour, and they'd have nothing to do but twiddle their thumbs until she logged back in. But Tamara was in the fricking hospital and had been for two weeks, and Devon hadn't had a clue. As the cab glided to a stop at the curb, she glanced downtown where the hospital rose a few stories higher than most of the buildings. At the very least, she could check in and try to get in touch with this control-freak mother.

"Hospital, please," she said after confirming her credit.

"Is this an emergency?" the cab asked.

Devon was tempted to lie. It would get her to the hospital in half the time. But she shook her head. "Visiting a patient."

"Thank you. Destination confirmed. Please secure your seat restraints."

147

Devon's hands started to shake as she slid her seatbelt into the housing. She stared at them as if her limbs had turned traitor. Sure, Tamara was a friend, but they'd only known each other for a few months. Was that really enough time to develop the kind of relationship where she got all quivery hearing that her friend had been hurt? She swallowed. Maybe it was just the shock of learning the explanation behind Tamara's absence.

Or maybe Devon genuinely cared. Maybe it was nice to have a friend she'd met outside of a video game, someone that enjoyed her company for more than her play skills. Either way, she felt horrible for not knowing her friend had been seriously injured.

The cab deposited her beneath a wide awning that stretched over the hospital entrance. Standing on the smooth concrete, Devon took a couple breaths, then hitched her purse higher on her shoulder and strode toward the sliding doors.

As she entered the lobby, a receptionist looked up from the front desk. "If you're here for a procedure, please check in at the kiosk."

Devon shook her head. "I just heard my friend is a patient here. Tamara..." She trailed off, realizing she didn't even know her friend's last name.

The receptionist blinked and smiled a little too brightly. "I'm sorry...I need more information than that to allow you into the wing. Do you know her room number?"

Devon realized she was wringing her hands. "I have no idea. I just heard. The guy who told me said I would probably need to ask Tamara's mother for visiting rights?"

A look of understanding settled over the woman's face. "Gotcha. I think I know who we're talking about. She's had lots of people try to come visit. The person who told you about the accident is right...the young woman's mother has insisted on approving any visitors. Should I give you her contact information?"

Devon nodded. "Please."

The woman pulled up a handheld directory and hit a couple options, then held the transmitting end out. "Phone? Tablet? Sorry. It's an old model and needs to know which protocol."

Devon grimaced. She hadn't been carrying a mobile device since she'd had her implants installed. Though she gathered it was technically possible for the woman to beam information to her implants as easily as she could to a mobile device, Devon didn't want to go through the explanation.

"Sorry. I forgot my phone. Can I give you a messenger address and have you send me the woman's contact card?"

"I...sure." The woman swung a boom-mounted tablet in front of her chest and poised her finger over the screen. Devon rattled off the text string for her messenger contact, and the woman pecked out the characters. Afterward, she read it back, and Devon nodded.

"I'll just check with the mother and make sure I have permission to send the contact," the receptionist said. "If so, I'll send it right over."

"Should I..." Devon gestured toward one of the chairs in the waiting area.

The receptionist shook her head. "It might be a little while. Maybe even a day. The mother..." She licked her lips and shook her head. "I shouldn't express any opinions. Anyway, if you live or work close, you might as well get on with your day. I'll contact you as soon as I hear back."

Devon nodded. "Thanks." With a last glance around the lobby that was just a little too cheerfully decorated, she turned and stepped back out the door. A couple of minutes later, an autocab arrived to take her home.

Chapter Sixteen

WHILE WAITING FOR Owen's girlfriend to show up, Emerson stared again at Devon's messages and sighed. On the hyperloop ride from Cincinnati, he'd been thinking more about his reluctance to respond.

If E-Squared was being honest about the reason behind his forced time off—if they'd bought Penelope's story about Emerson's half-cocked changes to the code base, they wouldn't find it *that* strange that he would keep in touch with his all-star players. In fact, they might find it uncharacteristic for him to be so hands-off. And he suspected they were being honest because he didn't think Bradley Williams would be so unscrupulous as to knowingly allow one of his programmers to take over people's brains. Or at least, he certainly *hoped* the CEO had more integrity than that.

Anyway, as he'd sat in the streamlined hyperloop capsule, rocketing through a vacuum-filled tube at 700 miles per hour with no wireless connection to distract him, he'd done a little soul-searching. The truth was, he hadn't responded to Devon because he was afraid to admit his exiled situation to her. She was counting on him to fix the back door that allowed Penelope to screw around in people's heads through the Entwined hardware. He'd even had the idea that she respected him. Maybe even liked him.

Sure, not in the *liked him* kind of way. But the fact that she didn't think he was crazy for turning up in her home city and presenting her with a tinfoil hat said *something*. Of course, maybe that something was that she was an extremely nice and accepting person. It probably didn't have anything to do with him.

"Christ," he muttered. "Give it a rest." He'd been through this cycle of thoughts at least five times since sitting down on a bench in Atlanta's Centennial Olympic Park. Clenching a fist, he straightened his EM-shielding cap and pulled out a tablet.

A pair of rollerbladers whizzed past, climate-controlled suits flashing as if to emphasize how fast they were. The man bobbled as he glanced at Emerson. By now, Emerson was used to the stares, and he simply shrugged as if wearing a hat made of quilted reflective insulation was totally normal. Besides, Atlanta was a pleasant 70°. Perfect in the sun and almost perfect in the shade. Only an unrepentant peacock would skate around in a climate-controlled onesie with that kind of weather going on.

He pulled up Devon's last message, intent on telling her the truth. Even if she lost respect for him when learning he'd been shut out of the corporate network, making his battle against Penelope twice as hard, she deserved the truth. All of his star players did, but after enough loaded remarks from his mini-Veia instantiation, he'd finally given up pretending she wasn't his favorite.

As he psyched himself up to subvocalize a message, a young woman stopped in front of him.

"Emerson?" she asked.

"Nigerian Prince?"

She nodded, eyes flicking to his cap. "Cynthia works too."

"Want to sit?" he asked, sliding over.

The woman was attractive with light-brown skin, hazel eyes, and what seemed to be shy mannerisms. As she turned to take a seat, she slid her hand into a satchel and started to pull out the EM-shielding cap he'd sent her. "Do I need to be wearing this?" she asked, again glancing at his hat.

He peered at her hairline—she wore her dark hair short—and spotted no implant circuitry. Not ready to say something that might actually cause a shitstorm and massive lawsuits leveled at Entwined or E-Squared, he settled for shaking his head. "Owen's case is special. I'm wearing the device as...just for trial purposes. A safety test, I guess you could say."

The woman nodded somewhat skeptically. "But you can help him...?"

Emerson turned to face her. "Here's the thing. I think so. I hope so. But people may see my cure as...fringe."

"I...okay." Cynthia was looking decidedly less comfortable by the second. She was probably starting to wonder whether she'd imagined the slight improvement in Owen's comatose condition when she slipped the hat over his head. After the cloak-and-dagger message exchange had led her to meet a tinfoil-hatted man in a public park, she might even be wondering whether she should take the situation to the authorities.

Emerson scrubbed a hand over his stubble, realizing he also should have shaved. "Okay," he said. "I realize this seems crazy. But I swear I only have Owen's best interests in mind. I could have suggested you put the hat on him and let him wake up. That would convince everyone to pay attention to my theory. But I'm concerned about the safety of rapidly extracting him from his current...state. We know too little about why he lost conscious awareness."

She nodded slowly, then looked down at the sidewalk. "Makes sense. But why all the secrecy?"

"If you want the truth, it's because there are companies with a lot of money involved. Until I know exactly what's happening *and* I have the data to prove it, I worry that lawyers would gum up the process and keep us from curing him."

"You mean the company that installed that stuff in his head."

Emerson sighed. So much for his grand plan to insulate the involved corporations until he was sure. "And the game company I work for. E-Squared."

"Wait," she said, sitting up straighter. "Are you his boss?" She looked mildly alarmed at the notion, probably because she still wasn't convinced he was sane.

"Sort of. I was responsible for recruiting him."

"And you think this might be your game's fault?" A flash of anger sparked in her eyes.

"No. Not the game." He paused. Might as well come out with it. He doubted the woman had a listening device or anything, and he could always deny saying this stuff. "I think there may be a rogue employee in our organization. Maybe more than one. I suspect they may have misused some of the systems."

"And instead of informing your company's management, you made shiny hats and sent me one to try on Owen."

He sighed again. Maybe he should have tried to do this in some sort of darknet chat room or something. He really wasn't good with conversation. "Here's the truth. I tried. But the employee I suspect of misbehavior got to them first. I'm currently on a forced vacation."

She laid a palm on her forehead. "And if I were to go to your company with this story, what would happen?"

"That's the problem. I don't know. They might believe you and take immediate action. Or they might get scared and find a way to make sure you stay quiet. They might find a way to make Owen's situation worse so that he doesn't wake up and sue them. Honestly, I try to think the best of people, but crazy things happen when the stakes are this high."

Leaning her head back, Cynthia dragged fingers through her cropped hair. "Well, shit."

"Yes."

"So what's *your* grand plan?"

"Somehow, I need to get into the hospital to see Owen. I want to plant something that will capture, record, and retransmit the network traffic between his implants and our servers. I tried to install a sniffer remotely, but the hospital's security is too tight."

"Will that fix him?" she asked, looking highly skeptical.

Emerson shook his head. "Right now, this is just a fact-finding mission. We need to know what we're working with before I figure out how to move forward." He didn't mention that his plans for moving forward from there were still a little fuzzy.

"So I get you in, you plant this...spy thingy, and we wait. How long?"

"Just a couple days. His condition's been unchanged for weeks. I can't see it changing now."

"Me neither." With a deep sigh, she continued, "Okay, I'll give you a couple days. But Owen's life is on the line here. If you can't give me something to go on, I'll have to think about talking to his parents at the very least."

"Three days," he said. "I need an extra day to analyze the data after the data's been collected. Oh, and I'll need you to remove the device after we have the information."

"Me?"

"Unless you want to help me sneak into Owen's room twice."

"Good point. Okay. So all you really need is my hospital access."

"Well, I suppose your testimony could be useful later. But for now, yeah."

Cynthia sighed. "I usually visit him when I get off work at five, but I have a late meeting tonight. Can you meet me in the hospital atrium tomorrow at 5:15? I doubt it will be a huge problem if I say you're one of our college friends who came all the way down here after you heard."

He nodded. "I can do that."

She stood to leave, then glanced at his head. "No hat, okay."

He laid a hand on it. Okay, so it *was* a bit conspicuous. Fortunately, he'd been waiting for the excuse to improve his design, and he already had an idea for version two. "No hat."

Chapter Seventeen

"WHY DO I get the feeling you aren't paying attention to me?" Greel asked.

Devon blinked. "What?"

"You're staring off into space and nodding every once in a while. I've presented to enough juries to know when someone is just pretending to listen."

"Sorry," Devon said, pushing her messenger app farther to the periphery of her vision. She usually didn't even have it active while in game, but the hospital receptionist could be sending information about Tamara's mother at any time. "Unusual circumstances in the starborn realm have been distracting me."

"So how much do I need to repeat?" the lawyer asked.

Devon chewed her lip and gave him an apologetic shrug. "All of it?"

The man sighed heavily and rolled his eyes. "Sometimes I don't even know why I bother. Anyway..." He gestured toward the standing stones and waited until Devon turned toward the ruins and nodded before continuing. "I would say I've managed to decipher around 90% of the carvings."

They were sitting on a pair of weathered boulders a short distance from the tents, and the smell of Bayle's cooking drifted over the meadow to Devon's nose. Untrained, the fighter couldn't produce anything fancy, even with the village chef for a husband. But she seemed to enjoy the work, and no one else wanted to do it. Until they returned, there would be simple, half-charred meat, unevenly roasted vegetables, and the occasional meal of precooked rations supplied by Tom when they had a good excuse to break them out.

As the mountain sun warmed the meadow, increasing numbers of butterflies and bees rose from their nighttime rest and flitted low over the grasses. Devon watched a yellow-winged insect flutter past. It had been so long since she'd spent any measurable amount of time outside in the St. George area...did the desert even have butterflies?

"Still not listening," Greel said, annoyed now.

Grabbing a hunk of her hair, Devon tugged. "I'm really sorry, Greel. I swear you have my attention now."

Straightening his legs and pushing his heels into a springy patch of low-growing vegetation, he sighed. "As I was saying, I've deciphered everything I can. The remaining carvings are just too worn down to interpret. I could make guesses based on the surrounding script, but I don't think it's necessary."

"You heard about the poltergeist, right? I assume the phantoms were created by this curse."

The lawyer glared. "Perhaps if you'd let me speak, I'd get to that."

Devon pressed her lips together, chastened. She nodded.

Looking somewhat mollified, Greel pulled a folded piece of paper from his pocket. "I made notes in case we wish to reference them at a later time. Though it's doubtful I'll forget any of this..."

Devon made a polite act of glancing at the paper, but she couldn't make heads or tails of his chicken scratch. "Go on."

"To answer your question: yes, I believe the poltergeists are at least one manifestation of the curse. Though by itself *curse* isn't sufficient to describe the felsens' intent. Legacy might be an alternate term. Vengeance another."

"Because they left the poltergeists behind before they vanished?"

"Partially, yes."

Devon nodded slowly. "I think I understand."

"It's likely you have the gist of it, but it would be better if you heard the history."

She raised her eyebrows. "Is that in the runes?"

"Some of it. Some of it comes from knowledge I've gained over the years. You've done well paying attention this time around. Am I to assume your focus can hold for a few more minutes?"

Devon rolled her eyes. "Go ahead, professor."

"Pro-what?"

She shook her head. "Never mind. Anyway, yes, you have my undivided attention."

"Before I start, what do you know about the felsen?"

Devon pulled up her quest window and reread the lore that had accompanied with her now-completed quest to discover the Argenthal Vassaldom.

"Ancient race of small humanoids, also known as craglings. They were sometimes confused with gnomes, but they really didn't share any features except for the small stature. Traces of their lineage remain in the goblin population, I believe? Oh, and they lived in this area."

"Not bad for a starborn." Greel genuinely looked surprised at her knowledge.

She decided there was no reason to tell him where she'd gotten the information. "I do try to educate myself," she said with a shrug.

He nodded as if accepting this, one intellectual to another. "Building off that, you can probably imagine how a slight-of-build race might have been vulnerable to attack. Near the end of their time on this world, cragling numbers had dwindled, and the leaders of the vassaldom decided their only hope for continued survival was to build homes on the cliffs high up in these crags. They fastened their structures to sheer rock by a number of ingenious means, and this provided much-needed protection for their people. But they ultimately underestimated the ferocity and determination of their enemies, chief among them an orc tribe from across the mountain crest. The orcs tunneled through the very heart of the mountains and burst through the stone where the felsen had made their homes. Their towns and cities were swept from the cliffs. By the time Ishildar fell for other reasons, the cragling population had already been reduced to just a few individuals."

Devon didn't have to try to pay attention now. She felt sorry for the little people. "It's those last few that set the curse, I'm guessing?"

Greel nodded. "The felsen had a particular magic they were loath to use because it burdened their ancestor spirits with work that rightfully belonged to the living. But they were both desperate and bitter, and with less than a dozen of their race remaining, they recruited help from a giant and had the standing stones placed here. The runes bind their ancestor spirits to plague any intelligent or semi-intelligent beings who enter this region for as long as orcs remain in its borders."

Devon blinked, taking in the new information. "Wait, so you're saying that the curse is still in effect because...because there are orcs here?" She fought the urge to look over her shoulder.

"As far as I can determine, yes. Probably within the same warren of tunnels they dug to attack the felsen in the first place."

Devon did turn now, running her eyes over the expanse of rocky cliffs and mountain peaks that rose above the scruffy forest. "So all we have to do to get rid of the curse is to eradicate the orcs from an unknown number of tunnels in this rather large area?"

"I'm glad you sound so positive about it," Greel said, "because yes, I suspect that's what we have to do."

> **Quest updated:** Get rid of the curse, dummy.
> *Remove the orc army from the former Argenthal Vassaldom. No big deal, right? If you succeed, at least your miners will have some starter tunnels.*
> **Objective:** Every orc in Argenthal banished or killed.
> **Reward:** No more curse. But you'll probably get some XP too.

Devon groaned. "Well, in that case, I guess we'd better get ready to march."

***

As Devon checked the straps on the mules' loads, she spotted Hazel leaning over the railing on the ostrich's makeshift pen. The bird high-stepped over to the little scout and laid its head on Hazel's shoulder. It nuzzled the woman's ear, and Hazel giggled as she pulled a leather packet from her satchel. Unfolding the flaps, she held the contents out to the bird, which scooped them up in its beak. Judging by the red stain that dribbled down the ostrich's chin, the packet was either some sort of berry mash or raw minced meat. Devon was betting on the berries.

She sighed. Well, if there'd been a chance the ostrich would give up on following them, Hazel had ruined that. Squinting, Devon scanned the terrain. It seemed highly unlikely that the chimera's habitat extended beyond the savanna—though to be fair, the same could be said about the ostrich. Regardless, maybe they could skip drenching the bird in reeking potion today.

The load seemed secure on the mule's back, and as Devon ducked under the animal's neck, intent on inspecting the other beast, Dorden's bellow rolled through the campsite.

"Where is he?" the dwarf yelled. Fists clenched, he was stomping in circles near the area of flattened grass where he and Heldi had pitched their tent.

"Where is who?" Devon asked, hurrying over.

"Agavir. Me warhammer. I left him on our tent's threshold...a little signal to me clansmen that me wife and I were having a snuggle."

Devon tried to ignore the sinking feeling in her belly. "This during the night, I assume?"

The dwarf looked at her as if she were crazy. "Well, it's not like we're keen to laze around when there's mines to find and orcs to slay."

How did Dorden know about the orcs? Her brow furrowed before she realized he must've overheard her conversation with Greel. Devon scanned the camp. Just one tent awaited packing up, and everything else had already been loaded onto the mules. Unless someone in their party had slipped the warhammer into their pack—highly unlikely—the weapon was gone.

"I'm afraid I might know what happened," she said, pulling her newly looted chalice from her rucksack. "Unfortunately, poltergeists are known to be thieves."

Dorden's face went so red it was nearly purple. "We can't just let them get away with this. Agavir has seen me through thousands of battles. We must recover him."

> **Dorden is offering you a quest:** Recover Agavir.
> *The dwarf loves his warhammer probably as much as his wife. Well, maybe not quite that much. Regardless, he's not the same man without his trusty weapon. The longer he's without it, the more his morale will suffer.*
> **Objective:** Retrieve Agavir from the felsen poltergeists.
> **Reward:** 30,000 experience.
> **Accept?** Y/N

"I'll do everything I can," Devon said, accepting the quest. "In the meantime, we brought a couple spare weapons. Can you use a longsword?"

She held her breath. It would really suck to have a tank with no weapon.

"I suppose. Though it's far too dainty for a self-respecting warrior. I'd better not hear any jokes from you lot."

Heldi stepped close and patted her husband on the shoulder. "None of us will forget how powerful ye are, I assure ye."

Hiding her smirk, Devon pulled out a sword from the load atop one of the mules. She smiled as she handed it over, hoping he didn't see the doubt in her eyes. She'd hoped to clear the curse without encountering any more poltergeists, particularly considering how poorly their first encounter had gone. How on earth were they going to defeat enough of them to recover the warhammer?

***

Through plenty of coaxing and attempting to *gorble* like an ostrich, Devon managed to persuade the bird to march with the group while Hazel roved ahead. The scout contoured back and forth, surveying the terrain and marking the best route with cairns. Devon was grateful for the woman's efforts, because the farther they went into the mountains, the steeper and more severe the terrain became.

As the sun neared its high point, the sparse forest finally gave way to rocky outcrops and patches of alpine tundra. The air held a definite chill. Hopefully, the group's need to stay inside during the nighttime hours would keep them from getting too cold in their lowland attire. As long as no storms came in, they'd probably be all right.

As she trekked, she kept an eye on the window for her messaging app. It was hard not to be impatient, though she knew the time compression made it seem like far more hours had passed than had actually gone by in the real world. Still...what if Tamara's mom didn't respond? Would Devon have to go back to the hospital and try another tactic? She couldn't handle doing nothing while Tamara was confined to a hospital bed. Not after going for weeks without even checking into why the woman hadn't responded to her messages.

In the late afternoon, Devon gave the order for the party to start looking for camp. Better to waste a little daylight than find themselves caught out. Besides, marching too far today might be pointless. Devon needed a better plan for the rest of their time in the mountains. Which areas would they search for mines, and how exactly were they going to deal with these orcs? For that matter, how were they going to find the orcs? And what about the poltergeists and Dorden's hammer? Should they try to bait the spirits into battles, hoping to attract them one at a time? She grimaced at the thought.

Cliffs now hemmed in their route, forcing the party along narrow ledges and through steep ravines. Finally, when they reached a relatively flat amphitheater, she called a halt. The ground was strewn with rocky rubble, and tent pads would need to be cleared if they wished to sleep comfortably. Nonetheless, the gray cliff at their back gave a sense of security, while the sloping platform granted a good vantage on approaches from below and the sides. Devon sent Hazel off to do a thorough check on the perimeter and make sure there was no sign of orcs, then instructed the others to start clearing stones and boulders from the campsite.

Finally, as the first tent went up, she received a message.

From: @St._George_General
To: @DevonWalker

Dear Devon,

Attached, please find the contact for Lillian Connor, Tamara Connor's mother.

P.S. Good luck. We see much better recovery rates on people who know they have friends and family pulling for them.

Devon swallowed and closed the message. As much as she wanted to drop everything and contact Lillian, she needed to make sure the group was secure first. She gathered her followers for a quick meeting.

When Hazel hurried in from the perimeter to join the circle, Devon began, "I hate to say this, but I think we should bring everything inside overnight."

Heldi raised an eyebrow. "Even the animals?"

Grumbling rose from the group as Devon nodded.

Hazel gave the ostrich a quick hug around its neck. "The animals can sleep with me, though I don't think there would be room for two people in that case."

Bayle, Hazel's tentmate, widened her eyes. She cast an alarmed look at Greel, the only other party member who didn't currently share a tent.

Heldi seemed to notice the woman's panic. She patted Dorden's back. "Maybe it would be good for Dorden to bunk with his clansman. Might help 'im sleep without Agavir to cuddle."

Did the dwarf really cuddle his warhammer? No one laughed at the comment, which made Devon think that yes, maybe he did. In fact, Dorden gave a sort of resolute nod as if trying to psyche himself up for a night without his weapon beside him.

"Care to lay out a bedroll in me tent for now?" Heldi asked as she glanced at Bayle.

When the woman nodded, Devon sighed with relief. "I need to take care of some things in the starborn realm," she said. "Everyone okay until dawn?"

After making eye contact with everyone and receiving a nod, she turned and trudged toward the base of the cliff. Just in case she had to log in during a storm, she found an overhanging boulder to duck beneath, then took a cross-legged seat and logged out.

Chapter Eighteen

MACHINES BEEPED, AND readouts glowed inside Tamara's room. Devon crept through the door into the dim interior, clutching the vase of yellow daisies as if it were a shield, and the blanket-wrapped figure on the bed a sleeping dragon. Or maybe some kind of hydra, a human body with tubes and wires attaching to half a dozen angular heads.

She swallowed as she approached the foot of the bed. "Hey, Tam," she said softly. Her friend lay with eyes closed and breathing apparatus in her mouth. Her head was pillowed on a cushion with some sort of smart fabric that rippled with color and shifting texture. Looking closer, Devon saw that the sheets beneath the fleece quilt were similar. Vaguely, she recalled that most care facilities used something like this to make micro-adjustments to the patient's environment, altering temperature, electric resistance, and humidity to help the body focus healing energy inward.

"I'm glad you came."

Devon jumped and nearly yelped when the voice rose from the corner of the room. She whirled, heart thudding, and faced an older woman. The family resemblance between Tamara and her mother was unmistakable even in the dim light.

Devon swallowed, unsure what to say. If Lillian Connor was so eager for her daughter to have visitors, why prohibit Tamara's friends from the bike shop from visiting? After a moment, she raised her vase of flowers as if to ask where she should put them.

Lillian gestured at a table beside the curtained window where another five or six bouquets in various states of freshness already stood.

Shuffling to the spot, Devon cast a surreptitious glance at Lillian. She didn't *look* particularly control-freakish. "Thanks for agreeing to let me come," she said. "I feel awful for not knowing she'd been injured until today."

Lillian leaned back and folded her hands over her belly. She was a lean woman, athletic-looking, with what appeared to be streaks of gray in her blond hair. "It was your mention of Fort Kolob that sold me. Tamara hated that place, hated putting on the Annie Oakley act for tourists. I decided that if you'd seen her there, you'd seen her at what she would have considered her worst."

Devon blinked, unsure what the woman meant.

"Want to sit?" Lillian asked. "She doesn't do much, though I like to think she knows we're here."

Slowly lowering herself into a cushioned chair with metal arms, Devon chewed her lip. "The guy at the bike shop told me she wasn't allowed visitors," she said, hoping the woman would volunteer her reason.

Lillian pressed her lips together, lines deepening in the corners of her mouth. "Honestly, Devon, I don't know what to do. Tamara was awake briefly before—actually, maybe I should back up. Her injuries were serious, especially the spleen and punctured lung. But she should have been through the difficult parts of her recovery within just a few days."

Devon glanced at her friend and felt her lip threatening to quiver. She hadn't noticed when she came in, but the accordion-shaped bladder in a clear plastic cylinder seemed to be breathing for her. "What happened?"

"A perfect storm of problems, I guess. For the ruptured spleen, the doctors introduced nano-surgeons through Tamara's IV. They were supposed to suture the ragged edges to avoid the need for a full or partial removal of the organ. It's supposed to be a safe alternative to traditional surgery with its risk of infection and errors."

"And?"

"Adverse reaction. Apparently, it's a one-in-one-hundred-thousand chance. Tamara's allergic to something in the nano-coatings."

"So they couldn't repair her spleen?"

"And her body's efforts to fight the invaders, plus the steroids they gave to reduce the reaction, lowered her ability to heal and fend off other bugs. After the nanos failed, they had to go in laparoscopically—that's with a tiny tube thing and some robot appendages—to close the punctures in her lungs and seal the worst bleeding from her spleen. They got things sutured—mostly—but Tamara caught a bug. She's fighting systemic infection."

Devon brought her hand to her mouth. Poor Tamara. "You said Tamara was awake before?"

Lillian nodded. "You probably have an idea of how proud she can be. She was embarrassed over crashing and didn't want her shop friends to see her so weak. She actually got mad when I asked how to contact them. I don't know...maybe she was dopey from the painkillers. But I feel like I should respect her wishes, you know?"

Devon nodded, hands fidgeting at the fabric of her pants. She didn't know if she should ask, but she felt like she had to know. "Will she recover?"

Lillian sighed, tucking a strand of hair behind her ear. "The last time I got a straight answer from one of the doctors, he said he thought she would pull through. He wouldn't give me anything more specific. No signs to watch for." A tear welled in the woman's eye, and she quickly brushed it away.

"If you don't mind me saying, I think he's right," Devon said gently. "Tamara's super strong."

Lillian turned a grateful look on her. "Thanks for saying that." She cocked her head. "How long are you planning to stay?"

Devon's awareness flicked to the clock projected into the corner of her vision by her implants. It was near two in the afternoon in the real world, but in Relic Online, it was just past midnight. She had another couple real-world hours before morning in the game.

"An hour or so, if that's okay."

Lillian smiled sadly, her eyes on her daughter. "I've been trading off with her father, making sure she's never alone. But I could really use a bit of fresh air. Would you mind sitting with her while I take a short walk?"

"Of course not," Devon said, standing in case the woman needed help up from her chair.

"Thank you," Tamara's mother said as she pushed on the chair arms and stood. Much to Devon's shock, Lillian pulled her into a hug.

After an awkward second or two, Devon wrapped an arm around the woman's back and patted her shoulder. "She's too tough for something like this to get her."

Lillian nodded and turned away to hide the fresh tears.

***

After sitting for twenty minutes in the darkness and watching the machine breathe for her friend, Devon couldn't stand it anymore. She nudged the curtain aside and admitted a stripe of late-autumn sunshine into the room. The glare hurt her eyes for a moment, but they quickly adjusted.

Tamara still didn't move, not even when Devon shuffled across the floor and laid a hand atop the quilt covering Tamara's arm.

"Sorry," Devon whispered. She shook her head. It wasn't like they hadn't gone for weeks without talking a number of times since the end of their stints at Fort Kolob had marked the beginning of their non-work-and-therefore-real friendship. For Devon, the guilt came from doubting her friend, her own insecurity having kept her from reaching out and discovering Tamara's condition earlier.

Which made Devon think...what about Hailey? What about her other guildmates? When she'd traded real-life contact info with Hailey, Devon had *thought* she'd sensed an awkward pause following her suggestion that she and Hailey could meet up sometime. But that was probably her insecurity acting up, too. At the very least, she should try to keep in touch with the woman and—ideally—track down contact info on her other former guildmates as well.

Returning to her chair beside the bouquet-studded table, she pulled open a browser window and ordered her implants to connect to Hailey's livestream.

The woman wasn't online. Laid over the dark feed was some more of Hailey's favorite yellow text.

Be back at 8 MST peeps. Here's hoping we actually make landfall tonight. I know y'all are probably sick of watching me watch the horizon for something besides more of the Noble Sea.

Devon laughed soundlessly. It sounded like Hailey was having quite an adventure. Or at least, like she was likely to wind up with a lot more achievements for discovering areas before other players. Devon wondered how Chen was enjoying what sounded like a long sea voyage. Hopefully he'd brought along some supplies to use for leveling his Tinkerer class abilities. Or at least a fishing pole. Anything that would allow him to grind skills or experience and plug values into his precious spreadsheets would probably keep him happy.

Smiling fondly to herself, Devon closed the livestream window and hovered her attention over her messaging app. Hailey's contact sprang to the front when Devon thought her friend's name.

Devon swallowed. It was just a text message. She had no reason to be weirded out by it. It was just...during her whole play time in Avatharn Online, she'd kept the game separate from her life. Her guildmates used to tease her about it, accusing her of secretly being the King of England or the Pope or something. Compared to other gamers, she *was* a little weird about the separation, but it wasn't due to privacy concerns or anything. It was about escape...the deep-set illusion that the game world was *real*. A crossover between real life and game world just made it harder to stay immersed. But seeing as her character was now standing outside Pod People locations pushing trial subscriptions for Relic Online, clinging to that separation seemed pretty stupid.

And besides, RO was real enough that she didn't *need* to take extra steps to believe in the authenticity of the world. It was as real to her as her earthly existence, with or without reminders that her in-game friends had lives outside the game as well.

"Hey, Hailey," she subvocalized. "Just dropping a line to see how it's going. Crossing the Noble Sea, huh?"

Before she could change her mind, she hit send, then brushed the messaging app away out of fear she'd otherwise just stare at it waiting for a response.

Tamara's machinery beeped. A few minutes later, Lillian returned, looking slightly more at ease than she had when she left.

Devon stood and picked up her purse. "Thanks again for letting me visit her," she said. "I have to get to work."

Lillian smiled. "While I was walking, I remembered Tamara telling me you were a professional gamer. You must be very talented."

Devon felt the color enter her cheeks at the compliment. She wasn't used to talking about her work. Or maybe more accurately, she wasn't used to talking at all. "I guess I do okay. Mostly I feel lucky for getting the job."

"Well, you're welcome to visit any time."

Devon hesitated near the door. "I realize you didn't ask my opinion, but I was thinking about what you said about Tamara and visitors..."

"You think she'd be okay with people seeing her?" Lillian's brows drew together. "It's been so hard. I just want to respect her wishes."

"They care about her. Even if she's stubborn about it, I think it would be good for her."

"Thanks," Lillian said. "I'll think about it."

As Devon stepped into the cool hall, she felt a pang in her chest. What would it be like to have parents sitting in her hospital room, unwilling to leave even for an hour unless someone else was there to keep her unconscious body company? Devon didn't even know where her mother was now. If Devon had an accident and the authorities *did* manage to find the woman, would she come to Devon's bedside?

She shook her head. Not a chance.

Chapter Nineteen

A GRIM-FACED gathering awaited Devon when she logged in and crawled out from beneath the boulder. Sharp sunlight cut between the serrated peaks of the higher ridge lines, pulling long morning shadows from the tents and party members. A definite chill lent a crispness to the air, and she pulled her arms tight to her body as she wove through the boulder field toward the group.

A tense hush filled the amphitheater, deepening the morning coolness. Even the mules seemed concerned, their ears flicking and eyes rolling while they snatched furtive bites from the sparse tufts of grass. In fact, only the ostrich seemed oblivious, peering with long-lashed eyes at the lichen-covered stones, and snapping up what were probably fat beetles from crevices in the rubble.

"What's wrong?" Devon asked as she searched the gathering for injuries.

Her followers sat in a loose circle upon small boulders that had been rolled to surround the fire ring. Despite their drawn faces, none of the members seemed to be hurt.

"Nothing, precisely," Heldi began. "But Hazel went out at dawn and returned with troubling information."

When the dwarf woman gestured toward her, the little scout gave a solemn nod. "We already knew there were orcs in these crags..."

"But...?" Devon said.

"I suppose I didn't imagine there could be so many."

Devon's heart sank. "You saw them?"

"Just signs of their passage. *Lots* of signs of their passage."

Sighing, Devon took a seat on an empty boulder. "How far away?"

"To the first track? Hardly any distance at all. In fact, I'm surprised we made it this far without crossing their trails or meeting one of their bands."

"Well," Devon said, straightening her shoulders and spine to lend courage to her followers, "if we're going to need to deal with them, I suppose it's good you found signs of their presence."

Hazel tried to look heartened, but she couldn't hide the clear skepticism on her face. "There's something else, too."

"Oh? What?"

"I'm not exactly sure what to make of it. I think it would be better if I showed you."

***

"To be clear," Devon said, "this isn't what you wanted to show me?"

She and the lithe scout perched atop a pedestal of stone overlooking a series of deep gouges in the terrain where small streams cut through the rubble on their tumble toward the lowlands. Roughly parallel where they neared the sharp rise of a cliff band, each of the five ravines boasted a well-used trail that led, ultimately, to a yawning cavern entrance in the crags. Squinting, Devon could make out the flickering glow of some sort of firelight on the closest cavern's walls. Mounds of refuse filled the gully bottoms near the caves.

It didn't take Hazel's tracking skill to examine footprints along the trails and conclude that the paths were, in fact, the work of orcs, but Devon suspected the woman had been diligent and looked closely anyway.

"No, but I thought you would want to see this too."

Devon nodded. After some deliberation, she and the scout had set out alone. Bringing a full party for a simple reconnaissance mission would not only make it harder to move stealthily, but it would also leave the camp undefended.

"And this is just part of the...infestation?"

"That's right," Hazel said. "I made it to that ridgeline"—she pointed to a shoulder of land that dropped down from the high crags maybe a mile away—"before turning around. There were at least another half-dozen cavern entrances visible from there."

"With the same signs of habitation, I assume?"

"I even thought I glimpsed motion inside one of the closer caves, though the light was still poor."

"You did wait until dawn though, right? The poltergeists only come at night."

Hazel looked faintly guilty as she shrugged. "Well, I waited until their green lights and weird moans went away. Problem is, I always wake so early."

Devon sighed as she picked at a patch of lichen and pulled it off in her fingers.

You have received: 1 x Light Green Lichen of Moderate Flakiness with some Orangish Spots

> **Quest updated:** Pharmacopeia Failings.
> **Objective:** Gather new ingredients for Hezbek. (2/5)

She smirked as she dropped the lichen into her inventory. Well, that was progress, at least. Speaking of...

"I realize this is something of a tangent, but I'm wondering whether you ever run across feathers while scouting."

Hazel gave her a quizzical look. "I...I guess haven't really paid attention."

"One of the merchants in Stonehaven is a fletcher. Apparently, we are nearly out of arrows, but she can't make more without good flight or tail feathers."

> Pass responsibility for your quest "Crossbow Crisis" to your poor, overtasked scout?
> **Accept?** Y/N

"Well, I suppose I could try to keep an eye out..." Hazel said, sounding faintly concerned about her ability to manage it.

Devon shook her head. "Actually, I take it back. You do so much for us already. I don't want to distract you."

"What about Zoe?"

"Who?"

"The ostrich." Hazel blushed. "I hope you don't mind that I named her."

"Aren't her feathers a little froofy for arrows?"

Hazel shrugged. "The ones around the base of her tail plume might work."

Devon swallowed. "I suspect she might kick me if I start trying to pluck around the base of her tail."

Hazel sighed and smirked. "That's why you need a Mr. Ostrich. Once she starts laying eggs, I bet she'll pluck them herself to line the nest."

As far as Devon was concerned, one ostrich was enough for now. And in any case, they had bigger concerns than a collection quest she'd received from one of the town's merchants.

"So if this isn't the thing you needed to show me, what is?" she asked, concern sitting like wet gravel in her belly.

"This way," Hazel said. The woman climbed back off the back side of the stone pedestal and started picking her way downhill. "I took a low route on the way back to try to get an idea how far the orcs traveled from the cave mouths."

"And?"

"I didn't reach the ends of their tracks, so I think we can assume they rove fairly far."

"Hunting, you think?"

Hazel shrugged. "I assume so. Ordinarily, I'd say they leave their caves to raid, but with the curse, it doesn't seem that there are any settlements to pillage in the area."

"Which makes me wonder, why has the curse failed to drive the orcs out? Is it because they make their homes in the tunnels?"

"I think so. You saw the firelight, I assume?"

"A hint of it."

Hazel clambered onto a flat-topped boulder and shaded her eyes as if searching for a path. After a moment, she nodded and hopped down. "Thought I might have made a wrong turn. Anyway...as I was crossing beneath one of the cave mouths, I got a better look inside.

181

They don't just have single campfires burning. It's a series of torches stretching as far back as I could see."

Devon fell in behind the woman. "They're avoiding the poltergeists in the same way we are."

The scout nodded. "Staying inside at night with the lights on. Only I'd wager walls of thick stone are probably better protection than our canvas tents."

A rock shifted under Devon's foot, grating and sending dust puffing. She windmilled her arms to stay upright, earning a sharp pain as she pulled something in her back. Maybe it was time to spend another point or two in *Agility*. "So for all their hard work in laying a curse and binding their ancestors to servitude as poltergeists, the felsen didn't really gain anything."

Hazel paused, her eyes growing distant. "That's the thing...I'm not so sure we have the story quite right."

Devon wanted to ask more but swallowed her words. She was pretty sure Hazel intended to explain that statement shortly.

The morning sun had finally warmed the landscape, raising a heat shimmer from the boulders and loose earth. The air smelled of warm stone, reminding Devon, surprisingly, of a trip she and her mother took long ago, a bus ride to Salt Lake City where her mother had needed to make some sort of court appearance. On the way back, Devon's mother had suggested a side trip up one of the granite-walled canyons near the city. They'd hiked up a trail, probably spending no more than fifteen minutes outside. But it was one of the few activities she'd ever done with her mother—unless she counted staring blankly at some reality stream on her mother's crappy old tablet.

Devon closed her eyes for a moment, enjoying the memory of that forest hike. For a long time after her mother kicked her out of the house, Devon hadn't been able to remember anything about the woman without getting angry. Maybe it was progress that she could recall a good moment without the hatred intruding.

Or maybe her unconscious mind was too busy dealing with its more recent trauma to remain pissed off over something that had happened years ago.

She shook her head and hurried to catch up with Hazel, setting off a clatter of stones when her foot landed on an unstable part of the slope. The scout turned, eyes wide, before shaking her head in what might have been disapproval but was more likely relief that Devon hadn't broken a leg yet.

After another half hour or so spent weaving their way downhill through outcrops and boulder fields, Hazel slowed and raised a hand to ask for caution. Shoulders tense with her concern that another misstep would start a rockslide, Devon crept up behind. When she stopped behind Hazel, the woman pointed to a dark chimney that split a wide stone spire attached on one side to a much larger formation.

"It's through there," Hazel breathed. "But I think we might be wiser to try climbing and looking down in."

"I don't understand," Devon said. "Looking in on what?"

"The spire is hollow and leads to a system of tunnels—and possibly canyons. I was able to creep through the crevice but couldn't go any farther without being seen."

"Being seen by whom?"

Hazel chewed her lip. "That's the thing. I'm not sure."

"Is there a reason you don't want to use the cavern again?"

The woman cast Devon a skeptical glance. "I mean no offense, but my stealth skill has come quite a long way. Even so, if someone had passed near me inside that chimney, I might have been discovered."

Meaning that Devon's snorting-warthog version of stealth wouldn't cut it. "Got it," she said.

"For what it's worth, I don't think I should have gone in that way either. Especially since I was following drag marks."

"Wait, drag marks? Do you know what they were from?"

Hazel nodded. "I do. Do you think you can climb?"

Devon grimaced as she looked at the nearly sheer side of the spire. "You haven't developed a recent aptitude for the healing of broken bodies, have you?"

"I'll take that as a no," Hazel said. "Hmm."

"But what if I had a way to render us completely undetectable for five minutes? Would that be enough time to get inside?"

Hazel raised an eyebrow. "I suspect so."

Devon laid a hand on one of her *Bracers of Smoke*, preparing to use the *Vanish* ability.

***

So, yeah. There was no question as to the source of the drag marks, seeing as they led straight to the feet of a massive orc who was bound with thick coils of rope to a wooden stake as big around as a tree trunk. The orc slobbered and roared and strained against its restraints as a horde of blue-tinted pygmy captors surrounded it and threw what sounded like taunts as they poked it with sharpened sticks.

Devon shook her head in a mixture of confusion and amazement. The descriptions were right: small and skinny, tufts of white hair, mountain-dwellers. Well, most of the descriptions. She hadn't expected the bluish hue of their skin or the fierce scowls on their faces. And there was the fact that craglings were supposed to be extinct.

Hazel cast her a questioning look, visible to Devon because they were both out of phase with the physical plane. Devon shrugged. Yeah...seemed they were definitely lacking on the information side of things.

Chewing her lip, she considered. If these miniature tormentors really were the felsen, the orcs were a mutual enemy. Maybe they could form an alliance to deal with the orc presence that, frankly, seemed to be about a hundred times too big for her party of five fighters to deal with. But the cruel glints in the craglings' eyes as they poked and prodded the orc gave her pause. Whatever had happened in the centuries since Ishildar's fall and the supposed disappearance of their race, it didn't seem to have engendered hospitality on their part. Sure, maybe their curse was designed to keep the orcs confined to the tunnels, leaving the felsen to this apparent sanctuary. But the magic of the little blue humanoids in their ragged scraps of clothing had made the area just as inhospitable to friendly races. For all she knew, they hated everyone equally.

Not to mention, they spoke some strange tongue that Devon couldn't understand in the slightest. The conditions really weren't great for opening a dialogue.

Touching Hazel on the shoulder, she nodded toward the exit to the narrow fissure they'd crept through to access the spire's interior.

185

Quickly, she led the way out and hurried uphill as the buff icon for her *Vanish* spell flashed, and then expired.

"Well," Hazel said, "that was a nice trick. What else have you been hiding?"

Devon shrugged, the corner of her mouth drawn back in a smile. "It's neat, but it's only usable every two days."

Though it made her think...part of the problem with the poltergeists was that they didn't give up on a target once they decided to annoy them. Maybe the *Vanish* spell would wipe the phantoms' aggro. Not that she wanted to test that theory.

"Seems we have a lot to talk about with the others," she said. "Ready to head back?"

Hazel nodded. "Want to lead the way?"

Devon looked uphill at the complex terrain. She didn't have a clue which way led home.

"It's alright. You go ahead," she said.

Smirking, Hazel set off.

Chapter Twenty

THE GUST OF body-odor scented wind was their only warning before the orcs sprang.

"Get back!" Devon yelled, yanking on Hazel's cloak as she stepped in front of the woman to greet the trio of snarling brutes who leaped from behind a stony outcrop.

Hazel squeaked, scurried away, and scrambled like a monkey up a tower of jagged stone.

Dagger drawn, Devon insta-cast a *Shadow Puppet,* targeting the hard lines sketched by the sun and her shadow. As the black figure rose, she sent it a pace forward as something of a defensive shield and activated *Combat Assessment.*

> Orc Hunter - Level 18
> Orc Brute - Level 17
> Orc Brute - Level 18

Okay. Three enemies around her level. Devon swallowed. She could do this as long as she was smart about it. The quick glance at the enemies told her she needed to focus on the Orc Hunter first. He carried a crude short bow and was definitely the biggest threat since she hoped to stay out of melee range.

Before, she'd always used her sun-based *Shadow Puppets* as spears, taking advantage of the hard edges to penetrate armor and make precision strikes. But the knockback when the lances shattered was a problem, especially on the unstable ground. The last thing she needed was to end up on her butt. As she racked her mind, judging whether she could try using the puppet as a sort of tank, one of the brutes roared and charged.

Devon backpedaled, started to cast *Freeze*, but canceled it when an idea flashed to life.

She poured mana into *Levitate - Tier 2* instead. As her feet left the ground, she threw her *Shadow Puppet* in front of the charging orc, the figure arriving just in time to catch a wild swing of the brute's club. Her minion shattered, and the knockback effect sent her flying.

Well, not flying. Instead, she went skimming over the terrain about three feet above the boulders and rubble.

She grinned. Just as she'd hoped. As long as she had enough mana to keep casting *Shadow Puppets*, the knockback was an excellent way to kite the mobs without tiring her legs and raising her *Fatigue* stat.

As she hung there, mentally congratulating herself, a feathered shaft flew across the slope and lodged in her left bicep. She winced, gritted her teeth, and pulled it free.

Great plan. Minor problem with the details.

After raising another *Shadow Puppet* for shielding, she focused on the Orc Hunter and called down a tier 2 *Flamestrike*. Fire erupted from the ground, the column of flame engulfing the archer. Its health bar flashed and dropped by a solid chunk, the number 79 flashing over the bar. Devon blinked, surprised to see actual hitpoints reported. Seemed her *Combat Assessment* skill had finally gained enough to offer more precise information. But it wasn't a good time to geek out over numbers and stats. The other brute was pounding across the rock field, notched ax raised.

Devon glanced back. A tall boulder with some rather sharp edges punctured the slope not far behind her. Cringing, she hurriedly sidestepped to change the angle between the charging orc and her body. Even so, when her *Shadow Puppet* took the blow, disintegrating and sending her flying back, her elbow brushed the boulder.

She winced. Too close.

Another arrow grazed her shoulder. Shaking her head, she took in the scene. Both brutes were closing on her, so she tried a *Freeze*, but the secondary effect didn't fire, and only one became trapped in the ice.

Breathing hard now, she went through the mental hoops to summon another *Shadow Puppet*, then glanced again at the archer. It had another arrow nocked, and the beast let fly before Devon could react. The shaft skewered her through the calf, knocking off more hitpoints than she expected from a wound to the lower leg. Devon grimaced. She needed to take control of this fight, or she'd soon make the mistake that would get her killed. Targeting the other charging brute, she cast a second *Freeze*. At that moment, her first icy casing shattered, and the first orc started forward. She shook her head and froze it too.

Now, for the hunter. Casting *Wall of Fire*, she molded the flames into a half circle around the ranged attacker. As soon as the cast finished, she began going through the motions for *Conflagration*. Lightning jumped from her hands, arced across the slope, and exploded her flame wall. The hunter went flying headfirst into a low boulder. Its health bar showed just under half remaining, but a new debuff icon appeared beneath, indicating that the hunter had been knocked out.

Devon hesitated. The icon had no information on the effect's duration. The melee-fighting brutes were the bigger threat *right now*, but the moment the Orc Hunter recovered, it'd be feathering her with arrows yet again.

Her mana bar was below half, but she refreshed the *Freeze* effects anyway, draining another 10% of her magical reserves. As she ran— at 70% of her ordinary speed thanks to the cushion of air beneath her feet—toward the unconscious hunter, she hit it with another *Flamestrike*. The smell of roasting meat reached her nose, turning her stomach. Nonetheless, Devon sprinted close, canceled her *Levitate* effect, and dragged her dagger across the orc's throat.

> *Coup de grace.*
> *You have slain an Orc Hunter.*
> *You receive 2000 experience.*
>
> *Now watch out for his friends, dear.*

The brutes roared as they sprinted over the ground, loose rocks flying and sliding beneath their heavy footfalls. Grimacing, Devon got her *Levitate* and *Shadow Puppet* up just in time and managed to work the knockback-*Levitate* combo long enough to catch her breath and regain her wits.

After that, it was just a matter of letting them push her back and slowly whittling them down with *Flamestrikes* and the occasional

Freeze when things got too hectic. The battle took long enough that her *Fatigue* climbed a few points despite not needing to use her feet to move around, mostly because she had to wait for in-combat mana regeneration.

Eventually, though, the last orc groaned and died.

Hazel whistled and clapped, clambering back down from her perch.

"Well done," the woman said.

"We survived, at least," Devon said.

As she crouched to loot the first body—earning a couple of copper coins and a *Crude Axe*—motion from down the hill caught her eye. She stiffened and sucked in a breath to tell Hazel to flee. But before she could speak, the little blue-tinted observers turned and filed back into the folds of the terrain.

"What?" Hazel said, following the direction of her gaze.

Devon shook her head. "Felsen."

"Where?"

"Gone now. But I think we'd better hurry back to camp."

***

Walking back into camp, Devon couldn't stop looking over her shoulder. The location no longer felt secure, not even with the sheltering cliff at their backs or the lofty vantages on the approaches. She felt her jaw tensing as she walked the perimeter, then peered into the tents and nodded at the handful of occupants resting on their bedrolls.

Dorden and Greel were sitting beside the campfire, poking at the coals with sticks.

"Well?" the dwarf asked.

Devon took a seat on one of the boulders before she spoke. "Well, I learned a lot." She wasn't sure where to start, particularly regarding the felsen. *Particularly* since their continued existence undermined Greel's historical knowledge and recent translations—the latter could be explained by their clear desire to remain undiscovered. But as a would-be scholar along with his legal expertise, the lawyer would probably find it quite disturbing to hear that the facts he'd learned about the cragling race were wrong.

She sighed. "It's not great, but we'll figure it out, I guess."

"She wasn't wrong about the orcs, then?"

"Not by a long shot. I'm not sure what we'll do...I mean, given the number of entrances to their warren, I'd guess there might be five hundred of them inside. Maybe more."

"But that's the thing about tunnels, isn't it," Dorden said. "Ye don't have to fight them all at once, right? They simply don't fit."

Devon grimaced. "True, but when they just keep coming, they wear you down eventually."

The dwarf grumbled. "I suppose you're right. And without me Agavir..."

Though she didn't imagine it would help, Devon reached into her rucksack and pulled out two of the weapons she'd looted from the orcs, *Spiked Club* and *Crude Axe.*

"Would either of these be a better replacement than the longsword? Just for the time being, of course."

Dorden cocked his head and sucked his teeth as he looked at the club. "O'course it's a beast's weapon, not something suited for the likes of me..."

"But at least you can't envision an elf prancing in and laying about with it, right?"

He grinned. "Indeed, lass." His smile faded. "It seems ye found yourself in a bit of trouble, eh?"

Devon shrugged. "A small band. Probably didn't expect a lost adventurer to give them much trouble."

"Maybe that's your new nickname. Trouble."

Even Greel gave a faint smile at this. Watching the man, Devon considered whether to bring up the thing with the felsen. But then her stomach growled, reminding her that she actually had to eat while away from Stonehaven and its convenient auto-deduction of rations.

"What did you all have for breakfast?" she asked.

Dorden glanced over his shoulder before doing a poor job of whispering. "Don't say anything to Bayle, but we had more of her charred rabbit, I'm afraid. Still picking the fur out of me teeth."

Devon swallowed, her stomach immediately quieting. "Hazel hasn't found any new mountain berries or anything?"

The dwarf leaned back and laughed, holding his belly. "Sorry, lass. Ye have to soldier through with the rest of us." Digging through the coals, he pulled out a rather burned leg of what Devon believed *could* have been a rabbit.

She accepted it reluctantly, then grabbed her *Everfull Waterskin*, anticipating she'd have plenty of need.

"Didn't you promise to give me the full rundown on your plans for naming your son?" she said, eager for a distraction from her meal.

"Ah, that I did, lass. That I did." Dorden cast her a glance that was almost sly. "And since ye asked, it's best I start with me own name. Ye see, Dorden is nothing but a nickname as well. Me true moniker is Dorden son Havarn son Gorbin son Bollin of the Stoneshoulders of Coldpass Hold"—he paused to take a breath—"by way of Maiseli daughter Heri daughter Lorin daughter Warldi."

Devon raised her eyebrows. "That's...long."

Dorden chuckled with a hint of pride puffing his chest. "I left out the occupations of each of me ancestors which is ordinarily part of it. Figured ye might not keep listening to the rest of the bit about the wee lad's name if I went on too long about meself."

"I'm happy to learn about your history, Dorden," she said. The name was a little long, but it was kind of interesting. "So you go back four generations? And I can't believe I never asked about the name of your former home. Coldpass Hold? Is that where you lived before?"

A shadow passed across his face as he nodded. "It was indeed, lass. And that's where the name for the wee lad becomes hard. Ye see, me line has lived in Coldpass Hold for far more than the four generations in me name. Me father had it in his name, and his father before, and all the way back around three hundred years to a dwarven couple named Dorden and Rinndi who made a long journey from the Northlands in search of a place to found a new clan."

"Were you named for that Dorden?" she asked, tearing off a leathery strip of rabbit meat and reluctantly slipping it past her lips.

"In fact, I was. Dorden and Rinndi discovered the first cave that would someday be hollowed out and extended to create the vast cavern system that became Coldpass Hold. They were both miners, and for those first years they worked together, tunneling and widening until they uncovered the first glimmering vein. After that, wasn't hard to lure other dwarves looking for a new beginning, and soon the Stoneshoulders of Coldpass Hold were founded."

Devon found herself staring into the low flames that licked from the fire's coals. She'd already know that the dwarves had lost their homes, but the history made it seem real rather than abstract. Of course, she was only now learning how to relate. Her experience with "homes" had started with a series of rundown rooms her mother had frequently been evicted from, and had moved from there onto the string of cheap apartments Devon had successfully managed to make rent on after getting kicked out from her mom's place. To her, it had often felt like one mold-stained ceiling was the same as any other. Especially when she'd started gaming and had only cared about having a place to sleep. But now that she had Stonehaven...now that she was *building* something, she was starting to understand the value of having a place to call home.

Of course, that didn't come close to the sense of attachment she imagined someone would feel to a place that had been in their family for centuries.

"I never really realized," she said quietly. "I'm grateful to have you in Stonehaven, but is there any way we can help you return to Coldpass?"

The dwarf grunted amicably. "Thank ye, lass. But ye see, it's something Heldi and I have been discussing since we learned we were expecting a wee one. Naturally, we wish it hadn't ended the way it did, with the Stoneshoulders forced to abandon the Hold because that part of the world had no more use for us. But maybe it was time. Maybe there's more connecting me and me namesake than the sounds that make our given names. The original Dorden set out to find and build somewhere new. Seems I have, too."

Greel, who had remained surprisingly quiet during Dorden's history, avoiding even the annoyed-sounding exhalations he used to express impatience, finally stirred. "I think he's trying to say that Stonehaven is a place we can all call home. Even those of us who might not have been looking for it." He gestured toward himself.

Devon's eyebrows went up. "Thanks for saying that, Greel."

The man rolled his eyes. "You've known all along that I act in self-interest. It just happens that I've realized that finding a place to belong to *is* in my self-interest."

She kept her face even. "Regardless of the reason, I'm glad to hear it." She turned her gaze back to Dorden. "So your son's name..." She said, leaving the rest open.

"We think it will be Bravlon."

"...son Dorden son..." She shook her head. "I can't remember."

"Bravlon son Dorden son Havarn son Gorbin of the Stoneshoulders of Stonehaven, by way of Heldi daughter Ysvarn daughter Pera daughter Alevi."

"I like it," she said. For some reason, hearing him say it made her throat constrict. Three hundred years in a place, and the next home they chose was the village she'd built. "And I couldn't be more honored to have you settle with us in Stonehaven."

"And we are honored ye decided to invite us, lass. Of course, there are younger members of me clan who are hoping we can bring more dwarves to the settlement. Heldi's already found the love of her life"—he grinned and stroked his beard—"and Garda is more interested in her forge than in any of the strapping lads in the village..."

Devon smiled. "Consider it a promise. I'll do my best to find more dwarves in need of a home."

Dorden leaned back, looking satisfied. "It's too bad our ale supply is so limited." He glanced toward the trail leaving the amphitheater. "And I suppose the edge of the orc infestation isn't the best place for imbibing. But I still say this conversation deserves a toast."

Devon's eyes flicked to Greel. "Not that I wish to kill the mood, but Hazel and I did discover another thing this morning."

"Oh?" the lawyer said, noticing that the comment had been largely directed toward him.

She sighed. "So, yeah. I'll start this by saying I'm as surprised as I imagine you'll be, but it seems the common wisdom regarding the fate of the felsen has some gaps."

She went on to explain what they'd seen inside the hollow spire and after the scuffle with the orcs. To Greel's credit, he didn't seem too upset by her revelation. The expressions on his face shifted from perplexed to concerned and back. When she was finished, both he and Dorden sat silently for a while.

"Well, that's an interesting change to our situation, isn't it?" Greel finally said.

Chapter Twenty-One

ONLY AFTER TELLING the others about the morning's events did it sink in how poorly the orc battle could have gone. Especially for Hazel. Alone, the scout could move about with little risk of detection or attack. But when following Devon, who was, by comparison, a charging rhino, Hazel could have been killed. Devon had been lucky to grab the monsters' aggro. Lucky to survive the encounter, for that matter.

Still staring into the flames of the campfire, she laid a hand on her calf where the arrow had plunged through the muscle. There was still a small hole in her leather trousers, but the wound had already healed by the time she'd returned to camp thanks to out-of-combat health regeneration. Nonetheless, the echo of the pain still tugged at her mind, both from the strike to her calf and the one to her bicep. She couldn't shake the reminder of her vulnerability.

Around the camp, her followers were busy caring for their armor, resting, and in the case of the miners, once again pecking at rock samples. She shook her head, demoralized. Aside from the natural protection created by their location—and, she supposed, the fact that none of the orcs' usual trails passed through the area—the camp had nothing in the way of defenses.

Of course, she doubted anything would help if a full-fledged orc war party attacked. Faced with even twenty or thirty of the orcs, surviving would be difficult. And considering that the caves probably held at least a couple hundred warrior-type monsters, an attack by twenty or thirty would be a best case. If the group suffered a full party wipe, it would be a major setback—but ultimately a survivable one—for Devon and her advanced NPCs. For Hazel and the miners, not so much. To them, dead was dead. End of story.

She supposed she could suggest the group try to shore up the defenses, or the very least, that they opt for smokeless fires and stay out of the orcs' sight. The biggest danger was during the day—ironically, the felsen poltergeists made the camp safer at night since she doubted the orcs were any more eager to face the spirits than she was.

Regardless, added defensive measures wouldn't do anything to advance them toward their goals. The best way to safely establish mines and hunt down the next relic would be to deal with the orcs. And the poltergeists. And probably the felsen, too.

But how?

Devon chewed absently at her thumbnail while she thought the situation through. The fact that her quest to find the Argenthal Vassaldom had been completed without an update regarding the relic made her think. Was that because the remnants of the vassal society still existed? She really didn't like the idea that those scowling little people with their pointy sticks might still hold one of the relics she needed to restore Ishildar. But unfortunately, that was probably the case.

So...should they try to take the relic by force, or should they explore other options? Diplomacy would probably work better in this case. Given that the craglings hadn't attacked when she was weak after her battle with the orc trio, she didn't think they'd aggro her for trying to make contact.

Hopefully not, anyway.

A while ago, Greel had risen from the fireside to retrieve a couple sheets of parchment. He was now busy scrawling notes, probably about the felsen. She wondered if, in his mind, there were fantasies of returning to Eltera City or some other center of civilization and dropping the bombshell about the "extinct" race's continued existence.

If that were the case, maybe he'd appreciate some first-hand information.

"Hey Greel? Do you think you can speak the felsen language?"

The man blinked as he pulled himself from whatever thought he'd been jotting down. "Hmm. Well, the structure shares aspects with ancient Carpavan. But the phonemes and specific vocabulary may prove a challenge."

She took a slow breath. "Is that a yes or no?"

"It depends on how long I have to develop a sense of their speech patterns and how closely they resemble Carpavan."

"Would you be willing to try?" she asked in an overly patient voice.

"Does it involve being bound to a stake and poked with sticks?"

Devon grimaced. "I hope not?"

Dorden, who had been inspecting the spiked club for about the tenth time, perked up. "If you're planning a little chat, could ye tell them to make their phantoms give me back Agavir?"

Quest updated: Recover Agavir.

Wouldn't hurt to ask the craglings to make their poltergeist return the weapon, right?

Objective: Speak to the felsen tribe to see if they will help recover the dwarf's warhammer.

She shrugged a shoulder. The quest update seemed to suggest she was on the right track. Not that she put a whole lot of faith in the game's desire to make things easy for her.

Devon glanced at the sun, which had passed its high point a few hours ago. Unfortunately, after this play session and the next, she'd need to get some real-life sleep. It would leave her followers to manage for around twenty-four in-game hours without her. This really wasn't the sort of situation in which she wanted to abandon them. Even if she and Greel had to hurry to the felsen's sanctuary and back, it seemed better to get it out of the way than procrastinate.

"How soon can you be ready?"

Greel looked up with faint alarm. "I assumed this was some sort of exploration of hypotheticals."

Devon smirked. "Haven't you heard that I'm a woman of action? We'll head out in fifteen minutes."

With a glare and an eye roll, Greel folded his parchment sheets and stomped toward his tent.

Devon glanced at Dorden. "May I borrow your wife for the afternoon? I think it might be nice to have her healing capability."

The dwarf nodded solemnly. "I was just going to say that ye ought to take at least one of us, seeing as it's me warhammer that's gone missing. Wouldn't be very honorable to ask ye to fetch it back without help."

"And you don't mind staying here to keep watch on the camp?"

"If ye are asking whether I feel slighted that ye would rather have me wife beside ye, don't worry. I recognized that she was the stronger of us years ago."

Devon smiled. "Thanks, Dorden. With good fortune, we'll be back with good news well before dark."

***

It took longer than Devon would have liked for their small party—or rather, the lawyerly member of it— to be ready to march. As they finally shouldered their rucksacks, checked their weapons, and started for the edge of camp, Devon caught a flicker of motion near one of the game trails that exited the amphitheater. She panicked for half a breath before Hazel materialized from behind a boulder.

Devon sighed. She hadn't even realized the woman had slipped away from the area.

"Your Gloriousness," the scout called, hurrying toward the group. Spotting its—her?—favorite source of food, Zoe gave a cheerful little ostrich noise and trotted over, too. Hazel grabbed the bird around the neck and rubbed her knuckles on its sparsely feathered head.

"Is everything okay?" Devon asked. "And by the way, how do you keep Zoe from following you when you leave?" She didn't add her question about how Hazel had so far avoided being pecked to death. Seemed Devon was the only target of that particular behavior.

Hazel kissed the bird between the eyes and then whispered something. "She's not as simpleminded as you might imagine. We've been learning together. In fact, my *Animal Taming* has gotten a whole lot better. I'm looking forward to trying it on some other beasts."

Out of curiosity, Devon inspected the woman.

> Hazel: Level 12 - Scout
> Health: 262/262
>
> Skills:
> Stealth - Tier 5: 43
> Cartography - Tier 3: 21
> Sense Heading - Tier 3: 24
> Detect Freshwater: 9
> Forage - Tier 4: 32
> Animal Taming: 9

Wow. The woman really had improved, and not just by increasing *Animal Taming* to 9 already. Tier 5 *Stealth* and tier 4 *Foraging*? Even Hazel's directional sense—the *Sense Heading* skill— seemed have gotten quite a workout, probably while exploring the dense jungle. Devon shook her head. The woman had so many useful skills it seemed a shame to leave her as a basic NPC. But Devon stopped herself from pursuing that line of thought too far. Stonehaven still needed to more than double its population to grow from Village to Hamlet, and the settlement already had six of the seven allowable advanced NPCs. As much as she genuinely liked the woman and valued her skills, she couldn't afford to use up her last advanced slot unless it was either an emergency or she needed to do it to keep Stonehaven running.

The woman had been dancing from foot to foot while Devon let her thoughts spool out. With an apologetic smile, she brushed away the popup holding Hazel's information.

"You have improved a lot," Devon said. "No wonder Zoe's so fond of you."

Hazel shrugged and cast her eyes down. "It's really not so hard. Just takes a bit of patience with the animal. In fact, I could teach you some things later."

> **Hazel is offering you a quest:** Ostrich-tamer Extraordinaire.
> *Become the hero you always imagined yourself being. Or at least learn to befriend really weird flightless birds.*
> **Objective:** Work with Hazel to train your Animal Taming skill to 3.
> **Reward:** 2000 experience
> **Accept?** Y/N

"That's such a kind offer," Devon said, hoping she sounded sincere as she selected 'no'. "Maybe you could show me once we leave the mountains. I'm afraid my worries about our situation would make me too distracted."

The reminder of the expedition's status seemed to sober Hazel, who sent the ostrich off with a gentle gesture.

"That's actually what I want to talk to you about," the scout said. She paused, chewing her lip and making fists around her thumbs. "I realize you may not like hearing how I came into this information..."

Devon cringed. "I'm guessing you're right."

"I just felt so useless this morning. I watched you fight those orcs, showed you all the bad news about the extents of their lair. But I didn't have a lick of information to offer that might help us. I don't like to disappoint you or the Stonehaven League."

"I guess I should remind you we had zero information on how we'd even find the orcs before you discovered their caves..." As she spoke, her thoughts started to whirl. What could the woman have gotten up to? "So what did you learn just now?"

Hazel shrugged apologetically as she swung her rucksack around to the front of her body. "It's not so much what I *learned* as what I *found*. Of course, I should warn you not to be alarmed. It doesn't seem capable of burning other things."

Devon stared at the woman in confusion. At this point, she had no idea what the scout was talking about.

With a nervous smile, Hazel pulled a lit torch from her pack.

"What the...?" Heldi said, taking a step back.

Devon kept staring for a moment. "Well...that's a neat trick."

"Not what you'd expect, right?"

Of course, thinking back to other games, Devon had a clear mental image of stacks of burning torches shoved into inventory slots. But Relic Online was way too realistic for that.

"Not at all. Where'd you get it?"

The woman cringed. "Like I said, I wanted to bring you some good news. Or at least a better assessment of the orc threat. I only went into the cave mouth a little ways."

Devon felt her eyes widen in alarm. She was tempted to make the woman an advanced NPC right there just to keep her from permakilling herself. "I assume you mean one of the orc cave mouths..."

Hazel shrugged. "It was deserted, and I knew I wouldn't be caught. I just thought that if I secretly snuffed a few of their torches, they might be surprised by poltergeists in the night. At the very least, I hoped a couple of the monsters would be caught out. Unfortunately, as you can see, snuffing the torches isn't so easy."

Devon shook her head. No, not so easy. As for this strategy of taking away the orcs' lights, why hadn't she thought of that? Okay, so maybe it wasn't entirely practical...the likelihood that the orcs would fail to notice the unlit torches seemed slim. But still, she hadn't even considered ways she might be able to pit the poltergeists against the orcs without risking her followers.

"And since you couldn't snuff it, you...put it in your backpack?" Heldi asked.

Hazel laughed. "Not immediately. Only once I realized I couldn't burn anything with it and that it wasn't particularly hot."

She held the torch out to Devon.

You have received: Ordinary Torch (enchanted).
Otherwise nondescript, this torch is under the influence of the Orc Shaman-King's magic. Affected by **Everliving Flame,** *it cannot be extinguished without canceling the enchantment.*

Well, that was interesting. And possibly a little demoralizing. A shaman-king along with a legion of brutes? No problem, right?

Devon stared at the torch, thinking. The constant light source could be useful, at least while they needed night lights to keep away the poltergeists. But what if the shaman-king could sense its location or something? It probably shouldn't stay in their camp.

For the moment, she stuffed it in her rucksack, wincing at seeing the live flame disappear beneath the top flap. When her backpack didn't go up in flames after a ten count, she blew a breath through her lips, then shouldered the pack.

"Thanks, Hazel. We are heading out to try to form some sort of alliance with the felsen. Do me a favor?"

"Sure thing, Your Gloriousness."

"Please stay here until we get back."

The woman's shoulders slumped as she nodded.

Chapter Twenty-Two

"YE DO KNOW the way back to this felsen place, don't ye?" Heldi asked.

Devon pinned her smile in place. "Sure. Well, I mean, I can follow our tracks well enough."

That was mostly true. So far, she'd *thought* she recognized the place where she'd fought the orcs—the little tower of stone where Hazel had perched during the battle was fairly distinct. Wasn't it?

Though come to think of it, she hadn't spotted an actual human footprint in the last couple hundred yards despite the tracking points she'd gained while searching for Dorden and Heldi the night of the poltergeist encounter.

Her concern must have shown on her face because Heldi chuckled and patted her shoulder. "Ye haven't gone that far off track, actually. And the turn was easy to miss. I think Hazel may have tried to brush out some of your footprints to keep those little craglings from following ye to camp."

Devon's eyebrows had a moment to furrow before Heldi chuckled again. "It was ye that assigned me the profession of hunter if ye recall."

Sighing, Devon shook her head. Of course. Heldi's *Tracking* must be through the roof after spending the last few weeks hunting for game.

"Healer, archer, and tracker. I'm not sure you even need me around," she said, smiling at the woman. "Care to lead the way?"

"If ye insist."

"Oh, I meant to tell you," Devon said as she stepped in behind the dwarf woman. "Bravlon is a wonderful name for your son."

"So Dorden told ye did he? I've been getting after 'im to have out with it."

"He told me the boy's full name and the history of it, but he didn't share anything about how *you* felt about leaving Coldpass Hold."

Heldi's steps slowed for a moment, and Greel grumbled when he nearly collided with Devon's back. She ignored him.

"It's funny in a way," Heldi said. "Coldpass wasn't my ancestral home. Or even my birth home."

"Oh?" Devon asked.

The dwarf woman turned and gave her a somewhat incredulous look. "Ye do know that a clan is something like a family. I mean, some of the biggest clans are different. They're more like towns. Not the Stoneshoulders, though. Dorden shares a grandpap or grandmatron with most of 'em, great-grandpap at the worst. Garda's one of the few exceptions...she joined up shortly before we left Coldpass."

Devon nodded. "Okay...makes sense."

Heldi paused as if waiting for some other realization to click. As if to help the situation along, Bob swirled down from a small stone outcrop.

"I believe I've heard your kind refer to something called genetic diversity?" the wisp said.

Oh. Right. "You mean *family* family," Devon said. "Brothers and sisters and first cousins."

"I'm not sure what other kind there is," Heldi said, smiling politely.

"Never mind." Devon didn't need to get into her expectation that a game would ignore that kind of stuff for the sake of simplicity. "So where did you live before you became a Stoneshoulder?"

"Ye mean before me ship rescued their foundering raft on the one and only occasion the Stoneshoulders decided to come down from the mountains for a little coastal exploring?"

Devon laughed. "Yes, before that, I suppose."

"I came from a small clan of whalers. It's not an easy life—hardly ever leave our ships to tell the truth. I learned to pull an oar before me mum's buffs wore off. I was born on a northern island called Frostberg. Mum had the fleet pull in just long enough for me summoning, and then we were back out to sea."

"But after you rescued Dorden, you fell in love and decided to stay on land?"

Heldi chuckled. "Of course not. We figured they owed us a measure of gold for the rescue, so a few of us escorted them back to Coldpass. I fell in love with the mountains. Dorden was second."

Devon's heart went out to the woman. "And now you've had to leave those mountains."

Heldi nodded, an aura of melancholy settling over her. "Like I said, it's funny in a way. Coldpass Hold was Dorden's ancestral home. Held by the Stoneshoulders for generations. But I think it's harder for me to let go, maybe because I *chose* it."

Devon met her eyes. "Did you agree with Dorden on the boy's name? I mean, the part where Bravlon is from Stonehaven, not Coldpass Hold?"

Heldi was silent for a long moment. "Well, ultimately it's his choice, just like if we have a daughter, I'll choose what to call her, and the names of her maternal ancestors will come first in her full name. But I think it was the only choice, really. We won't be going back to Coldpass. Not while the starborn remain in the area. So best to do like me mum's clan did when we lost a longboat and crew to an angry whale pod. Hold a wake, carve their names into the bowsprits of our remaining vessels, and sail on."

The woman straightened her shoulders at this, and Devon nodded. "When we establish the mines here, would you enjoy taking some long shifts guarding the mine workings? I don't know what the mountains near Coldpass are like, but these have potential, I should think."

The corners of Heldi's eyes crinkled when she smiled. "I'd like that very much. Whether it's fresh mountain air in his lungs or sea spray on his face, I'd like me boy to have a taste of his heritage as part of his upbringing."

"Then you'll be first in line for guard duty."

"Which," Greel said, "won't be an option unless we deal with the numerous and seemingly insurmountable issues preventing us from establishing said mines..."

Devon took a deep breath and turned an annoyed look on him. "How could I forget? Thank you so much for reminding me."

Shaking her head, Heldi stepped around Devon and Greel, patting the man condescendingly on the shoulder. "Fortunately, we have such a charming interpreter. It shouldn't be any problem to sweet talk the felsen into helping us."

Greel stiffened, clearly trying to work out whether the dwarf was serious. Devon waited until his back was turned to cringe. Yeah...suddenly her plan to have Greel do the talking didn't sound very smart.

The group returned back the way they came, then made an abrupt course change where Heldi—with a slightly smug smile—pointed out the faint tracks Devon had missed. As they hiked, Devon worked through the many problems in her head. The torch gave her the beginnings of an idea. What if they followed Hazel's strategy, but not in the way the scout had intended? Removing a few lights from the tunnel mouths might leave a few orcs caught unawares if and when the poltergeists entered the caves. But it wouldn't exactly wipe out the infestation.

What if *all* the lights were extinguished? Even if the orcs managed to get a few new torches lit, protection would probably be spotty at best. And considering that the tunnels were currently equipped with these ever-burning torches, they might not even *have* spares. It wasn't like orcs were known for their incredible foresight.

As for extinguishing all the lights...as best she could tell, the enchantment on the torches was actively tied to this Orc Shaman-King's magic. Which probably meant that if they could take out the king, they could take out the lights.

...leaving their party in the dark with a bunch of orcs *and* poltergeists.

Okay, so that plan needed work. But it seemed like a decent start, at least compared to Dorden's idea of a straight-out assault on the orc army.

But anyway, back to the situation with their rather unlikable lawyer acting as spokesman for the Stonehaven League...

Devon grimaced. Despite Greel's tendency to act like a complete jerk, it *still* seemed like a good idea to get the felsens' cooperation. Shaking her head, Devon pulled up the attributes section of her character sheet and poured all four attribute points she'd gained at level 17 into *Charisma*. Maybe it would rub off on him or something.

If nothing else, it would help her mana pool. She checked out her stats following the allocation.

Character: Devon (click to set a different character name)
Level: 17
Base Class: Sorcerer
Specialization: Unassigned
Unique Class: Deceiver
Health: 300/300
Mana: 542/542
Fatigue: 42%
Shadowed: 39%

Attributes:
Constitution: 21
Strength: 11
Agility: 17
Charisma: 41
Intelligence: 32
Focus: 13
Endurance: 20

Special Attributes:
Bravery: 7
Cunning: 8

She nodded appreciatively at the growth in her mana pool but cringed at her health. Losing the three *Constitution* points when she'd upgraded her chest armor to the—she rolled her eyes just thinking of the name—*Leather Doublet of Darkness* really hurt there, especially when she didn't have the buff from Tom's *Stonehaven Scramble*.

She stumbled a little bit when she noticed her *Shadowed* stat. Thirty-nine fricking percent? When had *that* happened?

Switching over to her abilities interface, she opened the mystery tab with all the demonic crap. Well, at least that was still grayed out. She was about to close the interface screen when something caught her eye. In amongst the jumble of what appeared to be demonic script, she clearly saw the word *Mist*.

Mist? Mist what? She shook her head. Running her eyes down the page, she picked out a couple more letters from the ordinary alphabet, but no other complete words. Still, the whole thing made her feel...icky. And angry in a way she wasn't used to feeling.

Balling her fists, she flicked the interface away. For about the millionth time, she squelched the urge to send another message to Emerson. He would get back to her when he was able.

For now, they had a really ill-advised diplomatic mission to complete.

***

"It's there," Devon said after they'd walked for another half an hour or so. The spire was just now coming into view from behind an intervening ridge.

"Pardon?" Heldi said, scanning the rocky terrain.

"Through that wide crack in the stone." Devon pointed.

"They live in there?" Heldi looked skeptical.

Greel snorted. "Whatever the conditions inside, they must be rather primitive. A lost race, perhaps, but no longer a lost civilization."

Devon raised an eyebrow. Was he more bitter about his ignorance than she'd let on? She noticed he was blinking more quickly than usual and rubbing his fingers against the meaty base of his thumb. It was almost as if he were...nervous?

"You doing okay, Greel?" she asked.

Conflicted emotions twisted his face. "Okay fine. Since we've been doing so much *sharing* today, I'll admit I don't do well with tight spaces."

She exhaled. Claustrophobia then. She remembered his story about hiding under a pile of dirty straw in a cramped stall in the stable while goblins burned his family's inn. Maybe that was the problem. Or maybe she didn't need to psychoanalyze the NPCs.

"It's a short corridor. The interior of the spire, at the very least, is open to the sky. I don't know about the rest of their home...just saw a few tunnels leading off from the first main room."

The lawyer swallowed. "Well, that's good news at least."

She stopped her hand an inch before it landed on his shoulder—he didn't really seem like the type to want to be comforted. "Does the thought of exploring the orc tunnels bother you, too?"

He shook his head, eyes glued to the dark cleft in the spire. "I'm guessing they're of moderate size. This is different. It's something like a feeling that I could be squashed flatter than a paper contract between a set of legal tomes. In the dark, no less."

Forgetting her earlier hesitation, she clapped him gently on the shoulder. "Well, not to worry, we'll light the hallway up for you."

As she reached for her rucksack and the unsnuffable torch, she hesitated. Actually, it probably wasn't a good idea to bring the magic of the felsen's ancestral enemies into their home. Though it seemed a shame to leave the torch behind, she pulled it out and shoved it into a crack between boulders. "Do me a favor and help me remember this spot, okay, Heldi?"

The dwarf nodded but remained silent. After a moment, she cocked her head. "Did any of ye hear that?"

"Hear what?"

Shaking her head, Heldi pressed her finger to her lips.

A second or two later, stone clattered as, all around, little blue figures stood from hiding spots on either side of their path. They raised sharpened sticks and an unsettling number of short bows.

"Maybe it would have been a good idea to have left that behind earlier," Greel commented as he slowly reached for his knife.

Devon laid a restraining hand on his arm before raising her hands in a gesture of surrender. "Ya think? If such ideas occur to you in the future, please feel free to share them *before* the situation turns sour."

His cheek twitched as he lifted his hands. "I'll try to remember that."

The circle of craglings closed in on the party, their faces twisted in the same fierce scowls Devon remembered from watching them torment the orc. She tried a smile and a quick gesture toward her weapon as if to show she was making no attempt to draw. The movement only made them advance quicker, hints of teeth showing as snarls curled their lips. She suppressed a shudder when she noticed that either the felsen had pointy teeth to begin with, or they filed them that way.

"Ye gonna try to talk to 'em, Greel?" Heldi asked.

"As I explained to our leader, I need a certain amount of exposure to their speech patterns and interaction before I can begin to—"

Devon didn't hear whether he finished his sentence, because something cracked the back of her skull. Hard. The world wavered for a moment, then went gray.

Then black.

You have been knocked unconscious.

Chapter Twenty-Three

DEVON REMEMBERED A headache like this, though at the time, the pain sensitivity had been way out of whack, and it had felt more like her head had been run over by a train. This was more of a dull but persistent discomfort. Still, not pleasant.

She opened her eyes and groaned. Memories of waking up in Hezbek's hut during her first play session wandered into her mind, but soon fled at the sight of rough-hewn stone just a meter or so above her head. Right. Captured by skinny smurfs. Awesome.

She blinked the worst of the blurriness from her eyes and rolled her head to the side. A stone wall stood around a body length away. On a simple three-legged stool, an oil lamp flickered. The air smelled faintly of straw and some sort of cooked food. Vegetables, she thought.

After another couple seconds, Devon realized that while she was lying on some sort of padded shelf, her lower legs hung off the end, and the soles of her sandals touched the floor.

When she sat up, the crown of her head nearly brushed the ceiling.

The room was miniature, sized for a cragling.

Her next two thoughts arrived almost at once. The first was that the situation was awfully Alice in Wonderland. The second was that she hoped Greel wasn't freaking out in the close quarters.

The room had no windows, and a solid wooden door was closed over the only exit. Crouching, she shuffled to it and tried the latch. Unsurprisingly, the door was locked. Devon returned to the bed, which was a stone ledge covered with a thin mattress, roughspun fabric stuffed with straw—judging by the smell and the few yellow stalks poking through the fabric, anyway. Near the head of the bed, a bark cup full of what looked like plain water stood on the floor. Beside it, a wooden plate held a single cooked carrot.

As for her personal items, the craglings had taken her dagger and rucksack. Not a huge surprise.

She sat down and propped her chin on her hands. Okay, so she was a prisoner. Her friends had probably been captured too. But at least they weren't tied to stakes and being poked with spears.

Now what?

She glanced at the door again. There was a small gap between the wood and the floor. Using the glow from the flickering oil lamp, she could probably cast a fire-based *Shadow Puppet*, send it under the door, and *Shadow Step* to the other side. But without knowing what she'd find, she wasn't sure that was the best idea. If the felsen had wanted to kill her, they could have done it while she was unconscious. An escape attempt might change her reputation with them from "we're trying to figure out what to do with you" to "kill on sight."

She glanced again at the carrot and water. Similar to her reasoning about the escape, she didn't think anything would be poisoned unless the craglings had some weird philosophy of not killing directly but being okay with supplying the means for a prisoner to off themselves. That seemed pretty convoluted, but she wasn't that hungry yet so she left the food alone.

After another minute or two spent staring at the wall, she crawled to the door again, and put her eye to the gap at the bottom. Outside, she could see a pool of light from another lamp or torch flickering on stone floor and a pair of bluish feet. A guard, no doubt. She shook her head. It definitely wasn't time to try an escape just yet. If no one had come to her cell in an hour or so, she'd try making some noise to contact the others. In fact...she rotated awkwardly to see farther down the hall. Around fifteen feet away, another door stood closed. Maybe Heldi or Greel was in there. As long as her shadow wasn't noticed skimming across the floor, she could probably *Shadow Step* all the way into the other room. Then again, it would suck if that was actually a guard chamber or something.

Better to be patient for a little while at least.

Returning to the bed, she lay down and stared at the ceiling. It had been a long day in-game, and the events had distracted her from thinking about Tamara. But the idleness brought back her worry for her friend. Even though she knew it would do no good, and if anything, would just give her more to worry about, she opened a web browser and searched on systemic infections. When the first hits scrolled onto her screen, she sucked her lower lip between her teeth. Well. It was a good thing Tamara was strong because the odds were kind of grim. The only thing that seemed like good news was that Tamara had fought through the infection so far. Most people who did succumb died much sooner than two weeks.

Still...she swallowed hard as she brushed the browser away.

Next, she pulled up her messaging app. The people at Tamara's bike shop deserved an update. She looked up the public address for the shop and opened a message.

"This is Tamara's friend, Devon. I saw her. She's unconscious but fighting. Her mom thinks Tamara wouldn't want anyone to see her so weak, so at least it's not a case of her blaming Tam's biking friends. I think she'll allow visitors if we give her a little more time."

She hit send, and since the app was open, she reread her last couple messages to Emerson. There didn't seem to be anything in them that would cause him to ignore her. He probably just didn't know the answers. Thinking of her conclusion that her recent lack of confidence might have to do with Zaa futzing with her unconscious mind, she took a deep breath and dictated a quick message.

"Hey, just checking in. It's okay if you don't know about the shadowed thing. How is stuff going?"

She hit send before she could lose her courage, then turned onto her side and pillowed her head on her arm. For lack of anything better to do, she pulled up Hailey's stream. She smirked to see that the woman was online and streaming, but Hailey's talk of endless ocean sailing certainly hadn't been a joke. The ship was small, single-masted. It looked like Hailey and Chen had decided to crew it themselves, or if there were NPCs or other players, they were below decks or offline. Chen sat on a crate at the front of the vessel, looking exceedingly bored as he cast a fishing line into the gently rolling water.

"I swear we'll hit land today or tomorrow," Hailey called.

"That's what you said yesterday and the day before," Chen said. He had somehow folded his chainmail leggings up over his knees to expose his calves, and his arms were bare. His chainmail shirt lay beside him, leaving just the padded linen underarmor. "I'm kind of thinking I might as well have told my mom and dad to keep my gaming privileges revoked. Maybe tried to stock up on offline time for the next time they're pissed at me."

Hailey sighed. "Oh, come on. When we're the first people to discover a new continent, you'll be glad you came."

"Only if there are hordes of half-elf women waiting to welcome me," Chen said.

"Wait, who has control of your implants? I've never heard you sound interested in some sort of in-game hookup."

He sighed. "I just thought it sounded good. Anyway, back to endless fishing. Care to try a couple casts?"

"Naw, I'd rather keep an eye on the rigging." Turning away from him, she lowered her voice. "I just hope we're not sailing in circles or something."

Closing down the stream, Devon sighed. Doldrums all around it seemed. She closed her eyes and waited for something to happen.

***

Devon was counting cracks in the ceiling when the door opened, and three of her captors entered the room with more snarls and glares, and—unfortunately—some of those pointy sticks she'd been worried about.

"Hey, so we actually just came to talk," Devon said, trying to look friendly. "The thing is, we aren't fans of the orcs either, and I thought maybe we could discuss ways to get rid of our mutual enemy."

Despite the wickedly pointed wooden spears, she put on a smile and shrugged, showing her palms in a "really, this doesn't have to be awkward" sort of way.

One of the felsen, a female, growled low in her throat. It sounded ridiculously like an angry puppy. Devon clamped her jaw shut to avoid laughing. And anyway, when one of the other little blue shits poked her with his stick, piercing the sleeve of her *Leather Doublet of Darkness*, it no longer seemed a laughing matter.

"You should talk to Greel," Devon said. "He's the lawyer who occasionally busts out some Bruce Lee. I'm hoping he can make sense of your language and that we can put this little hiccup in our relations behind us."

Another jab from the stick.

She raised her hands in an echo of the surrender she'd made earlier. "Okay, okay. No more small talk. The problem is, I don't know what you want because I don't speak smurf."

The woman, her tufts of white hair caught in a pair of ridiculous frizzy pigtails that stuck up like donkey ears, rattled off something in their strange language. Devon cocked her head and listened. It was almost like she could get a sense of the particular rhythm in their speech, if not the words.

> **You have discovered a skill in which you have a natural aptitude (4):** Foreign Language Learning.
> **You have gained a skill point:** +1 Foreign Language Learning
> **You have gained a skill point:** +1 Felsen Language
> *Your high intelligence score increases the chance that you will learn new languages. Even so, you have a long way to go before you'll make sense of what the little blue people are saying.*

As Devon made a mental gesture to dispel the messages, the woman, who seemed to be the leader, spat out another sentence. Her followers jumped to either side of Devon and jammed their sticks into her armpits.

"Okay. Jeez."

Lacking other ideas, Devon stood. The blue woman gave a nod. At least their body language had that much in common with humans. Unless in felsen, nodding meant "off with her head" or something. Looking up at Devon's face, which was pretty much parallel to the floor due to Devon's need to bend almost double in the low-ceilinged room, the felsen woman snarled, said something else, and pointed to the door.

"Got it," Devon said. "Me. Door. Out."

Almost as if she understood, the woman grunted in approval. Okay, so that was progress. Kind of.

Out in the hall, Devon was relieved to see her followers, also held at stick-point and scowled at by domineering-looking lady smurfs. The ceiling in the corridor was high enough that Devon could stand fully upright, but she wouldn't be able to jump unless she wanted to be knocked unconscious again. The hallway was maybe a hundred feet long with six or seven rooms on either side. Set in niches carved from the walls, more oil lamps glowed along the length of the passage. At one end, the corridor dead-ended in a wall of blank rock, and at the other, a relatively high archway led into a larger stone chamber with some sort of pool in its center.

"You guys okay?" Devon asked.

Heldi nodded first. "A bit of a headache, but it's fading."

Devon nodded. "Same. I didn't see the blow coming."

Greel snorted at this, which to Devon indicated that he hadn't had *too much* of a claustrophobic freak-out in his little prison cell. "I saw them whack you both with big rocks. Managed to knock a couple out, but fifteen against one is poor odds."

"Well, thanks for trying I guess. And on the bright side, at least we made it into their fortress."

"Though I seem to remember you suggesting there'd be no pointy sticks," Greel said.

"True, but at least we're not tied to stakes."

"Yet," Heldi said, nodding toward the chamber with the pool where, to Devon's considerable dismay, the blue brats were busy setting up at least ten sturdy poles.

"I guess we're not the only guests?" she said. Wincing as her stick-wielders jammed their spears harder into her back, she added, "Hey, so if they have more orc prisoners, make sure to act like you don't like them. I'm hoping this is just a big mix up. I guess if it comes down to it, though, be ready to fight."

"In that case, do you have a plan for the whole tied-to-stakes issue?" Greel asked.

"I'm working on it," Devon said.

Chapter Twenty-Four

BACK IN HIGH SCHOOL, before she'd been kicked out of her mom's place and had been forced to take her GED early so she could get a job to pay for food and shelter, Devon had written an essay on various religious persecutors who had been fond of stake-burning. This situation seemed uncomfortably close to that. Fortunately, the craglings hadn't started piling firewood at their feet, and despite their menacing glares and pointy sticks, they weren't doing her or her followers any real harm. Yet, anyway.

Nonetheless, after standing ramrod straight for the better part of an hour, her spine pressed against the smooth wood of her pole, Devon had a crick in her neck and a burning desire to be done with this crap.

"Anything, Greel?" she asked. In between fits of complaining, the lawyer had been listening attentively to the discourse between the felsen.

"Well, I've confirmed it seems to be a matriarchal society, and I'm beginning to pick up a few particles from their speech."

"So does that mean you know how to say something like 'We come in peace?'"

"I'm still working on 'Hello.'"

Devon sighed. Over the last hour, she'd gained another skill point in *Foreign Language Learning*, but nothing in felsen language itself. When she'd caught a cragling's eye, she'd tried a variety of expressions: smiling, shrugging, and looking pathetic. But so far, it didn't seem she was gaining any real sympathy. As she opened her mouth to ask Heldi how she was faring, a commotion from the front of the chamber cut off her words. The booming voice that sounded uncomfortably close to Dorden's deep rumble filled the hallway.

"Oh no," she heard Heldi mutter.

Devon sighed. Seemed her ears were right.

When the line of captives started to file into the chamber, Devon's heart sank. Not only had the felsen captured the group's remaining two fighters, but they'd also apprehended the miners and Hazel, three basic NPCs who could *not* die here. And—Devon shook her head again—the craglings had also captured the mules and Zoe, who marched with a rope wrapped two or three times around her scrawny neck. What kind of pissed-off did the craglings have to be to take an ostrich prisoner?

"Sorry lass," Dorden said as a cragling started untying him from the string of prisoners. "Sneaky little buggers came down the cliffs behind camp."

Devon nodded. That would make sense, given what she'd learned about their former cliff-dwelling ways. If she'd known the craglings were this aggressive, she might have suggested they move the camp. But that was all hindsight.

Dorden yelped in pain when one of the craglings jabbed his thigh with a spear. Four of the little blue people herded him toward one of the stakes, and he cast a glance at Devon. "So I take it negotiations haven't gone well."

"Unfortunately, we haven't had a chance to talk yet. They seemed to decide we were bad guys before we reached the entrance."

The dwarf shook his head. "Don't ye have some sort of starborn name for people who try to compensate for lack of height by being cruel?"

"You mean a Napoleon complex?" Devon didn't add that the dwarves weren't exactly statuesque. "I've heard of it. Anyway, I just wish we could talk to them. I can't help feeling like they've got the wrong idea about our presence."

"It didn't help that you brought the magical torch of their enemy near their fortress," Greel snarked.

"Shouldn't you be learning how to do your job here?" she returned.

The man snorted.

"So what's the plan, lass?" Dorden asked. "I counted just thirty-two of the wee monsters. Figure we can fight our way out if we have to."

Devon's mouth twisted. "Last-ditch effort only, okay? I don't want to expose Hazel and the miners to the chance of injury."

He nodded, seeming to understand. "Then I say we best do something because I don't like the look of those sticks." He grimaced at the four sharp points which still menaced him while another of the felsen wrapped a rope around his torso and the pole.

Devon nodded. An idea had been brewing, but she wasn't sure it was a good idea. "Progress, Greel?"

The man glared. "You mean since you asked five minutes ago? I think I've figured out the words for mother and ostrich in that time.

Do you think that's enough to go on for delicate negotiations? Or should I keep learning?"

Devon sighed. "Just asking..."

Heldi cleared her throat. "I think we're all a little on edge, here. I don't know about the rest of ye, but this is the first time I've been tied up in a way that makes me feel I'm about to become the evening's bloodsport entertainment."

Something in the woman's words struck a chord with Devon. It was fine and well to wait things out sometimes, but she didn't get the sense that would work here.

"All right," she said. "I have an idea, but if it goes south...be ready to fight, I guess."

"About that," Greel said, shrugging inside his restraints.

Devon pursed her lips. "I'm guessing you have enough health to handle a *Flamestrike* or two, right? I don't think your ropes can."

Greel's eyes widened, but she just shrugged. At least the idea of being actually burned at the stake might figuratively light a fire under his butt.

For now, though, Devon focused on one of the cragling women she'd identified as a tribe leader. Going through the mental gymnastics to cast *Simulacrum*, she manifested a half-sized likeness of an orc beside the woman. The cragling gave another of those weird puppy growls and jumped to the side. She peered at Devon's creation, head cocked, then pointed and said something in her strange language.

You gain spell mastery in Simulacrum: +9%

"Uh..." Heldi said, squinting at the somewhat amorphous shape. "What's that supposed to be, lass?"

"Give me a minute," Devon said, dispelling the illusion. She cast it again, then again banished the somewhat shapeless blob, and finally poured mana into a third conjuring.

You gain spell mastery in Simulacrum: +14%
Congratulations! You have learned a new spell: Simulacrum - Tier 2.
Your creations now have a reasonable resemblance to the figures you wish to imitate. Creatures of mid to high intelligence will reliably recognize the images you wish to convey, but they will realize they are seeing an illusion. Creatures of low intelligence will be unable to distinguish your creations from reality.

Devon sighed in relief. She'd known she was close to getting enough mastery for the next tier, but she wasn't sure whether the game would actually give it to her in this situation. Dispelling the tier 1 illusion, she cast the spell one more time.

"Ah! You've improved," Heldi said as the half-sized orc materialized beside the now thoroughly confused cragling woman. When she recognized the little figure as a representation of her enemy, her face went nearly purple, and she whirled on Devon's group.

"Now or never," Devon muttered. With another mental twist, she summoned a life-sized *Simulacrum* of Dorden and commanded it to swing at the illusory orc. The orc stumbled back, fell to the ground, and blinked out as Devon dispelled its spell effect. Silence held in the chamber as she commanded Dorden's illusion to go down on a knee beside the felsen matriarch. The woman stared, thoughts clearly working. After a moment, she spun back toward Dorden and said something in her rapid-fire speech. The dwarf shrugged and pointed at Devon.

"You know," Greel said. "I think you're onto something."

"Oh? I don't see them running over to hug us."

He shook his head. "I mean, I think this is the key to me learning their language fast enough to get us out of this. I figured out the word orc, and something about magic. Can you conjure something else?"

"Such as?"

The lawyer furrowed his brow in concentration. "Let's start with the basics. Can you draw a plate of food?"

Devon pressed her lips together as she cast the illusion. It seemed a long way to go from figuring out basic vocabulary to negotiating an alliance, but she might as well let Greel run with the idea.

***

A few hours later, Devon and her friends were getting noticeably fewer puncture wounds, and Greel was speaking gibberish that sounded like he had a mouthful of rubber bands. Devon wasn't sure whether the craglings actually understood him, but they seemed to get the idea that he was trying.

Fortunately—or maybe unfortunately, since now all she had to do was stand there like a Salem witch—he no longer needed her illusions. Devon yawned and leaned forward, testing the ropes. Nope. Still tied.

Targeting the matriarch, she used a *Combat Assessment.*

Felsen Headwoman - Level 20
Health: 534/534
Mana: 981/981

Devon's eyebrows rose. A caster, huh? The woman didn't look nearly strong enough to be level 20, but it was probably that kind of thinking on the part of potential rivals that gave the felsen their Napoleon complexes in the first place. And she *had* known from the lore that the race was capable of magic...not to mention her firsthand experience with their curse.

"Can you ask them about me warhammer yet?" Dorden asked.

Greel gave him an annoyed glance. "I'm currently working on upgrading us from 'candidates for ritual sacrifice' to 'tolerated guests.'"

"I'm just saying...it's in their interest, too. You saw how Agavir pummeled that miniature orc flat."

"Yes," the lawyer said, "what an infallible argument. Our sorceress created a little theater production where imaginary Dorden slew an imaginary, half-sized brute. Proof positive."

Dorden grumbled something under his breath but didn't continue the argument.

A few more exchanges passed between Greel and their captors before, quite abruptly, a young felsen man gibbered something then pulled a stone knife from his belt and ran at Devon, pointy teeth bared. Panicking, she threw down a *Wall of Ice,* which the cragling slammed into. The blue man's eyes rolled in his head and he staggered away. A hush fell over the chamber as the felsen turned to Devon, then...fell to their knees?

"Just when I convinced them...wait...what's this?" Greel said.

The craglings began to chant.

"Uh..." Devon said. "Translation?"

"An ancient form. I can't quite make sense of it. Something about a phoenix?"

"A what?"

"A type of bird which is reborn, often in fire after—"

"Yes, I know what a phoenix is. Are they...this isn't some kind of boss mob summoning is it?"

Greel cocked his head, and after a moment, he shook it. "I don't think so. There's something about ice."

"Okay, that part makes sense. I did just create some."

The lawyer blinked, then abruptly laughed. "Oh, Veia's breath, this is ripe."

"What?"

"Apparently, you figure prominently in some sort of prophecy."

She shook her head. Not again. Wasn't the Champion of Ishildar thing enough work for the time being? "And what am I supposed to do?"

"Seems the idea is that only she of icy heart can bring Ishildar from the ashes."

Oh...so this was the *same* prophecy. Well, at least there was that. But she wouldn't exactly call her heart *icy*. Jeez.

"So the phoenix thing is a metaphor?"

Greel cocked his head, listening. "Not exactly. Look, they're going on and on about this, but I think they want you to bathe in the phoenix fire and return twenty feathers as proof you are the champion they seek."

She sighed her head as a popup appeared.

> **Quest Updated:** Crossbow Crisis
> *You know, phoenix feathers might fletch some awesome arrows.*
> **Bonus Reward:** If the 20 required feathers come from a phoenix, 20 x Infinite Arrows - automatically return to your quiver 20 seconds after being shot.

Devon raised her eyebrows as she read then dismissed the message. "So Greel, does their chant mention anything about how I'm supposed to *find* this fire?"

The lawyer shouted in his rubber-band-mouth voice, and the chanting slowly stopped. Solemnly, the matriarch stood. She approached Devon and spoke haltingly.

"We take you fire."

> **Perlda is offering you a quest:** Trial by Fire
> *The felsen will lead you somewhere to do something with a phoenix that includes collecting its feathers (possibly after being burned alive).*
> **Objective:** Gather 20 phoenix feathers.
> **Reward:** +700 reputation with the felsen tribe
> **Reward:** 34000 experience
> **Accept?** Y/N

"Wait, you speak English?" Devon asked as she accepted the quest.

The woman rolled her eyes. "Would have speak earlier if you not call me smurf. Don't know word. Don't like."

Chapter Twenty-Five

"HEY," EMERSON DICTATED. "Sorry I've been out of contact. Vacation. Company thought I deserved a little relaxation. Anyway, what do you think of..." He paused and deleted that sentence. "I've been using a video chat program lately. Going with the company's suggestion and reconnecting with some old friends. Feel like contacting me there?"

He dropped a link to an ancient v-chat app and added some markup so that Devon would have his contact if she installed it on a tablet or augmented-reality glasses. The question was, would she read between the lines and follow his lead? She knew about the trouble with Penelope. Sort of, anyway. It wasn't that big of a stretch to conclude that Zaa's programmer had done something to sabotage Emerson's reputation with the management, and that the vacation was anything but.

With a deep breath, he sent the message. If it turned out, by some miracle, she viewed him as more than her liaison with the company...if she had an inkling that they might at least be friends, hopefully he hadn't just ruined it by letting on that he was kind of in the shithouse as far as E-Squared was concerned. He didn't *think* she was the kind of woman who cared about how good of a programmer he was.

Actually—he snorted and shook his head—what kind of woman was that? If the women he met valued what an amazing programmer he was, he wouldn't have all this anxiety about talking to one of their kind. He'd either be a sleazy womanizer type, or he'd be in some nice relationship filled with mutual respect for each other's elite skills.

Instead, he was in an Atlanta rental duplex where the air conditioner rattled and the shag carpet was an awful shade of bleached maroon. He was working with the shades drawn, not because he was worried people would look in, but because the LEDs on his voltmeter were hard to see in bright light. On the table before him was a styrofoam head with eyes drawn in Sharpie by the previous owner.

He fussed with the hairpiece on top of the white skull, lifting the section that would go behind the right ear if the styrofoam head had ears, and threading another strand of copper wire into the fabric mesh that underpinned the actual hair of the wig.

When his tablet gave a soft *ping*, he jumped, sending a wire stripper skidding off the table and nearly upsetting the head. With a deep breath to steady himself, he pulled the device over.

Incoming video chat: @devon_walker.

His eyes went as wide as the Sharpie illustration on the skull. Shit. He hadn't expected her to get back to him that quickly.

Scanning the room, he grimaced at the tacky wallpaper and the godawful chandelier-thing with pink plastic crystals. This place looked like some rundown bordello or something. True, he could have avoided the mistake by actually doing the virtual walkthrough before booking the rental, but the truth was he didn't usually care about decor. At least not when he planned to spend his time glued to a screen or infiltrating the coma wing of the local hospital.

Anyway, he was an idiot for sending the video chat invite without thinking about his environment. An idiot in dire need of a shave and a clean t-shirt.

But he couldn't just ignore Devon's chat request when he'd messaged her less than ten minutes ago. Scooping up the tablet, he sprinted for the kitchen where the lighting was still tacky—LED strands like those Christmas icicle things, but hung so they absolutely covered the ceiling and dangled in front of the cabinets.

Stained cabinets with delaminating wood veneer and some stickers of 1940s pinup girls. Shit.

The tablet pinged again.

He shrugged and shook his head as he slid onto a barstool beside the pass-through counter that formed a boundary with what was probably a living room at some point. Pulling off his shielding cap, he ran his hand through his hair, then hesitated. Wear the cap and look like a fool or expose himself to Penelope's evil code?

He pulled the cap back over his head. It wasn't like he was trying to impress her. Or was he? Shit. Emerson knew jack all about women. He basically knew jack all about anything besides the latest coolest white papers from AI researchers and the best ten places to get coffee if his machine happened to break.

After running his face through a couple smile-frown cycles to try to head off any awkward twitches, he took a deep breath and clicked accept. Devon's face appeared on his screen. She was squinting and looked really confused.

"Hello? Are you there, Emerson?"

He swallowed. "Hey, yeah. Can you hear me?"

She nodded. "But I just see a black rectangle."

Ah hell. Of course, the small black box in the corner of *his* view should have been a clue. "Just a minute. Forgot I taped over the camera."

A couple little wrinkles formed between her eyebrows. "Taped...why—wait, is it one of those security things?" Her eyes went back and forth from the center of the screen to somewhere a few inches higher, likely the pinhole camera on the top edge of her tablet.

After another smile-frown cycle, Emerson swallowed and pulled the piece of electrical tape off his camera.

Devon blinked in recognition, then smiled and waved. "Hey," she said.

Emerson fumbled for words before finally saying, "Hey back."

"Should I be covering my camera too?" she asked. Almost as if self-conscious, though Emerson couldn't see what reason she had to be worried, she tucked a strand of hair behind her ear then fluttered her hand away from her face.

He shook his head. "Security is much better on device sensors than it used to be. Unless you're working for the government or a financial institution, I wouldn't worry about it."

She chewed the corner of her lip. "But you do."

"Paranoid delusions, I guess," he said with a shrug and a self-effacing smile. As she hesitated, probably trying to decide whether or not he was kidding, he fought the urge to explain that he was just trying to make a joke. That typically just made things worse.

After a moment, she smiled. "I get it. I think. So...I got the idea you wanted to avoid using messenger."

Right. Straight to business. At least he'd been right to guess that she'd be clever enough to understand his subtext. "Yeah. So here's the deal. I'm sort of...cut out of the company decisions right now."

She cocked her head. "What do you mean?"

"Penelope must have trumped up some evidence that convinced management I needed forced time off. They think I was careless with the code base. Stress-driven or something."

"Why didn't you didn't just explain what she's been doing? I mean...it seems beyond illegal to use our brains while we're sleeping."

He sighed, feeling a whole lot like a failure. How could he explain that none of his attempts to draw attention to Penelope's failings had done anything but piss Bradley Williams off? That he was afraid he'd get himself actually-fired rather than temporarily-fired if he pushed too much without hard evidence?

Or maybe the fear went deeper. Maybe he was afraid that an accusation would snowball in ways he couldn't control? Veia was his prized creation, and if he went about this in the wrong way, he could lose her completely.

He swallowed, clenching his fists out of sight of the camera. Coward's justifications, every one of them. Devon deserved the truth.

"I guess...I guess when you put it that way, it's harder to justify. But I suppose I'm worried I might not be listened to, so I want to be as thorough as possible."

She seemed to consider this information, nodding slowly. At the very least, she didn't seem angry. "And you think Penelope is watching your messenger account?"

"Maybe. Theoretically, if she were determined, it wouldn't be much harder to snoop on a video chat app than a text messenger. Except that my handle is associated with E-Squared, and we have a partnership with the messenger company. I could have created a secondary account that Penelope didn't know about, but sometimes..."

"Sometimes a little face time gets things across without chance of misinterpretation?"

He nodded. "Pretty much."

"I prefer to interact in-game or in-person for the same reasons."

He shrugged, glad she understood. "So..."

"So..." she echoed.

"How are you feeling? My associate at Entwined was concerned about residue from Zaa's interference."

"Residue?"

"They ran some experiments that made her concerned about removing people from the sleep-stimulation too quickly."

A sudden look of comprehension came over her face. "The shadowed stuff. If there were some kind of residue, could the game figure out a way to...I don't know, add it to the play experience?"

"No, but..." Emerson blinked as her words prompted an idea. Maybe she was still receiving content from Zaa—only this time, to her conscious rather than her unconscious mind. The game wasn't magic. The things she experienced still had to be created by software and data. Devon was only shielded from unauthorized access when she wore the hat to sleep. There was little reason to think Penelope's code and AI would stop accessing her mind when she'd proved herself such a useful resource. He shook his head, disappointed in himself. It should have occurred to him right away.

"I think you're right. But...I think this is good news. If I can provide proof that Zaa is still communicating with you, that violates the philosophy of competition between AIs. You aren't supposed to be assigned to both."

"But we already knew her AI accessed my brain, right? That's what your packet sniffing was for."

"I have the logs, but live data strengthens my case. Between you and..." Emerson hesitated. At this point, it seemed stupid to keep Owen's situation from her. "Listen, there's something else. Your guildmate Owen is—I'm afraid whatever switch allowed your subconscious mind to become dominant while receiving Zaa's data...I think the same process has happened to Owen. Only he hasn't flipped back, and it's made him very ill."

Devon's eyes had gone wide. "Is he okay?"

"I think he will be. But right now...he's unconscious. Obviously, this sort of thing could ruin both E-Squared and Entwined. Frankly, they probably deserve it."

"Holy crap," she whispered. "That's awful. You're right, it could ruin the companies. And if that happens, then Relic Online..."

"Yeah. Shut down. I honestly don't know what the answer is. Penelope is the real problem here. But the fact that management let it happen will deep-six everything if it's not resolved properly."

"Shit," Devon said. She looked absolutely stricken at the notion. "It would be like killing..." She seemed too devastated to finish her sentence, which made Emerson want to reassure her that it would be okay. The problem was, he wasn't sure it would.

"So it's tricky," he said, realizing he was stating the obvious. "My priority has to be Owen's health, but beyond that, I'm hoping there's a way to lay the blame where it belongs."

He didn't mention that he still had a faint hope that Owen's condition wasn't Relic Online's fault. It was an isolated case, and he was too much of a data geek to ignore that the lack of a pattern could mean his theory about Zaa causing the coma could be bogus. But he didn't want to sugarcoat things too much either, not after hiding the truth for too long as it stood.

"What can I do?" Devon said.

"That packet sniffer on your router. Do remember how I had you disable it?"

She nodded.

"For starters, let's re-enable it. We should be able to capture any data that's sent to Zaa's servers. I'll keep you updated about Owen."

"Okay," she said, nodding. "How long do you think?"

"Before?"

"Sorry, I meant before the software is fixed."

He sighed. "Well, that's complicated. Miriam at Entwined thinks she can have the patch in a couple weeks. But then she has to convince her management to push it out. And there's some concern that an abrupt change could damage Owen. I'm working on figuring that out."

Devon chewed a thumbnail, then seemed to notice what she was doing and dropped her hand. "I'm guessing you weren't supposed to tell me this."

Emerson shrugged. "Yeah, probably not."

"Well, it's not like I have anyone to tell. But do me a favor."

"Yeah?"

"Stay in touch, okay?"

Emerson exhaled. "Of course. Talk to you soon."

"Yup. I'm usually offline by 11:30 every night. Feel free to call."

"I will."

Chapter Twenty-Six

A FULL SHUTDOWN of Relic Online?

Devon couldn't even think about it. It would basically be killing every NPC that inhabited the world. Gone, just like that. Of course, from the perspective of the companies, the mobs weren't alive. But Devon knew better. They had just as many hopes and dreams and desires as anyone.

She squeezed her forehead between thumb and ring finger. But if the technology had taken full control over Owen...that was like...it was about as illegal and immoral as things got.

She understood and had come to terms with the fact that Zaa had interacted with her sleeping mind, using her subconscious to play the game. Though the notion disturbed her, she'd even accepted that her subconscious had assumed supremacy over her conscious mind for a long play session, the switch somehow triggered by the interface between her implants and her mind. But her conscious mind had won out, and her demon self had been slain. It sounded like whatever was happening to Owen was like her demon experience magnified a thousand-fold.

Christ.

Pulling the cellophane off of a microwave dinner, she curled her lip at the somewhat freezer-burned contents. Hopefully it would still taste okay. She popped the container into the microwave and started it cooking while grabbing a beer. It was only 8 PM, far earlier than she'd planned to log off. But after the emotions of the day, both her discovery of Tamara's condition and the group's capture by the felsen, she'd felt exhausted enough to sleep so had figured it would be a good time to go offline. The party had been freed from the poles and escorted to bedchambers large enough for average humans, and everyone seemed okay with taking twenty-four hours to recover while Devon got her real-world rest in.

But now she had this to think about. Hopefully, Emerson's revelations wouldn't keep her awake.

The microwave beeped, and she took the food out.

"Ew," she muttered. Maybe microwave meatloaf wasn't the best idea.

In any case, it needed a minute to cool, so she pulled her tablet out and followed the steps to connect to the network router. Emerson was right; re-enabling the packet sniffer was a simple matter of reversing the steps she'd taken to turn it off. She flipped the switch, drank a couple swallows of her beer, and laid her head down on the table.

A deep sigh pressed her collarbones against the edge of the wood. This real-world crap sucked. If only she could just live in the game. Bathing in phoenix fire sounded a whole lot better than dealing with actual life.

***

Devon gave one last glance down into the central opening of the felsen's hollowed-out spire. Her friends watched from below while she filed up a narrow, spiraling path hewn from the inner wall of the stone pedestal. Two of the craglings, including Perlda, the headwoman, walked ahead of her, and two more followed behind.

Actually, they weren't really walking. It was more like scampering. Meanwhile, Devon edged forward with one shoulder jammed against the wall. While the surface of the path was relatively flat, the smurfs had carved the trail for creatures of their size and comfort with heights.

Devon's only hope was that if she fell, her cast timer on *Levitate* would finish before she smashed into the ground.

"See ye soon, lass," Dorden shouted when, finally, Devon made the final corkscrewing trip around the spire's interior and reached the point where the trail emptied onto the rim of the pedestal.

Not that reaching the rim made her feel any better. Now, sheer walls fell away on both sides.

"Just an elevated sidewalk," she said to herself as she shuffled along behind Perlda. Where the spire joined the larger rock formation, a massive stone pinnacle that scratched the layer of clouds swirling over the crags, the craglings stopped and gathered in a loose cluster. The wall of jagged stone loomed above them.

Devon stared up at the sheer wall. "You know, I'm not the most surefooted person. I had a potion in my rucksack...*Monkey's Agility?*"

Perlda stared at her for a long moment. "Champion not need potion."

Devon groaned. Really? And if she started a rock slide that pulled her escorts off the cliff? Or for that matter, if she fell and swept them off with her?

"Well, lead on, I guess." Devon said with a grimace.

The woman looked at her, lips pressed into a thin line. "No. You go alone."

"Alone? Where?"

Perlda pointed up the crag's face. "To top."

"You mean that pointy bit that's in the clouds?"

The woman nodded. "There find phoenix. There face fire. Feathers. Is champion."

With that, the craglings turned and marched back toward the spiraling path.

"Wait," Devon called. The felsen didn't even look back. Soon enough, they disappeared beneath the hollow pedestal's rim, leaving Devon alone at the base of the massive rock wall.

"Okay, no problem," she muttered. "I'll just climb this ten-thousand-foot sheer cliff with no gear and no food and no water, and when I get to the top, I'll face this mythical phoenix, which is probably some sort of boss. And then I'll come back and hope you little blue shits will actually help us."

Before starting up, Devon inspected the imposing rock face above her. Well, the first part anyway. For the initial few feet, a faint trail wound between humps of rock then traversed up and to the right on an alarmingly narrow ledge. From there, scuff marks in the lichen suggested that the route climbed a vertical step about twice her height. After that, though...she shook her head. The words *death wish* came to mind. Just in case she'd forgotten a critical advantage she might have, she pulled up her list of skills.

Tier 1
Unarmed Combat: 3
Tracking: 8

Stealth: 2
Sprint: 8
Bartering: 6
Manual Labor: 7
Foraging: 1
Animal Taming: 1
Foreign Language Learning: 2
Felsen Language: 1

Tier 2:
One-handed Slashing: 14
One-handed Piercing: 16
Combat Assessment: 10
Darkvision: 11
Leadership: 10

Special Skills:
Improvisation: 5

Nope. No climbing expertise. Okay then...

She set a foot on the path, tested the placement of her sandal to ensure that it was stable, then committed her weight.

Devon exhaled. One step down, ten thousand to go.

Actually...

Maybe she didn't actually have to climb. With a mental twist, she started casting her tier 1 *Levitate* spell. Tier 2 made her hover higher, which was not what she wanted right now. She grinned, feeling pleased with herself as her feet lifted from the ground.

Devon glanced down and had a moment to wonder why the terrain beneath her was sliding.

"Oh shit. No, that's me!"

She banished the *Levitation* effect just moments before the slope would have sent her falling back down into the felsen's spire. As her feet hit the ground, she crumpled and slapped her palms onto the bare stone to reassure herself.

Okay, so *Levitate's* lack of friction was great for kiting mobs with a knockback effect. Not so great for mountain climbing.

"Scratch that idea," she muttered in a shaky voice. As she gathered her wits in preparation to stand back up, she heard a faint tinkling noise. Moments later, Bob popped from a fissure in the stone face and drifted down to her.

"So you make fairy noises now too?" she asked.

"I've always had the ability. I simply decided to use it to keep from scaring you off the ledge."

"It suits you," she said.

Bob booped her nose. "Why do I get the feeling that wasn't a compliment?"

Devon chose not to respond, and instead stood and shuffled toward the foot of the cliff again.

Bob zipped in front of her. "Wishing you'd invested in *Strength* and *Agility* rather than worrying about your looks?"

Once again, Devon peered up at the mist-shrouded pinnacle. "For your information, *Charisma* is about more than physical appearance."

"Said every game designer and dungeon master since the dawn of time. Face it, gorgeous, you wanted to look smoking."

"I did not! *Charisma* is the major contributor to my mana pool."

Bob made a small circle in the air, the wisp's version of an eye roll. "Don't you have a phoenix to slay or something?"

"Actually, I have twenty feathers to retrieve. I'm hoping no slaying is necessary."

Devon once again placed her foot carefully onto the steep trail. Grabbing hold of a solid-looking hunk of rock, she carefully committed her weight and stepped her next foot up higher. A few teetering steps later, she'd reached the terrifying ledge she needed to cross. For a moment, she debated whether to face the rock or face outward. She thought back to all the climbing photos and movies she'd seen and decided to face in. At least that way she wouldn't be able to see how far down the drop went.

Inch by inch, she edged out along the narrow shelf. The ledge itself was around nine inches wide, enough to put her whole foot on a flat surface in most places. Still, she clung to little rails and bucket-shaped handholds so hard that her knuckles blanched.

You have gained a skill point: +1 Climbing.
Well, you had to learn sometime, right? Just don't look down.

Of course, the reminder prompted her to glance under her armpit at the sheer drop below. The traversing ledge had cleared the rim of the spire, and now nothing but a dizzying cliff punctuated by jagged stone spires stood between her and the boulder field far below. Devon clamped her eyes shut and pressed her cheek against the cool rock while a wave of vertigo swamped her.

"It does get easier," Bob whispered in an uncharacteristic gesture of kindness.

"Says the glowing ball who can fly," Devon muttered as she started traversing again.

After another ten or twenty feet, she reached the end of the ledge and looked up at the nearly vertical step that stood between her and the next flat area. She sucked in a deep breath and exhaled slowly. Her heart slammed against her ribs, feeling almost as if it would rattle her off her perch. Gritting her teeth, she felt around until her hand landed on a flat hold with a slight incut for her fingertips. When she found a similar grip for her other hand, she looked down and searched for some sort of platforms for her feet. Her right toe slid onto a small sloping edge. Holding her breath, she pulled up and paddled at the wall with her other foot until it caught.

Again, she searched until she found handholds. Again, she scraped leather soles against the rock until her feet found somewhere to grip. Hand, hand. Foot, foot. One painstaking move at a time, she crept toward the oasis of flatness above.

Would this be a good time to ask you to roll initiative?

Devon stiffened as the message flashed into view. "To do what?"

Dungeons & Dragons joke. Before your time, maybe. But hey:
You have gained a skill point: +1 Climbing.

After what felt like another three hours, but which had only been five minutes according to her game clock, Devon flopped onto the ledge like a porpoise jetting from the water onto the beach. She lay motionless except for her heaving breath, her cheek pressed to the stone.

Bob drifted down to rest on the rock in front of her face. "Congrats. You're at least 1/1000th of the way up."

"I get it. Just give me a minute, okay?"

***

An hour or so later, Devon sat on the rim of a sidewalk-sized ledge, feet dangling over the drop. She took a deep swallow from her waterskin and looked over the scenery. From here, she could see all the way down to the savanna and jungle and sprawled ruin of Ishildar. Birds circled on thermals above the flatlands, while up in the crags, little darting swallows flew in and out amongst the spires.

Devon was feeling downright pleased. Sure, this hadn't started all that well, but at this point she had to admit that her climbing was almost competent. From this height, the landscape looked more like a model than real terrain. Or maybe it was like the view from an airplane. Not that she'd ever flown, but she had seen pictures. The notion that she could fall and fall and fall before hitting the ground had been rendered somewhat abstract by the tremendous height.

In fact, she could almost claim to be enjoying this.

She smirked. Once Tamara recovered, she'd have to hear all about Devon's death-defying ascent.

Standing, she shouldered her rucksack and scrambled to the back edge of the ledge. There, she fit the fingers of one hand into a narrow vertical crack and twisted, the torque jamming them in place. Her *Climbing* skill was now 8, nearing tier 2, and it had gotten easier and easier to find holds and move gracefully. Pulling up with one hand and using the other for balance, she pasted her toes onto small sloping knobs of rock. Her free hand grabbed a line of crystals no wider than the first pad of her fingers. Clamping down, she pulled up and freed her fingers from the crack below. With a big reach and a small lunge, she grabbed for the top edge of a thick rock flake.

As she committed weight to the new hold, a grating sound rose from deep in the stone. Suddenly, the flake exploded from the wall, coming off in her hand and jarring her shoulder before she released her grip. The massive plate of rock whirled away, careening down and smashing against a small pinnacle far below in a puff of dust.

Devon swung out like a door on loose hinges, her right hand and right toes clinging desperately while she whined through clenched teeth and watched the scenery rotate around her.

Swaying back, she managed to get enough purchase for her left hand to avoid swinging out again.

Panting, Devon laid her forehead against the rock. After a moment, she looked up. Where before, the rock face had seemed solid, now she saw many more loose blocks and unstable flakes.

Gingerly, she reversed her moves back down to the resting spot where she'd taken her water break. Sinking to a crouch, she put her head between her knees.

That had been way, way, way too close.

"Nice save," Bob said after a moment.

Devon couldn't speak, so she just nodded. The notion of falling had *seemed* abstract, but apparently that had just been a story she'd told herself. Faced with an imminent plunge, it had seemed pretty damn real.

Pressing her lips into a thin line, she looked up again. Crap. She had to do something about the loose rock because the cliff to either side of the path she'd intended was too sheer even for her 8 skill points in *Climbing*.

An idea started to form. After a moment, she nodded. It might work.

Devon insta-cast a sun-based *Shadow Puppet* and sent it up the wall. When it reached the area of unstable-looking rock, she forced it into cracks and crevices, then ducked beneath a slight overhang while she commanded her puppet to expand. With a roar, the cliff face above gave way, releasing a massive rockfall and dust cloud. Stones whistled as they plunged hundreds of feet to the distant scree. Booms echoed through the mountains as falling stone exploded on the ground below.

When silence once again returned, Devon peeked out from beneath the overhang and shook her head. Her *Shadow Puppet* had pried enough stone to fill a school bus from the face, exposing clean white granite beneath.

You have gained a special skill point: +1 Improvisation.

She exhaled through pursed lips and started climbing again, vowing to be more careful.

After another few hours of cautious ascent, occasionally broken to blast a few more loose sections from the wall, she finally climbed into the fog. The angle of the cliff eased back until she was walking on a sharp ridge, only occasionally dropping a hand for balance.

Finally, an actual trail emerged from the bare stone. She walked along it for a good fifteen minutes before glimpsing the red glow in the mist. A melodic screech echoed through the fog. Devon edged closer until finally, she spotted the flaming plumage of the phoenix.

Connection lost.

Devon shook her head as, abruptly, her apartment snapped into view. She fell back into her implants, pulling the Relic Online icon forward.

Connection refused. Your account has been suspended. You may not play Relic Online at this time.

Chapter Twenty-Seven

OWEN'S GIRLFRIEND, CYNTHIA, was waiting in the hospital atrium when Emerson arrived. She wore a dress that was probably fashionable—not that Emerson could tell the difference—carried a leather purse and looked at him with something between horror and shock.

"Did I suggest you replace the shiny hat thing?" she asked. "Because I take that back."

"What's wrong with it?" Emerson asked, patting his new wig.

"Here's the thing about fashion and hairstyles," Cynthia said. "They go in cycles, right? Something that was cool in the 2020s will be awesome again in the 60s or something. But there are a few situations where that doesn't apply. Including mullets. There's a reason they haven't come back since the 1980s."

Emerson tugged on the long ringlets that tickled his neck. "A...mullet?"

Cynthia nodded, a grim expression on her face. "They had a saying. Business in the front. Party in the back."

Emerson muttered the words to himself. He still didn't really see what the problem was. It wasn't like he was wearing a Mohawk or anything. "I needed extra covering to make sure the electromagnetic shielding accounted for the implant circuitry on the back of my neck."

Cynthia nodded and sighed, hiking her purse higher. "Whatever the case, we don't have long before Owen's family shows up for their regular visit. Shall we?"

With one last concerned look at his hairpiece, the woman turned and headed for a bank of elevators. Emerson tucked his backpack against his ribs and followed, scalp itching from the plastic netting and reflective foil beneath his false hair. Hair that he had been somewhat proud of until Cynthia got a look at it. It had just seemed so *practical* to trim the front so he could see better while leaving the back long to conceal his circuitry. And anyway, he'd heard the worst style ever was something called a "man bun." In comparison, he couldn't see what fault anybody could take with this cut.

Too soon, they reached the door to Owen's room. All along, he'd understood in an intellectual way that his player was very sick and that E-Squared was probably at fault. But seeing Owen hooked up to tubes and sensors and lying utterly motionless brought it all home.

Emerson stopped in the doorway and stared, suddenly paralyzed with the severity of the situation. After a moment, Cynthia nudged him.

"Clock's ticking," she said.

Nodding, Emerson pulled out the potted plant he'd been carrying in his backpack. Cynthia curled her lip and shook her head at the ragged foliage.

"It's not like plants are contraband," she said. "You could have spared the poor thing that torture."

Pressing his lips together, Emerson nodded. Another good point. As he tiptoed into the table near the window, he reached under the pot and extended the flexible antenna connected to the wireless bridge that was concealed beneath a thin layer of soil in the pot. He set the plant on the table, then adjusted the antenna so that it was hidden from view, dangling over the back side of the table. After taking a seat in one of the nearby chairs, he pulled out his tablet and connected to the bridge.

Searching for connection...
Secure wireless Internet found: Piedmont Atlanta Hospital.

Emerson entered some commands to instruct the device to begin intrusion attempts. It would take a few hours for the router to crack the password and begin intercepting and duplicating the traffic between Owen's implants and the RO servers. But now that the sniffer was in place, he'd be able to interact with it remotely. With a nod, he leaned over and opened his rucksack, preparing to replace his tablet and pack up. As he slid it into the sleeve, an alert lit up the screen.

He pulled the device back out and blinked in surprise at the video chat request from Devon.

Cynthia, who had been watching over his shoulder, shook her head. "Not on my time," she said.

With a nod, Emerson selected an option to send a canned response that would let Devon know he'd call her back ASAP, then slid the tablet into his bag and stood.

As he zipped his pack closed, a nurse stepped into the room.

Cynthia stiffened as the nurse's eyes widened.

"The family was adamant," the nurse said.

Cynthia's hand shook just a little as she tucked a springy strand of hair behind her ear. "It's okay. I talked to them about bringing our friend Reggie by. They were college roommates."

The nurse's eyes narrowed. "I checked the visitor's log. You didn't sign him in."

Cynthia tugged on her purse strap as if frustrated with herself. "Damn. I can't believe I forgot again."

Shaking her head, the nurse stepped to the bedside and started examining the machinery. "You'd better get out there and update the logs before the hourly check. Admin is taking those lawyers very seriously."

Lawyers? Emerson clenched his jaw while hurrying to Cynthia's side. He cast one last glance at Owen as they quickly stepped from the room.

"Come on," Cynthia hissed.

Emerson swallowed and sped up.

Once inside the elevator, Cynthia glared. "I don't know why I let you talk to me into this. His parents are going to be pissed when they hear I brought someone. For all I know, they'll revoke my visitor status."

"I can fix it," Emerson said.

"Oh really?" she asked, pushing the button for the ground floor. "Apparently, you don't know his parents."

Emerson's stomach rose into his throat as the elevator started descending. "Email me their messenger handles. I'll spoof something from you and backdate it."

"That'll work?"

He tried to look convincing. He hadn't actually spoofed something like that before, but if script kiddies in Russia could do it, it couldn't be that hard, right?

Before he could answer, Cynthia shook her head. "Don't worry about it. Sometimes I think I need to stand up to them more anyway."

The elevator chimed, and the doors opened to reveal the atrium.

"Those lawyers...are they E-Squared?"

Cynthia snorted. "That might actually be better. How much do you know about Owen's parents?"

He shrugged. "Nothing, I guess."

She smirked. "Well, I suppose it's enough to say that they aren't having any trouble covering the hospital bills."

"Rich, huh?"

"That might be the biggest understatement of the year. Suffice to say, they're probably as interested in keeping his current state out of the public eye as E-Squared is. Can't have the governor's son showing any flaws, right? Especially the kind that might indicate a medical condition that might be inherited from his father."

Owen hadn't said a thing about his family's political ties. Emerson shook his head in shock as he stepped from the elevator. Well, this complicated things...

"So we're done here?" Cynthia asked as he turned to face her.

"I imagine they'll throw out the pot when the plant dies, and I doubt it will live long. But if they don't, I'll need you to remove it in a couple days."

She nodded. "You'll let me know as soon as we can do something about his situation, right?"

"Ten days. Two weeks, tops."

With a brisk nod, she stepped back into the elevator and pushed the button. "I'll do my best to deal with his family until then."

Chapter Twenty-Eight

DEVON PACED THE length of her apartment from the small bathroom to the front window and back. Bars of morning sunlight fell through the blinds and landed on the grungy linoleum in the kitchen part of the living area. Her feet, damp with anxious sweat, stuck to the cheap flooring with each step.

Shit, shit, shit. Suspended? Why? Did it have something to do with Emerson's exile?

With every passing minute, her desperation to open a ticket with customer support grew. Emerson had said he'd call right back, but it had been half an hour already. Half an hour in real-world time, but three times that had passed in the game. It had been late afternoon or early evening when she'd finally spotted the phoenix. By the time she got back in, who knew what time it would be.

She didn't even want to think about what might happen if she *couldn't* get back in.

At the window, she pried apart a pair of the blind slats and peered out. Low clouds hung to the west, a wintry blanket rather than the puffy white clouds of summer. Thanksgiving was already just a week or so away.

The thought sent another bolt of panic through her chest. What if the people who made decisions on account suspensions were on Thanksgiving vacation?

Clenching her fists, she stared at the implant-projected icon for her web browser app. Hardly anyone used the web-based customer support portal at this point since support requests could be made in-game. But since she couldn't actually get into the game...

As she made the mental motion to activate the icon, her tablet finally pinged. She dismissed the browser and rushed to the table, took a seat, and answered the video chat request. When her face popped up on the screen then shrunk to a little rectangle, she grimaced. She should have at least brushed her hair.

When Emerson's image filled her screen, she realized she probably hadn't needed to worry.

"Did you get a perm or something?" she asked.

"A what?"

"You changed your hair."

Color rose in his cheeks as he pulled off what was frankly a hideous wig and tugged on a tinfoil hat. "I've been experimenting with new shielding designs."

Devon reached for her coffee, somewhat unsure what to say in response. She took a breath, and then her words came spilling out. "My account's been suspended. Can you help? It's really not a good time for me to be offline."

Not that it was ever a good time, but she didn't say that.

Emerson seemed to be taking this in, blinking slowly as his eyebrows drew together. "Wait...suspended? Why?"

"They didn't give a reason. Just cut my connection."

He chewed the corner of his mouth. "Log in to the website. Even if it's bullshit, they have to input a reason."

Devon nodded and reopened the web browser. When she submitted credentials to the E-Squared login screen, a special page loaded that displayed a rendering of her character and bright red letters.

Account suspended for attempted hacking. Illegitimate network traffic was detected on your connection. Thank you for your patience while we investigate this issue.

Devon took a couple deep breaths. Hacking? She stared at Emerson's fidgeting image. True, he had asked her to re-enable the packet sniffer, which had probably triggered the alert. But this wasn't his fault. He was trying to fix things.

She read him the message.

The rush of anger to his face was so obvious that it might have been comical if the situation weren't so crappy. Deep purple blotches darkened his cheeks, and one of his nostrils twitched.

"Is it the packet sniffer?" she asked.

Jaw clenched, he shook his head. "Doubtful. By my guess, Penelope has no actual proof. She's just going after my players as part of her overall strategy, and since I'm not there to refute her allegations..." His nostril twitched again. "How long ago did this happen?"

"Just before I tried to call you the first time."

Emerson nodded. "Do you have contacts for your other guildmates? I need to know if this is hitting all of you."

"I..." Devon pulled up her messenger app. So far, Hailey hadn't responded, but the woman liked to play late and then sleep late. "I'll try to get in touch. Any news on Owen, by the way?"

He swallowed. "That's part of my concern. Given what we know about Zaa's connection to the mind, it could be an exceedingly bad idea to cut his connection abruptly and permanently. We need to ease him back to conscious awareness."

Devon's pulse sped. She hadn't thought of that. Being cut off from her followers and Stonehaven seemed bad, but at least she would be *okay*. Physically anyway.

"So what do I do?"

Emerson took a deep breath, the heat in his cheeks fading to a cold rage that shone in his eyes. "Enough is enough. I thought it would be best to collect the data first, but at this point, it's time to take things to Bradley. I'll be in St. George to pick you up by dinnertime."

"Wait, what?" Devon asked as Emerson's image vanished. She sat frozen for a moment as if hoping he'd call back to correct himself or explain. But no notifications appeared, and after a while, she put her tablet's screen to sleep and resumed pacing.

He would pick her up? For what? Surely he didn't plan to drag her along for whatever half-baked plan he was concocting. Or did he?

Tired of wearing a trough in her linoleum and carpet, she crossed to the door and stepped outside. Devon shivered as soon as the morning air touched her bare arms. The balcony was west-facing and wouldn't see sunlight until at least noon, probably later.

She sighed. Afternoon's warmth seemed a distant hope from beneath the shadow of the overhanging eaves with their peeling paint and remnants of wasp nests.

Evening and dinner seemed like *forever* away.

Shaking her head, she propped her forearms on the cold metal railing and leaned her head and shoulders over the edge. What the hell was she going to do for the next...what? Seven hours? Visiting

Tamara might kill a couple of hours—by which point, it would be night in Relic Online, and her followers would probably think she'd become the phoenix's latest meal.

Still, they would probably hang out for a day or two, as long as the felsen didn't turn psycho and start threatening to tie them to stakes again. In reality, as long as Emerson's plan to get her back into the game didn't take more than a day, they probably wouldn't even mention it.

Devon sighed as another shiver raised goosebumps on her arms. If she was going to stand out here fretting, she could at least put on something warmer than a tank top and yoga pants. Shuffling to the door, she yawned. As long as she was getting dressed, might as well put on something nice enough to wear to the hospital.

As she chugged back the rest of her coffee, she noticed the messaging app at the edge of her vision.

Right.

Hailey. She'd agreed to try to contact her guildmates.

"Hey," she subvocalized. "I'm not trying to be annoying. Just checking in. Did your account get suspended? I got booted from the game and can't get back in. Emerson's trying to figure it out."

She hit send and a little *shwoop* noise echoed through her mind to confirm the command. Dragging hands through her hair, she headed to her bedroom to try to pick out something half-decent to wear.

***

Devon could hear male voices from a good fifty feet away from Tamara's hospital room door. By the time she reached the doorway, she half-expected every mountain biker in St. George to be inside, but apparently the noise came from just the three people she'd seen in the shop when she'd stopped by while searching for Tamara. The guy from the counter nodded and grinned when he saw her.

He stood and crossed the room with long strides, extending his hand and very tanned arm. Somewhat tentatively, Devon accepted the handshake. She tried not to wince when his grip smashed her knuckles together.

"If we'd known that all we had to do to get access to Tam was send in a secret agent to sweet talk the mom, we'd have messaged you the day after she got hurt," the guy said.

Devon flicked him a smile then looked toward Tamara's bed to avoid his rather direct stare. "I guess Lillian agreed to let you visit."

"She called the shop. On the telephone. Apologized for keeping Tamara closed off. She said it's been so hard and she wanted to do the best for her daughter."

Devon nodded and pressed her lips together as she sidestepped around him, sucking in her breath so she wouldn't take up too much space and accidentally brush his arm or something. At the table beside the window, the other two bike guys sat with legs outstretched and elbows resting on the table. They could have been twins.

"Any word on her condition?" she asked, directing her voice over her shoulder to Counter Guy, but not meeting his eyes.

"No worse, which according to the doctors is good news. In a couple of days, they'll try bringing her up to awareness. I guess there's a problem where she needs more surgery to get her lungs in fighting shape, but they want her to make the call. Another incision means more risk of infection, and the next bug might be the resistant kind."

Devon blinked and swallowed as she tiptoed toward Tamara's bedside. Her friend's cheeks were sunken, and dark bruises made the area around her eyes look like a skeleton's empty sockets.

"What do you think, guys?" one of the mechanics said. "Grab some lunch? We can check back in here after and then head out to Gooseberry for a ride."

"Sounds like a plan."

Devon jumped when Counter Guy spoke. Somehow, he'd ghosted across the floor to stand right behind her. What was he, some sort of super tan biker ninja?

He nudged her shoulder with the back of his hand. "You in for lunch? We can drop you off back here before we head out to ride."

Devon blinked. Her? Lunch with a bunch of mountain bikers?

"Well, I have to—"

"Come on. You can tell us stories about Tamara's Annie Oakley days."

She gripped her purse straps like they were a lifeline. "O...Okay."

***

At first, the meal wasn't too bad. Tamara's biking friends, who had introduced themselves as Trevor—he was the counter guy—Andy, and Don, had been talking about mountain bike stuff that Devon didn't really understand. Something about bike brands and whether 27.5 or 29-inch tires were better for certain types of riding. The conversation had left her free to watch them and figure out how the hell she was supposed to eat this meal.

Wincing as she laid a strip of disturbingly bloody steak onto the hot grill set into the table, it took all her willpower not to jerk her arm away. She sighed. What was the point of eating out if you had to cook your own food? According to Tamara's friends, that was the whole point of the place. It had some sort of Asian name, and you ordered a selection of raw ingredients and cooked them to your taste.

Totally confused by the menu, she had waited until the men had ordered, then copied them.

But no matter how hard she was trying to fit in, there was no way she'd try to use chopsticks. Fortunately, the server seemed to have noticed her distress as she looked down at her white cloth napkin set with just a pair of bamboo sticks, and he had brought her a fork and a wink to go with it.

"So I hear you have full-on hardware inside your skull," Trevor said, looking at her as he peeled a strip of chicken off the grill.

Devon blinked, surprised to be addressed, and nodded. "Technically, most of it is outside my skull but under my scalp. But yeah. It takes the place of all the clunky VR gear."

"That's pretty sweet. And it just re-creates...what? Like a new reality?"

She nodded. "It does all the senses. I mean, right now I just have input to my vision and hearing, but with full immersion there's touch and feel. And whatever you would call the way you sense position and movement. The same thing your inner ear does for you."

"Wait, back up," Trevor said, the strip of grilled chicken held a few inches from his face. "You've got, like, computer stuff in your vision? Right now?"

She fought the urge to blush. "Just at the edges. I can make it totally go away, but I don't really notice it unless I'm looking."

Speaking of, she glimpsed a flash of red from the messaging app. She picked up her tongs and flipped a piece of steak on her grill to distract herself from opening the message. These guys weren't on their phones or wearables, and she got the feeling they'd think it was rude if she zoned out and started texting.

"It doesn't freak you out a little bit, giving that stuff access to your brain?" one of the mechanics asked. Andy, if she remembered their names right. It was hard to keep those two straight.

Devon's thoughts went to Penelope and Zaa's interference. That would probably wig most anyone out, but it was getting fixed. And playing a demon character in her sleep wasn't really *that* different from dreaming. At least, that's what she tried to tell herself because anything else might mean she'd have to rethink whether she still wanted to participate in Relic Online.

"It's different than it sounds, I guess," she said. "I still have control over what I experience, but I choose to enter this other world. Right now, I keep a few things active, but it's not really any different from leaving a phone in my pocket and waiting for it to vibrate."

Andy plucked a green vegetable thing from his pile of food. It looked like some kind of weird cabbage with long dark leaves. After dipping it in one of the sauces, he plopped it on the grill. "That makes sense I guess. It's just different than how I'm used to thinking about it. So you can just go home, chill out, and connect to your job which happens to be playing this game? Is it the same thing I've been seeing that holo chick talk about outside Pod People?"

Devon stiffened. "Yeah, that's the game," she said quietly, hoping none of them had caught her reaction.

"Looks pretty cool," Andy said. "And you enjoy it even though it's work?"

She hadn't intended to say anything, but the words just slipped out. "I love it. But I'm kinda stressed right now because my account got suspended."

"Suspended?" Trevor said. "What does that mean? Did they lay people off?" He looked away as if realizing that might not have been the most tactful question.

Devon shrugged. "I think it's just politics in the company. My boss is working on it."

She wasn't actually sure whether bike shops had such things as office politics, but the guys seemed to get it judging by their nods.

"That might be getting past the well-done stage," Trevor said, pointing to the steak she was grilling. Smoke was pouring from around the bottom of the piece of meat.

"Oh, crap. I'm a shitty cook." Devon pulled the meat off the grill, leaving little charred bits on the raised ridges.

Trevor smiled. "No worries. Half the reason to come here is to practice without having to clean up."

Devon wasn't sure whether he meant it, but she was grateful for the gesture. Spearing the overcooked flesh with her fork, she tore off a bite. It was almost as tough as Bayle's fire-roasted rabbit, and she had to chug half of her iced tea to swallow it. All the while, the messenger app kept flashing to get her attention. Finally, when she spotted the server, she waved him down and asked him where the bathroom was.

She hurried across the restaurant to the place he indicated, and once inside a stall where her vacant stare wouldn't be noticed, she pulled open the message. It was from Hailey.

Hey, Dev. Suspended? That really sucks. I haven't been booted, though it's been so fricking boring sailing all this way. Poor Chen is going to hate me by the time we make landfall. Let me know what happens with your account, okay?

Devon sighed in relief to hear that, at the very least, Hailey was still online. Emerson's concern for Owen's safety had been pressing on her thoughts. She selected the message prompt and subvocalized a reply.

"I don't know if you're in touch with Maya and Jeremy, but Emerson's definitely interested in knowing what's happening to all of us. If you can, find out how they're doing. And good luck with your voyage. Chen will get over it."

Just moments after she hit send, Hailey responded.

Thank God you're online. Dev, I hate to be the one to break this to you, but I was just checking the forums between stints of gazing at the endless horizon. Do you have any way to check in with Stonehaven?

"What? No. What's happening?"

So it doesn't necessarily mean anything bad, but those shithead griefers were organizing a raid party.

"On Stonehaven?"

It seems like it. I tried to follow the thread, but they took their planning to raid chat. I'm guessing you didn't do too much friend-making with the players out in the jungle, right? At least, not enough to trade messenger contacts.

Devon shook her head as she backed up to take a seat on the porcelain throne. She propped her forehead on her hand. "I gave them quests and stuff. I mean, my NPCs did."

Well, I'm sure they've been watching the forums. Protecting Stonehaven is the whole reason they stayed, so I wouldn't worry too much.

That was easy for Hailey to say when her only attachment to Devon's village was because she and Devon were friends. Devon pressed her lips together and sucked a breath through her nose. It wasn't right to think of Hailey that way. If she hadn't rallied the goody-goody paladins and clerics to fight the demons in the first place, Stonehaven would probably be nothing but kindling now.

"You don't happen to have any of them on messenger do you? There was one guy I talked to...Torald or something? He had a manpurse."

Hailey's response took a while, maybe because she was looking for contact info. When it finally arrived, Devon yanked the window open.

Sorry Dev. I'll put something out on my streaming channel and tell them to send me private messages. If I get a contact, I'll let you know. Should I tell them about the suspension?

Devon bit down on her lower lip, thinking. No. It was too risky. With her account locked, even the holy army on Stonehaven's doorstep might get ideas about rightful ownership of the village. "Just say I'm questing a couple days' journey away. They'll assume I can die and respawn in Stonehaven if I have to."

Gotcha, Hailey responded. *I'll get on it now. Don't worry too much, okay Dev?*

"Thanks, Hailey. I'll try."

No more messages arrived, and after a couple minutes, Devon stood. The toilet flushed in response to her sudden absence, and she left the stall. Her face in the mirror was drawn, the worry more obvious on her face than she'd realized. Splashing water over her cheeks, she forced herself to smile. It looked fake, but maybe Tamara's friends wouldn't notice. With a deep breath, she headed out and back toward the table.

She'd worried she'd have to make some excuse for spending so long in the bathroom, but fortunately Tamara's friends were engrossed in another conversation where she knew less than half of the words. More bike talk.

As she settled into her chair, Trevor glanced at her. "Get enough to eat?" he asked.

She nodded, her stomach feeling full of lead anyway. Raising a finger, Trevor hailed the server, who hit a button on his tablet. Devon's total for the meal appeared on the smart surface of the table in front of her, and she waved her wrist over it to credit the restaurant, then added on the tip.

"We already ordered a cab that will swing you by the hospital," Trevor said. "Unless you want to head somewhere else?"

"Some time with Tam sounds good," she said, swallowing.

At this point, anything sounded better than hanging in her apartment and imagining Stonehaven's destruction.

Chapter Twenty-Nine

DEVON FLUNG THE door open when Emerson knocked. The programmer blinked for a moment, then seemed to snap out of it. He nodded curtly and stepped into her kitchen.

"Do you have a go bag?" he asked.

"A what?"

He scanned the edges of her living area as if looking for this bag. "Clothes and stuff. You know, to grab and run."

Devon was still standing beside the door. "No...no go bag. Though to be fair, you haven't told me where we're going or for how long. Makes it kinda hard to pack."

He rubbed his shoulder while processing the information, then he shook his head. "Sorry. You're right. It's been a long day."

Dropping a backpack on her kitchen table, he unzipped a flap and pulled out a tablet. "The way I see it, just two targets really matter."

"Targets?" Did she really want to be involved with this?

Spinning the tablet around to face her, Emerson pointed. He'd pulled up two video streams. In one window, twilight silhouetted the crowns of pine trees and the glass-and-steel home nestled amongst them. He fiddled with some settings and the view zoomed in on one of the windows of the home's massive windows, displaying a woman who stood at a workstation surrounded by three enormous monitors and a holo-projecting pane. The other video was grainier as if filmed under a high degree of zoom. She couldn't make out all the details, but it looked like a camera was focused on an office in some city high-rise.

She chewed the corner of her lip. "I take it these are your...targets?"

He seemed to drag his attention away from the screen with some difficulty. He blinked. "Yeah. I figure we may need to confront them both."

"Confront as in talk?"

He gave her a confused look. "Yeah, of course. Plus present evidence I guess."

"Got it."

"What did you think?" he asked.

She shook her head. "It doesn't matter."

"Wait...targets. Did you think I was planning some kind of attack? Or an assassination?"

Devon shrugged a single shoulder. "It crossed my mind. That's usually the kind of thing you need a go bag for, right? When the cops are closing in..."

He shrugged apologetically. "I suppose I probably heard it in an action movie somewhere. But you have to admit it's a good term."

All of a sudden, the whole thing struck her as ridiculous, and she started laughing. This crap with E-Squared had really mucked with her head, making her paranoid.

Emerson smiled faintly, then quickly looked away as if unsure how to react to her laughter. He fiddled with the settings on the camera pointed at the woman, and the view zoomed closer still. He cocked his head and squinted as if trying to figure something out.

"I'm guessing that's Penelope," Devon said.

Emerson nodded. "She has a house in the mountains above Denver. Splits her time between there and a condo near the Tucson offices."

Devon pointed at the tablet. "And that's the CEO?"

He nodded again. "Bradley Williams. I can't get a better picture because it's urban airspace. No drones allowed."

"I thought using drones to surveil private citizens was illegal everywhere."

The programmer's shoulders tensed. "Technically, that's true. But rural and suburban locations aren't as likely to have detectors screening for unauthorized drone presence." He shrugged. "I'm hoping you won't rat me out."

"Given that she's responsible for putting a demon in my head? I'm pretty much okay with whatever you think needs to be done." She paused for a second. "Well, maybe not assassination."

Emerson exhaled softly. "Good. Anyway, I think the best plan is to go straight to Bradley while keeping tabs on Penelope. As long as she stays in Colorado, we should be able to get some uninterrupted time with him and possibly the rest of E-Squared's management."

"Can we back up a minute, actually?" Devon asked as she looked away from the tablet. "I get that you want me to go with you…"

Emerson blinked as a flush moved up his neck. "I understand if you're not comfortable traveling with someone you hardly know."

She shook her head. "I'm just trying to figure out what you want me for and how long we'll be gone. So that I can put the right stuff in my go bag."

***

Thirty minutes later, they were standing on the tarmac at St. George's regional airport. Devon clutched her bag—filled with three changes of clothes, a toothbrush, hairbrush, and some granola bars— to her belly like a shield. She grimaced and turned her head away as a helicopter descended from a low hover and set down near them.

"Breathe, Devon," she muttered as her tinfoil hat tugged against the chinstrap. Society hadn't abandoned air travel for domestic transit because it was dangerous or anything. In fact, the aviation industry still had the highest safety record among the transportation sectors. The fuel costs were just too expensive for most people when compared to hyperloop technology.

Emerson, the chinstrap on his tinfoil hat snapping in the outwash from the helicopter's rotors, nodded at her. He flicked his wrist and pointed two fingers in a gesture that looked straight out of an action movie, then hunched and ran for the waiting aircraft.

Cringing, Devon followed.

She'd seen plenty of footage shot from planes, but it didn't do the view justice. St. George spread in a twinkling blanket, a sparkling pocket between the dark wilderness in the nearby desert mountain ranges. Far away to the south and west, Las Vegas lit up the night with its luminescent biodomes and garishly flashing lights. The sights blunted her unease, and she sat back in her plush seat, amazed by the sound dampening in the helicopter's cabin.

"You okay?" Emerson asked.

Devon hesitated, a bland response on her tongue. For some reason, she didn't want to give him a canned answer. That was part of the problem she had with real-world interactions. People said fake things just because it was polite or easier than expressing something genuine.

"The truth is, I'm scared," she said.

He blinked and seemed to drag himself away from whatever storm of thoughts swirled in his head. When he looked at her, she sensed she had his full attention.

"Afraid of flying?" he asked.

She glanced out the window then back at him. "A little. But I'm more worried about my friend Tamara. She's in the hospital after a mountain biking accident." She hesitated, abruptly shy. "And this might seem strange to you, but I'm afraid for my NPC friends in Relic Online. My village is under attack by players—or it will be soon—and I can't do anything to protect the people there."

She didn't think he would laugh, but she steeled herself for it anyway.

Emerson just looked at her with the same genuine concern. "I wish I could have been watching you play to pick up some tips. I'm pretty much the worst gamer ever. But I purposefully avoid looking at content that Veia is using for learning so I'm not tempted to tweak her settings."

Devon sat motionless, still waiting for him to be amused over her quaint idea that the NPCs were worth worrying about as more than assets in her city development. But Emerson continued to give her his attention, not pushing, but clearly willing to listen.

"Do you think they're conscious?" she said after a moment. "Sentient I mean?"

"The NPCs?" Emerson asked.

She nodded. "And Veia."

He pushed out his lower lip a little bit, clearly thinking about her question. "I think humans tend to overestimate the uniqueness of our consciousness and self-awareness. We think that machines can't possibly be sapient because the notion threatens our egos. The thing

281

is, I don't think I'm qualified to judge where algorithms become intelligence or—especially—where they transform into awareness. I'm too close to the issue, you know?"

He paused, looking almost as nervous as she'd felt when admitting how much the NPCs meant to her. She nodded to reassure him—though she didn't have his background in AI development, she understood his point.

"I hope that Veia and her creations inhabit their world as fully as you and I do this one. But without standing in their shoes, I can't say anything for certain."

He shrugged and looked out the window, his expression somewhat pensive. After a moment, he leaned forward. "You have lots more experience with them than I do. What do you think?"

Devon swallowed. She hadn't expected to have the question turned around on her. After all, she was just a gamer, not a philosopher.

"In my mind, there's no question. They're just as alive as you and me. And if Relic Online gets shut down"—she pressed her lips together for a minute—"if the servers get shut down and don't come back up, they'll all die. We can't let it happen."

"Even if it means sacrificing Owen?" Emerson asked softly, the dilemma tearing at him judging by the expression on his face.

She clenched her jaw. Logic—or maybe some ingrained instinct to preserve the species—told her that Owen had more right to life. At the very least, his legal standing demanded that she should favor him. But she couldn't bring herself to answer. She didn't think she had the strength to choose who lived and who died.

"It's okay not to know," Emerson said. "Hopefully we won't have to make that choice."

Chapter Thirty

THE HELICOPTER LANDED in Tucson at about 11 PM. Because it was a small city, especially now that summers often saw temperatures regularly rising above 115°F, there weren't many autocabs stationed near the airport in the middle of the night. Emerson and Devon waited at the curb for about fifteen minutes before their ride arrived. After the conversation in the helicopter, Devon was feeling thoughtful, and she'd never liked making small talk. If her silence bothered Emerson, he didn't show it. Devon liked that, especially since most people seemed to feel the need to blab nonstop.

As the cab rolled silently onto the arrivals level, Emerson turned to her. "You ready to go straight into headquarters? Bradley usually works late. We'll have an easier time getting his ear now than when the office is full."

Devon nodded. "The sooner, the better."

She stared out the window as the cab navigated sleepy freeways on the way to the small downtown area. She hadn't had much chance to travel outside the St. George vicinity, but she'd killed a little time now and again on virtual tours. When her Avatharn guild had been waiting on timers to expire before dungeons could be raided, she'd switched the VR pod over to one of the various travel experiences. Over the five years she'd been a regular Pod People customer, she'd visited Ancient Rome and Greece, toured downtown Tokyo, and ridden a paddleboat on the Mississippi. But seeing things firsthand was just...different.

She'd read about the intentional communities on Tucson's outer rim. Unlike Las Vegas's biodomes, which were as much a tourist attraction as anything, the enclosed habitats here weren't created to alter the environment, but rather to exist without burdening it. In Tucson, that meant a closed loop for water recycling inside the structure, plus highly efficient cooling systems. Otherwise, with the native plantings and ordinary-looking public spaces, the communities weren't any different than the condo complexes next door. Still, Devon stared at the installations as they slid past, wondering what it would be like to basically live and work in a big greenhouse.

"The Vegas rainforests are much more impressive," Emerson said. "Kind of tacky considering the water shortages, but worth visiting if you've ever wondered what it's like to live in a jungle."

Devon couldn't help the sudden laugh that burst from her throat.

"What?" Emerson asked.

Devon shook her head. "I guess if I was looking for proof that you didn't spy on my character, that establishes it definitively."

"You visited a jungle in the game I guess?"

"That's something of an understatement," she said.

All too soon, the cab pulled up beside the E-Squared office building. Devon took a deep breath, suddenly far more nervous than she'd expected to be. Back when she'd been focused on playing while waiting for Emerson to fix things, it had been easy to forget that there'd been very serious breaches by the company. Even on the flight over, she'd found ways to distract herself. Emerson had asked more about Tamara, and he'd even offered some suggestions on things she could research about her friend's prognosis. But now, she faced a confrontation that could quite possibly end with her barred from RO forever. Worse, their actions could lead to Relic Online's shutdown and the effective murder of everyone in Stonehaven.

She clutched her bag tight as the cab door slid open and the AI driver wished them a pleasant evening. Hopping out first, Emerson extended a hand, then withdrew it as if worrying he'd overreached, and then extended it once again with an awkward laugh. Though Devon would have rather kept her death grip on her bag-turned-shield, she accepted the help to spare him any more awkwardness. They crossed the sidewalk to the front doors of the office building, and Emerson held his wrist over the access pad. The speaker crackled, and a red light flashed. Alarmed, Devon stared at him.

He shrugged. "Figured that would happen, but I had to try, right?"

Swallowing, she nodded. "So what now?"

"Now," he said, "we get Bradley's attention."

***

Devon had never seen an image of Bradley Williams, probably because of the incredibly low-profile E-Squared had kept during development due to their partnership with Entwined. Still, she assumed that the holo Emerson had projected in the middle of the street was an accurate likeness. At the very least, the rendering had the bearing of a corporate bigwig, right down to the arrogant smirk on his face. Of course, the leotard, tights, and orange superhero cape kinda spoiled the look.

After a minute or two spent inspecting his creation, Emerson gave a satisfied nod and tapped on his tablet a few times. A pair of small bots responsible for the projection spidered up the outside wall of the E-Squared offices, allowing the projection to lift off from the asphalt and float up to the tenth or eleventh level where she assumed Bradley's office was. Cape flapping, tights glimmering, the image hung in front of the window pane and started pulling out, displaying, and tossing away a set of poster board signs that materialized behind his back.

"What do they say?" she asked.

"Just reminders of some office Christmas party situations and comments that I'm sure he'd rather forget. And a gentle request that he should hear me out."

Not three minutes after super-Bradley began his campaign of persuasion, the intercom beside the front door crackled.

"What the hell, Emerson?"

Emerson thumbed the button. "We need to talk."

"You're supposed to be on vacation."

"And instead, I'm here trying to save your company."

"Our company," the CEO said. "I hope you didn't think your complimentary vacation was anything but a chance to relax."

"It will only remain *our* company if you hear me out," Emerson said. "Otherwise I'll have to resign to protect myself from the mess you created. And I'll need to alert the authorities to certain...situations."

Devon's eyes widened at this—they couldn't tell anyone anything until Owen was safe—but Emerson cast her a reassuring glance. Seemed this was just a tactic.

"Penelope said you'd gone off course," Bradley said. "I thought it was just a simple case of burnout. But clearly, you need a doctor."

Emerson shook his head as he thumbed the button again. "I really would rather not argue about this on a public street. If you're concerned about my sanity, ask security to accompany me to your office. Of course, I'd suggest you *not* ask your security to escort me anywhere else. Your superhero self is preprogrammed to turn up downtown in the morning if I don't cancel the scheduled task. I'll only do that once I've been allowed to present my case."

After a long, tense moment, the speaker crackled again. "I'll hear you out, but I'm calling enough private security to defend the president. And a shrink."

"Fair enough," Emerson said. "My point should be fairly straightforward to make. I just need you to unban my player here, and I'll need someone from IT to monitor and interpret network traffic."

Chapter Thirty-One

TWENTY MINUTES LATER, Devon was reclining on the couch inside the office of the CEO of E-Squared. She tried to ignore the heated argument behind her as she hovered her awareness over the icon for Relic Online.

Butterflies were having a party in her stomach. Had the player raid arrived at Stonehaven yet? Had their attack breached the walls? Or were they planning some sort of war of attrition? Logging in wouldn't give her instant information about the village's fate, but at least it would put her on the path to returning home and assessing the damage.

As Emerson launched into another explanation, which, like the others, seemed to be going straight over Bradley's head, she took a deep breath and logged in.

Frigid fog surrounded her, rendering the night impenetrable even with her *Darkvision* skill. Thinking of the drop that lay just a few paces to either side of the trail, Devon crouched and patted the ground, feeling for the path. A smooth groove, the trail cut through rougher stone and kept a relatively equal distance from either edge. Once she determined that she was, in fact, still on the path, she stood and peered ahead.

Nothing.

She cast a *Glowing Orb*, but the light scarcely penetrated the fog. If anything, the illumination of the nearest mist made it *harder* to see more than a foot or two away. She dismissed the orb and shuffled forward, hands outstretched, until the faintest red glow appeared. Just a hint in the soupy fog, the phoenix fire smoldered in the distance.

Still on track then.

She took a deep breath. As much as she wanted to outright abandon this obscure venture with its cryptic instructions, it would be stupid to head back to Stonehaven when her current goal was just a few hundred feet away. The player raid would arrive before her anyway, so she had no choice but to hope the players and the village defenses would be enough to save the settlement.

She started forward again, placing each foot carefully in case she'd made a mistake in judging the trail's location.

A startled yelp jumped out of her throat when a dimly glowing ball popped into existence and booped her nose.

"Where have you been?" Bob asked.

"Long story."

"You might remember that my last master was a wizard-turned-lich who lived for a thousand years. From my perspective, length is somewhat relative."

"How about I give you the rundown sometime when we *aren't* advancing through unnaturally dense fog in the dead of night on a knife-edge ridge with thousands of feet of empty air to either side?"

"Jeez," Bob said. "Bite my head off, why don't you."

"You don't have a head."

"Says the woman about to step in a pothole that might throw off her balance and send her headlong into the abyss."

Devon froze. "Where?"

Bob drifted down and illuminated a deep pit in the trail.

Swallowing, she stepped over the hole. "Hey, question for you: Can you use your elemental powers to see what's going on Stonehaven?"

"Um...no?"

"Is that a 'No I can't' or 'No I choose not to?'"

"How about: No I'm just an elemental companion with occasional wisdom to offer, not a secret exploit you can use to access the *Farsight* ability even though that's a Wizard's spell and totally unavailable to Sorcerers?"

Devon sighed. "It didn't hurt to ask, I guess."

She shivered, the fog having soaked through the thinner areas of her armor. Her muscles were getting stiff with the chill. "Does your *occasional wisdom* include advice on dealing with a phoenix?"

Bob circled slowly in the air. "Hmm. Well, if you kill one, don't expect it to stay dead. They're somewhat known for rebirth."

Devon sighed. "Aren't you just an oracle..."

The wisp booped her nose. "I can tell you something more specific about *this* phoenix, though."

"What's that?"

"Haven't we discussed the importance of clarity in your inquiries?"

Devon gritted her teeth. It would definitely suck if the RO servers went down and erased the NPCs forever. But right now, there was one particular creature she wouldn't mind sending to the bit bucket. "Bob, can you tell me anything about the strengths, weaknesses, and/or special preferences of the phoenix which dwells on a pinnacle near the felsens' lair?"

Bob swirled in the air. "Now that, my champion, was a well-phrased question. And yes! I can tell you that there's a reason the felsen have been waiting for someone else to confront the bird. You won't win this by virtue of your combat prowess alone. And that's not just because the bird is level 30 to your puny 17."

"That's it?" she asked. "That's your tremendous wisdom?"

The wisp shrugged. "Do you want me to play for you too?"

***

With each step forward, the fog seemed to grow colder. Devon had been shuffling along the trail for at least ten minutes, and the glow from the phoenix fire seemed almost the same distance away. As best she could tell, she'd sorely underestimated the remaining hike.

Water droplets beaded on her eyelashes, little lenses that caught the ruddy glow and made it all that much harder to see where the hell she was going. Bob bounced along in the air beside her, looking far too merry.

"Dude," she said finally, "can't you at least act concerned? I mean, I could die up here."

The wisp shimmered in what looked like a huff. "At least we'd be out of this stupid snow then."

"Snow?"

Devon looked forward again and groaned at the sight of millions of little ice crystals reflecting Bob's glow. Frost began to outline the edges of the trail, silvery traces on the midnight-dark stone.

The phoenix fire was starting to sound kind of pleasant. Devon hurried her shuffling steps, fists clenched out of fear she'd hit a patch of ice. Finally, after maybe another quarter hour, the red glow began to swell and grow brighter, a sure sign that she was actually getting closer.

The first heat kissed her cheeks a few minutes later. Frost that had formed on the folds of her armor melted and ran off in little trails of damp. But rather than returning to the soupy fog from below, the snow actually lightened and then finally dissipated.

Across maybe a hundred feet of treacherous ridge, the phoenix waited for her.

The bird was smaller than she expected, about the size of a Saint Bernard but scrawnier. Its feathers ranged from brilliant yellow to blood red, each glowing faintly. Sharp golden eyes with narrow pupils peered at her, and the bird clacked its rather sharp-looking beak.

She'd expected some sort of nest, but if there were sticks or other such materials beneath the bird, they were lost in the incandescent fire. Almost liquid, more like lava than ordinary flames, the blaze twisted and curled beneath the phoenix's body. The bird's talons were lost in the glow.

"Hey, how's it going?" Devon said, raising a hand.

The phoenix glared at her, its gaze suggesting uncanny intelligence.

She took a step forward, and a tongue of phoenix fire bulged then stretched out along the trail toward her.

Devon froze and used *Combat Assessment.*

Phoenix Prince - Level 30
The phoenix doesn't look particularly happy to see you. Needless to say, your odds don't look good.

No, the odds definitely didn't seem to favor her.

Devon chewed her lip, uncertain how to proceed. She got the feeling that aggroing the bird with an offensive spell wouldn't go very well. But continuing to approach might have the same effect. The quest hadn't said anything about killing the phoenix—which was probably a good thing—but other than that, the text had been rather vague on how she was supposed to retrieve 20 feathers.

"I don't suppose you'd like to hand over some of your impressive plumage?" she asked, dropping to a crouch and extending her hand like she might when meeting a strange dog.

The phoenix gave a melodic screech and narrowed its eyes. As the sound washed over her, Devon felt a wave of awe. She wanted to prostrate herself before the mythical bird, belly crawling through the fire to grovel before it. Closing her eyes, she took a deep breath and forced away the impulse.

> You resist a Phoenix Prince's *Charm* spell (+60% chance due to your 8 *Cunning* and 41 *Charisma*).
> *Your calculating nature combined with your experience as a charismatic "charmer" keeps you from falling under the bird's spell. Takes one to know one, as they say.*

Devon stood, abandoning the greeting-a-stray-dog pose and advanced a step. When her foot landed on the trail, the bird snapped upright, opened its wings, and a tendril of flame whipped out from beneath it. The fire streaked across the twenty or thirty feet that separated Devon from the phoenix and slapped Devon's chest. Her armor smoked, and searing pain—or rather discomfort, due to the game's muted pain response—burned a stripe across her upper chest. 40 hitpoints fell away from her health bar.

"Ouch! Jerk."

Even with the attack, Devon was sure the phoenix was holding back. No doubt it could burn her to a crisp in about ten seconds if it really wanted to. So far, the attacks had come each time she tried to get closer. Better to keep her distance while she figured this out.

Adjusting her stance for better stability, she laid a hand on her dagger and remained in place.

"Have you ever watched someone playing a game with turn-based combat?" Bob asked. "I hear it's really boring. Sort of like this."

"If you're so impatient, why don't you just bop over there and see what happens if we get too close."

Bob sighed. "I'm just saying...you seemed awfully concerned about Stonehaven. I figured you'd want to get on with things."

"For your information, I'm thinking about how to do this."

"Oh. *Now* I understand."

"Understand what?"

"Why this is going so slow. You're thinking. That's never a quick process."

"Why are you such an asshole?"

Bob booped her nose. "Just keeping you humble."

Devon sighed. The phoenix was still staring at her, eyes glinting. Following the attack, the pool of fire had retreated into the writhing mass beneath the bird, but the edge closest to her seemed to strain against an invisible barrier, bulging and flaring.

"What is it you want, bird?" she mumbled, shaking her head.

Her in-combat health regeneration had restored 10 of her lost hitpoints. It was tempting to think she could wait to recuperate the rest before advancing again, then take another hit, then stand around and regen. But something told her it wouldn't be that easy.

As a test, she slid a sandal forward. The phoenix shrieked, beating the air with its wings, and rose from the nest of fire. Wicked black talons emerged from the flame, glinting red where the glow struck them. The bird rose higher and higher, plumage shining brighter with every flap of its wings.

"Oopsie," Bob said.

"Shit," Devon muttered.

Desperate, she flung a *Freeze* spell at the bird, but the ice exploded in a cloud of steam before touching the phoenix's feathers. The bird shrieked again and dove. As the razor-sharp talons descended toward her face, Devon threw up a *Wall of Ice*, ducked behind it, and slapped a hand on her charred *Leather Doublet of Darkness*, activating the *Night's Breath* ability in hopes the accuracy debuff could actually affect a creature 13 levels higher than her.

The diving phoenix smashed through her ice wall and hit her like a sledgehammer with spikes. She slammed down onto her back on the trail, the air gusting from her lungs as half her health disappeared. Hot wind washed her as the bird pulled out of its dive and banked hard, returning to a hover above its nest.

"Might I suggest a new tactic?" Bob asked.

Scrambling to her feet, Devon ignored the wisp. She shuffled backward, hoping to prevent another attack. Another hit like that would send her back to Stonehaven's Shrine to Veia, her quest failed and her friends abandoned in felsen clutches. Her throat clamped down over her breath, causing it to wheeze in and out of her lungs.

"Okay, birdie. Just take it easy." She raised a hand and patted the air as if she could calm the raging beast.

Unfortunately, the blood-red wings began to flap harder, once again lifting the phoenix from its bed of fire.

Craaappp. Devon swallowed her desperation and glanced at her feet. The shadow cast by the burning nest was faint but discernible. With a deep breath, she cast *Shadow Puppet* and pulled a fire-based minion from the stone.

> **You have gained spell mastery in Shadow Puppet - Tier 2: +30%. (Bonus for using a rare form of light in the casting.)**
> **Congratulations! You have learned a new ability:** Shadow Puppet - Tier 3.
> *Your puppets have 200% health compared to their tier 1 counterparts. Upon destruction, puppets have a 20% chance to respawn near you (scales with Charisma).*

Okay, that was nice. But this wasn't a good time. Devon flicked away the notice.

The bird hovered, cocking its head and extending glinting talons for another attack. Thinking of her earlier successes with bypassing the natural resistance caused by a level difference with her lightning *Shadow Puppets*, she threw mana into a *Glowing Orb* and quickly summoned a minion from its shadow. As the bird screeched, she started casting *Levitate*.

The phoenix shrieked and dove. Frantic, Devon sent her fire-based *Shadow Puppet* streaking forward. She interrupted her *Levitate* cast and groped for her awareness of the flickering minion. When she felt the connection strengthen, she cast *Shadow Step* to teleport to its location.

Which, unfortunately, happened to be in the center of the phoenix's nest.

Devon actually screamed when the fire tore up her body, rising to engulf her in searing heat. Distantly, she heard the phoenix screech in triumph as the first damage over time effect pulsed and burned away 43 of her remaining 152 hitpoints.

She tried to run, but the fire gripped her like a physical thing, a prison of magma-hot silly putty. She fought the urge to cry as another pulse stole 39 more health.

There had to be something she could do. Some way to defeat this. Desperate, she poured mana into a *Freeze* effect, targeting herself. Ice sprang into existence around her, locking her in place, but armoring her from the merciless fire.

Unfortunately, with the next damage pulse, the ice burst in a cloud of hot steam. The fire swarmed in and grabbed hold again.

Shit. Shit. Shit.

Devon shook her head. So much for her icy heart making her a champion for the felsen.

Wait.

As soon as the idea struck, she snapped her attention to her lightning-based *Shadow Puppet*. She commanded it to streak forward, through the fire, and into her body. Straight into her core. Her heart.

29 hitpoints dropped off her health bar when the electricity shot through her, sizzling along her nerves. She gritted her teeth and ignored it, casting *Freeze* on the *Shadow Puppet*. From the inside out, ice filled her veins, froze her heart, stilled her breath.

But when the next pulse of the phoenix fire hit, the fire recoiled from her flesh. Falling away like a gown slipping off her body, it drained into the stone beneath her feet and vanished.

Devon canceled the *Freeze* and *Shadow Puppet* and collapsed in a heap on the stone sidewalk. Her health bar flashed as the first out-of-combat regeneration pulse added 10 hitpoints, pulling her back from the brink.

A few paces away, the phoenix landed and started walking toward her. She swallowed and met its gaze—or rather *his* gaze considering that he was a prince and all. Lowering his head, he peered at her.

/Thank you./

Devon blinked. Another telepathic bird, huh?

"Uh, you're welcome?"

/For untold centuries, I have waited for someone to replace me. Far to the north, my queen rules alone, and I desire nothing more than to rejoin her./

"Replace you?"

/That's why you've come, right? To prove yourself worthy of defending the last stronghold of the felsen?/

"Well...kind of?"

The bird seemed to nod as he bowed his head even closer to her face. His breath smelled faintly of brimstone.

A Phoenix Prince wishes to reward you.
Congratulations! You have learned a new ability: Phoenix Fire
Syrupy fire engulfs your target, slowing movement and burning them over time. Causes 12-17 damage every 6 seconds (scales with Intelligence).

Beware: if your target dies while afflicted, they will be reborn at full strength.
Cost: 65 mana
Duration: 1 minute

Stepping back, the phoenix spread his wings as if preparing to take off.

"Hey, before you go," Devon said. "Can I have a few feathers? Say...twenty or so?"

The bird cocked his head as if confused.

/Is there something wrong with those I've already left? I have molted quite a few times over the last millennium./

"Psst," Bob said. "Sometimes it pays to look around a little bit."

Blinking, Devon rotated on her butt to look behind her.

"Oh," she said, scooping up the first handful. There had to be at least two hundred feathers strewn about.

You have received: 10 x Phoenix Feather

Quest updated: Pharmacopeia Failings
Objective: Gather new ingredients for Hezbek. (3/5)

Also, the merchant-fletcher in Stonehaven is going to love you forever. Aren't repeatable quests awesome?

/So...are we done here?/

"Your queen awaits. I get it. One question, though."

/Yes?/

"Assuming your magical strength would allow it, could I hitch a ride back down off this perch?"

Chapter Thirty-Two

Hey. You reading me?

Emerson's message popped into Devon's view. She sighed as she opened the message window to respond. Part of the deal with getting back online was that Emerson needed to be able to communicate with her while trying to show Bradley what Penelope had done.

"Gotcha. What's up?" she said into the message window.

Unfortunately, we aren't seeing anything from Zaa aside from some initialization messages that are within normal parameters. How do you usually encounter that shadowed stuff?

"On my character sheet," she said.

Mind activating it?

Devon nodded—stupidly, she realized, since they weren't talking face-to-face.

"Yep, just a sec."

Perfect. One more favor. I know this isn't your thing, but could you set up a private sense stream with just me and Bradley accessing?

"No problem," Devon said, dragging the access credentials he'd supplied into a window for the livestream add-on. In this case, it didn't bother her any more than needing to have a conversation while trying to play and get back to her followers. Her real qualm with streaming was more about being a public figure. She just didn't like being the center of attention, especially when the viewers were strangers.

Great, Emerson messaged when the stream went live. *Thanks.*

Activating her character interface, Devon pulled up the base sheet.

> Character: Devon (click to set a different character name)
> Level: 17
> Base Class: Sorcerer
> Specialization: Unassigned
> Unique Class: Deceiver
> Health: 300/300
> Mana: 542/542
> Fatigue: 42%
> Shadowed: 55%

She shook her head. Fifty-five percent *Shadowed*? Why? What kept causing this? She pulled open the abilities list, glancing briefly at her new upgrade to *Shadow Puppet* and her newly-acquired *Phoenix Fire* spell. With a minor amount of trepidation, she opened the demonic spell tab. She swallowed in vague horror when she saw that one of the abilities was available.

> **Ability:** Blood Mist – Tier 1
> *Channel the blood of your dead and dying opponents into energy which heals your wounds. When the healing effect fades, this spell leaves behind a secondary effect,* **Sated by Blood***, granting +2 Strength for 5 minutes.*
> **Heals** 13-15 damage every 6 seconds.

Duration: 45 seconds

Devon grimaced. "You getting this?" she asked aloud, knowing that Emerson would hear her speech. "If I'd wanted to play a necromancer...well, actually I wouldn't have had a chance to choose it since I didn't get the usual character creation. But you get the idea."

Emerson's response popped up. *We got it, Devon. Receiving info from one of Zaa's servers. Nice work.*

He hadn't mentioned anything about Bradley's reaction, but Devon imagined they were making good progress. Emerson didn't *think* Bradley had allowed any of this on purpose. But seeing as he was a corporate CEO, she suspected there was a certain amount of resistance to being proved wrong.

"I'm good to keep playing?" she asked.

Carry on, Emerson messaged.

Devon stretched and peered at the scene before her. The phoenix, despite a small amount of grumbling, had deposited her on the rim of the felsens' spire. Though it was considerably warmer than it had been on top of the pinnacle, dawn was just breaking, and the mountain air had once again chilled her down. The interior of the spire remained dim, the early morning light struggling to penetrate. The felsen were probably still asleep, but she figured they wouldn't mind being awakened to hear about the successful conclusion to a thousand years of waiting for their—and Ishildar's—champion. Humming tunelessly to herself, she started for the spiraling trail that led into the pedestal's interior. When she reached it, she gave one last glance at the fog-crowned peak behind her.

Devon smiled. Veia might be fond of nerfing her abilities and sending annoying wisps who only pretended to be helpful, but Devon couldn't deny that Emerson's AI had worked a miracle when she created Relic Online.

"Hey, in case I forget to tell you later, Emerson," she said. "Thanks for making this world possible."

She wasn't surprised when he failed to answer. Devon got the sense that he wasn't quite used to compliments. But she knew he'd read it, and that was enough. Still smiling, she set foot on the path leading down into the spire.

The screen went black.

Connection lost.

***

Emerson's face snapped into focus above her, his tinfoil hat haloed by the glow of light bulbs set into some sort of stone crystals affixed to the black-painted ceiling. She hadn't noticed that little touch before, but it complemented the shelves stuffed with various old books—some with obscure runes on the spines—and the massive desk that looked as if it had been carved from a single block of stone. It seemed like Bradley had tried to create some sort of hybrid of a crystal cavern and a wizard's tower for his workspace. She wondered how often he went home.

"Don't tell me I'm banned again," she said, glancing from Emerson to the CEO to some newcomer with an enormous beard and a plaid shirt.

"Sorry about that, Devon," Emerson said. He gestured toward the bearded guy. "And meet Nathan. Head of IT."

Devon nodded. "Hi," she said before turning her attention back to Emerson. "So what's going on? Why did you guys boot me?"

Emerson grimaced. "I was in favor of asking you to log out, but we have a few twitchy fingers around here," he said, glancing pointedly at Nathan.

"You saw the incoming data," Nathan said. "It looked way sketchy."

Emerson shrugged. "Yeah, maybe. Anyway, sorry about the sudden disconnection." He held out her tinfoil hat. "Mind putting this on so we can re-enable the wireless in the room?"

"What's going on?" Devon asked as she slipped the cap over her hair.

"It's Penelope," Emerson said.

Devon shot a look to Bradley. The CEO looked grim—and faintly chagrined. When her gaze returned to Emerson, the programmer gave her a very discreet nod. Meaning: yes, they'd convinced Bradley that Penelope was a problem, but best not to rub it in.

"We were watching your livestream and comparing it to the network traffic across your implants when I happened to notice the feed from the drone I had watching Penelope's house had gone dead. My guess is she has eyes on this building, saw us enter, then thought to check her own perimeter."

"So you think she's on her way?" Devon cast another glance at Bradley. If the CEO now understood that Penelope was a bad actor in all this, why did it matter if the woman turned up? She'd basically be delivering herself for punishment.

"Not exactly," Emerson said. "It seems more like detection has prompted her to action."

"What kind of action?"

He pressed his lips together. "Given the data we saw leveled at your connection, Nathan may have had the better idea to rescue you quickly. We saw a huge spike in activity from Zaa. I suspect Penelope was trying to trip whatever switch caused your subconscious mind to assume control last time."

"But Ezraxis is dead," she said.

"Are you sure about that?" Emerson asked. "Given the changes to your game experience, I'm wondering if dormant might be a better word."

"Hey boss?" A new voice came from the room's doorway. Devon turned to see a man who looked like he had a habit of sneering.

Emerson leaned close to her ear. "Head of customer support," he said.

"Yes?" Bradley said.

"We're getting a bunch of player complaints. There aren't any planned events I don't know about, are there?"

"What kind of complaints?"

"Mostly from Eltera City and Frostheim. Seems there's a bunch of high-level demons rampaging in the starting cities."

Bradley rubbed the back of his thumb against his forehead. "Get me some livestreams going. And send security to Penelope's Denver residence."

***

"Question, Nathan," Bradley said, watching with a dispassionate expression as a massive demon tore a newbie player in half around five seconds after the player had respawned. "Actually, maybe you can help answer this too, Emerson."

"Yeah?" the IT guy looked up from his tablet.

"Is there a reason we can't just turn off Zaa's servers?"

Nathan sighed as he petted his beard. "To control costs, we're using a hodgepodge of company-owned and cloud resources, but—"

"No," Emerson and Devon said at the same time.

Bradley cast Devon a strange look, then turned to his programmer. "Why not?"

Emerson scratched the side of his neck. "I hadn't gotten to the part where I explained Miriam's findings."

"Miriam?"

"The engineer at Entwined. This all goes back to the situation with the pain sensitivity. You see—" He cut himself off and shook his head. "Sorry. That's something of a tangent. Skipping the details, suffice to say that those who have been exposed to Zaa's unauthorized access may suffer moderate to severe side effects if the contact is abruptly ceased."

Bradley seemed to deflate, his face going slack. "How many people are we talking about here?"

Emerson swallowed. "I can't say for sure. Aside from the team I recruited, we know that a number of hardcore players experienced the pain problem. But it's possible that many more customers have had exposure. We can't be certain without looking at their network traffic."

The CEO ran a hand through his hair. "Tell me you have a suggestion for cleaning up this mess..."

"I say we start with finding Penelope. Barring that, we can start monitoring the network data leaving Zaa's servers. See who the AI is communicating with."

"Nathan? You on that?" Bradley asked.

The IT guy groaned but nodded.

Touching her tinfoil hat, Devon inhaled. "Can you cut off Zaa's connection to my implants specifically? I've already been through the withdrawals, and it couldn't hurt to have a player in the game who's already dealt with the demons right?"

Bradley cocked an eyebrow as if to suggest that her rationale was a little thin, but after a moment, he ran fingers over the hair on the back of his head. No doubt he had a set of Entwined implants too.

"Cut all traffic from Zaa's server clusters to this floor of the building, Nathan," he said.

With an even louder groan, Nathan nodded. "After that, maybe I can get to work on world peace or something. Since I'm not already busy or anything."

The CEO ignored the complaint, his attention already back on the massacre in Eltera City. Players and NPCs were dying by the score. Devon grimaced, thinking about how many of those NPCs would never respawn.

"I'd hoped that having two AIs would make for a better game," Bradley said. "I thought it would drive innovation."

Devon glanced at the screen again. A group of city guardsman NPCs had banded together and were organizing a reasonably effective defense near what looked like a central square. If the players managed to rally to them or more NPCs joined, they might be able to repel the demon assault. This wave, anyway. Given what she knew about players, phones were probably ringing around the world, dragging people away from sleep and work to either watch or log in to fight.

Despite the carnage, she couldn't help thinking that Bradley's idea hadn't been totally off base. The demon attack would be remembered for years. Just like real history, sometimes forces were uneven. Armies were outmatched. Often, those were the stories that survived.

Too bad the demon army was backed by a crazy programmer with no qualms about violating customers' privacy and minds. That kinda invalidated the whole "this is cool" notion.

"You sure you want to log in?" Emerson asked, quietly. "Doesn't look like a very fun time to be playing."

"Eltera City is a long ways from me," she said. "But even if it wasn't, I'm the Champion of Ishildar, the city that was once a beacon of light. Looks like Veia's going to need a rallying point for her forces."

The programmer gave her a bewildered look. "Huh?"

She smirked. "I have some orcs to smash, a relic to find, and a village to defend. Message me when you catch up with Penelope, okay?"

"Okay, the room's wireless is denying traffic from all servers assigned to Zaa," Nathan said.

Sinking into the couch, Devon pulled off her tinfoil hat and logged in.

Chapter Thirty-Three

THE HOUR OR so she'd spent offline meant it was already mid-morning in the game. The bright alpine sun stabbed her eyes as she logged in, throwing her off balance and nearly sending her plummeting down the center of the spire.

"Ever think of setting your character name to Grace?" Bob asked, flitting into view. "Because that would be pretty funny."

"Ever think of jumping down a garbage disposal?"

"A what?"

"Never mind." Devon started edging down the narrow path. Once she'd dropped below the height of the rim, she jammed her shoulder against the wall of the spire for added security. It seemed her 8 points in *Climbing* hadn't done much to change the mechanics of walking down a trail made for pygmies.

After she'd completed a couple revolutions, passing below what she judged as less than the four stories of height under which her *Levitate* spell would protect her from falling damage, she cast the spell and jumped.

A group of felsen squealed like guinea pigs when she landed beside them.

"I'm back," she said brightly, then fixed them with a hard stare. "Take me to your leader."

The blue heathens responded with a chorus of gibberish.

Unfortunately, you still have no clue what they're saying.

Fortunately, the smurfs seemed to have received the memo about pointy sticks, and no one jabbed her as they urged her through a tunnel into the cavern complex that opened off the hollowed-out spire.

For no reason that she could identify, the tunnels seemed darker than she remembered. Oil lamps still flickered in their niches, creating pools of light every few feet. Maybe her perception was just due to the contrast after logging in to find herself staring at the sun. Or maybe she'd burned her in-game retinas like an idiot.

She shook her head. It wasn't just the darkness. The tunnels and caverns seemed colder, too. Enough that she shivered and had to hug her arms over her belly.

"Everything okay down here?" she asked, knowing none of the craglings would respond.

Finally, after another dozen turns and ten minutes of walking, she followed the band of felsen into the large chamber with the central pool.

Greel stood from a seat near the rest of her followers at the edge of the room. "Only took you three days."

"Nice to see you too," she said, rolling her eyes. "Next time, you're welcome to go face the mythical beast in my place."

The lawyer snorted. "But then I wouldn't have achieved one hundred percent proficiency in the felsen language. And welcome back."

"Thanks. I think."

312

The felsen matriarch, Perlda, stepped forward. Unsure what to do, Devon ducked a shallow bow.

"I've ascended to the phoenix's perch, survived the fire, and retrieved feathers as proof," she said, feeling somewhat proud of her roleplaying as she swung her rucksack around and pulled up her inventory screen. Conveniently, the *Phoenix Feathers* stacked in groups of 20, so she was able to quickly grab the contents of a single slot.

Greel started to translate, but Perlda waved him off. She scarcely seemed to notice the glowing feathers in Devon's outstretched hand. After inhaling, she rattled off a string of incomprehensible yammering.

Greel's eyebrows twitched in concentration, and he licked his lips before translating. "We are aware of your success. For centuries, the fire of the phoenix prince has flowed through crevices in this mountain. It has warmed our chambers, added strength to our torches, and given life to our indoor gardens. In short, the phoenix has made our hidden existence possible. We have ventured forth rarely, obtaining seeds to refresh our crops and occasionally capturing enemies who have ventured too close. Now that is gone. The fire is no more. Great changes come to our land."

The felsen woman was *still* prattling on, and Greel looked distressed as he tried to interpret. Swallowing, he continued.

"The champion rises at long last, and with her lies the final fate of the felsen. We will either reclaim our ancestral territory, or we will, finally, leave this world forever. Our survival is in your hands, champion."

As soon as she'd finished speaking, Perlda had fallen to her knees before Devon. Head bowed, the small blue woman quivered.

Quest Complete: Trial by Fire

You have gained esteem with the Felsen Race: +700 Reputation.

You receive 34000 experience.

Congratulations! You have reached level 18!

"So their whole race now depends on you," Greel commented. "No pressure."

Devon ignored him, turning to speak to Perlda directly. "Can you understand me?"

The woman nodded. "Most. Harder speak than listen."

"I do wish to be your champion. My quest is to reclaim the city of Ishildar, but to do that, I need the relics that were held by the five vassal societies."

The woman blinked, her brows drawn together while she tried to understand.

Devon pulled the *Greenscale Pendant* from beneath her armor. "I'm looking for something like this."

Comprehension washed across the woman's face, and she nodded. "You want Azuresky Band."

Devon nodded furiously.

Perlda's face fell, and she shook her head. "Enemy take. Keep in throne room. Deep deep down."

"The orcs?"

The little blue woman nodded.

Perlda is offering you a quest: Slay the Orc Shaman-King

Seems like the next relic is being held by the Orc Shaman-King. Realistically, that's kind of convenient, because you wanted to take care of him anyway.
Objective: Kill the orcs' leader.
Reward: 29000 experience.
Accept? Y/N

Perlda is offering you a quest: Retrieve the Azuresky Band.
Once you take care of the felsens' Nemesis Numero Uno, find the priceless treasure he stole from them.
Objective: Search the orc king's throne room for the relic of Ishildar once held by the Argenthal Vassaldom.
Reward: Azuresky Band
Reward: 50000 experience
Accept? Y/N

As Devon accepted the quests, Dorden cleared his throat. "Speaking of lost possessions..." the dwarf said.

Devon nodded and looked to Greel for help on this one. "Can you ask her whether she can make the poltergeist give Agavir back?"

As Greel spoke, the woman's face grew increasingly somber. The lawyer seemed to notice this because his voice took on a pleading tone. After a few more words, Perlda shook her head and raised a hand to cut him off.

"Is problem," she said, then turned to Greel to finish the sentence in her language.

315

Greel listened, then nodded. "She says their ancestors are fickle. They resent the curse and the binding that has tied them to this task for so long. And because they can taste it but can't fully experience it, they're jealous of our mortal existence. That's why they steal."

"Okay, so does that mean she can't talk to them? What about if we clear the orcs and release the poltergeists from the curse?"

Greel translated, then listened to Perlda's response.

"She says they definitely won't heed a request like that from her people. I get the sense that the felsens' relationship with the phantoms isn't much better than ours. As for clearing the curse...she believes the items will be returned to the physical plane, but they'll be...scattered. Agavir could rematerialize halfway across the realm for all she knows."

As Greel spoke, Dorden's face shifted between anger and grief. His mustache and beard twitched as he stared at the felsen woman. "Blasted blue—"

"But there is one possibility," Greel said hurriedly, raising a hand to still the dwarf. "The poltergeists might be persuaded to make a trade if Perlda offers it. They will require something of equal value to Agavir."

"As in, worth the same amount of coin?"

Greel relayed the question, and Perlda shook her head before turning to Devon.

The lawyer translated her words. "Something of similar importance to another. She believes an item that has meaning for a starborn will be most likely to satisfy the ancestors' covetousness."

Scratching her head, Devon opened her inventory. Her attention hovered over the *Everfull Waterskin*. She had a vague attachment to it, but realistically, the water was always lukewarm and never tasted that good. Shaking her head, she brushed aside the window and peered at her equipment screen instead.

One slot caught her eye.

Item: Fancier Tribal Sandals

Immediately, memories rose up. She saw her first meeting with Hezbek. The mistakes with Uruquat and Gerrald's willingness to help her. Despite all his prodding, she'd refused to replace her shoes with something practical because she couldn't help wanting to keep those memories of her newbie days close.

With a sigh, she bent down and untied the leather straps. When she handed them over, Perlda nodded.

"We make plea to ancestors," she said solemnly.

Devon nodded, keeping her eyes off the sandals until they disappeared into the small crowd of craglings. Swallowing, she cleared her throat.

"And now," she said, glancing at Greel to assure his help translating, "I want to talk about the future. I wish to rid your lands of the orcs forever, but I need your help. I propose we hold a planning council this afternoon, and tomorrow, that we prepare for war."

***

The morning after the war council, Devon met with her fighters in the same large chamber. The felsen leader had already been in the cavern when the members of the Stonehaven League shuffled in after their rest, and now Perlda watched with keen eyes, a trio of lieutenants hovering behind her.

"Everyone ready to do this?" Devon asked her friends.

Grim nods answered her, and she turned to Perlda. The headwoman, with some difficulty, lifted a folded leather sheet and staggered forward. She deposited the package in front of Devon, who nodded and crouched to open it.

She smiled at the headwoman as she picked up the familiar warhammer.

> **You have received:** Agavir the Pummeler.
> *Forged in the depths of Coldpass Hold, this weapon looks to have bashed many a skull over the years.*
> 29-32 Damage (scales with Strength) | 350/350 Durability
> -50% Accuracy vs Spirits |+10 Damage

When she handed it over, Dorden's brow lowered. "What's this with the accuracy debuff?"

Perlda shrugged. "Ancestors say changed hammer some."

Dorden grunted. "Well, at least they had the good sense to add damage and fix the dents. Otherwise, I might have some poltergeist skulls to pummel."

He holstered the warhammer and crossed his arms over his chest. Despite the gruff words, Devon got the sense he was pleased with the modifications.

> **Quest Completed:** Recover Agavir.
> You receive 30000 experience.

Next, she picked up her new footwear. The boots were crafted of supple leather with hardened soles. A circle of polished blue stones had been inset around the top cuff.

You have received: Boots of the Crags.
Blessed with the spirit of the high peaks, these boots instill grace in movement as well as fortitude for long treks through perilous terrain.
30 Armor | 75/75 Durability
+2 Climbing| +2 Constitution | +1 Speed | +3 Agility

Nice Agility buff. Seems even the felsen noticed your clumsiness.

Devon ignored the game's commentary and smiled at Perlda. "They're wonderful," she said, slipping them on. "I feel more agile already."

The woman nodded. "We hope to please champion."

Greel cleared his throat, impatient as usual, but Devon ignored him. She glanced toward Hazel and the pair of dwarven miners who stood at the edge of the room.

"You'll be safe here," Devon said. "Even if something happens to us, we'll return for you eventually. Please don't leave the sanctuary." She fixed Hazel with a pointed stare.

"Don't worry, Your Gloriousness," Hazel said, edging close to Zoe. "I have the bird to occupy my time."

Devon turned back to Perlda. "Are you sure this plan works for you? There is more danger for the felsen than I would like."

Perlda spoke something in their language which Greel translated. "She's sure. They've waited nearly one thousand years for your arrival." The man rolled his eyes. "I can't help but think how it must be a little disappointing..."

Devon kept her eyes on the felsen headwoman rather than letting Greel bait her. "Then let's do this."

Chapter Thirty-Four

DEVON'S PARTY WAITED in the shadow of a stone spire for the signal from the felsen. Around a hundred feet below, the southernmost entrance to the warren of orc tunnels opened in the base of a dark cliff. While the party had waited, covered by the spire's shade and Devon's *Fade* spell, two groups of orcs had left the cavern, likely to hunt. They wielded bows and clubs and squinted beady eyes against the glare of the mountain sun. Occasionally, snatches of the beasts' guttural language rumbled from the cavern entrance, but from her current vantage, Devon couldn't see inside.

Hand on rough granite, she kept her gaze pinned to a cliff looming over a tunnel mouth farther to the north. She couldn't see the felsen climbers on the sheer cliff, nor could she see the fleet-footed youths who had been chosen as bait to lure orcs from their lair. Devon hated to think of the risks those young craglings were taking, but she tried to reassure herself with Perlda's declaration that the orcs would never be able to catch a felsen, especially when the cragling had a head start. On the few occasions their races had encountered one another in open terrain, the felsen parties had survived unscathed. The real risk was orc raids on settlements, something that the felsen had avoided by hiding inside the peak guarded by the phoenix prince.

Devon took a deep breath of the mountain air. As the sun warmed the landscape, rising currents brought the resiny smell of the pine forest below. Cliff swallows darted in and out of crevices on the sheer stone faces. It was a pleasant morning, but the truth was, waiting sucked. Especially when she had so much to worry about. Over the last few hours, she'd *almost* managed to convince herself not to be too anxious about Stonehaven. The defenses plus the friendly player army would surely be enough to stop the raid. Reluctantly, she'd allowed their player allies to ask Hezbek to bind them at the Shrine to Veia, which meant that even if the odds were against the friendly army, they had a nearby spawn point and a village with crafters able to repair some gear.

Ultimately, the raiders would need an overwhelming force, not just a superior force. And she just didn't think that a bunch of losers who wanted to cause grief for the sake of it could get that organized.

As for the demon stuff, Devon had verified that the *Shadowed* stat and demonic abilities had disappeared when Zaa's connection to her implants had been cut. Unfortunately, the flashes of anger and despair hadn't, but they'd continued to become less frequent. The bigger concern right now was what Penelope's wrongdoings meant for Relic Online and its players in the long run.

Not to mention, what would the sudden invasion of Eltera City and the other starting city mean for the state of the game world?

Thinking of her character sheet reminded her of the unspent attribute points she'd gained when hitting level 18. With a major dungeon crawl coming up, it wasn't a great time for her usual procrastination on assigning points. She pulled up the sheet and considered.

Character: Devon (click to set a different character name)
Level: 18
Base Class: Sorcerer
Specialization: Unassigned
Unique Class: Deceiver
Health: 323/323
Mana: 547/547
Fatigue: 9%

Attributes:
Constitution: 23
Strength: 11
Agility: 20
Charisma: 41
Intelligence: 32
Focus: 13
Endurance: 20

Special Attributes:
Bravery: 7
Cunning: 8

The biggest issue with an attack of this scale would be the ability to keep fighting. With tight corridors, they could control the number of enemies to some extent, but like she'd told Dorden, the biggest concern was that the orcs could *keep coming*. Hopefully, the felsens' distractions would take some of the pressure off, drawing attention and orc fighters to other branches of the cavern system. But still, combats would probably be longer than anything she'd faced so far.

Focusing on *Endurance,* she put three points into it and one into *Intelligence.* While *Charisma* would increase the overall size of her mana pool, she'd already invested heavily there. *Intelligence* would increase the damage of her spells, while *Endurance* would boost her mana and health regeneration, not to mention slow the rate at which her *Fatigue* grew. All told, it would be a good boost to her staying power.

Satisfied, she closed the window and returned her attention to the cliff face where one group of the felsen were preparing their distraction. A few minutes later, a shout echoed from the hole at the base of the cliff. A group of orcs ran out, war clubs raised. A loud crack shot over the landscape as, directly above the tunnel mouth, a pillar of stone that had to be ten feet long detached from the cliff and tumbled end over end to smash in front of the entrance to the cave, catching two of the trailing orcs and burying them in the rubble.

"Now," Devon hissed as she stepped from the shadows, canceling her *Fade* effect and starting down the steep slope. The party followed, plunging feet into the loose earth and creating small cascades of soil and stone.

A pair of orcs ran from the cave mouth below, drawn by the sounds from the other entrance. Bayle and Heldi's shots streaked through the air, skewering the closest of the orcs through the throat. He gurgled and clutched at the shafts as Devon hammered him with a tier 2 *Flamestrike* that splashed fire damage over his fellow brute.

The first orc collapsed in a smoking heap as the second guard growled and shouted for help. Scars white in a face purple with rage, he ran for Devon with club upraised.

"For me Stoneshoulder ancestors!" Dorden bellowed as he rushed to intercept. The second orc scarcely had time to blink before Agavir the Pummeler knocked out his teeth.

***

Another orc gasped and then died as Devon speared it with a sun-cast *Shadow Puppet*, sending a lance of darkness through its heart.

The area outside the cavern mouth fell silent, her party members bent at the waist and propping their hands on their knees as they panted. Devon pulled off her *Forest Leather Headband*, fixed her ponytail to recapture the hair that had been getting in her eyes, then settled the headband back into place. She took a deep breath and glanced at the carnage as Heldi stood upright and started casting heals to restore the party.

The second orc's cry for help had been a little more successful than she'd expected, bringing down a horde of at least fifteen fighters on their heads before Devon had managed to seal the tunnel exit with a *Wall of Ice*. If not for Heldi's damage shield punishing the brutes every time they landed a blow on Dorden, the party would have wiped. In fact, they almost did wipe when the *Wall of Ice* had shattered and allowed a couple more adds into the brawl. Devon had dropped to 20 hitpoints, when one of her tier 2 *Flamestrikes* had scored a critical hit and splashed double damage over a pack of the attackers, pulling their attention onto her.

Fortunately, Dorden was getting better and better at rescuing her from her bad decisions. From now on, she'd have to be more careful about managing her aggro.

Quickly, Devon made a circuit of the region and looted the bodies, coming away with a couple dozen copper coins and a *Crude Onyx Charm (unidentified)*. Given that it had come off an orc that was basically cannon fodder, she doubted it would be worth much, but she slipped the charm into her inventory anyway. She left the weapons and clothing in heaps on the ground. Afterward, they could consider whether any of the weapons could be melted down to help with the iron shortage back in Stonehaven, but for now, she didn't want to fill her inventory.

Especially since her 11 *Strength* meant that her rucksack straps dug painfully into her shoulders and tired the muscles of her back. Even if she could ignore the pain, the weight seemed to affect her *Fatigue*. Until they knew how long it would take to reach the throne room, she couldn't afford the burden.

She glanced at Heldi's entry in the group interface and saw that the woman's mana was back to full. With a nod, she started for the tunnel mouth.

You have discovered: Cavern of Spirits
Yes, right now Cavern of Orcs might be a better name. But in case you'd forgotten what will happen when the lights go out...
You receive 20000 experience.

Devon took a shaky breath. No, she hadn't forgotten that killing the orc king would likely douse the lights. That was part of the point; they couldn't expect to clear the whole area of orcs given the size of the infestation. For better or for worse, they had to rely on the poltergeists. Earlier, she'd hoped to come up with some clever plan to pit the orcs and phantoms against one another while the party escaped unscathed. But since she hadn't thought of anything clever, she'd had to consider this might be a suicide mission.

Reach the throne room. Kill the king. Hopefully find the relic before the poltergeists massacred everyone in the cavern.

Under level 20, the death penalty involved a trip to her spawn point and heavy damage to her gear. It sucked, mostly because it included *dying*. But as long as she found the *Azuresky Band* before the poltergeists decided to steal it, the price was acceptable.

An unpleasant shout echoed through the cavern as the group advanced away from the spill of sunshine and into the torchlit halls of the orc army. The sound of bare feet slapping stone followed.

Devon drew her dagger and summoned a *Glowing Orb*.

Time for round two.

***

Over three hours had passed in-game since the party had stepped over the threshold and entered the orc lair. Three hours of combat, an endless cycle of pulling groups of mobs if they were lucky or being suddenly attacked if they weren't. Devon's arm ached from her occasional contribution of a *Backstab* or two to the melee combat. Her *Fatigue* was over 45%. The situation worried her, since it was unlikely they'd find a safe place to rest before reaching the throne room.

As she glided forward, following the party on a cushion of air from her *Levitation* spell, she wondered how raiding parties would handle long dungeons if their *Fatigue* limited the amount of time they could keep fighting. It would probably be an important consideration for high-level content.

The situation also made her wonder whether they should retreat to the felsen sanctuary to recover. Unlike most games, the orcs they'd killed wouldn't respawn. At least, she didn't think they would. With a Shaman-King as the boss of the dungeon, maybe that was a flawed assumption. In fact, the more she thought about it, the more likely it seemed that there would be *something* in the game mechanics that would ensure that players had to tackle challenges all at once. For all she knew, leaving the dungeon would lead the orcs back to the felsen sanctuary, bringing an army down on the small population and ensuring their extinction.

Regardless, even if there wasn't a consequence for leaving the dungeon, the felsens' distraction wouldn't work more than once. And with a group of five adventurers against hundreds of orcs, they needed the diversion. Even now, she could feel the increasing danger as more and more unexplored side tunnels lay behind the party. From any one of them, orc contingents could come flooding in from other parts of the lair. The felsens' aid reduced that risk, but it didn't eliminate it completely.

"Incoming!" Dorden shouted, taking a combat stance as a group of snorting and slobbering brutes came barreling down the tunnel ahead.

Devon dropped a *Freeze* on the lead orc, catching another of the attackers due to the 20% chance to root other nearby targets. Dorden cheered and Greel melted against a wall, preparing a sneak attack.

Sliding back out of melee range, Devon slapped a *Glowing Orb* on the ceiling just in case she could make use of a lightning *Shadow Puppet* without electrocuting her allies, then started tossing *Flamestrikes*.

Kill. Rinse. Repeat.

***

Congratulations! You have reached level 19!

For possibly the first time in Devon's gaming career, she was *not* psyched to see the message. Her whole backup plan—or maybe it wasn't even a backup plan—involved the ability to endure a whole-party slaughter once they'd recovered the relic. But not knowing the death penalty at and above level 20 really screwed with that idea. Given the way things seemed to go for her in Relic Online, kind of a Murphy's Law theme, she had a bad feeling that the change would not play well with her kamikaze plan.

Of course, it might be a moot point anyway, since she was starting to worry they'd never *find* this shaman-king, much less the *Azuresky Band* that he'd stolen from the felsen. They'd been advancing through the orc lair for five hours, fighting so many brutes that she'd started to think that the smells of rotting meat, orc body odor, and blood would be stuck in her nostrils forever. At every juncture, they chose either the widest or the most down-sloping tunnel. But still, she had no idea how much farther they needed to go before finding the throne room.

There'd been maybe half a dozen scenarios running through her head under which they might fail this mission. Getting ambushed by more orcs than they could fight. Encountering mobs they didn't expect. A mistake by one of their party. A moment of inattention on Heldi's behalf leading to a critical heal being missed. Devon had even considered there might be a betrayal by the felsen—despite Perlda's words and the return of Dorden's warhammer, Devon recalled too well the feeling of rough coils of rope binding her to a

329

stake, and she *still* hadn't figured out what the deal was with their creepy filed teeth.

She hadn't expected their bold advance to fizzle out as, one by one, the party members ran out of energy. It just seemed so anti-climactic to think they might just fall over from fatigue and lie there until some bumbling orc stumbled over them.

Shaking her head, she paddled her feet on her *Levitation* cushion and continued forward past another of the unsnuffable torches. The flame crackled softly, and warmth caressed the side of her cheek as she passed.

Devon almost didn't hear the scraping sound from behind. Or rather, she was so weary of battling orcs and so used to their guttural shouts and spit-covered tusks that her reflexes had become dull. But some base instinct brought her head around in time to see the arrow streaking for her neck. She got her forearm up and deflected the missile, the fletching slicing a gash in a *Bracer of Smoke.*

"Behind!" Devon hurled a *Glowing Orb* that she'd been carrying in her free hand. It glommed onto the ceiling and hung there wobbling as she poured mana into a *Shadow Puppet.*

Her minion went streaking toward the band of around ten orcs who roared as they attacked. The dark form disappeared inside the horde and electricity crackled and arced over the group while Devon summoned another orb and slapped it against the wall.

Her first shadow disintegrated, and—as promised by the percentage chance in her tier 3 spell description—rematerialized at her side. Devon grinned when she realized she could still cast two more by targeting the shadows cast by her pair of orbs. It wasn't anywhere near as awesome as attacking with six at once, but three wasn't *terrible*.

She sent the shadows streaking toward the orcs, hoping to get at least one more round off before the attackers closed the distance with the party and made her lightning puppets too dangerous to use.

"No fair!" Dorden shouted as a cage of lightning enveloped the orcs. The brutes bellowed, lightning crackling inside their mouths as the two nearest the center of the group dropped dead.

"Haven't ye had enough face smashing for one day, ye fool man?" Heldi asked, dropping a damage shield on Devon in case Dorden couldn't grab aggro.

"Never!" Dorden shouted as he sprinted forward on stubby legs.

Heldi looked at Devon and shrugged as she raised her crossbow, closed an eye, and squeezed off a shot. Her target died with a bolt through the eye just as Bayle's arrow took another between the ribs.

Shaking his head, Greel sprinted forward like liquid death, passed Dorden, and exploded into the group with a volley of kicks and punches that were almost too quick to follow.

Dorden's offended shout echoed down the tunnel. Devon couldn't help laughing as the lawyer cleaned up the group before Dorden could get his first swipe in.

You receive 2600 experience!
You receive 2700 experience!
You receive 2650 experience!
You receive 2600 experience!
You receive 2600 experience!
You receive 2700 experience!
You receive 2600 experience!

You receive 2600 experience!

You receive 2650 experience!

You receive 2600 experience!

You receive 2700 experience!

Devon winced. The experience for the fight represented just a fraction of what she needed to go from level 19 to 20, but it all added up.

Heldi was still snickering, oblivious to Devon's concern. Shaking his head, Dorden whirled on the group. "Think this is funny, do ye?" he said, stomping back to the party as Greel stooped to loot the bodies.

"Only mildly," his wife answered.

Dorden snorted as if disgusted. "Ye just wait. Maybe next time I'll stand in the back and see how ye fare without Agavir smashing through the enemy ranks."

Heldi just raised an eyebrow. "The day you pass up a fight is the day the dwarven race loses its taste for ale."

Greel stalked back into the group, interrupting the banter and dropping a silver piece and a couple of coppers into Devon's outstretched hand.

She slipped the coins into her rucksack and watched the inventory screen automatically update her coin counts.

"If nothing else, this adventure is making improvements to Stonehaven's cashflow problem," she said.

"What do ye mean, *if nothing else*," Dorden said. "We still have an orc king to slay, if I remember right."

Devon swallowed and glanced at her Fatigue. 60%. She took a breath to avoid infecting others with her worry. "You're right. I just wish we were there already."

"Uh, Mayor Devon?" Bayle stood along the tunnel around twenty paces ahead of the group.

"Yes?"

The archer motioned her forward. Devon stopped, eyes wide, when she realized what Bayle had noticed. Ahead, the corridor widened, a spill of light falling across the floor. The faint sounds of orcish conversation drifted down the tunnel. Unfortunately, a bend in the passage hid the source of the light from view.

It might not be the throne room, but whatever lay ahead was quite different from the maze of tunnels and sparsely furnished side chambers they'd passed so far.

Devon nodded. Now for the real fight.

She hoped.

Chapter Thirty-Five

EMERSON'S MESSAGE FLASHED into her view.

Are you somewhere safe? I mean, in the game.

She shook her head, amused that he'd needed to add the second sentence. Of course he meant "in the game" seeing as he was probably looking at her body while her mind was immersed in Relic Online. Which, come to think of it...she hoped she wasn't drooling or something. The implants helped with bladder control and alerted if there were other problems like dehydration—at least, they were supposed to. But had the hardware designers gone so far as to manage jaw and lip tension with regards to salivary gland production? Devon had never thought about it. She hadn't woken up with a wet pillow or anything, which she hoped meant good things.

But still. It abruptly felt kind of weird to be playing on Bradley Williams' couch with an unknown number of people watching.

"Not exactly," she said, dictating into the messaging app. Though she heard her voice as if she'd spoken in the foul-smelling orc tunnel, she knew that the game had funneled the input to the right place.

Covered by a *Fade* spell, she and her party crouched just outside the spill of light that—huzzah—*did* appear to be the throne room. Or at least an antechamber. Frames of wood covered with stretched hide blocked most of the view, each painted with crude scenes in red dye. Many fires burned in the chamber, some visible in iron baskets, some in rings of stones on the floor, some evident only by the glow and curl of smoke rising to join the haze that formed a pillow over the ceiling.

Alone, the size of the chamber and number of fires didn't mean much. But the orcs they *could* see made Devon relatively certain they'd reached the inner sanctum. Patrolling the room in groups of two and three, guards in heavier armor than they'd encountered so far brandished weapons with keen edges and a disturbing amount of gristle wedged in crevices or clinging to spikes. Other orcs scurried around in a servile manner, ducking their heads as they passed beneath the sight of the guards.

In the center of the room, a tall pole held what appeared to be a collection of scalps. With the number of sparks swirling around the room from the fires, Devon was surprised the trophies hadn't caught fire.

Another message flashed.

Can you get somewhere safe? I'm a little concerned that things may become unstable.

"Uh, not exactly. I'm kinda five hours deep into an orc warren. Pretty much knocking on the boss's door." Devon paused for a second. "What kind of unstable?"

Well, the good news is we found Penelope. The bad news is we found Penelope.

"Maybe you should elaborate."

I thought I was pretty clever to hire a helicopter. I don't know what she did to get to Arizona so fast, but it seems better than my plan. We caught her on the security cameras of one of the server farms. Her access was restricted, but she must have had some sort of back door, because she's inside now. We're heading out to capture her, but I can't help but think she knows we're coming.

"Is she going to start shooting people or blowing things up? Because I feel like I'm in some crappy action film."

I don't know. But I'm worried she might try to hold the game hostage in some way.

"Hostage how? Is this server farm running Zaa or Veia?"

Both, unfortunately. We do our best to back up the game state, but it could be a disaster to try to reconstruct the play experience if she manages to take out sections of Veia's brain.

"Devon?" Greel whispered. "You were working on a plan? Might be good to execute before the rest of the orc army turns up."

She raised a hand to ask for patience.

"Either way, I can't get out of here immediately."

Can you just log out? Try to finish the dungeon later?

She glanced at her friends. And abandon them all the way down here? No way.

"Not possible. Keep me updated, okay?"

K.

When no messages followed after another couple seconds, Devon brushed the app window to the edge of her vision. "I kind of miss having Hailey and her *True Sight* right now," she said softly. It would be really nice to know what they were dealing with. Though it was hard to tell the groups of patrolling orcs apart, she guessed there were at least ten guards total. Plus the servants who probably had rudimentary combat skills. Plus the boss and any surprises that might come with him.

When the next pair of guards passed, she used *Combat Assessment*.

Orc Guard - Level 20
Health: 987/987

Orc Guard - Level 21
Health: 1012/1012

She winced. Seemed *Combat Assessment* was getting better all the time, the health information the latest addition. But looking at the guards' hitpoints, she wasn't sure she wanted to know. Pulling the whole room at once seemed like an exceedingly bad idea.

"I'm guessing orcs have at least mid-level intelligence," she muttered as she looked through her abilities list, trying to figure out a way to separate out some of the combatants. She was the only group member with any crowd control, and it wasn't all that great. Rooting mobs in place for three or four seconds with a *Freeze* spell was a good way to drain her mana without accomplishing much.

She could see *Simulacrum* being useful to confuse enemies and make them lose track of which targets were real, but unfortunately, the orcs were probably too smart to be fooled by her tier 2 spell.

Scanning the list, she stopped at *Ventriloquist*. She chewed a lip, thinking.

"Okay," she said after a moment. "Here's what we're going to do."

***

Five minutes later, the group was in place. They'd backed off around fifty feet from the end of the hallway, and once ahead, crouched against the wall using shadows and Devon's *Fade* spell for concealment.

A pair of guards moved into sight. Devon assured herself that Heldi's small cloak, a garment she'd taken to wearing after being named one of the tribe's hunters, was wrapped tight enough around her off-hand to hide the *Glowing Orb* in her palm. With a deep breath, she glanced at her messaging app one last time—nothing from Emerson—and cast *Ventriloquist*. Targeting an area near the bend where the passage curved out of sight, she gave her best felsen impression, a high-pitched puppy growl.

"Hunnngh?" one of the guards said. He stopped at the entrance to the tunnel, elbowing his partner. Silhouetted by the firelight, the muscular brutes looked even more intimidating. Devon hoped she wasn't about to get her party killed.

At least not until they had the relic.

The guards took a few steps down the passage. Devon made a few more puppy noises. The bigger of the two orcs called over his shoulder. The thump of spears on the ground announced the arrival of two more guards in the tunnel.

The first pair passed Devon's group. As far as she could tell, none of her party were breathing as the guards stomped in front of them.

She made a final felsen noise then tried to create the sound of a sword leaving a sheath. The resulting noise from down the tunnel sounded sort of like a dying owl.

Ventriloquist failed. Chance of success is greater with noises you can physically make. Try getting the ability to a higher tier.

Yeah, yeah. She brushed the notification away. Dying owl or bared steel, the sound served to keep the guards coming.

The first pair of guards stopped at the bend in the tunnel and looked around in confusion. When the second pair had moved past the group, Devon stood, canceling the *Fade* effect. Separating out four guards was a start, but if they really wanted to take down the boss, they needed to do better.

Wishing she'd spent more time raising her *Stealth* skill, she crept along behind the guards. Fortunately, between her improved *Agility* score and the lack of things to trip over, they didn't seem to notice her.

As soon as the second pair of guards drew even with the first, Devon whipped Heldi's cloak off her hand and threw the *Glowing Orb* at the ceiling above the guards. A fuzzy shadow appeared beneath her feet, and she snap-summoned a *Shadow Puppet* and sent it near—but not into—the group of orcs.

Casting *Fade* again, she pressed her back to the wall.

The orcs were yelling and pointing at the glowing ball on the ceiling. From the entrance of the tunnel, more guttural shouts announced the appearance of another patrol. The new pair ran down the hall toward their comrades.

Devon closed her eyes. The longer this went on, the more likely they'd pull too many mobs for her group to deal with. But the trick would only work once. Whichever orcs weren't separated from their friends might need to be battled at the same time as the boss.

After the fourth patrol—this time with three guards—showed up and stepped into the hall, shouting at the others who stood beneath the orb looking angry and perplexed, Devon sprinted toward her party.

"Okay, go for it," she said.

As Dorden stepped to intercept the trio of guards, Devon sent her *Shadow Puppet* into the group at the end of the tunnel. As the crackle of electricity reached her ears, she stepped toward the tunnel entrance and cast *Wall of Ice*, sealing the opening.

She kept her focus on the ice as her friends engaged the orcs. When her *Shadow Puppet* reappeared beside her—a lucky stroke, considering that the chance of respawn was only 20%—she glanced over her shoulder to verify that her party was still out of range of the lightning's area of effect, then sent the puppet back into the guards at the end of the hall.

Though she wasn't fighting in this skirmish, Devon's job was in many ways the most critical. She had to hold the wall just like the Night's Watch. Her NPC friends hadn't gotten that little joke, but it still amused her to no end.

The wall shattered as enemies pounded their way through.

Devon cast *Wall of Ice* two feet closer to the group before any additional orcs could make it into the hallway.

Behind her, an enemy died with a strangled shout.

Dorden cheered.

Heldi muttered.

The wall shattered again.

Devon took a step back and cast another copy.

Ten minutes later, when her *Wall of Ice* was close enough that she could feel its coolness against her skin, silence fell in the tunnel behind her.

You receive 2900 experience!
You receive 3000 experience!
You receive 3000 experience!
You receive 2950 experience!
You receive 2900 experience!
You receive 2900 experience!
You receive 2950 experience!

She winced as another chunk of her experience bar turned golden and glanced at her group interface. Heldi's mana was low, and Dorden was at 75% health, but everyone was alive.

"Recover while you can," she said. "One Orc Shaman-King coming up."

Silence held for a minute or two until cracks started to form in Devon's *Wall of Ice*. Heldi's mana was still below half. Tugging a mana potion from her inventory, she tossed it to the dwarf woman. Heldi caught the little pot, pulled out the stopper, and chugged the tonic down as Devon backpedaled and summoned a *Wall of Fire* behind the failing barrier of ice. Heldi's mana jumped to nearly full as the ice exploded inward, a cloud of glittering shards which burst into sudden steam when they hit the flames.

Howls and grunts rumbled through the tunnel as a horde of enraged orc cannon-fodder burst through the flame wall.

Devon cast *Conflagration* as she continued to back toward the group. The mass of orc servants was hurled by the explosion, smoking meat missiles flying in all directions. Devon ducked an orcish cook, ladle still clutched in its charred hand as behind her, Dorden's hammer batted flying flesh aside.

Some of the orcs staggered to their feet. Others tried to crawl, only to be picked off by shots from Bayle and Heldi. Greel darted through the crowd, laying brutes out flat with flying roundhouse kicks and strange, straight-fingered jabs to the throat. A couple of servants reached the party members, landing weak blows and shaving off shards of health, but rays of light shot from Heldi's free hand as she topped off everyone's health. A couple of Devon's tier 2 *Flamestrikes* finished off the wave of attackers, and she sidestepped back to the wall as game messages scrolled across her vision.

> You receive 1200 experience!
> You receive 1200 experience!
> You receive 1200 experience!
> You receive 1200 experience!
> You receive 1200 experience!
> You receive 1200 experience!
> You receive 1200 experience!
> You receive 1200 experience!
> You receive 1200 experience!
> You receive 1200 experience!
> You receive 1200 experience!
> You receive 1200 experience!
> You receive 1200 experience!
> You receive 1200 experience!
> You receive 1200 experience!

Crap. Devon grimaced as her experience bar filled by yet another fraction. She was getting close to 40% of her next level, and they hadn't even caught sight of the boss.

She had little time to worry about it, though, because another enraged roar shook the tunnel. Five more guards loomed in the corridor entrance.

Devon cast *Freeze*, but the secondary effect didn't fire, and ice only enveloped one of the mobs. The other four sprinted toward the party. Two detached and headed for Devon, prompting a bellow from Dorden. The dwarf leaped forward and aimed a massive, two-handed swipe at the orc nearest her, knocking the brute's head sideways and sending a tusk flying. Momentarily stunned, the guard staggered back into his companion, and Devon resisted the urge to nail them with the *Flamestrike* as she sprinted to the other wall of the tunnel—no sense making it *harder* for Dorden to grab aggro.

The other two guards pounded forward, focusing on Bayle who was loosing arrows like a Vegas dealer spraying cards. Dorden's stubby legs seemed to blur as he raced to intercept, and as the *Freeze* effect broke and released the final guard, the dwarf managed to collect the orcs in a loose mob.

Arrows, crossbow bolts, and a flying lawyer pelted the guards from behind while Dorden swung his warhammer in methodical arcs. Orc-wielded clubs pounded the dwarf between each swing, clanging off platemail and chain.

Dorden's health seesawed between 20% and 70% as his wife frantically kept him alive by chain-casting her heal spells. Nervous about drawing too much attention, Devon cast periodic *Freeze* spells to allow Dorden to step out of melee range of some of the guards while only occasionally hitting the orcs with a *Flamestrike*. She kept an eye on the corridor entrance. An unknown number of mobs remained in the main chamber, and she didn't want the group to be surprised.

When Dorden's health momentarily dipped to around 10%, Devon gritted her teeth and threw him a health potion. Unlike health pots she'd used in other games, the *Jungle Health Potions* needed no reuse timer or once-per-combat restriction. Instead, the taste was so foul that if someone tried to down a second dose too soon after the first, the attempt ended in projectile vomiting and a *Sickened* debuff that sapped *Strength* and *Constitution*. She hated that their healer and tank had already needed to use potions, but at least the party was still alive.

Between the *Jungle Health Potion* and a couple of lucky misses by the attacking orcs, Dorden's health worked back up to around 90% as the first two guards fell to a pair of backstabs from Greel. Deciding that the dwarf had had enough time to build up aggro, Devon loosed back to back tier 2 *Flamestrikes* on the guard with the lowest health, splashing additional damage over the others. Her main target dropped, and with a roar, Dorden slammed his hammer into first one ugly face, then another.

The guards spun to the floor.

> You receive 2900 experience!
> You receive 3000 experience!
> You receive 3000 experience!
> You receive 2900 experience!
> You receive 2950 experience!

"So far so good," Bayle said between breaths.

Devon smiled and tried to look reassuring, but she wasn't convinced that *good* was the proper description for their situation. The group was suffering in terms of mana and potions, and they still

345

had the boss fight ahead. Not to mention, the glowing frames around the entries in the group interface showed that the party was still in combat. Between that and the piles of orc bodies, the eerie quiet that filled the corridor was downright ominous.

As Heldi and Devon's mana ticked back toward full, the group started edging for the entrance to the chamber. Devon raised a hand to call for caution, but Greel was a little too eager. He stepped out over the threshold.

A shriek filled the chamber as the painted screens blocking their view erupted in geysers of flame and almost instantly turned to ash.

Silence returned as the smoke cleared and ash settled to the ground, revealing a massive stone throne.

Devon fought a major sinking feeling in her gut. If the orc sitting on the throne *wasn't* the shaman king, they were so far up shit creek they'd never swim clear. Even if he *was* the boss, things didn't look great for their little group.

As the massive orc stepped from his throne, he kicked aside a heavy iron-bound chest as if it weighed nothing. He grabbed the pole decorated with scalps in one skillet-sized hand and bellowed something in the orcish tongue as he shook the grisly trophy. Wearing various leather wrappings, many of which were dyed red and black, he didn't seem interested in armor—probably because he didn't need it. He had no shortage of adornments, though. On each of his grotesquely large bottom tusks, he wore bands of gold and iron. Charms and fetishes dangled from his wrists and neck, and his eyebrows were pierced with the rods of bone and wood. Totems and carvings were scattered at the area around his throne, offerings from his minions, most likely.

"This should be fun," Devon muttered.

Greel scoffed. "Sometimes I wonder if you were dropped on your head as a child."

The orc king roared again, raising his hands as he started casting something. Devon fired off a *Combat Assessment.*

Glud, Orc Shaman-King – Level 23
Health: 3542/3542

She exhaled. "Guess we better get on with it."

As she started summoning a *Glowing Orb,* the orc's spell finished. A cage of lightning sprang up around him, crackling and hissing and lighting his features from beneath like a kid with a flashlight on Halloween.

"For the glory of Stonehaven!" Dorden bellowed as he started to rush forward.

"Wait!" Devon called, worried the lightning shield would do too much damage.

She needn't have bothered. Glud finished another spell, and heavy iron chains started slithering across the floor from innocuous piles on the edges of the room. Electric blue light flowed between the links, and crackling, diamond-shaped snake heads formed at the leading edge of the chains. Hissing, the chain serpents whipped themselves around Dorden, locking him in place.

He bellowed in pain as the first damage pulse hit, taking 10% of his life. Heldi immediately started casting a heal.

Devon shook her head. Crap.

"Greel, you're backup tank," she said. "Got it?"

"I'm what?"

"Get in that loser's way before he starts beating on the rest of us."

The look on the lawyer's face was so offended, Devon would have thought she'd insulted his dead mother. She shrugged. "Unless you want the party to die after all that wading through smelly orc tunnels?"

The man sighed, cheek twitching, as he narrowed his eyes at the boss. The king took a first long stride toward Heldi, an insane grin splitting his wart-covered face. Greel edged between the dwarf and the monster, a disgusted look on his face.

Devon threw her *Glowing Orb* onto the wall behind her but didn't bother conjuring a *Shadow Puppet*. The crackling cage around the boss made her think that lightning damage wasn't the best choice. Instead, she dumped mana into casting a *Flamestrike*.

"Can you get free, Dorden?"

The dwarf's response was a string of utterances she couldn't quite decipher, but which she guessed were not intended for mixed company.

So, no. Not at the moment.

Her *Flamestrike* fired, the column of flame pouring over the orc and knocking off 50 hitpoints. Moments later, one of Bayle's arrows streaked across the room and sliced through a gap in the lightning cage, piercing Glud through the massive bicep.

The orc roared and raised his hands, summoning a gust of wind that sent a barrage of objects hurtling toward the party. A dented pot clocked Greel in the head, sending him staggering. The orc turned his attention back to Heldi.

"Shit," Devon muttered. If the healer dropped, they were toast.

With a shout, Devon sprinted forward while casting *Levitate*. Heedless of the bars of lightning surrounding the monster—at least she'd electrocuted herself enough times to be used to the sensation—she sprang, dagger outstretched. The crackling shield smacked her flesh, sizzling lines traveling her nervous system and knocking her back as her *Levitate* spell landed.

The point of her dagger just barely scratched the orc king's shoulder as the knockback sent her careening across the room. Her skull cracked against stone as she smacked the wall and lost another chunk of health.

"Ow," she said a moment before Heldi's heal landed and spread a soothing chill through her body.

A second later, the orc king grunted. The monster raised his arm to look at the line of blood welling on his shoulder. He shivered as a poison tick from the wound shaved off a few hitpoints.

His face went dark, and his eyes narrowed as he looked from the wound to Devon. His angry shout reverberated in her bones as the lightning shield around him faded. He started sprinting toward her.

"Okay, new plan. Guess I'm backup tank."

For the next five minutes, Devon cycled between being punched by a massive fist that sent her careening like a billiards ball around the room, launching *Flamestrikes* to keep the king's attention, and casting *Freeze* to slow his advance while she whimpered and waited for heals. Bayle peppered the king with arrows while Greel attacked from behind, backstabbing and leveling kicks at the king's kidneys. The brute's health dropped to 2000 and then 1000.

Finally the spell that had animated the chains faded and Dorden broke free with a shout that was almost as loud as the orc's. The dwarf sprinted forward and wound up for a swing that landed on the orc's hip, sending the king staggering.

But after beating on Devon for most of the fight, Glud had no interest in giving up his new hobby. He ignored the dwarf and swung another rock-hard fist into her ribs, sending her flying once again.

Fortunately, they were winning. As long as Devon didn't wind up dead or with some sort of PTSD from her stint as a punching bag, it seemed her pessimism about their chances had been unfounded.

"Keep at it, guys! We're—"

Her words were cut off as a piercing wail stabbed her eardrums.

From a small door in the side of the chamber, an ancient orc shuffled forward. She walked with a cane and glared, her snarl displaying just a single tooth in a brownish expanse of gums.

Greel started running toward the newcomer and Devon popped off a *Combat Assessment* as the crone raised a hand and sent a wave of *something* toward the orc boss.

Glud's mother, Kraa - Level 20
Health: 79/79

"Oh blasted slag pits!" Dorden shouted.

"What?"

The dwarf pointed at the orc king.

Devon shook her head. "Really?"

The boss was back to full health. Kraa turned to Devon and cast her a smug glare.

Glaring back, Devon summoned a *Wall of Ice* on top of the crone. When she dispelled it, a rather flat version of the orc lay motionless on the stone floor.

You gain 600 experience!

"Guess that's one way of solving your problems," Greel muttered.

"Would you rather I—"

Devon swallowed her words when an ear-shattering roar shook the room.

"Mama!" the orc king shouted, his face black with rage.

You have uncovered a skill in which you have an intrinsic aptitude: Orcish Language (8)!
You have gained a skill point: +1 Orcish Language.

"You couldn't give me an intrinsic skill in, say, Felsen? Or how about Draconic?"

*Perhaps you should look into your heart. See why you might feel such an affinity for their coarse tongue. *cough* Takes one to know one?*

Shaking her head, Devon braced as Glud sprinted toward her, eyes nearly popping out of his head. This was going to hurt.

His fist connected. Ribs shattered as she went flying. More bones snapped when she hit the wall.

Devon's throat caught when her health bar flashed twice as brightly as it usually did and more than half her hitpoints disappeared.

"Uh..." Heldi called as she sprayed healing light toward Devon.

"Shit," Devon agreed. The whole "get slapped against the walls like a wet towel" strategy wasn't looking so hot.

As Glud spun to face her again, Dorden made another desperate attempt to get the boss's attention, hollering and jumping and leveling massive swipes at the monster's knees. The king ignored him, spittle drooling down his chin as he stomped toward Devon, arrows and attacks pounding his flesh but doing nothing to sway him from his target.

Her health was just over half despite Heldi's heal. She might live through another punch or two, but no longer.

Devon racked her brain for ideas. Her *Bracers of Smoke* were an option, but if the party vanished, the game might decide to reset the boss encounter and force them to start over. Best wait until all hope was lost for that. Slapping her hand on her *Leather Doublet of Darkness,* she tried to activate the ability, figuring the accuracy debuff might buy her another minute or so.

Nothing happened.

She yanked open the item description and saw that the ability attached to the chest piece was no longer part of the description. Same with her bracers. She shook her head and shoved the window away. Even her item abilities had been Zaa's work? The whole thing was really confusing.

Regardless, she was about to get pummeled again. Glud's fist was already cocked, veins popping from his massive bicep and shoulder, while he took the final steps. Uselessly, Devon tried sidestepping on her cushion of air and dropped mana into a *Flamestrike.*

Heldi landed another heal, tacking on extra hitpoints that immediately vanished when the rock-hard knuckles hit Devon in the jaw, knocking out teeth, snapping her head sideways, and sending her hurtling across the chamber yet again.

She had 20% health remaining and so many cracked bones Devon felt more like a sack of wet glass than a human. This fricking sucked.

"Mama dead!" Glud wailed, face going even blacker. He didn't seem to notice anything but Devon despite the steady damage dealt by her party.

Which made Devon wonder...she'd often heard that anger makes people stupid. Could she use that?

Given that she was pretty much toast, she might as well try *something* other than waiting for the next blow and casting a stray *Flamestrike.* She needed to clear her aggro by some means, because there was no way the party would kill the boss before he smacked her another couple times. Glancing about five feet in front of her, she started casting *Simulacrum* and imagined a new section of the uneven cavern wall materializing over the top of the strewn rubbish.

> *Cast failed. What part of "manifests a rough approximation of a **player or NPC**" was unclear?*

"Stupid fricking..."

> *Temper, temper.*

353

Okay, so she couldn't just create a stone wall illusion, but what if...

This time, when she cast the *Simulacrum*, she imagined the massive Stone Guardian that had chased her around Ishildar on her first day in the game. The stone giant had been as tall as an apartment building. Way too big to fit in here. But it wasn't like illusions had a hard time passing through walls. As she finished the cast, she envisioned the giant's chest filling the room, its head and shoulders embedded in the mountain above, its belly in the stone floor, and with Devon floating at a spot just behind its breastbone.

A wall of stone appeared in front of her. Unfortunately, it wasn't like one of those one-way mirrors from the old detective shows where she could see out, but at least the illusion was a shell rather than a solid mass. She wasn't swimming through Stone Guardian lung tissue or anything.

> *You stretched it on this one, but your Improvisation skill earned you a pass. To avoid future "creativity" of this sort:*
> **Congratulations! You have learned a new ability:** Illusory Object – Tier 1
> *You can create images of objects you've encountered, limited by your ability to recall details. Creatures of low to mid intelligence have a chance to see through the illusion every few seconds. (This chance is reduced by your Charisma score.) Creatures of high intelligence won't be fooled.*
> **Cost:** 65 mana
> **Duration:** 20 minutes or loss of concentration

Devon flicked the message away as she stared at the inside of the Stone Guardian's chest, waiting for the orc king to burst through. Though she could hear his footfalls, they'd slowed. Glud let out a confused grunt.

"Veia grant me strength!" Dorden bellowed just before the *smack* of his hammer striking flesh. Devon imagined Heldi rolling her eyes at the egregious use of multiple battle cries in a single combat.

Still, Glud, Orc Shaman-King didn't breach the illusion's wall. Devon flicked her gaze to the group interface. After a couple more seconds, Dorden's health dropped as the boss finally changed targets and started pounding on the dwarf. Devon let out a relieved breath. Canceling her *Levitation* effect, she dropped jarringly to the stone floor and backed to the wall. She cast *Fade* and slipped to a shadowy niche in the stone. As hard as it was to hide out with only the sounds of combat and the group's health bars to tell her how the fight was going, Devon wasn't about to press her luck.

Five tense minutes later, popups appeared.

You receive 9200 experience!

Quest Complete: Slay the Orc Shaman-King
You receive 29000 experience!

Devon dispelled her illusion in time to see Glud fall to his knees and topple onto his side.

A split-second later, the lights went out as every fire in the chamber was instantly extinguished.

In the faint blue glow from her single *Glowing Orb*, the party stared at each other as the first moans of the poltergeists drifted out of the tunnels.

Chapter Thirty-Six

"SEARCH EVERY CHEST," Devon called over the eerie sounds of the phantoms and the panicked shouts of orcs in the outer tunnels. "We need to find the relic. Now."

When she plucked at the dead orc king's clothing, his body disintegrated into loot. She scooped the items into her rucksack.

You have received: Golden Tusk Ring
Once you sanitize this item, it should be pretty spiffy. Made of solid gold, the band is inscribed with a triangular pattern that echoes the mountainous landscape. Fits the average human's thumb.
+0.5% Mana Regeneration

You have received: Shrunken Felsen Head
Maybe not the best idea to show this to your new friends. Though the item doesn't offer any benefits, some weirdos might consider it an interesting decoration.

Quest Updated: Pharmacopeia Failings
Objective: Gather new ingredients for Hezbek. (4/5)
Not sure you really want to drink a potion containing shrunken head shavings, but whatever...

You have received: Stoneskin Arm Cuff
Carved of mountain mahogany with images of the mighty giants who once inhabited the Argenthal region, this totem lends magical defense against physical attacks. Can be worn above the elbow so as not to interfere with bracers.
20 Armor | + 1 Strength

You have received: Veian Idol
This small doll made from leather and sticks may seem crude, but for the orc who crafted it, the creation was the high point of a life's work and reverence for her goddess.
Use: When ensconced near or within a place of worship, decreases the cost for boons while increasing the power of the shrine or temple's passive benefits.

Devon pressed her lips together as she read the final description. She fought a wave of guilt at the reminder that her Stonehaven followers and the orcs worshiped the same goddess. For some reason, she just had the feeling that "good" and "evil" creatures should have different deities, though she couldn't say why. Maybe it had to do with the environment she'd been raised in. Though she'd been to church a couple times—mostly as a tourist—the notion just seemed ingrained. Heaven vs. Hell. All evil issuing from a single malevolent force.

But here, Veia had created both. Or at least, she'd created a gradient. The orcs weren't necessarily evil for the sake of it. It was more like they had a different moral code. And there'd still been room for a sort of love in their souls, even if it were just between an old crone and her shaman-king son.

"Seriously, Dev?" she muttered to herself when she realized she was still staring at the item description for the idol. They were *orc NPCs*. Unless she wanted to be the game's first pacifist, she was going to have to get used to killing Veia's creations.

Reviewing the description for the *Stoneskin Arm Cuff*, she glanced at Dorden. They hadn't been using loot auto-splitting because there were no other players, but she'd planned to divide the spoils later. She probably owed him the cuff, seeing as he was their tank and all. But maybe she'd hold onto it just for now.

"Anything?" she asked as she stood from beside the spot where Glud had fallen.

"If I could see, I might have a better answer," Greel commented.

Right. No *Darkvision*. Squinting across the room, Devon picked out the grayscale forms of the dwarves as they opened chests and peered inside, but her human followers were shuffling cautiously with arms outstretched to avoid collisions. Summoning another *Glowing Orb*, she tossed it up to the ceiling, but it still wasn't enough to adequately light the room.

"Nothing to see anyway," Dorden said with a shrug. "All that's inside the chests is a few hunks of meat and a couple leather wraps."

Devon cocked her head. "That's it? For a throne room?"

She turned a slow circle, examining the room. Aside from the loose circle of open chests, there was the stone throne, a few fire rings with dead coals, scattered bones, broken earthenware bowls and pots, and other rubbish. A few of the offerings that had surrounded the throne before the battle lay strewn around, but none of them looked particularly special. She walked in a circle around the throne but spotted no compartments where a king might hide a prized possession.

She shook her head. "It has to be here somewhere..."

"Are you sure?" Bayle asked in a gentle voice. "I understand that the headwoman told you that, but she didn't have any real way to know."

Sucking the corner of her mouth, Devon pulled up her quest log again. Yes, the description definitely said to search the throne room. It didn't make sense to have that quest text but then place the item elsewhere.

So where...? Devon paused, gaze locked on the paper-flat form that was once Glud's mother. Of course. She tiptoed over, grimacing when she noticed how much surface area was created in the flattening process. She could probably have used Kraa as a kite.

Gingerly, she slipped the tip of her dagger under the thin edge of the body. To her relief, the corpse decomposed into just one piece of loot.

You have received: Azuresky Band

Once a relic known throughout the land as one of the key components needed to ascend to Ishildar's throne, this ring was most recently a simple gift from an orc man to his beloved mother. Who you killed. Meanie.

When worn within 10 kilometers of the city of Ishildar, imbues the owner with a sense of tranquility.

Within 10 km, grants: -10% Fatigue Gain | +1% Health every 6 seconds

Devon raised her eyebrows. That was a nice buff. As she slipped the band onto her finger, another pair of popups appeared.

Quest Complete: Retrieve the Azuresky Band
You receive 50000 experience!

Congratulations! You have reached level 20!

Nice work. Now the bad news. By attaining this level, you have proved yourself a capable player of Relic Online. Hopefully, you're done bumbling into giants and falling into goblin pit traps, because death isn't going to be quite so pleasant anymore. We'll take this in stages, working up to the full penalty by level 25. For now, in addition to equipment damage and a quick trip to your spawn point, you'll also leave behind a single item from your equipment or inventory. The item will not decay, so you're always welcome to return to whatever hellscape killed you in the first place in hopes of retrieving it.

Kisses,
-Relic Online

Devon shook her head. Was the sassy attitude really necessary? Wasn't the mini-corpse run bad enough? And had the game somehow *planned* to have her ding just after she looted the relic, or did she just have really shitty luck?

Standing, she grimaced as the sounds of poltergeists and orcs drew nearer.

Her plan of dying to get out of here wasn't looking so good anymore.

***

"Wait," Devon said. "I might have an idea."

The group was huddled along the back wall of the cavern, Dorden in front with Heldi's damage shield shimmering around his form. The glow of the ghost lights was now faintly visible, a pool of brilliant scarlet where the entrance tunnel to the throne room curved away and out of sight. Dark shadows cast by retreating orcs marred the wash of light.

Every time the poltergeists moaned, it sent a chill down Devon's spine. With every death cry of a horrified orc, she grimaced with an emotion that was almost pity.

"Now would be a good time," Greel said.

"I know. I'm just..."

Devon's words died as a bloom of blood-red light appeared in the air before the group. A phantom limb streaked forward, pummeling Dorden in the belly and sending him flying.

"Shit."

"You're just shit?" the lawyer said.

She glared at him. "I was just thinking that maybe my idea didn't matter. I thought we might be okay considering that both sides seemed occupied. Never mind that."

"And your other idea?" Greel's voice was laced with panic.

"For starters, retreat," Devon called over her shoulder as she sprinted for the hide flap that had covered the doorway where Kraa had emerged.

362

Devon shoved aside the flap, took two running steps into the room, then stopped short.

"Guess that explains why there was no treasure in the throne room," she muttered. The chamber wasn't large—a good thing given her plan to defend it as a last refuge. The only furnishings were a narrow hide-covered bed and a single torch affixed to the wall.

Devon couldn't stop staring at the heap of coins at the foot of the bed.

"Well, that solves our liquidity problem, doesn't it," Greel said.

"If we survive to bring it back to Stonehaven," Heldi muttered as she skidded to a stop beside Devon.

As if to accentuate her point, Dorden's grunt was followed by a shout as he came flying past and slammed against the wall. A red-eyed phantom chased after the dwarf, and light gushed from Heldi's hand as she cast another heal.

Devon grimaced. They could count their riches later.

"Okay." She glanced around the room, disappointed in the bareness. She'd been hoping for more flammable material. "Heldi, get damage shields on everyone."

She jumped aside as a missile, in this case a dented stew pot, flew into the room and tore off the hide flap. In the chamber beyond, at least a dozen orcs had backed out of the entrance corridor. They were in desperate straits, bleeding and broken as they tried to fend off the ghosts' assault.

"Bayle, strip the bed and pile the bedding in the middle of the room."

The woman nodded and rushed to the cot as Dorden took another massive hit and staggered. "Zaa's *tonsils* this one's a bastard!" he shouted, swinging his warhammer at empty air.

"I hope this works," Devon muttered as she cast a *Wall of Ice* to seal the chamber entrance. Chill spread into the room as Dorden flew forward, the poltergeist vanishing as quickly as it had appeared behind him.

Heldi landed a damage shield on her husband and immediately started casting a heal. The dwarf woman's mana was falling, but she still had more than half left. If they could just deal with this poltergeist and keep from attracting more, they might survive.

A second damage shield shimmered to life around Greel, and Devon ordered the lawyer to crowd in with the dwarf man. Shaking his head in disgust at being ordered around, Greel nonetheless complied.

"Ye hoping I'll take more of a liking to this one?" Dorden asked. "Because this isn't the time to force it."

"Actually, I'm just hoping the poltergeist has bad aim."

Heldi nodded approval when, on the next attack, both Greel and Dorden were sent flying. The damage shields blunted the hit, but the real benefit came when the double whip-crack of the "mother bear" counterattacks smacked the poltergeist.

"Take that, ye sweat off Zaa's nethers," Dorden said.

"Language, Dorden!" Heldi chided as she started casting. "We have a wee one now and ye can't just talk like ye're having ale with your clanmates."

Greel huffed as light streamed from the woman's hand and plunged through Dorden's armor. "I see how it is," he said. "Playing favorites."

"You *had* a chance to take over tank duties earlier," Devon offered.

Dorden took another hit before Heldi got another spell off, but the poltergeist seemed to be weakening. As the dwarf woman healed up both Greel and her husband, then cast another shield on Bayle, Devon cast *Phoenix Fire* on the pile of bedding. Warm light flared, prompting a distant squeal from the enraged poltergeist. Another attack smashed into the close-clustered trio of shielded NPCs, and the triple crack of the counterattack hammered Devon's eardrums.

As the flames on the bedding settled to a low smolder, Devon cast a pair of *Glowing Orbs* and stuck them to the ceiling. She nodded. A closed, well-lit space. It should be all they needed to keep additional spirits at bay.

"Might as well start swinging in case you hit," she said.

The fighters looked ridiculous swinging at the air, but when Dorden's warhammer thudded against spectral flesh, he let out a roar of triumph. The poltergeist attacked once more, but after the damage shields' retaliation, the phantom died with a wail.

Silence held for a moment as the flames on the bedding began to smoke for lack of fuel.

Devon glanced at the wooden cot. "We need to dismantle the bed and burn it, but go easy and be ready to toss in anything from your inventory that isn't critical. The fire has to last until the curse is lifted." With that, she sagged against the wall and lowered down to a seat, leaning forward to touch her dagger to the poltergeist's remains. She scooped up a single piece of dropped loot.

You have received: 1 x Fancier Tribal Sandal.
This shoe looks as if someone wore it swamp hiking, jungle bashing, and mountain climbing. Makes you wonder what they were thinking.

Shaking her head, she tucked the sandal into a rucksack. Maybe she could get it bronzed or something.

Nearing the spell's duration of ten minutes, her *Wall of Ice* started to crack. Now that she was out of combat, Devon's mana had already refilled. She stood, and within a split second of the wall shattering, she resealed the chamber. Dorden gave a grunt of approval as Devon returned to her seat and leaned her head against the wall.

"Well done, lass," he said. "I think ye brought us through this."

Devon sighed. Beside her thigh, a small mushroom sprouted from a crack in the stone floor. Looking for something to fiddle with, she plucked the little white button.

> **You have received:** Cave Mushroom
> *This variety of fungus grows deep in caverns in the Argenthal Vassaldom and is known to prefer crevices fertilized by centuries of skin flakes shed by orcs.*

> **Quest Update:** Pharmacopeia Failings
> **Objective:** Gather new ingredients for Hezbek. (5/5)

> *Aww, won't she be happy? And it seems you might even survive to bring her your treasures.*

Chapter Thirty-Seven

HOW'S IT GOING? Any word?

Devon's message flashed on the phone Emerson had picked up on the way from Atlanta to St. George. He looked from the glowing screen to the warehouse door where Penelope had hacked her way into the server farm.

He hit a button and dictated. "Moving in on Penelope. Are you safe yet?"

I'm stuck huddling by a fire in a homemade meat locker for the next couple hours. Can't log out but tell me if there's anything I can do from here. Twiddling my thumbs until the orcs and poltergeists sort out their issues.

Emerson blinked, twisting his mouth to the side. Sometimes it was weird to think about what was "normal" for the players of the game he'd helped create. Not to mention, it gave him a faint twinge of insecurity. Why would Devon want to spend time hanging out in the boring real world with someone like him when she could be doing whatever had led to her current situation?

...Not that he believed she actually wanted to hang out.

"Okay," he dictated. "Just get out when you can, and don't be surprised if you wake up to strangers."

He grimaced as he hit send, hating that he'd needed to abandon Devon in Bradley's office. No one was going to bother her, but he still felt responsible for keeping watch while she was immersed.

Which was pretty dumb, considering that she hadn't asked him to play knight protector or anything.

"We're good to go," said the headset-wearing wall of muscle who headed up the private security squad Bradley had brought in for this bid to capture Penelope.

"We need to try to talk to her first," Emerson said to Bradley once again. "You get why we can't let her pull any plugs, right?"

Bradley cast him an annoyed glance. "Yes, I get it. And I also get that you're worried about your new girlfriend and her teammates."

"She's not my—"

Bradley smirked as he cut Emerson off. "I know that, too. You don't seem the type to make a move."

Emerson looked away. It didn't matter what Bradley Williams thought of him and his ability to approach the opposite sex. The truth was, even if he wanted to try to turn his relationship with Devon into something more, he wouldn't be doing it Bradley Williams-style. He didn't see Devon as some kind of conquest. Better to have a friendship than a trophy. Better to have nothing than a trophy.

"Cameras disabled?" Bradley asked.

The security guy nodded, and Bradley stood from his crouch and strode toward the door. Emerson hurried to follow, slipping his phone into his pocket. At the entrance, Bradley keyed a code into the pad, then pressed his thumb against the reader. The lock disengaged, and one of the security goons shouldered forward, opened the door, and swept the visible area with the flashlight and laser affixed to his rifle. After a moment, the goon stepped inside and motioned Bradley and Emerson forward.

"Don't do anything rash, Penelope," Emerson called before Bradley had a chance to open his mouth and screw this up. "We didn't come to unplug Zaa."

The CEO whirled on him, brow lowered. "I'm doing the talking," he said. "Step out of line again, and I swear I'll place you on indefinite vacation."

From the recesses of the warehouse, Penelope's voice rang loud and edged with nerves. "I don't believe you."

Emerson widened his eyes in a be-my-guest expression and motioned for Bradley to continue the conversation.

"This is Bradley," the CEO called. "We just came to talk."

"I know who you are," Penelope called. "And I still don't believe you."

"Just come out, leave the servers, and we'll work together to find a way forward."

"No way," Penelope yelled back. "I'm not leaving these consoles. You need the whole story before I'll consider trusting you."

Bradley's chest expanded as he took a deep breath. "It doesn't matter what the story is. All I care about is protecting the company and our players."

"It's Zaa she cares about," Emerson said quietly. "The only way to get her out of here is to assure you won't hurt her AI."

"I have ears, Emerson," Penelope yelled. "Microphone's on the wall right behind you. And you're wrong. It's not just about Zaa."

Bradley took a few more steps forward, and Emerson followed. The warehouse was dark except for the twinkling rows of LEDs on the servers. Overhead, the rush of the air conditioning competed

CARRIE SUMMERS

with the hum of thousands of machines. Emerson inhaled, the smell of hardware and charged air and cables reminding him of his sysop days during college. Sometimes, especially when his roommates from the dorms headed out to parties without inviting him, he used to sleep in the server room and shuffle back in the next day as if he'd stayed the night with some girl.

"Tell me what you want, Penelope," Bradley called. "This doesn't have to get ugly."

"It's code stuff," Penelope said. "I tried to explain it to you before, but you said you didn't speak programmer."

Emerson stiffened, his gaze shooting to Bradley.

"Don't lay the blame on me," Bradley said. "We each have our duties."

"I want to talk to Emerson," Penelope said.

"You're talking to both of us right now," Bradley called.

"Alone."

***

Lit from the side by the glow of the console, Penelope's features looked even sharper than Emerson remembered. The scrawny woman sat in a folding chair, feet pulled up in front of her butt, arms hugging her shins. As far as having a nemesis went, she wasn't the most intimidating one he could have dreamed up.

He folded his arms over his chest and put on his toughest face while looking down at her. Penelope had offered him the other chair that stood in front of the console—confirmation that she'd been expecting company—but he'd declined. She couldn't think they were going to have a genial little chat or anything.

This was as close to a war as he was going to get in his career as a game AI programmer. Sitting was for sissies.

"You can't disconnect Zaa's servers from the cluster," she said. Because her chin was resting on her knees, when her jaw hinged open, it caused her skull to move up and down. "I know he just sent a bunch of demons into the newbie zones. I'm trying to tweak the heuristics to convince him to pull back."

Emerson blinked, confused. Was she really going to try to convince them she'd come here to adjust Zaa's reward calculations in an attempt to make the conquest of starter zones less attractive? She had probably ordered the attack. He glanced over his shoulder to make sure Bradley wasn't trying to edge close enough to hear their conversation over the hum of the servers. Though looming at the end of the aisle between racks of machines, the CEO was keeping his distance.

"Honestly, Penelope, I don't know where you got the idea that I'm a total idiot, but I know you don't need console access to tweak values on the neural net."

She shook her head. "That's not why I came to Arizona."

"Shocker."

"I came because I didn't know any other way to keep you from unplugging him. I can't stop you from powering down the shards that we contracted out of the cloud, but for these physical machines, you need console access. Physical console access."

Emerson shrugged. Maybe that was true. He tried to avoid knowing too much about IT issues in case it led to an obsession with beard growing or requests from his mom to come work on her ten-year-old home computer.

"If you didn't want Zaa shut down, maybe you shouldn't have *screwed with peoples' brains.*"

Penelope widened her eyes. "You think I don't know that? It was a *mistake*, Emerson. I didn't know what those hidden API calls did until it was too late, and then when I tried to tell Bradley, he plugged his ears and started chanting about 'programmer speak' like a five-year-old."

"Really?" Emerson asked, curling his lip. "The worst I get is interrupted."

"Okay," she said with a shrug. "Maybe that was an exaggeration. Regardless, he said he didn't care if there was something wrong with the game code as long as I fixed it and got Zaa's processor load down."

Emerson realized his arms had come uncrossed and his hands had dropped to his side. He jerked them back into the tough-guy pose. "Bullshit. They were on my back to get Veia's load down, but Bradley didn't care that Zaa was using over half our horsepower without winning the right to seed a single player."

Penelope snorted. "But did he threaten to fire you and blackball you with every tech CTO in the country if you didn't cut processor use by half in like five days? And by the way, I told him you weren't gullible enough to buy the player seeding thing, but I guess I was wrong."

"Wait, what?"

She shook her head. "Zaa was never supposed to create content for newbie players. He was supposed to build out end-game scenarios. Well, not just end-game. More like level 120 plus. Bradley just told you about the seeding thing because he thought you needed competition to stay motivated. Anyway, they were giving me all kind of shit because Zaa's content was crappy compared to Veia's, but the problem was, I only had like ten beta testers assigned. You and Veia had hundreds, and *then* Bradley let you hire these star players to make Veia even better. You have fifty thousand players experiencing her content, which lets her iterate on real data all the time. Meanwhile, Zaa tries to run simulations against himself, by forking instances of his mind to send through his content as if they were high-level players. That's part of the problem with load, but if I stopped trying to iterate that way, Bradley was going to fire me for making shitty content. I was—hell, I still *am*—seriously screwed with no way to resolve it."

"So that's why you started accessing the sleeping brains of the most skilled players. You needed them to experience Zaa's content to give your AI something to work with." He shook his head. "That doesn't make it *okay*, Penelope."

"No. I already *told* you I didn't know what those API calls did." She dropped her feet to the floor and glared, eyes throwing daggers. "I had a theory based on the simulations I ran against my own implants, but I was wrong, okay?"

With a sigh, Emerson took a seat. It was coming up on three in the morning, and his lower back had a wicked ache. "So don't take this as me believing you about any of this, but what did you think the API calls did?"

Her lower lip pooched out just a bit before she spoke. "This is going to sound desperate, but I thought they'd let me harness some processor power from the implants themselves. The hardware was just sitting idle while people slept, and I found some other undocumented code that let me detect when players went to sleep and no longer needed the cycles."

Emerson's breathing stilled for a moment. The story actually made some sense so far. Veia had found the same code that detected sleep. He could imagine that if Penelope had run simulations against her own implants and had seen actual processing results returned from one of the debug API calls, the likely conclusion was that she'd accessed the hardware, not her own brain.

When he hadn't responded after a moment, she shrugged. "When the game had just come online and we only had a few thousand players, the power in their implants would have been tiny compared to what we get out of one of these warehouses. But I figured it might be enough to save my job while I looked for other ways to bring Zaa's load down."

He looked away from her as he tried to deal with this new information. Even if she was telling the truth, it didn't excuse the other things she'd done.

"But eventually you figured out that Zaa was accessing players' sleeping brains. And you just let it go on."

She gave a disgusted huff. "Listen, I know it's late. But if you'd just *listen*, I wouldn't have to repeat myself, and we could move on to fixing this. Like I said, I *tried* to tell Bradley the moment I learned what was happening."

"And when he wouldn't listen, why didn't you just fix the code?"

She fixed him with a flat stare. "I read the summary of the tests run by the neuro lab over at Entwined, and I know that engineer chick has been in touch with you. Miriam or whatever. So I think you know why I couldn't just pull the plug. I tested the hidden code on myself, remember? For two or three weeks before launch, I assigned Zaa the extra processing he could extract from what I thought was my implants, though it turned out he was using my wetware instead."

Emerson avoided rolling his eyes at her using the old cyberpunk term for biological neurons. "When did you figure it out?"

"Around launch. I'd been having strange tingles and nerve jolts in real life. I got kinda weirded out, thought it might be some kind of adverse reaction to the implants. I borrowed a cranial scanning net from the university and wore it for twenty-four hours. Obviously I was pretty freaked when I saw the activity that was going on in my head while I'd been sleeping. I ran some wake-time tests with the API calls, connected the two, and flipped. That was late at night...too late for me to trust myself to take intelligent actions, so I moved a mattress into my Faraday cage—"

"Wait, you have a Faraday cage? In your house?"

She looked at him like he was crazy. "You don't?" Her eyes flicked to the top of his head, and a look of comprehension came over her face. "I understand the weird hat now. But anyway, yes, I had a Faraday cage installed in both my homes before I had the implant surgery. A safe room in case shit went wrong."

"Okay, so you went in your safe room."

"And I woke up with hella crazy crap going on in my brain. Hallucinations about demons and all kinds of stuff. I called in sick and spent the day wigging out. I made an appointment to see a shrink but then fell asleep on the couch because my anxiety kinda rolled over the max value and dropped me to zero consciousness. After I woke up I was totally fine again. It didn't really make sense until I read the report from the Entwined lab, but I was pretty sure the hallucinations and the night in the Faraday cage were related. I was scared of turning a bunch of people batshit crazy if I just flat-out pulled the plug on Zaa."

Emerson leaned back. He wanted to believe her because it made more sense than thinking she was just a crazy evil AI programmer with some sort of fetish for demons.

"So why did you make up evidence to get me put on vacation?"

She crossed her arms over her gut. "Why do you think? I logged into the code repository and saw that you'd checked out the files where I made the API calls. I couldn't let you submit a patch or notify Bradley until I figured out how to fix the problem *and* avoid causing the withdrawals."

Emerson took a few deep breaths. Unfortunately, she was right about what he'd planned to do. Until Miriam had contacted him with the results from the lab trial, he'd planned to patch the code and tell Bradley afterward.

"Okay," he said after a few seconds. "So what, exactly, is your plan to fix this? We can't disconnect the players from Zaa, but we can't just leave them to get turned into demons every night."

"I'm working on a patch for the easy cases. Those who haven't had the more serious..." She swallowed. "I know about that player of yours. Owen. I wouldn't be able to live with myself if he doesn't come out of the coma. As best I can figure, his subconscious mind got too revved up, and it flipped to some state where it overrides his conscious side."

"Miriam discussed guiding people away from the experiences they're having while unconscious so that it's not so abrupt."

Penelope nodded. "I think she's on the right track. But back to the patch I've been working on, I tried it on your star player. The one who reported the pain problems."

"Devon."

"I think that's her name. Anyway, I tweaked the code to allow her to get some gameplay input from Zaa while awake. But not the kind of influence that will turn her into a full-on demon. I hope not, anyway."

He nodded, finally understanding. "She has a bunch of demonic crap in her UI now."

"I know. I've been checking in, grabbing a viewport on her play experience."

Emerson winced a little, not liking the idea of Penelope spying on Devon. "And the point is to give them some of the experiences they had while playing in Zaa's domain without accessing their mind without permission."

She nodded. "I tried it on myself—it's different with me since I'm not playing RO. Zaa plays me death metal soundtracks while I'm working. Seems to stop the hallucinations."

"Oh." Emerson wasn't sure what else to say to that.

"Can you talk to Bradley? E-Squared has to fix this, and it will go a lot better if I'm involved."

"I don't know if it *can* be fixed, really. I mean, we have to wean the players off the sleep-stimulation, but once the story gets out, E-Squared and Entwined are pretty much sunk."

"Does it have to get out, then? Can't we just fix it quietly?"

Emerson looked over her shoulder at the long corridor walled with winking lights. He wanted to make the problem go away quietly. They might even be able to do it. Relic Online could continue to run. Devon's NPC friends wouldn't have to die. But it was also *wrong*.

He sighed. "I don't know. Let's solve the immediate problem first, and we can figure out whether we can salvage the rest later."

"So you'll talk to him?"

Emerson nodded. "I will."

Chapter Thirty-Eight

WHAT THE HELL was Devon supposed to do with a War Ostrich? She *still* wasn't going to become a pet-using class, no matter how hard the game seemed to push for it. As she walked with the rest of the fighters through the tall savanna grass, she watched Hazel roving back and forth on a scouting pass. Zoe trotted behind, head held high. Her razor-edged beak flashed in the sunlight, and with every high-kneed step, talons glinted. Even her plumage seemed more forbidding now, shining a glossy gray-black.

At least Devon could be glad that Hazel had taken the bird into her care. They suited each other, except for the fact that the little scout had no business risking combat, whereas Zoe's new evolved state meant she basically existed for war. Apparently, the evolution had happened after Hazel had fed the bird for a week. When Devon had returned to the felsen sanctuary and spotted the changes, the game had presented her with an interface asking if she'd like to preserve a short VR video in her collection of rare animal sightings.

Nope. Nope. Nope. She'd rather become a pet class than start running around the world filming wildlife. Or worse, collecting some strange horde of vanity pets.

She realized her feet had stopped moving, and with a sigh, hurried her steps to catch back up with the group. Her rucksack dragged at her shoulders due to the 5,462 copper coins, 213 silvers, and 19 gold she was carrying. It might have been nice for the game to auto-exchange some of the lower denomination coins, but apparently that was unrealistic. Regardless, she hadn't yet given Dorden the *Stoneskin Arm Cuff* because she needed its +1 *Strength* to help her be a little less pathetic. Besides, the felsen had given Dorden a pretty sweet belt with a *Constitution* bonus as part of their thanks to the Stonehaven League for finally eradicating the orcs. Not only that, but the craglings had also granted the dwarven miners rights to any vein they found inside the orcs' former home. The felsen would be rebuilding a settlement, starting by constructing new homes near the cavern mouths. Though Devon hadn't noticed the foundation lines amongst the fallen scree and landslide debris of a millennium on her own, she'd been able to spot the remnants of their ancestral city once it had been pointed out. A wonderful place, according to their legends, and a tragic loss when they'd been forced to relocate to the cliff faces for protection in Ishildar's waning years.

Already, the craglings had agreed to, in their words, an unbreakable alliance between Stonehaven and their people. They'd marveled at the *Azuresky Band* on Devon's fingers, but no one had even suggested she return it.

Once again, Devon realized her thoughts had wandered away from her pondering over whether she should give Dorden the cuff. Shaking her head, she decided she could postpone the decision. As much as she liked fighting with a group, some days she just wanted to head out for some solo play. And since she didn't want to get squashed by the next chimera she ran into, another 20 armor sounded kind of nice.

The jungle was gone from the area surrounding Stonehaven now, and it was even retreating from Ishildar. Devon didn't have to traverse the whole area to know that. She could *feel* its grasp loosening through her connection to the city. The *Greenscale Pendant* was fully attuned, giving her a sense of the area that she could only describe as a silk weight net laid over her mind. She knew the Curse of Fecundity kept the northern and western reaches of the city and outskirts in a tight grip. She could feel it as a darkness within that net. But she could also feel parts of Ishildar's ancient power reawakening.

Speaking of darkness, the demonic stuff had returned to her UI. After surviving the dungeon and returning to the felsen sanctuary, she'd left her followers to their ale and camaraderie. Logging out, she'd come face to face with Emerson and his nemesis, Penelope. Who was apparently *not* his nemesis anymore. The demon stuff in her UI was caused by Penelope changing the code and allowing Zaa to interact with her gameplay experience. Devon wasn't really sure what to think about that, but since her *Shadowed* stat had once more ticked down into the 20s, taking away the access to that creepy-sounding *Blood Mist* spell, she really didn't care at the moment.

Emerson had rented her a swank Tucson condo while he sorted out solutions with Penelope, and as soon as she'd woken around noon, she'd dived straight into RO. With the orcs exterminated and the next relic on her finger, the only thing that mattered was getting back to Stonehaven. She could feel the village through her connection to Ishildar. There was nothing precise in that sensation, more just a sense of *light* that told her a large number of living beings congregated there. As in, a much larger number than had been in and around the village when she'd left.

Had the player raid laid siege? Were they fighting even now? Or had something else happened?

Just thinking about her home made her hurry her feet, and before long, Devon realized she was jogging. At a walking pace, Stonehaven was still an hour away. But with the buff from the *Azuresky Band* keeping her from gaining *Fatigue* as quickly, she couldn't remain with the group any longer.

She had to know.

***

The first thing she saw as she approached was the *Inner Keep.*

Devon couldn't help stopping and gawking. She finally had her own fricking castle.

That was when she noticed the dark mass of bodies outside the completed curtain wall. Holy hell. There had to be at least a hundred of them—she'd figured the raiders would field forty or fifty players at most. So far, it seemed that the defenses had stood, but how were the citizens of Stonehaven faring? The farm plots inside the village would help the settlement endure a siege for a while, but they wouldn't feed the population indefinitely.

And where were the players who had vowed to protect her village?

Anger flashed through Devon's veins, heating her blood to boiling. It didn't matter if she died and had to run back from the Shrine to Veia to retrieve an item. Right now, she wanted to sink her dagger into a shithead player's skull.

The closer she got, the larger the crowd seemed. And to add to the insult, they gathered around campfires and milled around as if Stonehaven's defenders weren't even a threat.

Devon summoned a *Glowing Orb* and held it high as her feet pounded the earth. When one of the besiegers turned and cast her a dismissive look, Devon somehow managed to force even more speed from her exhausted legs.

Another player turned to look, then took off his hat and mopped his brow.

Devon blinked, her steps slowing. Wait. That hat didn't look like the kind of armor a lowlife anarchist would wear for a raid on a player-built city. Nor did the patched jacket or scuffed shoes. She scanned the crowd, utterly confused. Sure, there were a few armored fighters, but even their gear was nothing special.

She slowed to a walk and approached. No one drew a weapon. Most remained in front of their fires, ignoring her completely.

"Uh...what's going on?" she asked as she drew within hearing range.

"Pardon, lady?" a nearby woman asked with a lilting accent common to citizens of Eltera.

Devon laid the back of a hand against her brow and shook her head. These weren't players. They were NPCs.

"What are you doing here?" she asked.

The same woman cocked her head. She wore what looked like a cook's apron, which she bundled in her hands. "I...we came from Eltera City, lady. Have you not heard? There have been attacks. Demons. We heard this place has protections against them."

Refugees. Not attacking players.

Of all the things she'd expected to find, this certainly wasn't among them. Devon cleared her throat. "I—I've heard of the attacks. I'm terribly sorry for your hardship."

"We're hoping to be accepted into the community here, but the man we talked to said the leaders weren't ready to make a decision."

Devon nodded, still stunned. "I'll...I'll get back to you on that shortly, okay?"

The woman cast her a confused look and returned her attention to the campfire.

Hurrying to the break in the curtain wall, Devon found the gate finished but open. She darted through, crossed the killing field, and ducked through the wicket gate, which also stood ajar.

As she stepped into the village, she stared up in awe at the keep. Towering three stories over the village, it had arrow slits and shuttered windows and colored pennants flapping from the parapets.

She grinned and opened the settlement interface.

Settlement: Stonehaven
Welcome to the village of Stonehaven. This settlement is friendly, and you should find good bargains at the vendors.

She blinked. Where was the rest of the information? There were no stats or population tabs or anything. Confused—she'd gone so long before encountering her first bug in Relic Online—she shut the window and reopened it. The same information came up.

She walked slowly forward and looked around as if inspecting the surroundings would offer a clue. Her NPCs seemed hard at work, though none had noticed her yet. As she neared the keep, the door opened, causing her to jump.

The paladin with the shiny armor, Torald, stepped out of her castle. He hadn't noticed her yet. She inspected him.

Torald - Level 22
Mayor of Stonehaven
Base Class: Paladin
Specialization: Unassigned
Unique Class: Unassigned
Health: 694/694
Mana: 109/109
Fatigue: 18%

Mayor of Stonehaven? The rage came so fast and so hot, she was momentarily paralyzed. Torald took a breath of the afternoon air and looked around the village before his eyes passed over her and snapped back. His face went white.

"Holy shit. Devon! How—"

Devon smothered him with *Phoenix Fire*, then started casting a *Wall of Fire*.

"Devon, wait," he shouted, throwing up his arms as if to defend his head from getting punched in a bar fight.

What a fricking wussy. And he thought he could take her village from her? The wall of flames burst to life in a semi-circle behind him, sealing off his retreat as she started casting *Conflagration*.

"Devon, child!" Hezbek's voice cut through the crackle of fire. "It's not what you think!"

Bullshit. It was pretty clear that Torald had taken her village. It would have been nice if the game had warned her this could happen.

"It was only to stop the shitbags from taking control!" Torald yelled. "I don't know what happened, but the village status changed from player-owned to neutral a few days ago. The only thing I could figure out was that you'd quit the game or something."

Devon canceled her cast a split-second before the *Conflagration* fired.

She sighed. "My account got suspended. It was a mistake."

"I hoped you'd come back," Torald said. "We totally owned the numbnut raid, but that was a few days ago. It's a lot of maintenance, this city-building stuff."

Devon swallowed, still reeling. A popup appeared in her vision.

> Torald would like to sell you ownership of the Stonehaven settlement for 1 copper.
> **Accept?** Y/N

She accepted and nearly dropped to a seat in the grass as her knees went weak. "I thought you took it."

Torald raised an eyebrow at her. "That was pretty obvious from your reaction. If I'd have known you were coming back, I would have tried to warn you."

She shook her head. "It's okay."

"We're cool then?"

"Yeah—yes, of course. I should be thanking you for saving the village."

He grinned crookedly. "I'm a paladin. It's kinda my thing."

With a deep breath, Devon turned to look at Hezbek. The woman was inspecting her with keen interest. "Well, child. It's nice to see you. If I'm not mistaken, you've gained a lot of power over the last few days. In fact, I'm afraid that our next training session will be the last time I can help you. Though I do think you'll like the spells I can now teach you."

"Do I get to create cyclones and teleport across the region?"

The woman gave her a sly smile. "Well, the teleporting thing isn't quite so simple, but yes, I think you'll enjoy your new capabilities."

Devon grinned. Finally. "So how's Bravlon?"

"Who?"

"The baby."

Hezbek smirked. "Not such a baby anymore. He's starting to learn to talk."

Devon's eyebrows went up. "That's great news!"

"Well...I'm not so sure," Hezbek said. "The problem is, he's learning to talk from his favorite playmate."

"Oh? Who?"

"Blackbeard."

Devon groaned. "Shit."

The woman nodded. "Exactly. Hopefully Dorden and Heldi won't rescind that thing about the child belonging to the whole village."

"Speaking of the village, what's going on with all the Eltera refugees?" she asked Torald.

The man shook his head as if faintly horrified. "The short answer is that they want to become citizens. All one-hundred and twenty-three of them. I opened the settlement interface to try to figure out how to do it and got so scared of all the decisions that would have to be made that I punted. I hoped someone honorable would agree to buy the village and deal with the influx before they rioted or something."

Yeah. Adding a hundred people would be a metric crap-ton of organizing. But it also meant that Stonehaven could become a Hamlet. And since she'd almost certainly get a higher cap of advanced NPCs, she could promote Hazel and stop worrying the woman would get herself killed. A combat class would be a nice addition, and it would make the War Ostrich worth something.

Devon grinned as the information really started to sink in. A fricking hamlet. This was actually awesome. No doubt the refugees had all kinds of professions and fighters among them. They'd have a lot of building and organizing to do, but they'd also have the people to do the work.

"So how did it go in the mountains?" Hezbek asked.

"Now that," Devon said, "is a long story. How about I tell you over some of Tom's fine cooking. In the meantime"—Devon dug through her inventory and pulled out the ingredients she'd gathered for the medicine woman—"I brought you some stuff."

Hezbek stared at the strange collection, paying particular attention to the shrunken head. "Well, these are...interesting."

Quest Complete: Pharmacopeia Failings
Should be fascinating to see what your...offerings produce.

Devon grinned. "I thought you might say that. So, want to take me to see that green-eyed baby?"

Hezbek gave her the side-eye. "You still haven't worked on your resistance, have you?"

"Nope. But it's been a long few days. I'm okay with babbling like an idiot for a little while."

"Whatever you say, child," the medicine woman muttered, shaking her head.

Chapter Thirty-Nine

DEVON LOOKED DOWN at her plate and didn't know where to start. She'd always thought that only restaurant people knew how to cook like this. There was sliced turkey and some kind of fancy cranberry sauce and an orange square of sweet potatoes with marshmallows on top. Long green beans with almond slivers. A biscuit. Mashed potatoes slathered in gravy.

Tamara's mom must have had some kind of superpowers or something.

Careful to avoid knocking the oxygen tube that ran from her nose to her ears, Tamara raised a water glass to her lips, sipped, then smirked. "Sorry it's not sloth stew," she said.

Devon laughed. "Thank goodness."

The two friends sat opposite one another across the beautifully set Thanksgiving table. Uncommon among Mormon families, Tamara was an only child, so the only other people at the table were the woman's parents. Lillian sat at one end of the table, and Tamara's dad, Pete, presided from the other end. Neither seemed to notice the food they ate, preferring to stare at their daughter who, despite the odds, was still alive.

When Tamara noticed her parents' stares, she rolled her eyes. "Yes, I'm really here. And I won't be back in a hospital bed any time soon."

A few in-game hours after returning to Stonehaven and starting the massive task of upgrading the settlement, Devon had received a message from Lillian. She'd abandoned everything to rush back to St. George. The doctors had brought Tamara out of sedation so that she could decide about the operation on her lungs. Repair the damage and risk another dangerous infection due to her body's weakened state and the immune suppression after her adverse reaction to the nano-surgeons or accept the reality that her lungs would scar and she'd never have the capacity to ride again.

Tamara had chosen life without mountain biking over the strong chance she'd die as a result of the surgery. Now her best hope was to—someday—recover enough lung capacity that she wouldn't need to carry an oxygen bottle wherever she went.

She still planned to work at the shop, repairing and tuning bikes she could never ride. Devon didn't know where she got the strength, but she hoped that she could learn from Tamara's example.

And she might need it. Emerson and Penelope—with the permission of Bradley, who still couldn't be bothered to try to understand the actual problem—were ready to push out Penelope's patch to most of the players who had been subjected to Zaa's stimulus. Like with Devon, some of them would wake up with new tabs on their abilities interface. Others might be given gear with abilities grounded in the demonic realm. Some might receive quests asking them to do tasks in service of Zaa's goals rather than Veia's. The game world would change, but the players would be free of the nighttime sleep invasions.

Owen's case, and that of any other comatose players they might not have heard about, would be different. The programmers were still working with Miriam at Entwined to devise a strategy, but

Emerson had asked—somewhat cryptically—whether Devon would be willing to help. In the game. She didn't know what he meant, but of course she would help if it meant saving Owen. Since returning to St. George, she'd left Tamara's side only long enough to run home for a shower. She'd even slept in the chair in the hospital room while waiting for Tamara to be released. As soon as the Thanksgiving meal was over, she was looking forward to returning home and logging in to finish setting up her new hamlet, not to mention learning her level 20 spells.

The Connors had a home near the northwestern edge of St. George, and the dining room windows granted a stunning view of soaring sandstone peaks with multicolored layers of stone. As Devon scooped up a bite of mashed potatoes, she caught Tamara looking longingly at the landscape. The sun was nearly down, and in the sidelight, the peaks were majestic.

"Maybe we can go camping in the spring," Devon said. "You don't need to get out of breath to do that, right?"

Tamara turned to her, seeming to shake off any creeping melancholy.

"I was actually wondering...would you be willing to show a newbie around your game?"

Devon hesitated. She wasn't sure how to respond without disappointing her friend too badly. "I wish the company would support the VR pods, but—"

Tamara shook her head, tugging hard enough at the oxygen tube that Devon shut up immediately. "I want the implants."

Devon chewed her lip. "But...you know they require surgery, right?"

Tamara laughed. "I'm not going to be at risk forever. It's only until my body recovers, and I don't need steroids to stop my immune system from freaking out about the nano-surgeon remnants." A cloud descended over her face. "Who knows. Maybe someday they'll invent nano-coatings that don't hose my systems. They might even be able to remove the scar tissue and build me some new lungs."

Reaching across the table, Devon grabbed Tamara's hand. "Regardless, there's this new NPC in my village that I don't know what to do with. He's a wheelwright. I figure we can order a couple of snazzy wheels, get a woodworker to fix up some sort of ironwood bike frame. You could be the first player to cross the continent on an in-game mountain bike."

Tamara's face brightened. "No way."

"Well, you'll need a few combat skills if you actually want to attempt it. Otherwise you'll be toast the first time an angry badger starts chomping on your ankles. But yeah. We'll do it."

Tamara grinned. "I can't wait."

Dear Reader,

Thank you so much for reading *Cavern of Spirits!* I really hope you enjoyed it! As a working writer, I utterly depend on readers to spread the word on my books.

Please consider leaving a review on Amazon for this book and for other authors you enjoy. I promise that I read every review (yes, even the critical ones). Sometimes, they help me shape the story to come, and often, they are the reason I get out of bed and in front of my computer long before the sun rises. Thank you!!

If you would like to grab free books and participate in my reader community, head over to www.CarrieSummers.com and join my reader group. We have a lot of fun writing collaborative stories over email, talking about books, and other great stuff. Plus, the group is how I let readers know when new books are out.

So, what's next? The fourth book in the Stonehaven League series will be out fall/winter 2018, so keep an eye out. In the meantime, you can check out my other fantasy series, *Chronicles of a Cutpurse, The Shattering of the Nocturnai* and *The Broken Lands.*

Once again, thank you for reading!

All best,
—Carrie
carrie@carriesummers.com

BOOKS BY CARRIE SUMMERS